TAKE THE SHILLING

TAKE THE SHILLING

THE CONFEDERATED WORLDS BOOK 1

RAYMUND EICH

CHAPTER 1

THE RECRUITERS

TOMAS' nape prickled in anticipation. Every pair of eyes in the room would stare at him if he raised his hand. It would be so much easier to lie low. Madame Martin gave the room a final passing gaze, then moved the paper toward the corner of her desk—

He raised his hand. Someone near him murmured, and Madame Martin looked up as Tomas said, "I want to meet the recruiters."

She took a moment to reply. "You, Tomas? You aren't the type of young man to want an early dismissal from class."

His mouth felt dry. How could she think he wanted to shirk school? "I want to meet the recruiters."

A row in front of Tomas, one boy muttered to another. All the students aged about ten standard and up turned in their seats. His desire to speak to a military recruiter defied their stereotypes of him, and their guarded expressions and shared whispers showed how much they disliked his defiance. Even Véronique, who'd shared a few dances and even kissed his cheek at the last Harvest Fête, widened her eyes. Her hand rose defensively to the closed collar of her dark green jumpsuit. Tomas felt a trickle of relief at being in his final year at the *lycée* and having no one sit behind him.

"Quiet," Madame Martin told the other students. "You're disrupting the first years' work on addition." She cast Tomas an arch eye. Would she ask him if his mother knew? Instead, the quirked her eyebrows for a moment, then said, "You're old enough to make this choice." She picked up her pen and wrote his name on the paper with trim motions.

A few minutes later, the *lycée*'s secretary came in. She bowed to Madame Martin and took the paper. On her way out of the room, her gaze fell to the list and she hesitated with her hand in air near the classroom door's handle.

The same boy snickered and Tomas bent his head to his physics and current-affairs papers. The younger boy tried to catch his gaze but soon gave up. Tomas' face cooled.

He spent a few minutes skimming over a description of optical fibers. He gave a little more attention to a diagram of an array of fibers wicking light around a solid wall, but still set those papers aside as soon as he could. He turned to a current affairs paper about the Space Force's victory over a Unity relief mission near one of the artificial wormholes in the New Liberty system, but a movement outside the window soon distracted him.

The secretary swung open the wrought-iron gate, crossed the street to leave the *lycée*'s property, and took her phone from her handbag. She cradled the phone between her neck and shoulder and pulled out a paper. Calling the recruiters with the names of students from the *lycée* who would meet them later in the day, Tomas guessed. But when she lowered the phone, call complete, she kept it out, swiping across the touchscreen to place another call. Her eyes danced with excitement and she covered the mouthpiece with her free hand. *You won't believe what happened,* he imagined her saying to the other party. *The étranger twelfth year, Neumann, signed up to meet the military recruiters today!*

Soon everyone in town would know. Before long, word would reach his mother.

He forced his attention back on the printout, spending the rest of the time until fourteen o'clock rereading the article about the Space

Force victory. Tomas imagined the SF men, strapped into their gee fluid pods, lifting their strong arms against the acceleration generated by their fusion drives, pressing buttons, turning dials, flying their ship into battle. The colonels and generals commanding the ships and task forces inspired their men and outsmarted the enemy emerging from the artificial wormhole inbound from Nueva Andalucia.

Soon the SF would take the war into Unity space on multiple fronts and score a victory so great the enemy would capitulate. Within a few months, he could be there, part of the Confederated Worlds' triumph.

He reread again, skimming the paragraph about the Ground Force's continued mission to clear the remnants of Unity infantry from the surface of New Liberty. Wasn't it unnecessary? Couldn't the SF destroy the enemy infantry from orbit?

At fourteen o'clock, Madame Martin looked up from the civics lesson for the middle years. "Guillaume, Tomas, you are excused to visit the recruiters."

"Thank you, Madame," Tomas said. The other boy had already risen and started through the arrayed desks for the door. Tomas followed him into the hallway. The door at the far end already started closing on the view of green-black foliage and Guillaume's untucked shirt and rumpled trousers.

Outside, the indigo sky was cloudless. In the southeast, two-thirds of the way to zenith, Soleil-de-France's fat red disk hung above the engineered maples and elms lining the *rue des Lycées*. In six hours, the hazy blue bulk of the gas giant Napoléon would eclipse the red sun.

Tomas went out through the wrought-iron gate and turned east to walk down the *rue des Lycées* to the *Place des Citoyens*. The street in front of him was empty.

Puzzled, he stopped, turned. Guillaume scurried in the opposite direction, away from the recruiters. "You're going the wrong way," Tomas said.

Guillaume kept walking.

"*Place des Citoyens* is this way."

Shoulders hunched, the other boy stopped. He looked over his shoulder with a scowl. "Just 'cause you're a goody-goody doesn't mean

I am. I got out of school early, I'm going fishing at the river. Who cares about those recruiters?"

I'm not a goody-goody crossed Tomas' mind. The thought of the river, swimming to midstream with deep strong strokes, warmly bubbled up from his subconscious.

He sighed and rejected the thought. *I promised Madame Martin I'd see the recruiters. It would be wrong to not go.* Then another thought came to him. "Madame Martin can look down *rue des Lycées.* If she doesn't see you head that way, she'll know you're playing hooky. Follow me, then split off at *boulevard Hyperborée.*"

Guillaume grunted, then trudged toward Tomas. "Didn't think of that." The two boys walked down the street. Other than the churr of tires from passing automobiles and the harsh calls of grackles and crows, they started in silence. Tomas expected the other boy to want to talk. To forestall Guillaume, he looked to the eastern sky. Sometimes ships could be glimpsed on the transit between their colony on Joséphine and the artificial wormhole to the al-Aqsa system. Not today.

From the corner of his eye, Tomas glanced at Guillaume to see if he too watched the sky. The other boy instead kept his gaze on the asphalt skin of the living street. To the sounds of the town, from time to time Guillaume added the skitter of sloughed aggregate as he kicked small, tarry pebbles to the curb.

Guillaume finally spoke at the corner of *boulevard Hyperborée.* "Go talk to those recruiters if you want, but I still don't care about them." He headed south on the boulevard, toward the river. Tomas shrugged and kept going.

Rue des Lycées soon jogged to the left and climbed uphill. Eight hundred meters ahead, the Ecogenesis Ministry's local heatwick stood like a giant mushroom on the hilltop overlooking the town. The heatwick loomed over the granite-tile roofs festooned with solar panels of the town's wealthier houses on the upper slopes of the hill. The largest building in sight was the *Lycée Superieur,* two stories tall, fronted with diorite columns. The personal automobiles, coupes and sport sedans, belonging to the LS' upper year students formed a line at the sidewalk in front of the building. None of those smug rich kids would meet the recruiters. Tomas breathed a little easier when he remembered he could avoid the LS by taking a side street, *rue Saint-Girard*, to get to the *Place des Citoyens*.

He turned and halted at the sight of a familiar face. Etien wasn't a friend, exactly, but Tomas felt closer to him than any other teenager in town. Son of a government scientist from the capital, eccentrically dressed, he too didn't belong in this small town. "You aren't home-schooling today?" Tomas asked.

Etien lifted his kepi by the visor, then placed it back on his head at a jaunty angle. "I was going to accompany my dad on a survey of magma flows in his sector, leaving at eight o'clock, but his ornithopter's diagnostics flashed red before we took off. It's grounded until Ecogenesis gets a maintenance crew out here from Couronnement. My schedule's been open all day."

"Your mother didn't give you schoolwork to make up for it?"

"It's the will of Odin, she says in situations like this." An odd woman, from Midgard, Etien's mother wore dresses instead of jump-suits, drank beer instead of wine, and homeschooled her only child. Etien laughed. "I've been ambling since this morning. Despite your fears, my friend, my wanderings have even been educational; I just studied anatomy with the widow DuBois." He laughed again.

Tomas noticed a red smear on the side of Etien's jaw. Lipstick. He ducked his face, cheeks suddenly hot. Envy filled his crotch, but it was soon doused by fear that Etien would ask him about his amorous adventures, of which there had been none.

"Speaking of school, Tomas, what takes you away from Madame Martin's gimlet eye?"

The change of topic gave him a moment of relief. "I'm meeting the military recruiters."

The relief evaporated. Tomas expected Etien to put on a look of mockery, or at best, disbelief, but instead, Etien took it in stride. "I heard they were coming today. Both Space Force and Ground Force."

"I want to meet the SF recruiter," Tomas said.

"I believe you. Yet I'm sure GF serves some useful purpose, else the Confederated Worlds would have disbanded it." Etien shook his chronometer out of the sleeve of his Nehru jacket, then looked at the face on the inside of his left wrist. "You have fifteen minutes. I'll walk with you." He started down the street and Tomas hurriedly caught up.

Once abreast of Etien, Tomas studied the other's face. "You aren't going to ask why I'm meeting them?"

"I hadn't planned to. Enlisting to escape this vile ville would be reason enough. Whatever your reasons, clearly they are good. Otherwise, you wouldn't meet them."

As they neared the St. Girard church, the houses and their lawns on both sides of the street grew smaller, behind shorter, plainer fences of extruded mycocrete instead of wrought iron and quarried stone. At this hour, the street was quiet, with children at school and parents working in skilled trades in the industrial quarter down by the river.

The quiet soon gave way to a churring sound rising in volume, coming up the street behind them. Tomas glanced up as the car sped past: a red teardrop, two doors, with badges on the trunk lid from car designers throughout the Confederated Worlds. Even without the *Lycée Superieur* parking sticker in the back window, Tomas identified it as Lucien LaSalle's car. Probably on his way to lacrosse practice, or to help his father dun tenants for rent. Lucien had been born lucky and made sure everyone knew it.

Four hundred meters ahead, Lucien turned right on *boulevard Hortense*, away from the *Place des Citoyens*. Yet even after he left their sight, Tomas' gaze remained on the intersection as he talked to Etien. "Aren't you going to ask what my mother thinks of me meeting the recruiters?"

Etien frowned. "I hadn't planned to, but if you want me to—"

"No."

"Are you certain, my friend? You brought it up—"

"I'm certain."

"Fair enough." They approached the corner, passing through shadows cast by flying buttresses of the St. Girard church. "I'll take my leave, friend." Etien flourished his kepi. "I wish you a productive meeting with the recruiters." Etien moved to replace the hat on his head, but hesitated. "Since I hate receiving advice," he said, "I'm loathe to give it."

Would any other townsman than Etien hesitate before telling him what to do? Tomas said, "I'm listening."

"You might consider whether you're meeting the recruiters because you want to, or because your mother doesn't want you to. That's all. Take care." He flourished his kepi again, then seated it on his head and walked away down the boulevard.

Tomas turned the other direction and quickened his steps. *Boulevard Hortense* bore more traffic, from private cars and for-hire jitneys to bicyclists and pedestrians. Cafés and the showrooms of handcrafters lined the street, on the ground floors of buildings with walk-up flats and mansard roofs. The people sipping espresso at sidewalk tables, the shopkeepers plying custom furniture and clothing from their front windows, all glanced at him and then looked away. *Étranger*, foreigner. Observer. Preacher's kid. Not poor enough for social protection, but close enough. Not one of us. He hurried on, along the boulevard, across the lanes of the traffic circle at the boulevard's end, to reach *Place des Citoyens*.

Grass covered most of the plaza, except for the straight walkways leading to a small paved area in the center, in front of a statue of the symbolic empty throne, awaiting a legitimate heir of Bonaparte to take his seat. A dozen locals, ten boys and two girls, milled around the paved area. Two military personnel waited at the front side of the paved area, furthest from the statue. A woman, whose large dark eyes and faint unibrow looked al-Aqsan, wore a gray Ground Forces dress uniform with some chevrons on the jacket sleeve. Some enlisted rank. Next to her stood a male Space Forces lieutenant, his beard and turban suggesting he was from Navi Ambarsar, his dress uniform as deep blue as Joséphine's sky.

The SF lieutenant extended his hand. "Welcome to our presentation on military careers. The chief recruiting officers will be speaking in a few minutes." He lifted a tablet computer. "Your name, please?"

"Neumann. Tomas Neumann."

"Noy-man…" The lieutenant swiped his fingers up and down the touchscreen. "I don't see any Noyman on the list."

Tomas wanted to protest, but his mouth felt like a seized-up engine. *I'm on the list don't let your dangerous machine exclude me don't make me face my mother for nothing—*

"Lieutenant," said the Ground Forces enlisted woman, "if I may, look under n-e-u. You aren't native to Joséphine, Mr. Neumann?"

Tomas nodded. The motion freed his voice. "I was born on Sankt-Benedikts-Welt. We moved here when I was young, after my father died."

"There you are," said the lieutenant, "sorry." Someone came up the walkway behind Tomas. "Welcome to our presentation..." he said, stepping past Tomas.

"Thank you, lieutenant," the new arrival said. Tomas knew that smooth baritone voice. It belonged to a past builder of playground coalitions that excluded Tomas, a present-day charmer of girls whom Tomas fancied. "It's L-a-capital-s-a-l-l-e, Lucien."

"You're on the list. The chief recruiting officers will speak in a few minutes."

"Excellent. Pardon me, lieutenant, corporal?"

Tomas glanced over his shoulder. The SF lieutenant looked vaguely embarrassed and the GF enlisted woman stifled a frown when she noticed Tomas looking. He counted four chevrons on her sleeve and vowed to look up what rank that number signified after the meeting ended.

He avoided making eye contact with Lucien, but the other's smooth, hooded-eye gaze passed over him, then lurched back. "Tomas? I wasn't expecting to see you here, but what a pleasant surprise."

"I'm surprised too. Didn't I see you turn the other direction on *boulevard Hortense*?"

Lucien lifted a cardboard coffee cup. "My favorite café is a few blocks south of the Saint Girard church."

Tomas leaned back, wary of the other's motives in talking. "I hadn't expected you to be considering a military career."

A glint came to Lucien's gray-blue eyes. "Time and place came together. We LaSalles are well-known here on Joséphine, but I don't want to be just a member of the planetary legislature. I could gain a much higher office in the Confederated Worlds government, I'm sure, but I need some name recognition among the masses, plus contacts with the brokers of power. Service in wartime is a great first step to getting both. My father has a friend in Couronnement who can introduce me to an admissions officer at officer candidates school."

Lucien angled his head. *Now comes the mockery*, Tomas thought.

"You're interested in the Space Force?" Lucien asked.

Tomas replayed his words, looking for subtext in the other's tone but finding none. "I am."

"I knew it. It's the branch I'm looking at, too. By far, the more important one. I'm glad to know you could be serving under me. The physics you're learning is obsolete, but you're good at math, and they can slot technical skills into you easily enough." Lucien glanced at the dozen locals already waiting and lowered his voice. "I'd much rather have you than those hicks. Public schoolies, all of them, slotting in trade skills as if that's enough. You can't build a palace on a foundation of sand and you can't make a tech sergeant out of a cretin. Those ones are only good for the mudbugs."

Lucien glanced up, then slapped Tomas on the shoulder. "The recruiters are preparing to speak." He slipped forward, the local boys recognizing him and making way. Tomas drifted unnoticed to the rear of the crowd.

A riser had been placed in front of the statue of the Imperial throne. The two chief recruiting officers stood at the back of the riser, talking to each other in low voices, each with a tablet in hand. Both shook their tablets. After reviewing the results, the GF recruiter stepped back, and the SF recruiter smiled and strode to the front of the riser.

"As always, the Space Force is the first on the scene. Greetings, young women and men of Portage-du-Nord. I'm Major Bäckström." The SF recruiter looked to be from Österbotter, with steel-blue eyes and a fuzz of blond hair at the sides of his head, under his dress cap. He spoke Joséphine French with a precise, upper-middle-class accent. A Cross of Valor, second class, decorated his chest. "This is my first visit to your town, but judging from your display of patriotism, it won't be my last."

The major continued. "I'm certain you've heard about the vast opportunities an enlistment in the Space Force would open for you." He surveyed the crowd with an easy, confident manner. "I'm here to tell you they're all true."

The major spent the next minutes talking about benefits of service in the SF. Travel, technical skills applicable to numerous civilian careers, pride in defending the travel routes binding the Confederated Worlds together, respect and admiration from civilians in their ports of call. As he strode the riser, the rays of Soleil-de-France would sometimes glint in the Cross of Valor and dazzle the locals' eyes.

"There's danger, of course, given we're in wartime. But the risk is less than in—" He angled his head and motioned with his eyes toward the GF recruiter, "—other branches, and, the better you perform your task, the lower the risk. No other branch can say that. And no other branch will have as great a say as we will in bringing about a victory over the Unity. Does anyone have any questions?"

"I saw the news story about how you kept your men firing their gun in the first battle at New Liberty," said one of the local boys. "What's it like to be a hero?"

"I only did my duty to my ship and my service in spite of the damage we suffered. If you want to call that heroism, I can't stop you. Other questions?"

Lucien said, "Does the SF favor officers who graduated from the Space Force Academy over those who emerge through officer candidates school?"

The major paused, checked his tablet. "I assure you, Mr. LaSalle, whether you come to have a single brass bar or a flock of eagles on your epaulets, your rank is the only thing your men and your fellow officers will see. No other questions? Thank you for your attention. Let me turn the stage over to my colleague."

Lucien slipped back through the crowd as the recruiters changed places. "Why bother listening?" Lucien murmured to Tomas.

"It would be rude to slip away."

"Pff." Lucien shrugged. "It's your time to waste." He passed the lower-ranked military personnel at the back of the paved area on his way to his parked car.

The GF recruiter, a stocky man, had a captain's bars on his shoulders and a set of plain ribbons on the front of his dress gray jacket. "Hello, I'm Captain Schreiber. Before we start, I'd like to thank Lieutenant Singh and Staff Sergeant Bath-al-Uzzá for their efforts in organizing our meeting with you today. I also should thank Major Bäckström for his service as well."

Continuing in passable *joséphinais*, Capt. Schreiber said, "The major drew a lot of distinctions between what his branch can offer you from what the Ground Forces can. Even though he oversold some things—that travel he spoke of is in a windowless can from one space station to another—he got one thing right. The Ground Forces get their hands and their uniforms dirty. Even if you don't carry a rifle as part of your duty assignment—most GF soldiers don't—combat support personnel still face hardship and risk.

"That said," Capt. Schreiber added, "GF personnel can benefit in ways spacemen can't. The bonds you can form with your squadmates are stronger than any other, except the ones with your families. You can see the wide variety of human worlds and human beings, up close and personal. And though there's less glamour, the wisest civilians will commend your service, because they know the truth. All other combat arms, from the Space Force to the Intelligence Bureau to the Foreign Affairs Ministry, exist for only one purpose: to put the Ground Forces infantryman in sole possession of the battlefield."

Capt. Schreiber went on, his manner gruffly affable, and Tomas found himself warming to him and his branch. The captain's honesty refreshed Tomas, and made him wonder. What else had the SF major obfuscated or downright lied about?

After a public question-and-answer period at the end of his presentation, Capt. Schreiber said, "If you want to talk more informally with the major or me, we'll be around for a few minutes."

With that, the meeting broke up. Tomas stood in the same place for a moment. Most of the locals drifted away, but one figure strode effortlessly against the current: Lucien, returning for more face time. He went directly to Maj. Bäckström without a glance to either side.

Tomas swallowed once, his Adam's apple feeling thick, and walked to join SSgt. Bath-al-Uzzá and two local boys around Capt. Schreiber.

Soleil-de-France now hung a few hours away from Napoléon. A storm in the gas giant flashed lightning in its gibbous dark face as Tomas reached the group around the captain.

"But wasn't the major right?" one of the local boys asked. "GF is a lot more dangerous than SF, yeah?"

"If you look at total casualty rates, that's adding up killed, wounded, and taken prisoner, sure. But you can't be taken prisoner in a space battle, and you're a hell of a lot more likely to end up killed in a ship than you are wounded. Here, let me show you all something." Capt. Schreiber lifted his tablet, swiped the touchscreen, then turned it to them.

Tomas glimpsed a photo of a long black shape occluding background stars on the touchscreen, then shut his eyes and turned his head. *The photograph was the first step toward Earth's virtual fugue,* his mother had said a thousand times. *We may only look at what is, not what was, somewhere else, some time ago.*

"From this side, the ship looks intact," came Capt. Schreiber's voice. "Even from the other side, the only damage looks minor. Let me zoom in. See? Not much, right? Now, here are some photos the SF recovery team snapped from the interior, far from the hull puncture." A fingertip sounded on the touchscreen.

"Ugh," said the boy who'd asked the question.

"I don't feel good," said the other, voice queasy.

"There's lots of ways to die on the ground," Capt. Schreiber said. "But for your eyes to bulge and your lungs to hemorrhage, you have to be in space." He held a pause, then said, "We've excluded Mr. Neumann enough. Didn't know you were an Observer. I'll warn you next time."

Tomas opened his eyes. The tablet dangled in the captain's hand; the touchscreen showed plain text. "Thank you, sir."

Capt. Schreiber nodded in acknowledgement, then continued speaking to the group. "In Ground Force, you're a damn sight more likely to get wounded and live. Sergeant, you were in medical corps, weren't you?"

A faraway look passed over SSgt. Bath-al-Uzzá's face. "I was," she said quietly.

"I'll give you the honor of quoting medical corps' motto."

"'If they come to us alive, they'll stay that way.'" She blinked and turned away for a moment.

Capt. Schreiber held his gaze on the other boys in turn, then Tomas. "I can attest to the truth of that motto." His thick hands unbuttoned his gray jacket with surprising quickness. He handed the jacket to the staff sergeant, then opened the links at the cuffs of his white starched shirt. This close, his hands were visibly different: the left had thicker nails and larger veins than the right.

He pushed his sleeves back to his elbows. His right arm was fresher-looking all the way to the elbow, skin more pink, hair less gray. "There are civilian young ladies present across the way," he said with a nod at the cluster around Major Bäckström, "so modesty bars me from baring my chest, but you could see the beginning of my regrown arm right here." He gently chopped his right shoulder with the side of his left hand.

Tomas digested his words in a few moments of silence. "But still, a lot of Ground Force die," the second local boy said.

Capt. Schreiber gave him a firm look. "That's true. And? You think you're guaranteed to live a thousand years if you sit this war out? The more men we have who are unwilling to risk their lives, the more likely we are to lose this war. If the Unity wins, do you trust them to keep you alive? If you want guarantees, go listen to the major blow smoke." His expression changed to take in the entire group. "More questions?"

The first boy spoke. "The major made it seem like SF guys get—" He jolted his gaze to SSgt. Bath-al-Uzzá and blinked a few times. "—I mean, more, respect—"

"Spacemen get more *vulve*? Pardon my language, sergeant."

"I've heard worse, sir." SSgt. Bath-al-Uzzá sounded mildly amused.

Capt. Schreiber returned his attention to the boy. "I don't know if that's true. Now it may be that some dumb girls see Shirley Foxtrot in casual blues and give it up more easily, but I hear you can get all the *vulve* you want on Sol b." Earth, whose billions slept in virtual reality chambers while the real universe unfolded around them.

Was the captain an Observer? Or at least sympathetic to Observer precepts? Tomas wondered if his long-dead father had been as honest, as challenging, as worthy of respect as this man.

What the local boys might think now struck Tomas as irrelevant; his nervousness at school a few hours earlier now seemed unreal. "What about Observer doctrine?" he asked. "Can a man serve in the GF without being forced to see previously-recorded video or hear previously-recorded audio?"

Capt. Schreiber thought a moment. "He can. I have to tell you, some duties are impossible to reconcile. Others can be done, but you'd be in for a tough road persuading your commander you can hack it without all this." He lifted and waggled his tablet. "Live video and audio are okay for you?"

"They are."

"Then there will be duties to fit you." After a look around the group, Capt. Schreiber asked, "Nothing further? That's fine. GF isn't asking for a decision today. You have to earn your *baccalauréat* or your skilled trades aptitude cert before you can enlist. Let me print out or beam you my contact information. You can call or mail me anytime with any questions, or your decision yes or no."

He pointed at the far side of the *Place des Citoyens*, where a line of public hire jitneys stood at the curb opposite the mouth of *boulevard Hortense*. "For now, your ride home is on us."

A few minutes later, Tomas sat in the back of the jitney, heading north of town. He held the captain's business card between thumb and forefinger, flexing it. He paid no attention to the driver's route. They could be driving past the *Lycée Superieur* for all he knew, or cared.

A few minutes later, sweat broke on Tomas' forehead and the jitney's air conditioning blew louder from the vents. He neared the heatwick atop the hill on the north side of town. As they passed a hundred meters from it, a space between rows of black-green maples gave a glimpse of the heatwick's base, dirt piled up around it, graffiti staining the black ceramic. The heatwick blocked a wide swath of the eastern sky, as if the gas giant Napoléon had darkened and fallen to the world's surface.

Almost at the top of the hill, Tomas glanced over his shoulder. Portage-du-Nord covered the slope falling toward the Friedland River, three kilometers distant, with low roofs and clumps of elms and maples. He'd seen the town every day coming to school, but today, Portage-du-Nord seemed like a flattened stain on the terraformed landscape, insignificant under the indigo sky. Soleil-de-France shown amid the sparkle of a dozen bright stars, stars where he could serve, not as a cog in Lucien LaSalle's machine, but as a man with men like Capt. Schreiber.

He crested the hill and the town slipped from sight. The boulevard narrowed to two lanes. Its median tapered, then gave way to a yellow center stripe. The road now continued in a straight line as it rose and fell with the jumbled landscape. Cuts in ridgelines showed strata of primordial lava and compressed ash, splotched with moss and lichen and tufted with a few tenacious plants.

After half a dozen kilometers, the car climbed the tallest ridge since the Portage-du-Nord heatwick. Off to the right, the Observer parsonage showed as a small artificial block, in contrast to the natural lines of the ridge meeting the sky and the curves of the Observing pews. The driver slowed and pulled off onto the extra-wide shoulder approaching the driveway to the parsonage. "Take you to the house?" he asked Tomas.

"I'll walk. Thank you." The car stopped and Tomas climbed out. This far between heatwicks, the cool air made him shiver. He unlocked the gate across the driveway and went in, zipping his jacket after his first two steps.

His mother was supposed to be gone all day, Observing a funeral in Bois d'Orme, but as he paced up the driveway, he didn't relax until he noticed her car missing from the carport next to the parsonage. Relief hit him. He had a few more hours to work out what to tell her.

His relief faded when he came closer to the fence around the parsonage, carport, and lawn. The yellow flag on the gate post, next to his mailbox, had been raised. He trudged to a stop. Reluctantly, he lifted the mailbox lid and pulled out his mother's message to him.

We're doing a snap Observation of today's eclipse of Soleil. Clean the pews. Love Mother.

He frowned at the note for a moment, then slid it into the recycling bin and stalked down the path that led around the parsonage to the Observing pews. He kicked a pebble across the parallel yellow lines of the parking lot. Even though she was twenty kilometers away, he couldn't escape her commands.

Tomas yanked the microfiber mop from the custodial dugout

behind the pews, then let the dugout lid clang shut. The pews formed a semicircular amphitheater facing downslope. The main entryway was at back center, flanked by two diorite pillars bearing black and white *taijitu* symbols. He waved the mophead at the *taijitus* and entered. He glanced downslope, where a lectern bearing another *taijitu*, the receding line of sparingly-traveled road, and the distant heatwick over Portage-du-Nord were the only artificial constructs visible under Napoléon's looming bulk. The Observing pews gave a great vantage point, but a snap Observation? No one would hear about it in time to plan their attendance. Mother would be lucky to have three people make the drive from Portage-du-Nord or Bois d'Orme.

He lazily swept the mophead over the granite pews in the outermost ring of the semicircle. Dust could linger in the corners, who cared, why bother digging for it. But as he went on, habit kicked in, goaded by guilt. Cleaning the pews had been his chore since they'd moved to Joséphine. He couldn't help it. He pushed the mophead deep into the corners of the first pew in the second ring, then sighed out a breath and went back to the outermost ring to redo them.

Don't be such a coward. You'd rather give her what she wants then tell her it doesn't matter. Yet despite the thoughts passing through his mind, he persisted in sweeping the pews according to his mother's expectations.

About halfway through, another thought hit him. Even if cleaning the pews didn't matter, even if he left town the day after receiving his *baccalauréat* and headed straight to Capt. Schreiber's office in Couronnement, this was the duty assigned to him, and he owed it to himself to do it as best he could. The critical thoughts fell away after that and he found himself entering a rhythm, sweeping quickly and efficiently. He lost track of time. Surprise widened his eyes when he realized he'd reached the innermost ring of pews.

He sat for a moment in the right front pew, next to the central aisle. Joséphine's tidal lock to its primary meant the bottom limb of Napoléon always just grazed the top of the lectern as seen by his vantage point. The gas giant's face was dark and already it obscured a curved sliver of Soleil-de-France.

"You better be done cleaning if you're sitting around," came his mother's voice from the top of the amphitheater. A low wall behind the lectern reflected her voice as well, pummeling him from both sides. In addition to her brusque tone, she spoke in Sankt-Benedikts-Sprach, the language she normally used when she wanted to keep her words to Tomas unintelligible to locals.

Tomas lurched out of his seat and the end of the mop handle spun in a wide circle before he settled it. He winced that he jumped even when she gave no command and lifted his chin when he faced her. "I cleaned everything."

She came closer. Though ten centimeters shorter than Tomas, he still felt small in her presence. Her brown eyes were usually narrowed in a scowl, but now the expression was more intense than usual, with her lips pressed tightly together. "Even the tops of the *taijitus*?" She lifted her hand and pointed her forefinger at him. She wore a white glove, and her fingertip bore dust.

"Sorry, I must have missed there."

"We have to be attentive to detail. The local people will probably never meet other Observer ministers. If we don't show them the Observer way as perfectly as we can, they'll end up in virtual fugue and whose fault would that be?"

His heart thudded and he forced himself to look into her eyes. "I need to talk to you about something, mother."

She leaned back. "I don't have much time. I need to rehearse the homily for the Observation of the eclipse."

"It's important, mother." Tomas swallowed. "I want you to hear it from me and not from anyone else."

Alarm crinkled her brow. "What is it? Did you get one of those girls pregnant?"

"After I finish the *lycée*, I'm going to enlist in the Ground Force."

Her expression clouded. "No you aren't."

"I'm eighteen standard. When I have a school leave-taking cert—"

"You will go to the seminary on Péngláishān. You have a gift for Observing. You have to practice and perfect that gift for the people of the Confederated Worlds, to save them from virtual fugue." Her tone buffeted him with her certainty.

He clutched the mop handle. "I don't know if I have a gift."

"You have a gift. I've never lied to you, have I? Becoming an Observer minister is the best thing you can do."

A cold breeze flowed down the slope toward them. It lifted the ends of his mother's brown hair from her shoulders, but she stood still and her face showed no sign of distraction.

"I could always go to seminary after finishing my enlistment—"

"Enlistment?" She stepped closer and looked at him as if he suffered some grave illness. "You would throw your pearls before swine if you joined the Ground Force! All they want is boys with empty heads to give more room for their slotted skills and knowledge. Empty heads they can fill with lies of glory and sacrifice. Empty heads no one will miss when they're splattered across some foreign planet!"

Tomas flinched, then remembered Capt. Schreiber's comment to the second local boy. "There's risk in serving, but there's also risk in doing the same old thing."

His mother's head reared back and her eyes widened in passing. She groped for words. "This is your life we're talking about. You're eighteen standard. You think you're immortal and infallible. You aren't. You know you aren't. The local boys will clutch their napoleon medallions and their crucifixes around their necks, thinking divine favor will keep them alive when bullets fly around them. But you know those gimcracks make no difference. The emergence of each moment from the one before will cut down the pious and the impious alike—"

"If the GF medical corps finds a wounded man still alive, they'll keep him alive."

"And the people on both Earth and Heinlein's World count themselves kings of infinite space," she said in an incontrovertible tone. "People say all sorts of things, but saying doesn't make it true."

"They can rebuild arms and legs—"

"Can they rebuild heads? And I don't just mean you might get your head shot off. Do you know what war does to the men who fight?"

Tomas brought the mop handle, still clutched tightly, in front of his body. "They see bad things."

"Worse. They do bad things. They kill people. They destroy things. They harm the innocent. Most of the *joséphinais* who'll enlist will turn to drink or drugs to dull the pain of their memories." Her voice softened. "But you're an Observer. You see everything as it is. Drink and drugs are barred to you." She peered at him, and her tone grew cold. "Unless you renounce Observing, after all it has done for you."

He grasped the mop handle with both hand. "I can both serve in the Ground Force and be an Observer. Captain Schreiber said so."

"He lied. His only goal is to press the shilling on enough boys to meet his quota to his superiors. Soon as you would take it, he'd forget you. He'd love to get an Observer to enlist. The military wants to destroy us—"

"What? No!" She hadn't met the captain; she wouldn't say these things if she had. And she'd never denounced the military before.

"They want to revoke the limits we Observers call on our peers to follow, so they can misuse computers and time-shift recorded data to better make war. You think that's all? Do you believe you'll have any say in what they will slot into your brain? They'll make you watch and listen to recordings. They'll make you use computers for purposes other than reading text. You'll have no choice."

"I will too have a choice. Captain Schreiber told me." Anger overwhelmed meekness. He pushed the mop away. The wooden handle clattered against the nearest pew. "He's the only man I've ever met who's treated me with respect."

The corners of her mouth turned down, and her eyes looked as cold as the handful of stars at the indigo zenith. Voice dispassionate, she said, "You're just like your father."

Shame flooded him when she did that, as it always had when she'd said those words in that tone before. But now, he felt something else. The captain's demeanor was a lifeline as he thrashed to keep himself from drowning. "He was a man and I am his son. Maybe I should be like him."

"You should be a fool? Throwing his pearls to swine and getting trampled to death in the process? He had immature daydreams, just like you, and he didn't know what he was getting into, just like you. And he died for it, just as you are likely to if you enlist. You want to be a soldier? You want to come home in a plastic bag? Or with a mind forever broken by the shame and guilt your actions would earn you? Then in your last lucid moments, when you'll know your life or your sanity are ebbing away to never return, see how much it comforts you to know you're your father's son."

Her words stung him, but in a moment, his timidity fell away. *You know nothing about being a man,* Tomas thought, but then his anger faded. "Thank you for telling me what you think I should do. But I will enlist."

Her mouth opened without speaking, expressing disbelief. She blinked and her eyes glistened, and muscles momentarily worked in her throat. "Don't make me cry."

"You don't have to. I'm not dead yet."

She drew in a breath and peered down her nose, gaze suddenly hard. Arms folded over her chest, she said, "You're close enough. You're no longer an Observer. Get out of my pews."

CHAPTER 2

TAKING THE SHILLING

FIVE MONTHS LATER, Tomas stood in a line of recruits in the middle of the GF's main intake base, a space station in orbit high above Challenger, capital of the Confederated Worlds. From the exhaustion of weeks of travel getting here from Joséphine, the jet lag going from the standard day on board ship to the nineteen-hour Challenger day on the station, the heavy weight in the station's outer rings, and the bewildering mix of delay and hurry making up the intake process so far, the conversation going on behind him seemed unreal.

"Man, why'd they have to cut my hair?" asked a smooth-faced Österbotterman in school-slotted Confed. He rubbed his palm over the blond fuzz on his scalp.

"It's SOP," said an al-Aqsan. He must have been on the same ship as Tomas, but Tomas had first seen him at the start of intake a few hours earlier.

"But he's got all his." The Österbotterman nodded up the line, where a Navi Ambarsari waited. "A beard, and he's got hair under that headwrap, doesn't he?"

A Challengerite with a chummy manner leaned in. "I think it's called a turban." He caught Tomas' gaze and rolled his eyes without the Österbotterman noticing. The whites of his eyes contrasted with the massed green uniforms of the recruits lining the corridor behind him.

"Whatever it's called, it isn't fair."

"He gets a religious exemption from the grooming regs," the al-Aqsan said.

"Religious exemption? I checked 'Evangelical Lutheran' on the religious preference page and they still buzz-cut me."

Tomas remembered the intake form. He'd hesitated at the religious preference page for several seconds, before the intake sergeant on the other side of the table cleared his throat. Tomas' finger had hovered over *None*, spite toward his mother building up in his chest, before he shook his head and pressed *Observer*.

"They're stripping away our civilian lives," the al-Aqsan said. "Same reason we're wearing unadorned green with no rank insignia. We all start out as soldiers with nothing."

"Except our 2d barcodes." The Challengerite tapped his fingers against a dense black pattern on the left side of his chest.

"They had to cut your hair," said another Challengerite, a short fellow with dark brown hair and a bulbous nose, to the Österbotterman. "It's so they can drill the skill implanters into your brain."

The Österbotterman's eyes widened in passing, then a surly look formed around his mouth. "That's crap. They would've shaved the Ambarsari too."

The chummy Challengerite exaggeratedly shook his head. "For him, they'll have to use the penile catheter. That's why the girls got routed a different way for this part."

"In school they used medicine and video goggles," the Österbotterman said, disagreement in his voice but fear in his eyes. He looked around. "Hey, Saint Benny, isn't it like that here?"

Tomas couldn't remember if he'd only told the intake sergeants his birthworld, or if he'd also mentioned it to some other recruit. How had it gotten out? "I don't know," he replied. He winced at his poor fluency in Confed. Madame Martin didn't use any skill-slotting to teach her students.

"They've got to use more than grade school tech," the short Challengerite said. "This isn't about learning languages and arithmetic. It's got to take high powered stuff to make us soldiers."

A sergeant surprised Tomas, coming from the front of the line. His green fatigues showed a camouflage pattern with bright red bands around the arms and at the collar. "Listen to you lot. You don't even have your pubes yet." He brushed the back of his hand over Tomas' upper arm, where the solid green fabric lacked chevrons. "You know as little about skill-slotting as you do about pussy. At least you're going to find out about one of those today. To the chambers, now!"

The line moved forward in bursts. Eventually it led Tomas around the corner to another sergeant. He waved a plastic wand over the barcode on Tomas' chest. "Keep going."

Tomas went over a pleated plastic strip in the floor to a narrower, lower-ceilinged part of the corridor sloping upward. A wider, level space opened out past the top of the slope. Tomas climbed, the al-Aqsan and the Österbotterman behind him, when the sergeant paused the line. A wall hid the two Challengerites from view.

"Glad to be rid of them," the Österbotterman muttered. "From the capital and they think they're better than us—whoa!" All three of them reached for handrails. "Something happen to the station?"

Tomas remembered Capt. Schreiber's words about horrible death in space, yet he kept calm. The far end of their part of the corridor slewed over a thickness of alloy and nanotube fiber on its way to another wide, level space. "The station is okay. The corridor is moving from one destination level to another."

Another sergeant waited for them in the wide, level space. The light came dimly from ceiling bulbs and cast long shadows down his face. "One to a chamber." The sergeant jutted his hand toward six open doors on the far wall. "Lock it behind you, strip down, and climb in."

"Into what?" the al-Aqsan said.

"You'll see. Move it, prepubes!"

The doors seemed narrow, the spaces within dim. The air carried a sick-sweet smell. The scared speculation of a few minutes ago suddenly seemed plausible. "Have you seen anything like this?" Tomas said to the al-Aqsan.

"No—"

"The chambers, prepubes! And strip means *strip*! Bare-assed, on the double!"

Tomas went in and locked the windowless door. In the tiny room, he had to turn sideways to fit between the side wall and a table bearing a plastic box, over two meters long, about one wide, and sixty centimeters high. The box had an opened lid. The interior looked to be coarse black plastic with grilles and nozzles jutting into it from the box walls.

It's not a coffin, they won't kill their recruits. Though if there's a chance we'll die it would be easy to bury us.

Tomas shook his head to push the thought away. He would survive this. But another thought jolted him. The Österbotterman had talked about video and audio in skill-slotting. Those feeds had to be recorded. Didn't the recruiters know he was an Observer? The third sergeant hadn't scanned his barcode! A mistake, he'd go out and tell the sergeant—

He rattled the handle. Locked. Of course, he'd just locked it. Tomas took a breath, then reached for the unlock dial.

The dial refused to turn.

He tried again and again, putting more muscle into it each time, fear burning his chest. He had to get out. He lifted his fist to pound the door when a thought held him back. If he didn't go through with their skill-slotting, what would they do? Discharge him.

What would his mother say?

He opened his fist and turned to the coffin. He looked for video displays and audio loudspeakers in the interior. He knew what they looked like—his mother had let him watch live transmissions of public pronouncements, like the President's address upon the declaration of war on the Unity—and the coffin held none. The GF probably had better tech than a public school on a sparsely-settled planet and didn't need video and audio.

Or else most Observers weren't as fanatically against unreal images and sound as his mother.

Tomas stripped. He hung his plain green shirt and trousers on a hook on the door, then followed them with his underwear. Suddenly, the urge to piss struck him, but he glanced around and failed to see any bedpan or slot in the wall. *Climb in.* The GF had planned for this too. He could probably piss in the coffin if he had to.

He climbed and noticed another door, on the wall opposite the one he'd entered. He sat down in the coffin. The plastic felt warmer and softer under his ass than he'd expected. He stretched out. The plastic's soft warmth soon lost its luster. The room was cold. His *biroute* shrank and his scrotum pulled his balls toward his abdomen.

The second door then opened. Three figures entered in green fatigues with white trim at the cuffs and collar and red crosses on white circular fields just above the elbows. Even before he heard their first words, Tomas realized they were women. His cheeks grew hot. He pressed his legs together and cupped his hands over his genitals.

One woman, her blond hair tinged with gray and captain's bars on her collar, said, "The corporals need your arms."

"Arms? But—"

"We've seen more penises than a midwife. Arms, recruit. For the IVs."

"I need to—" He sought a polite word to use around women. "Urinate."

"You can wait ten minutes?" the captain said. "The urge will go away."

He wanted to appear in control. "I can wait." Tomas breathed shallowly, then pulled his hands from his crotch and rotated his arms to expose the veins inside his elbows. The corporals, one of them, from her dark skin tone, clearly native to Zion-against-Babylon or Garvey's World, pulled equipment from shoulder bags, plugged tubing into nozzles in the coffin's interior wall, and prepared his arms. Tourniquets squeezed his upper arms and evaporating iodine solution made his skin tingle. The needles stung when the corporals inserted them and then stopped hurting. Skintape, clicking plastic, swipes and taps on tablet touchscreens. More skintape followed, applied to sensor discs across his chest, abdomen, arms, legs.

While the corporals worked, the captain did too. "This is the TMI helmet," she said. With one hand she guided Tomas to lift his head, then pulled the helmet down. It fit snugly from occipital bump to eyebrows. She cinched a strap snugly under his chin.

"You really had to cut our hair for this," he said.

The captain ignored his words. "This goes over your mouth and nose." She held up a curved, lumpy piece of clear plastic. The lobate edge glistened with a bright blue gel. She pulled out a strap and nodded to bid Tomas lift his head. He did. She slid the mask over the TMI helmet, then guided it toward his lower face.

"Why not put on the mask before the helmet?" he asked.

She connected one end of a tube to the mask and the other to the coffin wall. Gas hissed as she moved the mask to his mouth and nose. The bright blue goop sucked itself onto his face. "Recruits are more likely to freak out from the mask than anything else." She plugged cables from the helmet into ports in the coffin interior and made a few motions on a tablet.

"Farewell, recruit." The lid swiftly lowered toward Tomas, then sealed him with thuds. Darkness. No getting out now. His breathing became ragged and he wanted to push on the lid. Not scared, just testing the situation… He resisted the urge. If the GF monitored his actions in here, he wouldn't show panic. And even if the GF wasn't watching, he watched himself. He remembered Capt. Schreiber. The captain had gone through this. Tens of thousands of other men had gone through this. If his mother thought him less a man than the all those other men, he'd prove her wrong. He might be afraid but he would stay calm.

The darkness was so deep his vision couldn't adapt. Eyes open or closed, the view was the same darkness. Tomas paid attention to his other senses. Pumps sounded in several spots in the coffin wall or nearby. Shouldn't something be happening? Did some defect delay the start? *Let's get this over with….*

His thoughts seemed stretched out. The touch of the coffin liner disappeared and a warm feeling spread up his flanks, his armpits, into his ears. Water? He thrashed his head, heard a few splashes. The feeling soon covered his eyes and all his skin.

He couldn't tell if he lay on the coffin bottom or floated in the water. Beats sounded, alternating ears, in a quick rhythm that set up a resonance filling his awareness. He couldn't tell if they came from hardware in the coffin interior or in his own head, induced by the TMI helmet. The need to piss had faded. He couldn't tell if his brain had heightened its control over his body or if his bladder had emptied into the fluid surrounding him. He couldn't find any of the answers, and it was no longer important to ask the questions.

Thoughts slowed and broke apart like crystals crumbling to powder. *What's happening? Did Capt. Schreiber get more recruits from Portage—any port in a storm—port—starboard—star—star....* His mind lost the ability to make words. Only sensory impressions remained: Soleil-de-France near eclipse. Véronique's shy smile before she pecked his cheek behind the bleachers at the Harvest Fête. Dead men in Space Force blue jumpsuits, lungs prolapsed out mouths frozen in screams. His mother's cold look. Beneath a waving oak under a golden sun, a man with brown hair and a narrow jaw, known with a sudden certainty to be the father he'd never seen....

A STRIP of light ran vertically through his field of vision, ends beyond the reach of his eyes. The strip widened, widened. Solid off-white in the distance, a triangle of yellow-white glow expanding as the strip widened. Faces, too, two pale, one dark.

Tomas blinked and started, pushing his weight into the coffin bottom for a moment before relaxing.

"Welcome, private," the captain said.

"Thank you, ma'am, corporal, corporal." The corporals touched styluses with glowing red tips to the skintape over his body. The skintape shriveled with a tingle over his skin. He was still naked, but unashamed. Not only had they seen more penises than a midwife, but he now knew women received recruit intake skills implantation duty after medical service in a field battalion. They'd seen more blood, torn limbs, and open wounds than even an armored grenadier or airmobile hussar.

"Doing our jobs, private," said the corporal from Garvey's World.

"Your fatigues are where you left them," the captain said. "Take five minutes to dress, then head out the front door."

"Yes, ma'am."

The skills implantation team left the room. Tomas climbed out of the coffin. Except for the taupe smears of hemostop over the IV needles' puncture sites in his elbows, his body looked no different. Yet he felt different. He stood taller, but there was more. New capabilities lurked in his muscle memory, ready to come out when needed.

He found his clothes on their hook. Underwear on, trousers on, tunic… He paused when he saw a sleeve. A single chevron pointed toward the shoulder seam. Private. He stepped into his boots and pressed the button inside at the top of the heel to tighten them, then reached for the door handle. It opened easily.

Where the mouth of the sloping corridor had been, a temporary wall stood, mounted in upper and lower tracks. In the wide, level space, four privates stood in a rank with their backs to Tomas, and as he stepped forward to join them, he realized they were his companions up the ramp.

The same sergeant waited, but this time, with three officers: two captains and a lieutenant colonel. Tomas came to attention and saluted.

"At ease," the lieutenant colonel said.

Tomas stole glances at the other privates. The Österbotterman stood two places to the right. He looked wiser than he had sounded waiting in line a few—

Minutes? hours? days? ago. How long had they been in the skills implantation chambers?

To his left, the final door opened. The al-Aqsan joined the rank of privates, saluted, was ordered to ease.

"Men, I'm Lieutenant Colonel Gallegos, commander of 1st Recruit Intake Battalion. Over the past two days, we have given you the skills to be soldiers. I know you can already sense some of the changes in yourself. There are even more you'll discover in the coming weeks, when you are assigned to a specialty, receive further skills implantation in that specialty, and get your first active duty assignment."

Lt. Col. Gallegos went on. "But there's more to being a soldier than what's in here." He tapped his temple with his forefinger. "Part of being a soldier is knowing you are part of a team, where all your team-mates, whatever their rank, their world of origin, their religious beliefs, have certain things in common. Here's one of them."

Slender fingers undid the top three buttons of his fatigues, then pulled out a polished gray medallion about three centimeters in diameter and a half-centimeter thick. Tomas recognized it immediately. "This is the Multi-Purpose Individual Data Acquisition Processing and Communication Device. Charged up by the motion of your body, it is a friend-or-foe beacon, a medical telemetry device, a short range communicator, and a dog tag. We call it the shilling."

Lt. Col. Gallegos shifted his weight. "One reason we call it a shilling is its shape, like a medallion or an ancient coin. But the other reason is a custom going back to ancient England. You see, even now, you can back out. Maybe you sense the changes we made in you are ones you don't want. Fine. The skills implantation team can take those soldiering skills out of you as easily as they put them in. A little bit of paperwork, you're discharged honorably, the end. But if you take the shilling, you're a soldier till your enlistment expires."

Blunt, truthful. Just like Capt. Schreiber. Maybe just like the brown-haired man with the narrow jaw. Was that really what his father had looked like?

"Take a minute. Think about it. If you take it, you've declared, to GF as a whole, to the men before you, to your fellow privates on either side, your commitment to serve. And most of all, you've declared it to yourself. If you make this commitment, there's no backing out." Lt. Col. Gallegos let his words reverberate in their thoughts for a time, then he, flanked by the captains and the sergeant, stepped forward to each man in turn. The al-Aqsan said yes, as did the next man.

When they reached Tomas, Lt. Col. Gallegos said, "Do you take the shill—?"

"Yes, sir!" His heart pounded.

"You're certain? 'Marry in haste, repent at leisure,' ever hear that one?"

"Sir?"

"Enthusiasm is good, but flightiness isn't. Do you understand what this means? For five years, Neumann, we will own you. Are you ready for that?"

Tomas drew in a breath and stood as tall as he could. He spoke in unaccented Confed. "I am ready to take the shilling, sir."

The lieutenant colonel nodded. "Welcome to our ranks, Neumann."

One of the captains handed Gallegos a chain with a shilling on it. The lieutenant colonel lowered the chain over Tomas' head. The shilling thumped gently on Tomas' chest.

The officers moved to the next private. Tomas laid the shilling in his palm and unbuttoned the top buttons of his tunic with his free hand. Regulations about proper care and safekeeping of the shilling passed just below consciousness, like a school of fish near an ocean's surface, and so too did protocols about supplemental charging and field reboots. Those thoughts faded as the polished gray metal filled his gaze. It had been proper and good, to receive the gift of new life in a womb from a woman; but even better and more fitting, to receive the gift of comradeship from a man.

THE NEXT DAYS BLURRED BY. Physical training in the morning, then breakfast, tests, lunch, more PT, more tests, dinner and a lecture on the GF's proper place in the Confederated Worlds' politics and society, yet more tests, thirty minutes of relaxation, then lights out. The shorter day carried a shorter sleep cycle, and Tomas went through the five minutes between reveille and the fall in for the march to the PT ground in a mix of exhaustion and epinephrine-boosted alertness.

PT was the longest length of time he got outside the barracks buildings, mess hall, and testing facilities, and under the transparent shielding roofing the station's rotating ring. Tomas couldn't remember ever seeing ground cover as green as the grass. If Tomas lucked into the timing, he would do crunches or weighted getups when Challenger, Epsilon Eridani d, was high overhead, just above or below the opposite side of the station's ring. He didn't dawdle when flat on his back between repetitions of any exercise, but he paid as much attention to the planet as he could. Clouds and deep blue oceans on dayside, the glow of a thousand cities on nightside. A hundred million people lived down there. The number boggled his mind. Half the population of the Confederated Worlds. Most of the privates hoped for a week of liberty on Challenger after finishing prelim training, but Tomas didn't. A week would barely get them up and down the space elevator to McAuliffe City. The glimpses Tomas took from here were enough.

The tests ranged from stylus-on-tablet to hands-on. Literally, in one case: a sergeant lifted a lid on a box full of parts and gave him thirty minutes to assemble a metals extractor. He worked the full time and still had a dozen pieces left over. Apparently he failed; the al-Aqsan talked a few days later about taking a second, comparable test while blindfolded.

Within a week, some of the privates received duty assignments and left the barracks, leaving only empty lockers and crisply-made beds for their fellows to find on returning before meals or at the relaxation time. Before long, it was Tomas' turn.

A sergeant stopped him on his way out of the mess hall after lunch. "Neumann, follow me."

They wound down walkways set in narrow lawns between buildings. Shadows cast by EpEri slid over their path. A turn and a glance over Tomas' shoulder showed the PT ground far up the ring behind him. At a double door, they entered a gray mycocrete building near one end of the facility.

The sergeant led him to a room with windows viewing an interior courtyard, then withdrew. A lieutenant and two enlisted stood near a major seated at a desk. The major brought a narrow-eyed gaze up from a tablet. Tomas saluted.

"At ease, Neumann. We've reviewed your aptitudes, and we are offering you a position in intelligence analysis."

In the ensuing silence, Tomas frowned. "Sir, permission to speak?"

"Yes?"

"I'm not ordered to it?"

"Normally we would, but there are some notes on your file.... You're an Observer?"

"Yes."

"And you don't look at images? Did our recruiting officer on Joséphine get that right?"

Tomas spoke quickly. "I avoid prerecorded photography and audiography. I may see and hear live transmissions of real events."

"Do you make a distinction between prerecorded real events and fiction?"

"Prerecorded events are fiction, sir."

The major leaned back in his chair. "Hell of a strict Observer you are, son." His gaze slowly cycled between Tomas and his tablet. "This is a tough situation. Intel can certainly use you, and you can use it. It's your best aptitude. But the task it needs you for is analysis. That means looking at prerecorded pictures, video, and audio. After intel, your next best aptitude is the armored grenadiers, so if you turn intel down, that's where you'll go."

"I'll gladly serve wherever I'm assigned."

The major had a sour look. "You ever break a bone? Get cut by a knife? Injured in a car accident?"

"No."

"Ever shoot a rifle? Go hunting? Get into a fight against someone armed?"

Tomas remembered Capt. Schreiber's words. All other arms serve the infantryman. He stood taller and put more emphasis in his voice. "No."

The major took off his cap and brushed brown hair back from his forehead. "Son, I'm not trying to burst your bubble. I think you could sack up and do infantry. But any infantry duty gives you a risk of death every day. Armored grenadiers aren't immune because they ride a battle wagon into the combat zone. Intel? You'd be in a secure area on New Lib or whatever planet we next liberate from the Unity. Clean beds, three hot meals a day, Daughters of Astarte on base, no one shooting at you."

"I didn't enlist for comfort, sir."

"You enlisted to grow as a man? Here's a chance to learn and practice skills related to the best aptitude you have."

Tomas said, "At the price of my spiritual beliefs, sir?"

"Spiritual beliefs change and evolve and… hell, I'm not selling you on it. Yeah, son, it doesn't fit with how you interpret being an Observer. Now the damn Unity would say to hell with that and force you into intel. We aren't like that. Being a soldier involves making tough choices, and we'll give you practice at that. Your best aptitude or your spiritual beliefs? Which will it be?"

There were other ways to be an Observer than the one his mother had drilled into him? The thought echoed in a mental space suddenly much larger. He could both follow his talents and conform to the spirit of being an Observer.

"Neumann, we need a decision now."

Whose spirit, though? How many Observers on Earth and Heinlein's World had, in all sincerity, acquiesced to photographs, recorded television, recorded music, virtual reality, and every other form of reality-denial leading to virtual fugue? The major was right, the Confederated Worlds were better than the Unity. The Confederated Worlds didn't force doctrines on its civilians or its soldiers.

So who was the major to tell Tomas the proper way to be an Observer?

"Neumann?"

Tomas snapped his heels together. "Thank you for allowing me the choice, sir. I will join the armored grenadiers."

CHAPTER 3

"GET ON BOARD!" the SF captain shouted in the holding area. He raised his voice over the rumble of the airlock door opening. "Come on, mudbugs, we aren't going to hold up ten thousand tons for your sorry asses!"

"Space Force hospitality never changes, does it?" shouted back a GF soldier in the middle of the crowd in the holding area.

"You want to be in a hurry dirtside, not up here!" called a woman.

"Yeah, I hear a Unity soldier was spotted within a thousand klicks of the spaceport!" yelled a man.

The SF captain looked annoyed, but no one had impugned his dignity as an officer. "Shut your pieholes, sweaties, and board the shuttle!"

Tomas stood up and hoisted his sack to his shoulders. Two months of being shipped around like talking luggage by the SF came to a close today when he landed on New Liberty and got a unit assignment. He moved with the other GF personnel, their travel slow, their chatter echoing off the holding area's nanotube alloy walls. Nervous energy rocked Tomas' weight from side to side every time the crowd halted.

At the airlock's open door, a GF lieutenant, a turbaned and bearded Ambarsari, swiped a scanner over the shilling hidden under each soldier's tunic. The SF captain looked bored as he swiped the touch-screen of his tablet. "The canned spam got to send a captain to do a lieutenant's job," muttered a GF private near Tomas in line.

"They do give us space supremacy," replied a captain with an airmobile hussar badge, an ornithopter above and to the right of a diagonal stripe, on his sleeve.

"If they're not too hung over to operate the lasers." The SF captain glanced up and the private blanked his face.

Through the airlock, they entered a pressurized tube the height and width of a narrow hallway, on the floor of the transport ship's docking bay. Two hundred meters square and fifty high, the docking bay was large enough to show the curvature of the transport ship's outer hull. A seam ran down the middle of the floor, where joined the two docking bay doors, now closed. A stalactite field of girders, flexible piping, and articulating arms jutted from the ceiling. Clangs of metal and throbs of fluid ran through the docking bay doors and up from the soldiers' feet.

The pressurized tube bent upward; the flat floor became a staircase. The clanging and throbbing faded. Banks of floodlights cast smeared shadows over the GF personnel in the pressurized tube. Between the lights, the press of people, and the shallow viewing angle through the tube's thick plastic wall, Tomas barely glimpsed the shuttle before he entered its airlock. He only noted a cylinder, wider than tall.

Inside the shuttle, GF sergeants stood throughout the corridors, guiding the new arrivals to a large round chamber in the shuttle's center. The floor was a black mesh and large blue sacks, roughly the size and shape of sleeping bags, hung on guide wires between the ceiling and floor. The sacks were arrayed in rows and columns like trees in an orchard, and each had two openings, a small hole about a meter and a half off the floor and a large slit running most of the way from the small hole to the floor. The sacks made Tomas think of a ruptured cocoon—

"Kali's yani," muttered a mustachioed soldier from Satyayuga.

An SF lieutenant, green-eyed and scowling, stalked between the sacks. "Pick a gee-sack. Clip your ruck on the back and get in. Stick your face out the hole, then zip up from the inside. Gee-fluid will fill up to your neck. You'll feel it pump when we're in free fall, and if we need to pull gees; this will help your heart and lungs, so don't panic. We've got better things to do than clean up mudbug puke."

The sacks hung so closely together his sleeves brushed clipped-on rucks and someone climbing into one jostled him as he passed. Tomas found an empty one and climbed in. As soon as he closed the zipper, fluid squished in, cold jets hitting his legs and torso. A far cry from the skills implantation couch back at Challenger.

Some soldier nearby called, "You want my hands in the sack? What if there's a rupture? How can I put on the emergency oxygen?"

"Sonofabitch." Tomas judged by the SF lieutenant's voice his scowl had deepened. "There's no emergency oxygen. If there's a rupture, the lack of hull integrity will tear the shuttle apart when we hit atmosphere. I'd rather pass out before getting ripped apart, how about you?"

The sounds of milling soldiers grew quieter. An SF sergeant stopped in front of Tomas, tugging on tubes connected to the back of the sack in front, checking a display on his tablets before moving on. Viscous gee-fluid sloshed around him. The gee-fluid felt warmer than at first, and the view of the backs of other sacks was monotonous. Someone nearby snored. Tomas' nervous energy faded. He almost shut his eyes—

A shudder ran through the ship, rocking him in the gee-sack. On the back of the sack in front, a video display lit up. In the corner, a clock showed current time in 24-hour standard, just past ten-hundred. Live? Girders and moving arms filled the display. One piece, in the center, remained fixed, while the rest slowly shrank and slid toward the center of the view and more filled in from the edges. The docking bay's ceiling?

Nanotube alloy walls came into view from the display's edges. Tomas put it together: an articulating arm held the shuttle by the nose and pushed it out of the docking bay. After a time, the dock doors and the transport's hull appeared on the edges of the display. The shuttle was clear of the transport ship.

Without warning, Tomas' stomach rose and his feet lost contact with the sack bottom. The video display showed the transport's hull scrolling up the screen, and then the scrolling sped up as a low mechanical sound came from somewhere in the ship. Tomas felt queasy and shut his eyes.

He wasn't alone. "Christ, warn a fella!" yelled a sickly voice from amid the sacks. The SF personnel made no reply. Tomas decided he would reopen his eyes, and keep them open as long as he could.

The transport ship scrolled off the display, leaving a view of the stars over New Liberty. Suddenly, a deep, loud rumbling filled the ship and Tomas felt heavy. The entry burn had started.

A countdown timer appeared in a lower corner of the display. 9:52, 9:51, 9:50.... The view of the stars remained unchanging. *Switching to simulated stern view* appeared, and below it the numeral 3.

"Simulated?" A wave of anxiety flowed through Tomas' torso. "Why simulated?"

2...

"You can't see a damn thing through the drive exhaust," came a male voice through a speaker somewhere in his sack.

1...

"It's a rare GF who even wonders why," the voice added.

Tomas shut his eyes. GF personnel around him talked.

"So that's what New Liberty looks like."

"Who cares? It's all green and gray on base."

"Some of us fight for a living, pogey."

"Why no lights nightside?"

"NL's too close to its primary," came the hussar captain's voice. "Tidal lock. Permanent dayside, permanent nightside. See that greenish-black band crossed by lakes and rivers just sunward of the terminator? The only place NLers live."

"Like Nuova Toscana," someone said.

Tomas had read up on New Liberty during transport from Challenger. Sounded like he missed nothing by refusing to watch the screen.

"Band? Like a landing strip?"

"Landing strip? That's how the local girls wear their snatch hair?"

"Like you'll ever know."

The shuttle kept rumbling, and the soldiers swayed in the gee-sacks.

"Where's the cities?"

Tomas spoke up. "Two million people on the whole planet."

"Two million? Don't lie to me. That's too small for the planetary gene pool."

"Not even close," someone said. "Learn some biology. Maybe history too while you're at it."

"Goodbye, McAuliffe City," came a wistful voice.

"Screw you, smarty pants."

"Small gene pool? That means they're all inbred?"

"Woohoo! Retarded girls are too dumb to guard their landing strips!"

"Damn, isn't it getting big?"

"It better," a woman said. "We're landing on it."

"How fast are we going!?"

"Slower every second, mudbug!" called the SF voice who'd spoken to Tomas.

The soldiers grew quieter for a short time, but soon their chatter returned. Tomas gathered the shuttle approached the landing cradle of the main GF base, just outside Reagantown, capital of New Liberty, population forty thousand, all of whom had welcomed the Confederated Worlds' forces not just as liberators, but as long-lost cousins.

The apparent gravity generated by the entry burn intensified. Waves sloshed through gee-fluid, pounding Tomas like a clumsy masseur, pushing in his stomach as he exhaled, ebbing as he inhaled. "Here we go!" someone shouted.

The shuttle's rumbling cut off and Tomas instantly felt lighter. He took a few breaths. In front of him, sacks twisted as GF personnel craned their necks to see how close they were to leaving the ship. Tomas kept still. So far, his military career had consisted mostly of travel, as much spam-in-a-can as the SF personnel around them.

The major's words at the time of choosing his duty assignment back at Challenger came back to Tomas. He might look back with longing on this time of doing nothing.

Tomas set aside the thought. A pump sounded nearby, pulling gee-fluid out of the sack. SF personnel moved among the sacks, checking their tablets, then unzipping soldiers from the outside.

"GF personnel, this way," yelled a GF sergeant somewhere behind and to the right of Tomas.

An SF sergeant let Tomas out of the sack. Walking felt easy, despite the surges in apparent gravity during the entry burn and the dregs of gee-fluid dripping from his clothes to the mesh floor. New Liberty's local gravity was about point-seven gee and the air was enriched in oxygen compared to Joséphine. He knew these facts in his head, but his first step outside the shuttle's hatch, onto a pedestrian bridge extended from the lip of the landing cradle to the shuttle, put the knowledge into his body.

The white ceramic parabolic dish that made up the primary capture system of the landing cradle poured heat up his body. Dregs of gee-fluid turned to powder and drifted from his clothes.

Tomas glanced to his left. New Liberty's star, locally called Constitution, was a red dwarf, dimmer and fatter than Soleil-de-France as seen from Joséphine. Dim, but bright enough to make him squint if he looked directly at it. Low in the sky, it cast long shadows across the landing cradles, driveways, and dark green fields of the spaceport. The planet's tidal lock meant the star would never appear to move. It was permanently late afternoon on New Liberty.

The sky was a deeper indigo than Joséphine's. High thin clouds streamed away from the sun. In passing they veiled bright stars.

A GF sergeant with a scanner waited at the other end of the pedestrian bridge. Just a sergeant—Tomas wouldn't see any SF personnel until he left the planet. After the scan, the right side of Tomas' shilling throbbed against his chest. He turned that direction, toward a large building nearby. He pulled out his tablet. On a map, a yellow line led through the building to a small auditorium inside.

He started off down a walkway. Scattered across the grassy field between him and the boundary of the spaceport, antimissile lasers were parked behind berms and under camouflage netting. Outside the door to the large building, he glanced back. The shuttle passengers had strung out along the walkway. In the distance, the shuttle had two pedestrian bridges connected to it. Two? The second reached higher on the shuttle than the one Tomas had taken, mating with a hatch on the opposite side of the ship. A few people walked in clusters down the second bridge, voices too distant to hear.

"What's that?" Tomas asked.

A corporal in the airmobile hussars, with a trimmed reddish-blond beard and weary eyes, trudged past. He glanced up, then said with a Midgard accent, "The bifrost bridge, virgin. Allows the orificers to descend from heaven."

"But a captain rode with us...." Tomas said. The door swung shut behind the Midgarder. It was an honest question. The Midgarder didn't have to be rude. Maybe the airmobile hussars had a chip on their shoulder. No matter. Tomas would join his fellow armored grenadiers soon.

Tomas went in and soon found the auditorium. Eight rows of twelve seats descended to a stage. Behind the stage, a large video display, mostly black, showed in large print the text *Infantry Replacement Sitrep*. Broad stripes of Confederated Worlds red, white, and blue ran up the windowless walls. Less than a dozen soldiers waited, scattered around the room, not talking to each other. Tomas looked for armored grenadier patches on his fellow soldiers' sleeves. He saw half a dozen, but no one met his gaze. Still, they were his comrades, so he sat near one on the second row back from the stage.

A few more soldiers came in, and then a door to the stage opened for a major, followed by a couple of aides, an enlisted man and woman. The soldiers in the auditorium stood and saluted.

"At ease. Good morning, I'm Maj. Mueller." He had a round, ruddy face and he sounded bored. "I'm going to brief you on the situation here, then give you your unit assignments."

The major cleared his throat. "At this time, our operational posture is the pursuit of remnants of Unity infantry formations in order to deny them an opportunity to reorganize and contest our dominance of NL." Thanks to his skills implantations, Tomas was able to translate the jargon into plain Confed. *Keep them on the run till they give up.* "Here's a map."

The display flickered, showed an image. Though no map was ever live, a map was a pictorial representation of data, not a photograph purporting to be reality. Tomas studied the map as the major spoke. "At present, intel has confirmed elements of five Uni regiments have pulled back to a mountainous region, the New Rockies Plateau, about six thousand klicks sunleft from here."

Instead of directions relative to planetary magnetic poles or the local or galactic ecliptics, and as people did on other tidally locked worlds, the GF referred to two of New Liberty's four cardinal directions as *light*, toward the local sun and *dark*, away from it. If the local sun was to one's left, one faced *sunleft*; if to one's right, one faced *sunright*.

"The New Rockies Plateau is roughly eight hundred klicks by a thousand. About two thirds of it lies darkward of the terminator and bears glaciation at higher elevations. The glaciation spawns a number of rivers winding through the plateau. The lightward third is heavily forested. The terrain favors the defense."

The major tapped his tablet. Five red icons, replete with alphanumeric codes, appeared on the plateau, amid smears of red crawling down valleys and fading the further the smears got from the icons. "All the Uni regiments are understrength as a result of sustained combat over the last standard year, so each is smaller than one of our brigades. Locations are approximate based on last best intel and models of Uni movement potentialities. Questions?"

"Sir, aren't they recruiting locals to replace lost manpower?" asked a fusilier.

"They can't," said the grenadier near Tomas. He had a faint accent Tomas placed to the continent of Endeavour on Challenger. "The locals are descended from Challengerites who came out here three hundred years ago to terraform. They're loyal to the Confederated Worlds. No one would join the Unity forces."

The major said, "To answer the original question, no. One disadvantage of the Uni forces' current disposition is the exceedingly sparse settlement of the plateau. There are no more than ten thousand civilians residing there, most of them in three towns." Another tap on the tablet and the three towns lit up on the map. All were on the light side, within a hundred kilometers of the flatter land around the plateau, on some of the few paved roads into and through the region. "So there's a small manpower pool the Uni forces could draw from. Plus, our civilian interface officers have repeatedly emphasized to the NLers this isn't their fight. If they stay out of it, we leave them alone. The vast majority of them heed that message."

"Sir?" asked the same grenadier. "They welcomed us as liberators. *Confederated Worlds Today* has always been clear about that."

The major looked pained, and his next words came carefully. "I don't know what the civilian news organs on Challenger base their reports on. All I can say is that the people of NL are generally neutral."

The grenadier's brows still furrowed. Tomas understood his puzzlement. Every news story about New Liberty's civilians—the people whom the war was described as liberating from Unity oppression—painted a picture of joy at the Confederated Worlds' presence on planet and in the system. Those were lies?

Tomas thought further. What if Unity forces from Nouveau-Normandie had occupied Joséphine at the start of the war? Would Guillaume or any of Madame Martin's other students joined them? Etien the ambler? Lucien LaSalle might have. Not out of cultural loyalty with other descendants of ancient France, though; only if the Unity showed itself as the stronger horse. "Most people want to live quiet lives," he whispered to his fellow grenadier. "Better the devil they know than the angel they don't."

The grenadier's puzzlement turned to a surly narrowing of his eyes. "Shit, what do you know, smartypants?" He looked away.

Tomas' face fell and anxiety knotted his gut. I'm on your side I'm one of you don't you see that—

"No one is at liberty for side conversations!" The major said. "You have something to say…." A glance at his tablet, then, "Neumann? Say it to us all!"

Tomas labored for words. "Sir, I was trying to inform a fellow armored grenadier—"

"What about the grenadiers on the far side of the room? And the hussars, fusiliers, engineers, and scouts? Do none of them matter? Speak!"

He swallowed. "People would rather be governed by the devil they know than the angel they don't. Sir!"

"Hmph." The major cocked his head. "You're wiser than you look."

Relief flowed through Tomas' limbs as the major said, "Let's move on to your unit assignments." He lifted his tablet, swiped. "Bannister. Third Scout Squadron. Beltran…" Tomas' heart quickened as the major moved down the alphabet, Jäger, McPherson, "…Neumann, 2nd Battalion, 21st Armored Grenadier Brigade. The Blackjacks, good unit. Quiñones…."

The major soon finished the list. "That's it. The sergeants here will guide you to your transport. Godspeed, men."

Thirty minutes later, Tomas trudged to an ornithopter waiting on a tarmac behind the building. A Bluejay, the smallest noncombat transport thopter in the GF's hangars, squatted on four legs. Heat poured from the reactor in the thopter's tail. Tomas winced and swung wider. A cool darkly breeze felt pleasant as he reached the boarding ramp in the middle of the fuselage under the wing. At the top of the ramp, his shilling throbbed from a scanner mounted in the doorframe.

Inside, the plastic mesh seats were laid out in banks on the sides of the cabin, eight facing the ramp and six on the other wall. About half had occupants, mostly toward the front. The Midgard hussar slouched down, rucksack under his seat and garrison cap down over his eyes. Tomas had to sit next to someone. Maybe he could connect with the Midgarder this time, during the next hours in the air.

The Midgarder stirred and lifted the front of his cap a few centimeters. "Virgin, word of advice." His tone was off-hand, but kind enough.

"Yeah?"

"Never pass up a chance to take a nap." He dropped the cap back over his eyes and settled deeper into the plastic mesh.

They waited for a time. "Come on, let's get going," said one of the men from the briefing. The scout, Bannister, Tomas remembered.

"Zip it, virgin," said a private in the engineers.

"I don't want to sit here all day. Do you?"

The engineer rolled his eyes. "We're replacing dead men. I'm in no hurry getting there."

Bannister looked abashed and grew silent. Eventually the copilot, a warrant officer, sidled through the narrow opening between the cockpit and the cabin. He looked at each of the men in turn as his finger tapped the air. At the end, he made a sour face. "Yeah, seven," he said over his shoulder, raising his voice above the whine of the reactor.

The pilot's voice, muffled by distance, obstacles, and extraneous sounds, said, "Damn it."

"You knew the shillings were counted right."

"I know. Where's that damn lieutenant?"

Motion on the boarding ramp caught the copilot's attention. "Officer up!" he said.

Tomas and the other men stood and saluted. The Midgarder rose rapidly from his nap, and the pilot too emerged from the cockpit with a salute.

"At ease." The lieutenant wore gray-green camouflage fatigues. The name *Tower* showed on his breast pocket and an armored grenadier patch, on his sleeve. His name poorly fit his presence; he was shorter than the Challenger average, and lacked the stockiness of most heavy world natives. As if to make up for a soft chin, his gray-blue gaze scowled across the cabin. "Mr.… Pilot, where's the officer seating?"

"Bluejay's too small a bird, sir."

"We don't deserve a bigger one for this flight?"

"Transport assigned our bird to this run today, sir."

"I see." He turned to the man in the most forward seat on the side opposite the boarding ramp. "Private, I'll take your seat."

"Sir?"

The lieutenant raised his voice. "Do I have to quote the manual?"

"Sir, of course not. Permission to remove my stow?"

"Permission? You mean to tell me you were thinking you'd leave your ruck under my seat?"

The man put on an innocent look. "Sir, I only sought clarity of the order."

The lieutenant kept his piercing gaze for a moment. "Is it clear?"

"Yes, sir." The man knelt at his seat, slid out his rucksack, and moved to the rear of the cabin. As he passed Tomas and the Midgarder, he whispered "Paper tiger" through gritted teeth.

Tomas frowned.

Amid the rustle of the men returning to their seats, the Midgarder murmured, "Graduate of the Ground Force Academy."

"I never heard that term for GFA grads."

"I know, newb. The skills imps only gave you knowledge the orificers want you to have. Remember that."

"I will," Tomas said, but how would he know what skills he really needed?

The pilot's voice came over the intercom. "We're lifting in fifteen seconds."

"Thanks, chief," called one of the experienced enlisted men. The ramp swung up. Tomas double-checked his seat belt. In preparation for launch, the wings beat, sending big chuffs of air downward and bouncing the thopter's suspension. The cabin sank for a moment, then the thopter sprung on its legs and sped up its wingbeats.

Tomas expected the Midgarder to already be asleep, but the other gazed at the live view from external cameras, displayed on video screens above the heads of the men on the opposite side of the cabin. Maybe he would talk more if given the chance. "Why does a paper tiger act so lordly?"

"All new louies have a touch of it."

"But Academy grads worse? They think a piece of paper makes them better than us?" His last sentence froze Tomas' thoughts. Part of the status of Joséphine's *lycées* lay in granting *baccalauréats* instead of the skilled trades diplomas granted by the public schools. He'd bought into that mindset. Maybe his mother had pushed it on him, but he'd relayed it out, expressing disdain for the public schoolies. Maybe some of the dislike he'd received from the locals in Portage had been in response.

"No." The Midgarder glanced at Lt. Tower. "They fear their lack of experience makes them inferior."

The thopter climbed higher. The display showed a view of the GF base, the spaceport, and Reagantown beyond. The thopter darted, sickening Tomas' stomach for yet another time this day, and the view abruptly gave way to a rolling plain, dark green made darker in spots by the permanent shadows of the terrain's relief. By the time fresh questions came to Tomas, the Midgarder's garrison cap was back down over his eyes.

. . .

"Squad," said Sergeant Johnson, "Welcome Private Neumann."

Tomas stood at the sergeant's side at the entrance to the shelter, a low structure of reinforced mycocrete bermed with a dried slurry of plowed soil and polymer. Blocks of armored, transparent plastic formed the shelter's windows. A shaft of sunlight from Constitution caught dust motes and compounded the late-afternoon feeling dragging down Tomas' eyelids and fogging his mind. Twenty-two hours on planet, sleeping fitfully as the thopter hopped from base to base near the main routes from sunright onto the plateau. Hard to believe it was oh-eight-hundred.

Sixteen pulldown cots lined the walls in the front and middle of the shelter. Half the cots were pulled down, where men sat with tablets and earbuds. Most glanced up from their music, videos, and letters, but after giving Tomas their once-overs and terse greetings, most turned back to their activities.

Sergeant Johnson led Tomas in. The sergeant had the darkest skin of any man he'd ever seen in the flesh. Johnson spoke with a lilt Tomas couldn't place, and used vocabulary and grammar far away from the textbook Confed he'd studied at the *lycée*. "Pick a spare cot." Tomas found one in the middle of the room. A blank video display on the bottom of the cot had a slot next to it. Tomas fished out his shilling and slotted it. His name appeared on the display. He stowed his rucksack in a locker mounted on the wall to the left. A display in the locker wall also showed his name, at eye level for a man of average height.

To the back of the room stood a door to the toilets and showers, a kitchenette, and a long table. Four men sat around one end of the table, hunched over tablets, engaged in some game. One, with pale blond hair and a narrow nose, looked up. "Where's the other spare part?"

"Voloshenko, we got one replacement. We make do." Sergeant Johnson raised his voice. "Idrin, make sure you get yourselves to the oh-nine-thirty inspection on time. We have a new platoon commander and we be turning out smarter than B squad." He left.

Maybe the disinterest would fade with the sergeant gone. *They want to meet me without any superiors present.* Yet most still ignored him. He grabbed the handle of the pulldown bed for a place to sit while getting ready for the coming inspection. The bed was lighter than he expected; the swingout leg clanged on the floor.

Men at the table chuckled. "Keep it down," said one, with black hair and sunken eyes.

Tomas ducked his head. He tapped the inside of his left wrist to call up a chronometer. The visually active fabric showed the time, and another tap gave a countdown till the inspection. Less than ninety minutes. He glanced around. Might as well get ready, even though everyone else remained leisurely. He rummaged in the locker for shoeshine, a rag, and a spray bottle of water, then sat and took off his boots.

Voloshenko and the black-haired man rose from the table. As they stepped closer, Tomas noticed the name *Alvarez* on his breast pocket. "Just what we need," Alvarez said. "Another virgin." He gave the name on the locker a cold squint. "Your name's New-man? Right as shit."

"It's pronounced *Noy-mun*."

As if Tomas hadn't spoken, Voloshenko said, "New-man wastes time on chickenshit."

"New-man wants to make us look bad," Alvarez said. "Suck up to the new louie. Were you the teacher's pet back in school, New-man?

The rest of the men took an interest now. Tomas couldn't muster a reply. He blinked a few times and realized he held his breath.

"Where you from?" Voloshenko asked.

Tomas relaxed a bit. "Joséphine—"

"Double shit," Alvarez said. "Josies are useless fuckups."

"I just went through skills implant—"

"Oh? Skills implantation? Why didn't you say so?" Alvarez's sarcastic tone filled the room. Everyone looked up now. "Goddammit, you think jacking off makes you less of a virgin?"

"What do you care?" Tomas said.

"About your ass, New-man? Not a goddam thing. You're going to be dead in a week and I'm not going to care. But if you take someone better than you with you to hell, then I'm going to care. Good men die when virgins fuck up. So stay the hell away from me."

Tomas wanted to reply, yet Alvarez's ire drove words away from his vocal cords. Before he could rally himself, a new arrival, a corporal, distracted him. He had a stout chest and a fair firmness to his features.

His voice sounded deep and profound. "Are you part of the solution or part of the problem?"

Alvarez looked sullen. "Just kicking the tires on the new spare part, Marchbanks."

"Jumping on a virgin for bullshining his boots? Maybe he knows something you don't."

"Like hell," Alvarez said.

Marchbanks went on. "I've been gathering scuttlebutt on the new platoon commander, Lieutenant—"

"—Tower?" Tomas said.

Some of the men in the background blinked, leaned forward. Alvarez narrowed his eyes. "What do you know about him?" Marchbanks asked.

"We took the same Bluejay here from the spaceport. Paper tiger. Orificer. Bifrost bridge." Tomas slowed his words. "He ordered a soldier to the back of the bus and called the Bluejay pilot 'mister' instead of 'chief.'"

The men in the background grumbled. One or two swore under their breath. Soon most of them, including Voloshenko and Alvarez, reached for their shoeshine kits, or called up the diagnostics apps on their tablets to check their fatigues for dead pixels.

Marchbanks stepped away for a moment, then returned to Tomas' cot with a shoeshine kit. "Here, let me show you the quick way."

"Sure. Thanks."

Marchbanks sat, pulled off his boots, dipped a rag in polish. "Nobody wants to get close to the new guy. Every man here has seen someone they like die and wants to armor himself against that much loss ever happening again."

"And new guys die a lot."

"The skills imps give you skills you need, but they can't teach you to work in a team. That's the second most important thing to do out here. Work as a team. No, wet the rag, not the boot."

Tomas sprayed the rag, applied it to the boot. His heart pounded.

Finally, he found the camaraderie he'd been looking for. "So what's the most important thing?"

"Keep your head down. No, not while bullshining. 'Hero' is a four-letter word for 'dead man.' I want all my men to tell their grandchildren what a good old sonofabitch I was. Remember, no one wins a war by dying for his country. You win a war by making the other bastard die for his."

Tomas glanced at Alvarez, who sat near the front of the shelter with buds in his ears and a comm cable between his tablet and the breast pocket of his fatigues. "What about him?"

Marchbanks glanced along the line of Tomas' gaze. "Both things I'm talking about set him off. Alvarez disliked the Josie from the start. No offense."

"About? Josie?" Not much. That's what men did, right? Break each other's balls? "No. Plus, I was born on Sankt-Benedikts-Welt."

Marchbanks smiled. "We're practically neighbors, then. I'm from Scotia." He dropped the smile. "So the Josie wasn't just a virgin, but you know how sometimes men start off on the wrong foot? Same with the Josie and Alvarez."

Marchbanks finished brushing his polish. His boots bore a dull coating. How would he get a shine out of that? He wetted a rag and gently rubbed each boot, talking to Tomas without looking at his handiwork. "I don't know why, but his first mission, the Josie went cowboy. I should've kept him in my fireteam. Dammit. Anyway, Josie ended up in a Uni foxhole against a machine gun crew. Killed two of them, silenced the machine gun. But multiple wounds himself, and for nothing, because our platoon sergeant took a round from a sniper, and our former platoon commander's vehicle hit a landmine."

"So the platoon retreated."

"First they tried to get the Josie to the ambulances."

Tomas nodded. "Never leave a man behind."

"Yes, and there's a counterintel benefit, too; someone badly wounded may be in too much pain to pop his memory disrupters. Unis have transcranial magnetic receivers, like the skills imps' TMI helmets in reverse. Read a prisoner's thoughts, we can do it too. Anyway, Alvarez's buddy goes out to recover the Josie, but then he takes a bullet to the head. His shilling broadcasts a medical emergency over the squad's channel, but he doesn't say a word. Very bad sign. Soon telemetry says both he and the Josie are dead."

"Alvarez blames the Josie." Dead men, the experience of combat, what could a virgin say? "Maybe there's a way to persuade—"

"Don't force it," Marchbanks said. "Alvarez will either warm up to you or he won't."

Tomas took a few breaths. He wanted these men to be on his side. At least Marchbanks was. "Your boots look sharp."

"Yours aren't bad, either. Now, Neumann, what are the two most important things?"

"Work as a team. Keep your head down."

"Exactly," Marchbanks said. "Stick with me and you'll do fine."

CHAPTER 4

NEW BOSTON ROAD

SEVENTY-TWO HOURS after crossing the line of departure, Tomas' experience of war was mostly limited to the cramped crew compartment of a Badger, the GF's primary armored fighting vehicle. Jammed shoulder-to-shoulder in the back, waste heat from the Badger's onboard fusion reactor parched their throats and made their feet swollen. The tracked Badger rode the asphalt like a boat on a rough lake, banging heads against the nanotube alloy side walls and bouncing butts on the plastic mesh seats.

At least there was live video. Displays on the inside of the rear door showed the views from the front of the Badger's body and from its turret. More displays on the side walls showed live views to those sides, overlaid with cursors showing the aim point of semiautomatic rifles mounted on the outside of the Badger. A computer somewhere processed visible light and infrared to yield composite images. The displays didn't show the plain truth, speaking strictly, but after a few hours of riding with eyes shut, Tomas told himself *the video is live, and you can't Observe anything if you're dead.*

There was little to observe. The road headed roughly sunleft and darkward, winding through valleys between eroded, forested hills on the way to New Boston, still a hundred klicks away. The valleys lay in shadow. Ahead of their vehicle, a platoon of Graywolfs, the GF's main battle tank, showed dark, boxy shapes, heat vents glowing in infrared. Grass engineered for permanent shade, low wide stalks of greenish-black, descended from the road's shoulders down drainage ditches, then climbed up the ditches to the forests on the higher elevations of the slopes.

Though unoccupied now, the terrain showed signs of human presence. Elevated conduits and standpipes fed water to the pines on the slopes. About every three hundred meters along both sides of the road, GF obs wheels stood on poles two meters high. The turret camera showed occasional glints of sunlight from more obs wheels amid the trees on the hilltops.

They came to a point where the valley narrowed and the hills steepened. "Great place for an ambush," Obermeyer said, behind Tomas and to the left.

"You always say that." Cohen, next to Obermeyer, sounded annoyed.

"You're from Shambhala, aren't you supposed to be detached from wanting people to change?"

Despite the banter, Alvarez snored.

Lt. Tower's voice came from above them in the turret, followed a moment later by his voice in their earbuds. "Scouts swept this whole area and mounted obs wheels per the book. No Uni ambuscades."

Next to Tomas on the left, Marchbanks arched his eyebrow. *Nothing more dangerous than a junior officer who read the manual*, he'd said outside the Badger on one of their breaks.

From Tomas' right, Sharma said, "Who's got the honeypot? Neumann?"

The honeypot was the MIUCS, mounted infantryman urine collection system. An ungainly contraption one stuck his *biroute* in to piss. Tomas had only used it the first time when the alternative was wetting his pants. "Not me."

"You assume the virgin's got a nervous bladder?" Marchbanks said. "It's mounted on the sterilizer rack."

"I don't care where it is, just hand it to me."

"You got to piss again?" said Obermeyer. "You've got the nervous bladder."

"I'm trying to stay hydrated." Sharma sounded bluffly confident. "I'll perform better—"

"Not if that water goes straight out your schlong."

Behind Tomas came the sound of the piss tube unreeling. Sharma reached behind Tomas for the funnel, pulled it to his crotch, unzipped—

"Platoon full halt," Lt. Tower said. The Badger stopped, pressing them into their seats, then lurching them back to the sound of a piss stream hitting the floor. Without the clack of the tracks, the compartment was mostly silent.

"Damn," Sharma said.

"What's going on?" Alvarez sounded groggy.

Delacroix, the Badger's gunner, up in the turret with the lieutenant, spoke. "Graywolf on point detected metallic debris buried in the road." The forward display showed the tanks stopped on the road. Their turrets slewed to left or right, ready to fire if some Unis had sneaked past the obs wheels. Their heat vents still glowed.

"Standard defensive position," Lt. Tower said. The turret swung to face the hill on the left.

"I'll bet ten confeds it's another dummy mine," Cohen said. The column had paused several times so far when the sensors in the lead tanks picked up potential landmines. All the ones so far had been crude hunks of metal and plastic, lacking explosives, but requiring a halt to make sure.

"Not even the virgin will take that bet," Obermeyer said. His voice sounded friendly and he nudged Tomas' shoulder with his fist. Sharma fumbled for the piss funnel.

"Graywolf platoon commander reports further analysis finds no explosives," Delacroix said. "Company commander authorizes continued advance."

"Platoon, get ready for travel." Lt. Tower sounded irritated at the delay. *No officer got promoted for standing still* was another nugget of wisdom from Marchbanks.

On the display, the tanks ahead of them began to swing their turrets forward and start moving—

"Missiles!" shouted Delacroix. Tomas lunged forward, eyes wide. "From our three and nine! Targeting the Graywolfs ahead, rear and flank! Attempting laser takedown."

In the floor of the Badger's main body, capacitors hummed and sharp cracking sounds marked fire from the anti-missile laser. A difficult shot by eye, even with his augmented reality display. "Missed!"

"Time to dismount!" Marchbanks shouted. The men around Tomas called out in agreement. An armor-piercing missile could destroy a Badger more easily than a Graywolf, generating jets of molten alloy killing or maiming men in the interior.

"Remain mounted while we break contact," Lt. Tower said. "B squad Badgers, suppress by fire—"

Flashes erupted on the display, followed a fraction of a second later by the roar of explosions outside the Badger and through the company's radio net. When the flashes faded, one of the tanks showed a dull bruise of heat escaping through jagged metal, while flame gouted from another Graywolf.

"Sir, I and I recommend dismounting." Despite his odd diction, Sgt. Johnson's voice came deep and calm over the platoon's radio net from his Badger, next in line behind Tomas'. "We face an ambush by anti-armor weapons."

"This is a break contact situation," Lt. Tower said. "Not an ambush. Can't be. Scouts set obs wheels by the book."

Marchbanks gave firm looks around the Badger's rear compartment, then stood up, hunching slightly under the vehicle's low ceiling. He put on his helmet, picked up his rifle from a rack along the side, and made a get-up gesture with his hand. He then pressed the cuff of his suit sleeve. A pattern flickered through the plain green and his suit, boots, and helmet went into full chameleon mode, wrapping light a hundred-eighty degrees around his body. He was only visible as tricks of shading and movement. Another quick motion and Marchbanks' rifle vanished into chameleon mode.

Marchbanks' confident motions pulled skills out of Tomas' brain and into his muscles. Secure helmet, set suit to chameleon mode, prep rifle… "Did I get it?"

Through the cameras mounted in his helmet, Tomas looked down at his barely-visible body. Video, yes, but live, and the only way he'd be able to see on the battlefield.

Marchbanks nodded. "You got it."

"Missiles, second wave!" shouted Delacroix. "Four hundred meters to our six. Targeting Supply Platoon, front and flank."

Sgt. Johnson's voice filled their platoon net. His lilting accent and odd vocabulary almost sounded normal. "They be trying to pocket us, sir. Looks an anti-armor ambush. Sir?"

Lt. Tower made no response over the radio net. Over the mechanical sounds of the Badger, a whisper floated down from the turret. "It's platoon break contact break contact oh Christ isn't it?"

"Sir, I recommend we lay smoke," Delacroix said.

More explosions, this time from behind them. Had those Badgers, and the mol fabs in their refitted rear compartments, survived? If not, had the men in those Badgers gotten out in time?

When would the Unis target his vehicle? Tomas wondered. He twisted his head to the side displays, looking for the glimmer of a missile launch. Both hills were dark.

Marchbanks touched Tomas' shoulder with one hand and, with the other, pressed his shilling through his suit to silence his radio pickup. He hissed past Cohen and Alvarez to the driver's compartment. "MacInnis, get the door ready."

"I'll press the button when I get the order," MacInnis replied.

"Sir," said Sgt. Johnson over the platoon net, "I and I suggest Badgers orient to provide fire support to our flanks and we dismount." Still no reply from Lt. Tower. Even the whispering had stopped.

A gruff voice burst in. Capt. Marcinkus, company commander. "Badger Two, what in the damn hell is going on? We're taking fire from both flanks. Base the vehicles to provide fire support and dismount your boots!"

"Yes sir!" Lt. Tower's voice wavered. "B squad, aim right, Johnson, your squad left. Prepare to dismount. Oh, yes, smoke."

A smoke canister *thwoomed* out of the tube. Delacroix said, "Sir, I suggest covering terrain."

MacInnis spoke over the vehicle's channel. "We can hull down in the roadside ditches and fire over and across the road."

Tomas visualized it. The maneuver would turn the Badger's thicker top armor to the enemy up the slopes, protecting the vehicle.

"Do it," Lt. Tower said.

"Do what, sir?" Sgt. Johnson hadn't heard MacInnis' suggestion.

"Badgers go hull down in the roadside ditches. Provide supporting fire across the road." Lt. Tower found more of his voice. "Let's move!"

As their Badger slewed backward, Tomas reached for a ceiling strap and missed. Cohen and Obermeyer jammed their hands against his shoulder to steady him. The tracks clattered on the living pavement, then made softer, wetter sounds when they hit grass.

The Badger tilted backward down the side of the ditch. Tomas said, "Whoa!" and leaned away from the doors with the rest of the men to compensate. He suddenly felt his cheeks grow warm. Had anyone else spoken? What would they think—

"My first was a hell of a ride, too," Marchbanks said.

The Badger slowed, stopped. "Dismounts, now!" Lt. Tower said. "Up the ditch, cross the road, then get to cover facing upslope."

"Sir," said Sgt. Johnson over the platoon net, "We can cross-support. B squad's Badgers face up the hill we can run straight up—"

"Stick with your squad's Badgers!" Lt. Tower shouted. "Dismount now!"

In front of Tomas, the displays cut out. The armored alloy door dropped open, hydraulics catching it a dozen centimeters above the ground.

I might be virgin, but I won't let my squadmates down.

Tomas sprinted out. Two steps on the open door, then a turn to the right. Loping steps up the side of the ditch to the road. Smoke teared his eyes and scratched his throat. Even with night vision, he could barely see through the smoke's thick roils. He could only hear, not see, Marchbanks and Sharma alongside him. His breath huffed through his open mouth.

Tension skewered him when he reached the road. Even with the smoke, Uni night vision or lidar might be able to pick up his silhouette, naked atop the living asphalt. *Go go go.* He glanced down and chopped his steps to clear the ruts of the Graywolfs and his Badger.

A sound boomed nearby. Tomas felt it in his chest and through his boots. His Badger had fired its main gun up the slope at the launch point of one of the missiles. Despite the plugs over Tomas' earbuds tuned to the unit's net, his ears rang. He took another step, another, then realized Marchbanks shouted for him. "Neumann, Sharma needs help!"

Panting, he turned. A vague human shape sat on the road, another crouching nearby. His helmet augmented the sight with Sharma and Marchbanks' names. *Sharma hit I never heard the Uni fire....* He went to the two men. The smoke was thin enough to see Sharma, pain on his face, and Marchbanks next to him.

"How bad?"

"Rolled my ankle," Sharma said. "Road's damn-all rutted."

The second wave of infantrymen, Obermeyer, Cohen, and Alvarez, hesitated. "Minor wound," Marchbanks said. "Get going, we'll need covering fire! Can you move?"

Sharma nodded. "I'll stick with you guys."

"Neumann, help me get him off the road. Other arm." Tomas went to Sharma's right side, lifted the man's arm across his shoulders, and put his left arm behind the man's back. Marchbanks took Sharma's other side. "Let's go."

They took a couple of careful steps when a flash and a shrill roar came from up the slope. "Missile!" Marchbanks shouted. "Cover, now!" He lurched forward and to the side, angling away from the front of their Badger. Tomas dug the fingers of his left hand into Sharma's suit and ran wildly over the gouged road. He stumbled but kept his balance until the edge of the road, then the three of them jumped onto the drainage ditch's bank.

The missile's scream grew in volume, until a flash and an even louder explosion came from the front of the Badger. Reactive armor—a layer of explosive on the outside of the vehicle, designed to destroy an incoming missile in the milliseconds before the missile's warhead penetrated the vehicle's armor. Fragments of the missile casing and the reactive armor would wound or kill a man too close, regardless of the body armor lining his suit and helmet.

"Anyone hurt?" Marchbanks said.

"I'm okay," Sharma said.

"We reached cover in time, right?" asked Tomas.

Marchbanks spoke grimly. "Enough alloy flying rapidly enough, no cover in the worlds will help you." He glanced up at the road. "Sharma, can you put weight on your ankle?"

"Enough," he grunted.

"Get to the tree line, lads. Let's go!"

They separated a few meters from each other, then crouched and trotted forward. The tall blackish-green grass scraped at Tomas' faceplate. Five meters into the woods, he dropped prone behind a fallen pine and aimed his automatic rifle over it, peering upslope. The smoke had thinned out enough to show a blur of pine trunks and undergrowth, dark and cool, seemingly empty.

More Uni missiles fired, this time from the valley's far slope. Tomas knew the sound now. The Badger's guns roared in response, booms echoing off the hills, and their machine guns chattered as well. In front of Tomas, shells detonated halfway up the slope, midway between the line of obs wheels along the roadside and the other line on the hilltop. Dirt rained down through the pine canopies and broken trunks collapsed. Tomas breathed easier for a moment. All four of his platoon's Badgers were still in the fight. In the lulls between the firing of the heavy guns, the automatic rifles of the other squad's infantrymen banged out rounds on the far side of the valley.

Where were the Unis in front of his squad? Tomas wondered. The Badgers' lidar units didn't pick up any, but between the smoke and the woods, lidar's effectiveness at picking up enemy infantrymen would be low. His own eyes were the best enemy detectors he had.

How good was chameleon mode on the Unis' suits?

"My team, call in," Marchbanks said through Tomas' earbuds.

"Here," Tomas said. Sharma, Obermeyer, Cohen, and Alvarez called in as well. All safe. Tightness in Tomas' chest relaxed.

Sgt. Johnson's voice came over the squad net. "Idrin, we will move uphill, squad in line, bounding overwatch. Marchbanks, your team bounds first."

"Roger." Over his team's net, Marchbanks added, "When I say go, go, low and quick. When I say stop, go to ground at the next tree." Back on the squad net, he said, "Team ready."

Their squad's Badgers fired their guns. "Go!"

Tomas set out, crouching. His gaze stayed mostly on the ground, looking for rocks and roots to step over, fearing trip wires and booby traps. An occasional glance up oriented him. Shells exploded over the same positions halfway up the slope, concussing the air, pounding the ground. How could anything be so loud? The vehicles' thirteen millimeter machine guns chuffed, firing at the Uni missile launchers. The squad's other team, led by Sgt. Johnson, aimed their automatic rifles and grenade launchers up the slope, but the Unis were quiet; Johnson's team held its fire.

"Stop!" said Marchbanks. Tomas dropped behind a pine's gnarled root and aimed his rifle upslope. What to aim at? Still no Unis in sight. High above, at the ridge line, an obs wheel glinted with Constitution's rays. How had it failed to notice the Unis on the slope below it? Behind him, automatic rifles and Badgers' main guns kept chattering, roaring. "Provide covering fire on my order."

More missiles launched from upslope, from fifty meters to sunleft, toward the front of the column. Moments later, more launched from a hundred meters to sunright. The missiles' exhaust sent bands of bright light and tree-trunk shadows racing through the forest. Explosions sounded behind and sunright from Tomas. The other squad's Badgers, in the ditch on his side of the road. Hopefully their top armor held.

"Ready now!" Marchbanks called over the team's net. Tomas aimed toward the gap in the trees torn by their Badger's main guns. His finger touched the trigger and he jerked it away, tapping the nail on the trigger guard. He wasn't going to be the virgin who shot his wad too early. Fire discipline separated soldiers from amateurs. He swept the muzzle ten degrees to each side. "Johnson's team has reached cover," Marchbanks said. "Prepare to bound. Just like before."

Lt. Tower burst in over the platoon net. "Johnson, what the hell are you doing?"

"Climbing the nine o'clock hill, sir. Squad in line, about twenty meters in."

"I see that from your goddam shillings. You have to move faster! Use your power bursts!"

"Sir, standard procedure is to save power bursts for when we need them."

Tower sounded livid. "We need them now! We have one damaged Badger! Knock out those missile launchers!"

"We be moving under bounding overwatch—"

"You've taken no small arms fire!" Tower shouted. "All they have is missile teams. They're only gunning for our vehicles."

"Unis may have small arms and good fire discipline, sir." The sergeant's voice was imperturbed.

"'Sir?' Are you mocking me? You think I'm a freshly hatched tiger cub who doesn't know his asshole from his elbow? Doesn't know how to lead?" Lt. Tower hesitated, and the tone of his next words showed he sensed how much weakness he'd shown the squad. "Get up that hill." The lieutenant dropped out of the net.

"Marchbanks, your team's next bound," Sgt. Johnson said as if Lt. Tower hadn't spoken. "Ready?"

"Speak up if you aren't, lads," Marchbanks said over the team's net. Then, to the sergeant, "Ready."

Each five second bound seemed to last forever. Dread spurted through Tomas every moment he left cover. It subsided slightly in the lulls when they covered Johnson's team, but not much. The Unis above them hadn't fired at their squad. Hadn't they? Over the din of the Badgers' heavy guns, the clack of surviving Graywolfs falling back from the point, and the roar of Uni missiles, would he be able to hear the chatter of Uni rifles targeting him? Would he only know the Unis fired at them when he was hit? Or not know, his brain splattered over the pine trunks before he could know what had happened—

Stop. Breathe. You have enough microphones on your side to pick up any small arms fire coming your way from upslope. Breathe more. Apply your skills. Cover, bound, repeat.

They were within fifty meters of the hilltop. The obs wheel glinted in the sunlight above them, canted at an angle by stray fire.

Tomas peered behind the last intact tree trunk. Ahead of him, Badger shells had torn pines apart like a giant snapping toothpicks, and beyond that, craters swallowed the dim light. "Final bound," Sgt. Johnson said. "Marchbanks, ready?"

"I'll go forward with Alvarez and Obermeyer to the shell craters. Neumann, Cohen, Sharma cover us. Ready? Go, lads!" The moving men bounded forward, crouched shapes in the infrared, names shown by the augmented reality display on the inside of Tomas' helmet. He kept his rifle aimed up hill. No Uni motion or fire, still.

"Rest of my lads, forward!"

The dread mounted, making Tomas' feet curl and his legs feel leaden. He slipped past torn trunks, crashed through falling branches. Even at a crouch he was exposed to every Uni soldier on the planet—

He jumped into a crater with Marchbanks. His foot touched something hard and jagged. *Land mine why aren't I dead?* and he lurched backward against the crater wall. His limbs shook and his breath came rapid and shallow.

"Lad, you with me?"

"Something in here."

"Irrigation pipe."

Marchbanks' tone of voice grounded Tomas. "Where are the Unis?" he asked.

"Buggered off when the guns opened up."

"Marchbanks, Sergeant!" Sharma's voice over the squad net. "Found a tunnel mouth in a crater. Maybe a service tunnel for their irrigation system."

"Throw a grenade in to keep them honest," Sgt. Johnson said. "Idrin, buddy up. One looks for tunnels and the other provides security."

More gunfire and explosions from the valley and the far slope echoed around their squad. Sharma's grenade gave a muffled blast inside the tunnel he'd found. Soon a man in Johnson's team found another tunnel, and another grenade went in. Tomas looked over the crater, poking cautiously with his bayonet. The blade struck something solid under five centimeters of torn soil and he jerked the rifle back.

"Clean it off," Marchbanks said. Tomas reached under his arm to a pocket and pulled out a small packet of nanotubes and memory plastic. A press of his finger transformed the packet into a spade. "Careful."

A few scrapes with the side of the spade revealed the jagged edge of a torn mycocrete casing. More scrapes sent dirt sliding down a meter-wide hole running about forty-five degrees into the hill. Dimly seen straight lines crossing the tunnel suggested steps.

"We found one," Marchbanks said over the squad's net. Aloud to Tomas, he said, "How the paper tiger's trusted obs wheels missed the Unis." Marchbanks reached into a pocket for a grenade and tossed it in. "The Unis are probably long gone, but it's easier to have Supply fab us more grenades than Medical graft us new skulls." The grenade detonated and the tunnel soon returned to silence.

The sounds of battle raged in the valley below. Tomas and Marchbanks crouched in their shell crater, watching for Unis. The damaged woods around them held only their squad.

"Is there something more we should be doing?" Tomas asked. He hadn't even slid his rifle's fire selector toggle off safety.

"We're staying alive, lad. There's nothing more we can do for the vehicle crews or the other squad."

Tomas swiveled his neck, barely keeping his eyes above the rim of the shell crater, looking up and down the hillside for Unis. Still none. A glance skyward showed three wheeling Kestrels, thopters loaded for ground attack. Constitution's rays lit up their wings. "Why aren't we getting close support from the air?"

"Takes time for battalion HQ to decide where to send them. Eyes on the ground, lad."

"Right." Tomas settled deeper against the crater wall. Still no Unis. The roar of guns continued, deep percussive blasts, until distant, deeper booms sounded from far to darkward.

"Arty incoming!" Johnson shouted into the squad net. "Down down down!"

"Ours or theirs?" Tomas said out loud.

"Nae matter!" Marchbanks lunged toward the bottom of the crater, then looked up. "Deep as you can, lad!" He grabbed Tomas by the arm, yanked him to the crater bottom. Marchbanks curled up, half over him. His jabbing knees and elbows drove Tomas to curl tighter—

The first Uni shell was louder than anything else Tomas had heard so far. The blast buffeted them and dirt showered down in thick fast clumps. He heard nothing but a ringing in his ears. Nothing, not even his own breaths.

The Uni shelling continued. Tomas felt their detonations through the ground, a giant's steps, poised to crush them underfoot. Tomas shrank in on himself, wishing he could be somewhere else, anywhere else. His rifle was useless against the distant guns and the hail of shrapnel. He could only cower and hope. Capt. Schreiber had said nothing about this. He was aware of Marchbanks' weight covering him, grateful he exposed himself to give Tomas a little more protection.

His hearing returned. The shelling seemed quieter. The crackle of splintering trees came from somewhere. "Unis be walking the shells toward our vehicles," Sgt. Johnson said.

Marchbanks shifted his weight. "They weren't after us?" Tomas asked, shouting to hear himself over the din of receding shelling.

"The Unis probably don't even know we're here, lad." Marchbanks winced as he spoke.

Sgt. Johnson said, "Marchbanks, casualties?"

A pause; Tomas assumed Marchbanks checked his team's medical status through his helmet display. "One very minor flesh wound, upper arm. We got lucky."

"I've got one dead, one severely wounded. Patch your man's flesh wound. I'm calling the platoon medic and an ambulance from company."

"Roger." Marchbanks winced again. "Help me with my first aid kit."

In his display, Tomas looked at his team's status icons for the pulsing red that meant a wounded man, when he realized what Marchbanks had said. "You?" he asked. Guilt gripped him. Marchbanks had taken that wound for him. "Absolutely."

Tomas fumbled with the hemostop, one ear out for more Uni shelling. More distant, deep thumps sounded. Tomas glanced up in alarm—

"That's battalion...light artillery company," Marchbanks said. "Counterbattery fire against the Unis."

Slightly more relieved, Tomas realized the ground attack thopters had disappeared. "Where are the Kestrels?"

Marchbanks popped a painkiller into his mouth and looked to lightward, past the canted obs wheel. "Heading for the other side of the valley. Hang on, this will get loud."

Tomas smeared hemostop on his fingertip and stuck it into the hole torn in Marchbanks' sleeve by the shrapnel. By feel, he smeared the hemostop over Marchbanks' wound as bombs shrieked down the sky. Detonations sounded from midslope on the far hill, louder than the din of the Badgers's guns, but much quieter than the Uni shelling. Or else his hearing had been wrecked. "I've heard worse."

Marchbanks chuckled. "You're one of us, Neumann. And thanks for dressing my wound."

Guilt returned. "You took it for me. I don't deserve any thanks."

"No, lad. I didn't take it for you." The sound of firing subsided. Marchbanks glanced across the valley. "I took it for me. Remember, I'm counting on you to tell your grandchildren what a good old sonofabitch I was."

CHAPTER 5

DAUGHTER OF ASTARTE

THE BLUEJAY GAVE a final beat of its wings, then settled on its landing feet. Around the cabin, men rose from their seats with smiles and cheery voices. No helmets, no rifles, no packs. A day's liberty, hundreds of kilometers from the nearest Uni forces.

"Chief, hold the door a moment!" Sgt. Johnson shouted to the cockpit. He gave a stern look to the men. "Set your countdown timers for twenty-three hours forty-five minutes. You will be back here then." The look grew more stern; Tomas imagined him preaching fire-and-brimstone in some Afro-Caribbean church. "If I and I have to hunt for you on base, or Jah help you, in the town, you'll be preferring combat against the Unis to I righteous anger! Be I and I clear?"

"Yes, sergeant!"

His look relented slightly. "You handled yourselves well in the ambush on the New Boston road, and you've been working hard in training since then. Go enjoy yourselves, idrin. You've earned it."

The ramp dropped. Obermeyer ran down and leaped to the tarmac. He looked back with a grin. "What are you fools wasting time for? The day is young!"

Cohen and Sharma trotted after him, followed by some men from Johnson's team. Tomas and Marchbanks followed. Tomas felt lighter, and not solely because he'd dropped twenty kilos of kit back at the battalion's forward base. He could be himself here. For a day, his implanted skills would go unused.

On the tarmac, warm and resilient underfoot, Tomas looked around. A cool darkly breeze stirred the Confederated Worlds' flag, the stars and rays, atop a tall flagpole next to a shorter one flying the Blackjacks' banner. Parallel fences topped with coils of razor wire stood at the airfield's edge, a rolling plain dense with dark green grasses beyond them. A solitary guard patrolled between the fences. The greater part of the base was behind them. "Where to?" he asked Marchbanks.

Alvarez had descended the ramp after them. "Too bad, boys, there's no such thing as Sons of Astarte. Wait, you've got each other."

"Toss off." Marchbanks watched Alvarez round the Bluejay's tail, then said to Tomas, "There are the Daughters of Astarte, of course."

"Of course," Tomas said. He hated the nervousness in his voice. Marchbanks must have heard it.

Marchbanks led them around the Bluejay. Puzzlement gave way to a kindly expression. "You've never hired a slattern before. No matter, it's just business, like getting slop at the chow hall. Is it against Observer precepts?"

"No," Tomas said, but his voice wavered. His mother would disapprove, and he imagined the man with brown hair and narrow jaw would too. Yet he had another reason for hesitating. "You call the new guys 'virgins' for a reason."

Marchbanks' mouth gaped, then he chuckled. "Lad, that's a good one." He peered at Tomas. "You're serious."

"Yeah." Tomas' cheeks felt warm.

"You're worried you won't know what you're doing? You needn't. They're professional ladies. They'll flatter a client to keep him returning."

Fear of failure hadn't inspired his embarrassment. "It's okay....?" Tomas didn't know what he wanted to ask.

"Okay that silly Josie lasses missed their chance to part their legs for so fine a lad as you?" Marchbanks waved the matter away. "We'll visit the Daughters, that's for aye, but we've some matters to take care of first."

Marchbanks led Tomas between airfield control and the maintenance hangars. The view opened up. The base stretched away to a bluff, at the bottom of which could be glimpsed a few roofs of the nearby town, Springfield, and a river in the distance. Most of the base's buildings were laid out to form a long quadrangle. A road ringed the quadrangle, surrounding a field where soldiers in gray fitness attire played pickup games of cricket, football, and ultimate flying disc. Jeeps plied the road, along with trucks and walking soldiers.

"This way," Marchbanks said, turning darkward. "Follow your nose."

Something did smell good. Bacon and eggs? "Is that—?"

"Yeah, lad. Forget the so-called food shat out of those field extruders. This is the real thing. They've got racks of incubators growing pork bellies, chicken breasts, and steaks. Get this, there's a farmer near Springfield who sells honest-to-God eggs! Squeezed out the twats of real live chickens! Vegetables, fruit, orange juice, coffee.... We've a busy day ahead of us and have to gird our strength."

The mess hall had more of those delicious smells, plus picture windows giving a view of the playing fields and the shadowed faces of buildings across the quadrangle, silhouetted by Constitution. Metal and ceramic clanked under warming lamps, where chubby soldiers, male and female, clad in plain, rear-area green crewed their stations.

The serving line was short. Most of the soldiers ahead of them had the jagged vee-shape of St. Martin's cloak on their sleeves. Supply and Support Corps. Tomas sniffed out a breath. We risk our lives and lose men while they eat three real meals a day.

Marchbanks leaned toward him. "Their service is important," he murmured, "even though not as much as ours. Remember SSC's motto. 'The spearhead needs the shaft behind it.'"

Chastened, Tomas said, "I hadn't thought of that." He mused a bit further. "How'd you guess what I was thinking?"

"I thought it too, my first time off the line."

They reached the serving stations, took trays. Despite a breakfast of extruded rations before boarding the Bluejay at oh-five-thirty,

Tomas ordered widely. Bacon, a mix of scrambled eggs and diced peppers called *migas*, melon cubes, a chocolate croissant. The servers aimed scanning wands at his shilling to register payment. The first few times, he glanced at the inside of his wrist, where his account balance shrank a little with each debit. Not much; he soon quit paying attention.

Drinks were available at the end of the line. Water, milk, plain coffee? A sign promising espressos and cappuccinos caught his eye. He gave it a skewed look. Joséphine had little to offer the Confederated Worlds, but at least it knew coffee. "Espresso." He received the cup with low expectations.

"Taking coffee liqueur in that?" Marchbanks asked.

"No."

"Ah, too early in the day for you." To the server, he said, "Your tallest draft stout." The server pulled the handle and soon set a liter glass on Marchbanks' tray.

Round tables, each seating eight, filled the space between the serving lines and the picture windows. Half the tables were empty, and the rest, sparsely occupied. Marchbanks started toward a table at the windows when two SSC men hailed them. "Care for some company?" they asked.

"We'd love it, lads." Marchbanks changed course and Tomas grudgingly followed. Even if the spearhead needed the shaft, he didn't need to talk to the SSC men.

He expected the conversation to cover standard stuff, *where are you from* and the like. But the first thing an SSC man asked was, "You're 2nd Battalion?"

"Aye. Foxtrot Company."

They winced in sympathy. The other SSC man said, "Bloody hell, I heard you drove into the worst of it."

"Our squad got away easily," Marchbanks said.

"Your rides, too?"

"Unis scratched the paint on our Badger."

The first SSC man shook his head. "There was a lot of mangled metal on that road, I heard. We were running the fabs as hot as we could to get Graywolfs and Badgers to you guys. Sounds like you didn't get one of ours, but have you heard any complaints from the guys in the new rides?"

Tomas put his fork down. He felt embarrassed at being rude earlier. "They're doing well in training, I hear."

"Glad to hear that. But let the guys in them know we had trouble scraping up titanium for some of the alloys. Local soil's depleted in it and the demand tapped our supply. We skimped a little on the rear armor. The drive sprockets in the tracks won't be as durable, especially off-road."

"We'll let them know," Marchbanks said. He lifted his beer mug.

Tomas frowned. "You didn't write that up?"

"What? Mate, of course we did."

Marchbanks firmly set down his beer, the motion and sound drawing Tomas's attention. "That information has to cross a lot of tablets before it reaches the crews driving those vehicles."

"Oh." Tomas felt more embarrassment.

"Don't sweat it, mate," said one of the SSC men. To the other, he said, "Time for us to clock in. Stay safe, mates."

After they left, Marchbanks finished his beer. Dregs of foam slumped down the inside of the glass. "I'm getting another. You've had a full meal, does that make it late enough to buy you one?"

"No, thanks," Tomas said. "I don't drink."

"I thought you were joking before, but now I know you have to be. Every soldier drinks."

Tomas shook his head. He didn't want to disappoint Marchbanks, but he had to speak the truth. "I've been taught alcohol distorts our ability to see things as they are."

Marchbanks' expression grew distant. He stared out the window for a moment, somewhere beyond the sporting soldiers and the buildings across the quadrangle. "Some things you don't want to see as they are." His face grew more lively. "Like an ugly face on a shapely lass. No drink? Your loss, Neumann." He left the table.

How big a blunder had Tomas made by declining Marchbanks' offer? *Mother would disapprove everything I've done since I enlisted. Why not add to it?*

Before he could change his mind, Marchbanks returned to the table, accompanied by Delacroix and MacInnis carrying heaping trays. Their food steamed and, once seated, they dug into it with vibrant eyes. After a few bites, they started to talk.

"Heard anything about Lt. Tower?" Delacroix asked.

"Me?" Marchbanks stifled a grin. "What makes you think I'd know anything?"

"You've got your ear to the ground," MacInnis said. He sipped coffee and kept his gaze over the cup's rim on Marchbanks' face.

"I saw him fly off for here yesterday, same as you did. I'd guess Brigade is reviewing his performance."

Delacroix sniffed out a breath in a chuckle. "I hope they axe him."

MacInnis looked sympathetic. "I heard him over the Badger's net, but you were stuck in the turret with him."

Tomas cleared his throat. "Was he that bad?"

"You're not a virgin anymore." Delacroix sounded peeved.

"I heard him same as MacInnis did. He was bad. Couldn't map the situation onto the categories in the textbook and needed the sergeant to tell him what to do. But how bad was he?"

"Bad enough," Delacroix said. "Why are you taking his side?"

"I'm not."

"You're trying to see good in everyone," MacInnis said. "I can't fault you for that. Yet it's not like he's a virgin rifleman. If a virgin rifleman fouls up, he ends up dead. If a virgin louie fouls up, we can all end up dead."

"We didn't."

"We weren't the target of the ambush," Marchbanks said. "The tanks and supply Badgers were. Though you make a good point, lad; he did listen to Sgt. Johnson."

"Do you think he can learn?"

Marchbanks paused, shrugged. MacInnis gave no answer. "I hope we don't find out," Delacroix said.

After a few more minutes, Marchbanks said, "We've enjoyed it, lads, but we do see enough of your faces in the squad shelter."

"Off to the Daughters?" MacInnis asked with a smirk.

"In due time, aye."

MacInnis raised his eyebrow at Tomas. "Your first, Neumann?"

Tomas blinked, tongue-tied. Marchbanks filled the gap. "When else would he've had a chance to visit the Daughters?"

"Neumann doesn't seem the type to hack the system," MacInnis said, "but he might have been the one man to find an exploit to visit them before joining us."

"Would that I had," Tomas said.

"You haven't heard their pagan claptrap, then."

Delacroix laughed. "You don't want to listen to them, Mac, but you have no qualms about taking what they offer? You know the word 'hypocrisy?'"

"They're priestess-whores of some false goddess. Better to slot it in them than some Presbyterian girl forced by circumstance into selling herself."

"I'll make sure Neumann ignores the pagan claptrap," Marchbanks said. "Later, lads."

Marchbanks and Tomas recycled their trays and soon were outside. Marchbanks led the way across the playing fields, passing between the cricketers and the footballers. "Thanks for distracting MacInnis," Tomas said.

"Distracting? It was the answer he expected. No matter, you're secret's safe, at least until we get you rid of your condition. Oh, nice cross into the box."

Tomas looked up. A footballer leaped up to the ball and headed it toward the far corner of the goal. The keeper backpedaled, then lunged too late. "Looks like he wasn't sure whether to play the pass or the shot."

"Better to follow the wrong course of action in time, then choose the right one too late," Marchbanks said.

They soon reached the road on the far side of the playing fields. "Where are we going?" asked Tomas.

Across the road, Marchbanks turned onto a sidewalk. A sign in front of a nearby building read *Brigade Headquarters*. "MacInnis has it off. It's not my ear, and it's not to the ground." Marchbanks led them away from the sidewalk, down a narrow lawn of dark green tinged by the rays of Constitution. He slowed his steps near a rear window and whistled a few bars of some Scotian-sounding tune.

Around the back of the building, he bade Tomas wait at the foot of a stoop. A few moments later, a door swung open and a woman, insignia and nameplate identifying her as Cpl. Metzger, came out. She had a turned-up nose and squinty eyes, and a squared-off cut of hair falling to her neck. "Les, good to see you. And your friend."

Marchbanks introduced Tomas to her, then said, "Has Brigade made our paper tiger cry yet?"

"Damn near. They're playing audio and video from the Badger's turret. He's a little red-faced ball, but he's kept his composure."

"Are we stuck with him?"

"It's looking that way. Sorry to have to tell you."

"My gut was expecting it. He got less than half of B squad killed. Not bad for his first time in the saddle." Marchbanks put on a leer. "Speaking of which, when are you off-duty?"

She set her fist to her hip. "After your appointment with the Daughters, I wager. You're going to lead this young man into sin?"

"I can't lead Neumann anywhere he doesn't want to go."

Cpl. Metzger shook her head. "If you can swear off whoring, maybe there could be something between us. I need to get back in before Brigade notices I stepped out."

"Always a pleasure, Corporal. I wish in more ways than one."

She *hmmph*'d and went back into the building. Marchbanks set his hand on Tomas' shoulder. "Time to get away before Lt. Tower has a chance to notice we were here."

Tomas followed, frowning. "You and Cpl. Metzger—?"

Marchbanks chuckled. "Lad, remember what I said about lasses with ugly faces? I haven't had enough beer to goggle my eyes for her. But she enjoys the game."

"Game?"

"I let her think I want to get in her pants, so she gets to show off her virtue in refusing me. And I find out what's happening in headquarters. Everyone wins."

Excitement and trepidation filled Tomas' chest. "Is it time to visit the Daughters?"

"Almost, lad. Let's get cleaned up first."

Part of Tomas felt glad to delay the visit for a little while. But another part of him bade him ask, "Would they turn us away if we didn't?"

"It's not for their sake. It's for ours. We'll feel more like men at liberty once we scrub off the field."

A hundred-fifty meters toward the front gate stood the base's fitness center. Marchbanks led the way past glass-walled rooms filled with kettlebells and free weights. Racquetballs ponged down a side corridor. Toward the back of the building, a clerk handed out towels and a toiletries kit.

Tomas took his kit into the locker room. At an open sink, he smeared depilatory over his face, softened the calluses on his hands, then cleaned his teeth. By the end, his gums throbbed and yellowish gunk glommed on the tonguescraper. He hadn't flossed since his last day in the transport delivering him to New Liberty. Amazing how dental hygiene could feel like such a luxury.

A sign in the showers showed a strict time limit. Ten minutes. He chuckled. After the spartan conditions up at battalion, a ten minute shower seemed indulgently long. Tomas soaped, rinsed, and almost stepped out halfway through his allotted time before remembering Marchbanks' words. He stayed under the showerhead, hot water streaming down his face, until the timer cut off the flow.

After meeting Marchbanks outside the locker room, Tomas followed him up the sidewalk, past Brigade headquarters, back toward the airfield. Their destination was a building like any other, two stories of mycocrete painted in a dazzle pattern of greens and grays. It lacked a sign in front, and maroon shutters covered every window. The only other indication it had a purpose other than military came at the front door. Mounted high on the inside of the jamb, a statuette of a nude, pregnant woman, breasts and belly swollen, head back, eyes closed, face contorted, showed a dilated *vulve* between lifted, parted knees.

"False advertising." Marchbanks shook his head. "You'll neither move their world nor get them with child."

They entered a vestibule, barely big enough for both of them. The shuttered window next to the front door, facing darkward, suffused the room with a dim glow, augmented by a small candle floating in a round globe filled one-third with water. A closed door at the far side presumably led deeper into the building. Tomas remembered the skills implantation chamber at the intake station. The few months since then seemed like half his lifetime.

Next to the door leading into the building, a tablet hung on the wall, alongside a wand like those wielded by the mess hall servers. The tablet showed abstract artwork, swirls of maroon, pink, and lavender. The artwork dissolved to show text. *Welcome to the Daughters of Astarte. Your donation will help us minister to the spiritual needs of people throughout the Confederated Worlds.*

"Donation?" Tomas asked.

"Saying that lets them pretend they aren't slatterns," Marchbanks said. "They even act shocked if you bring it up in the salon, or the private chambers."

"How much should I donate?"

"They say it doesn't matter. But it only stands to reason, the more you give, the more you can get them to do." Marchbanks moved closer, shoulder-to-shoulder. "If it's your first time, donate as much as you can."

Tomas checked the inside cuff of his left sleeve. "I've got about sixty confeds, but we still have meals and—"

"I'll take care of the rest of your food and drink while we're on liberty, lad. This time. Donate all you have."

"All?"

"After today, it may be… months before you get another chance to spend money."

Carried along by Marchbanks' words, Tomas went to the tablet, tapped the screen. In response to prompts, he worked his shilling out of his shirt and waved it at the wand. A glance at his cuff showed his account balance stood at a few cents.

"My turn." Marchbanks worked the tablet and wand like an old hand. Once he finished, the inner door opened.

Slow acoustic guitar music and a faint spicy scent greeted them. Maroon curtains hung from the ceiling, marking out sitting areas. The curtains and the dim light of candles and shuttered windows made the room look smaller than it was. Men's low voices murmured. Somewhere, a woman gave a high clear laugh.

"What next?" Tomas asked. Maybe it would be over with soon. Was that what he really wanted?

"We find seats and wait. Remember, they want to believe they aren't slatterns." Marchbanks led the way to an ell formed by two loveseats, each one backed by a maroon curtain. Tomas looked around. More high laughter. A woman in a simple yellow dress, her knees and elbows exposed, led a grinning soldier by the hand toward the back of the room.

"Les!" A woman came around the curtain behind Marchbanks. She had wide, innocent eyes and a pointed chin. Long silver spirals dangled from hooks in her earlobes. "I thought that was you!"

"Gloria, this is my friend Tomas. It's his first visit."

"Really?" She angled her head and playfully peered at him. He relaxed even more when she looked up, face bright. "Persephone might be just the lady looking for your companionship." She touched the spiral hanging from her right ear and muttered too quietly to be overheard. She then sat with Marchbanks, drawing her knees up on his loveseat and resting the back of her hand on his thigh.

Despite her body language, Gloria kept Tomas in her conversation with Marchbanks for a few minutes, until another woman sauntered up. Lean limbs, large teeth, curly blond hair; Tomas remembered a time he went swimming with Etien and they happened upon Véronique and her friends at the river bank. He'd dived deeply into the cold water and swum to the middle of the river to hide the erection distending his trunks. He shook his head to clear the thought, then stood. "Are you Persephone?" His heart thudded hard enough to rock his torso. Uncertain, he extended his hand.

"Hi. Tomas?" He nodded and she shook his hand like it was the most natural greeting in the world. She raised up on the balls of her feet and kissed his cheek. "Let's sit, and tell me about yourself."

As he did, his nervousness began to fade. Marchbanks and the other men had talked up the Daughters as something mysterious and powerful, yet Persephone was only a young woman, talking and listening in an idle conversation about his homeworld and places he'd seen.

At one point, Tomas mentioned his Observer upbringing. Behind his shoulder, Marchbanks gave a pained grunt and Tomas realized he'd made a mistake. Yet Persephone kept her smile and asked him more. She hiked one knee to the loveseat and kept her gaze on him, hands in her lap sinking into the thin fabric of her dress, playing absently with a bracelet of smoothed, polished stones around her left wrist. He couldn't phrase how, but he knew he was being tested, and he was passing.

"Care to go someplace more private?" she asked.

Disapproval burst from the mental model of his mother residing in the upper parts of his subconscious. He took a breath and slowly exhaled. He was a man, with a man's needs, and his mother would never know how he satisfied them. "I'd like that."

Faintly smiling, she took his hand and stood. He rose and followed her. A step later, Marchbanks roared with laughter. "Aye, lad!" Gloria playfully canted her eye at him.

Tomas' cheeks grew hot as he returned his attention to the back and side of Persephone's neck. "Sorry."

"About? Your friend?"

Nerves afflicted him again. "It's my first time."

She lifted a curtain across a doorway, waited till he came through, then dropped it. They were alone in a hallway with red, floral-print wallpaper and an open, wide staircase along one wall. "Gloria told me—"

"No. I mean, yes, my first time visiting you, but also, I'm a virgin."

A troubled look flickered over her face. "Let's not talk about the war and what it might do to you—"

"No…." Tomas grasped at more words, but none came to him.

"Oh." She paused at the foot of the stairs and gave him a look that seemed wiser than her years. "May I tell you a secret? Most men are, the first time they visit us. You're one of the few to admit it." She put her arm around his waist. "Upstairs."

Her room was small, a double bed with half a meter of open floor along the sides and foot. At the head, against the wall, stood a plain wooden slab, five iron rings across the top and a niche containing another statuette of the goddess high in the center. More red, floral-print wallpaper. A chandelier held a half-dozen floating candles.

Tomas returned his attention to Persephone as she lifted her dress over her head. The candles gently shadowed the lithe curves of her body. He had the firmest erection he ever remembered, throbbing, aching against his pants. She lunged at him, put her arms around him, covered his face in kisses. Her voice came hot, breathy, indistinct in his ears.

He fumbled at the front of his pants, but she took his hand away. "I'm ready," she whispered, "but for other girls you'll meet, you need to start someplace like here—" she guided his hand to her breast.

Would he ever meet another woman? He put the thought aside and observed his hand's motions.

After a time, she said, "—then here." She pulled his hand lower, over her belly, through the thatch of her pubes. He gasped as the outer petals of her vulve parted and his fingers slickened on her *l'eau venusianne*, water of Venus. Her hand on the back of his fingers guided him into a slow, rhythmic motion.

"While still working your hand, your mouth here." She turned her chest slightly toward him, jiggling her nipple.

He moved closer, hesitated. "But, nursing—"

"The goddess has given us a great gift," Persephone said. "A woman's body can unite with both a man's and her child's."

He darted his tongue out of his mouth to flick her nipple. She moved closer, pushing her breast at his mouth. She moaned a little and moved her belly to him. "Next, to the bed."

She stretched out and smiled as he climbed next to her. The sheets smelled fresh and felt warm. Now must be the time. His hand went to the front of his pants. "Still not yet." She guided his hand to her *vulve*. "A finger, inside. Two if she's a big girl or well excited. Stroke the cat's tongue."

Cat's tongue? Realization dawned on him when he found a raspy area on the front wall. He ran his finger over it.

"More firm. Once a woman's charged up enough she can handle it." Tomas increased the pressure and speed of his motion. "Yes. And now...." She laid her hand on the side of his head and guided him further, further. She wanted her *vulve* licked? He hesitated a moment, then lowered his face to her outer petals, his finger still working inside her. Her *l'eau venusianne* tanged on his tongue. She moaned again, louder, and lifted the small of her back off the bed. "Now let's get those pants off you," she said, panting.

They both worked at the snaps and buttons of his uniform, flung his shedded garments to the floor. She laid back and parted her legs for his knees. With a soft grip, he guided his throbbing *biroute* toward her *vulve*. "A little lower," Persephone said. "That's it…."

Nothing had prepared him for the feel of her moist inner folds around his *biroute*. All the times he'd masturbated couldn't capture the intensity of the experience. He knew he should work his hips, and did, slowly. His arousal pressed for release, and too fast or too deep a motion would burst the dam. But he could no longer help himself. As he moved, she rocked her hips to meet him. He could tell she wanted to go faster and he did, deeper and he did. His shilling slid between them as he thrusted into her.

He'd heard older boys on Joséphine talk about silently counting numbers to delay their orgasm, so he tried that, lapsing into Sankt-Benedikts-Sprach, *ein zwo drei…* and then her breath caught and the muscles around her *vulve* fluttered, pulsing against his *biroute*, and he couldn't help himself. His ejaculate spurted into her and he sagged onto her, his face against the side of her head, his breath ragged in her ear.

She shifted languidly next to him.

Now what? Though the boys in Portage, and his squadmates, talked volumes about their sexual exploits, none had ever spoken of what they said and did after the act.

Tomas propped his head on his shoulder and looked at Persephone. She gazed contentedly at the ceiling. She looked lovely. A sudden intuition told him he would never see her again.

Persephone turned her face to him and studied him. "The goddess has blessed me to bring my path across yours. You truly are unique, Tomas."

Pride swelled in his chest. "How so?"

"Some boys, and especially those whom I am blessed to initiate into the arts of love, turn lovestruck in the afterglow. It saddens me because I can't return their love. My commitment to the goddess forbids it—"

"I understand."

Persephone reached toward him and brushed her fingers through his chest hair. A vulnerable look flashed across her eyes. "Most others act as if they've bested me at a game. They've popped their corks and now are done with me."

She seemed complacent. Tomas crinkled his brow. She deserved better. "Doesn't that bother you?"

After a high tinkling laugh, she said, "The male pops his cork and pours out his tiny bit of acorn soup. It flows through me into the ocean of the goddess. Deep down he knows the truth, and hates and fears it. As well he should. She ebbs and flows unchanged long after his manhood softens." Gently, she trailed her fingers over his flaccid *biroute*. Her face grew sad. "Long after he lies in his grave."

Persephone shook her head and looked slightly alarmed at her most recent words. "Again, Tomas, the goddess has blessed me." She leaned toward him and kissed him. He read from her tone and her motions that she wanted him to say farewell.

"She's blessed me too." In formal *joséphinais*, he said, "*Adieu,*" and reached for his clothes.

LATER THAT AFTERNOON, in a lounge on the other side of the base, Tomas had a few minutes alone. After a hesitation, he pulled out his tablet and swiped his way through the apps and menus. *Compose letter, select addressee.*

*Annike Neumann, Portage-du-Nord, Joséphine

Mother, you were worried I couldn't remain true to our precepts. You can be glad that I have. I have seen combat as it truly is and I remain intact, both in body and in mind. He thought back to his final conversation with Persephone and his biroute stirred in his pants. And in the rest of the soldier's life, I see things as they are, and am a better man for it.*

He saved the most important question for last. *During skills implantation, I recovered a memory of a man with brown hair and a narrow jaw. Was that my father?*

CHAPTER 6

FRIENDLY FIRE

"Lad, I'd love to be twixt Gloria's thighs right now."

Tomas kept his gaze over the lip of their foxhole, watching the lightward horizon for movement. "Instead of waiting for the Unis to blunder into us? I'd rather be slotting your slattern, too."

Marchbanks caught his breath, then chuckled. "You're talking like a man, now. Yours must have truly done you right. What was her name? Penelope?"

"Persephone." He fell silent. Was that motion in the distance? Fuzzy warm spots danced on the display inside his helmet. Vehicles.

"You see them too," Marchbanks murmured, voice serious. "I make a company, in column."

Tomas studied the fuzzy warm spots, looking for the shapes of Uni fighting vehicles silhouetted in the infrared by their waste heat. Yet what else could be crossing this dark plain of near-black grass, the nearest NL town a hundred klicks away? "I concur. I'll call it in." Tomas groped in the dark for the handset. Wire had been buried back to Lt. Tower's position to remove the need for radio calls. Even if the

Unis picked up no content, they could still learn from radio traffic the GF was in the vicinity.

Time to pay them back for the New Boston road. An enlisted man at platoon headquarters picked up and Tomas whispered their sighting.

"Good eyes," came the reply. "Now hang up."

The lead Uni fighting vehicles were five thousand meters from Tomas' foxhole, racing darkward on a dirt road at sixty kilometers an hour. Thirty klicks to darkward, the GF partially surrounded a Uni regiment on three sides. When the breeze gusted, the cold wind carried the rumble of distant artillery. The oncoming Unis were elements of the 2nd Nueva Andaluciano Regiment on their way to relieve their pocketed comrades. Somehow the GF had scored an intelligence coup, exploiting a gap between Uni forces to place Tomas' battalion in a blocking position, dug in and hull down parallel to the dirt road, without Uni intel noticing.

"The Badgers and Graywolfs will throw most of the steel at them," Marchbanks said. "We just keep our heads down and wait for any Uni rifles to dismount." He fell silent and Tomas did as well.

A faint hum built up, slightly louder than the moans of the cold darkwardly wind. The lead Uni vehicles had closed to within a thousand meters of their foxhole. Between their infrared signature and refracted light from sunward, Tomas identified their outlines: Marlborough tanks, followed by DeGaulle infantry carriers. The vehicles rumbled closer, bobbing like boats on a choppy lake.

Tomas hunkered, his head against the wall of the foxhole. The rumble of the vehicles came through the ground. His first encounter with Uni tanks.

Sixty tons of metal and carbon nanotubes, what if they found his foxhole, drove over it, crushed it? His skills told him the engineers followed standard procedure when they'd excavated it; the foxhole would resist being collapsed by a vehicle… yet his subconscious knew only fear of the fast, massive machines. He wanted to melt into the rocky ground when the Marlboroughs passed a hundred meters from him. The rumble of their tracks filled his head and body, as if the sound bypassed his ears and went straight to his brain.

"Come on, lads, give it to them," Marchbanks said. Badger and

Graywolf gunners, he had to mean. Thoughts of *fire discipline* popped in Tomas' mind, like firecrackers on a sunny day. He knew the plan—let the Unis stretch out in front of their positions—but his legs and arms still tightened uselessly, wanting to take some action, do anything to distract the primate part of his mind from the fear of the massive, rumbling vehicles.

Tomas forced himself to step forward and peer out of the foxhole as a platoon of four DeGaulles passed. Dust settled out of the air, obscuring vision and piling on their foxhole's chameleon fabric cover, as more vehicles went by. A headquarters team came into position in front of Tomas and Marchbanks. Two DeGaulles, belonging to the Uni commander and his staff, were interspersed among eight supply vehicles. The latter, called Bismarcks, lacked turrets and had false guns aiming forward. The difference could fool a distant viewer, but from across the hundred meters of dark grass, Tomas saw it plainly.

Light flashed behind Tomas, throwing transient shadows on the front wall of the foxhole. A moment later guns' thunder and missiles' roar reached his ears. Their Badgers and Graywolfs had fired from behind their foxhole at the Uni column.

Explosions erupted on the road to their left and right. Some Uni vehicles swerved off the road, and others slewed on jammed or torn tracks. Blue-white lines jumped through the dust from Uni anti-missile lasers aiming wildly at the incoming fire. A few Uni machine guns chattered, and Tomas' skills identified the sharp bark of a Marlborough's gun, then another, soon drowned out by another fusillade from the Badgers and Graywolfs.

In front of Tomas, the Bismarcks around the Uni headquarters team milled in confusion. Supply drivers would be poorly trained for combat. The two DeGaulle fighting vehicles, though, looked to be driven by men with combat skills. They turned their heavier forward armor toward the GF line and fired their guns at the Badgers. One's machine gun ripped out rounds, smacking dirt within a dozen meters of their foxhole. Tomas shrank back, stupid instinct, too late to matter. The large caliber rounds could easily smash through their helmets and the body armor lining their suits.

"They've spotted us," Tomas said. His throat sounded dry.

"Stay calm. They can't hit us in our hole, lad. They'll need dismounted rifles to roust us."

Can't? Did he really believe that? But his comment about Uni riflemen reminded Tomas the best sensors to pick them up would be their own eyes. "You see any?"

Marchbanks peeked over the edge of the foxhole, ducked back down. "Nay."

Shells shrieked overhead on flat trajectories. More explosions sounded from ahead and behind. The GF vehicles were hull down, with just the muzzles of their guns poking over swells of terrain. Most would survive, unlike the Unis taken unawares.

He and Marchbanks were like flies, liable only to be swatted, powerless to make any difference.

"Your turn to look, lad. Only stay up a fraction of a second."

Tomas nodded. He glanced at the Uni headquarters team, then ducked back down, eyes closed as he made sense of what he'd seen. "Lot of smoke. Less motion in it."

Marchbanks took a quick look. "Aye, that's a good eye. Looks like the Bismarcks have buggered off and the DeGaulles will soon follow. Call it in."

Tomas fingered his shilling through his uniform. The need for radio silence had evaporated. He called Sgt. Johnson over the squad net and reported what he'd seen.

More GF guns fired, answered by a few Uni vehicles. Somewhere ahead, a DeGaulle fired its main gun. Soon after, a shell from a Graywolf shrieked into the smoke. The smoke muffled the shell's explosion, but Tomas could tell the Graywolf gunner had hit something.

The rest of the Unis followed their headquarters team's example. Smoke covered the road in thick billows, smearing light and infrared, muffling sound. Uni guns fell silent and the rumble of vehicles faded.

"They're all buggering off," Marchbanks said.

Tomas waited, taking longer and longer glances of the quiet road. The smoke remained strong in pockets, but wispy breaks gave glimpses of silent, immobile Uni vehicles. The holes pierced in their armor seemed tiny; blue-white flame licked at a few, but not even all. That couldn't be enough to kill a vehicle, could it? Then he remembered the photo on Capt. Schreiber's tablet he'd avoided seeing. Space Force and Ground Force had more in common than he thought.

"We be reconnoitering the kill zone," Sgt. Johnson said. "Teams by bounds. Don't go more than fifty meters past the road; that be the near boundary for our arty to mop up their retreat. Marchbanks, your team has first bound."

"Scope out some cover, then out of your holes, lads." Marchbanks covered his microphone with his hand. "See that thick tuft of grass at thirty meters?"

"Not much cover."

"Take it. I'll get another." He uncovered his microphone. "Ready?"

Tomas crawled out of the back of the foxhole, turned around, and started into a crouching run. The field between them and the road seemed impossibly broad. The near-black grasses blurred as he ran. He lurched headfirst to the ground behind the grass tuft and a memory of Persephone's bed stirred at the lower edge of his consciousness. He aimed his rifle into the smoke and caught his breath.

His next bound brought him to a Bismarck with a thrown track and a twelve-centimeter hole in the side armor. The smell of charred plastic warred with those of scorched reactor coolant and cooked meat. His team gathered around. "Who'll open the hatch?" Marchbanks asked.

Men looked to one another, faces showing unwillingness.

"It's a Bismarck. No ammo on board."

Still, no one else volunteered. Tomas lifted his chin. Finally he could do something, instead of letting the war happen around him. "I'll do it."

Marchbanks looked hesitant for a moment, then shrugged. "You'd see it later if not today. Steel your stomach, lad."

Tomas frowned. He could handle the sight of dead men. He'd avoided Capt. Schreiber's photo for being a photo, not for its contents. Squaring his shoulders, he reached for a rung of the Bismarck's side ladder—

And jerked his hand back amid chuckles from Obermeyer and Alvarez. Tomas winced at the burn in his hands. "Warn a fellow next time."

"You mean the skills imps didn't?" Alvarez chortled coldly as

Tomas pulled on thermal gloves from a pocket. He climbed, fuming at Alvarez. He wasn't a virgin anymore; he was part of the team. Despite the gloves and his boots, he felt heat coming through the ladder. Atop the false turret, he danced, unable to keep his feet on the hot armor too long.

He wrapped his gloved fingers around the outer handle of the hatch and lifted. Lighter than he expected, the hatch swung rapidly and he staggered back. The stench of the wrecked vehicle grew far worse, and hot air carried charred, ashen fragments out of the interior.

Tomas mounted his flashlight to his rifle's barrel and looked in the hatchway. Melted plastic and torn metal looked ashen gray in his flashlight's beam. *Did the crew escape?* and then he noticed shriveled, burnt mannequin parts littering the interior.

He looked closer while sweat poured down his face. Torn, blackened arms clutched the driver's controls. In the commander's cupola, teeth showed amid the crisped, split skin of the man's face. Even if they were enemy, they were men just like him. Tomas' vision swam and his stomach sickened. He inhaled the hot, stinking air and somehow kept himself from vomiting. This was the world he had entered. He could try to blinder himself by focusing on details, like a white gleam of bone in one of the driver's arms—-he took in the entire cabin. He wouldn't shut out his senses and think coolly about *make the other bastard die for his country.* He observed the scene as it truly was.

"I count two dead," he said to his team outside.

"Only two?" Marchbanks said. "They usually have a third crewman in the back, the fab technician."

"Can't see that far." He shut his eyes against another wave of nausea. Seeing it as it was didn't make the cabin less sickening.

"Come on down, lad. Someone pop the rear door."

Tomas climbed off the Bismarck in two jumps and sucked in cooler, cleaner air. Obermeyer grunted, tugging at the rear door hatch with gloved hands, while Alvarez sidled closer to Tomas. "Makes you hungry for *chicharones,* doesn't it?"

"*Chicharones?*"

"Fried pork rinds." Alvarez grinned, his eyes boggling.

"Och, you're a sick bastard," Marchbanks said. "Leave the lad alone."

Tomas peered at Alvarez. Sickness? Or a defense mechanism, to keep from thinking about the reality of the dead men inside the vehicle? If that's what Alvarez wanted, he could reply in kind. Tomas sniffed and managed not to wince at the stench. "Reminds me more of a Josie delicacy." He turned off his flashlight. "Calf's brain."

After a moment, Alvarez grunted in amusement. "I can almost believe you, Josie."

"Got it," Obermeyer said. The rear hatch fell to the ground. Backscatter from Obermeyer's flashlight shadowed his face. His cough sounded like he fought nausea. "Third crewman is dead."

Marchbanks nodded. "I'll report to Sgt. Johnson." He murmured into his microphone, then said, "Sharma, Cohen, you look in the next one. Obermeyer, Neumann, security."

A distant whistle of artillery sounded overhead, followed by the faint flash of explosions, then moments later, their sound. An attack on retreating Uni vehicles a few kilometers away.

The team next searched a DeGaulle five meters beyond the road, its gun pointing in the direction of the GF tanks behind Tomas' foxhole. A Graywolf gunner had scored a lucky hit, catching a chink in the vehicle's front armor. "Looks like their commander's ride," Obermeyer said.

"Be nice if we decapitated their unit," said Marchbanks.

Tomas rushed around the rear of the vehicle, rifle raised. The hatch was down, bending the grass. A few dim lights glowed in the DeGaulle's dark interior. "Someone might have gotten out," he said.

He looked in the direction the Unis had retreated while Cohen and Alvarez went into the rear compartment. Their flashlight beams danced in the corner of Tomas' eye. There was nothing to see in front of him, and when the two men tramped back down the ramp, he listened with most of his attention.

"Driver never knew what hit him, but he's the only one in there," said Cohen.

Alvarez' voice lacked the coarse tone he'd used to talk about pork rinds. "At least one man's bleeding." A flashlight beam swept back and forth on the ground in Tomas' field of vision. At its furthest, the light penetrated a few meters into the thick grass.

"And someone left his memory disrupter behind when he evacuated." Tomas stole a glance over his shoulder to see what Cohen talked about. A black bag, almost fully covered by Cohen's clutching fingers. Cohen shook the bag for emphasis and plastic rattled within.

Marchbanks reported their finding to Sgt. Johnson, then returned his attention to the team. "Alright, lads, next—wait."

The sergeant spoke over their net. "You might have found a hot situation. The Uni commander might be wounded and have himself a head full of knowledge of their plans. Track down that wounded man."

Marchbanks let out a heavy breath. "We might be chasing a phantom, sergeant."

"We can only find out by hunting. Get to it."

Marchbanks shook his head. "Obermeyer, Sharma, follow that blood spoor. Everyone else, security, fan out. We stop at the arty boundary."

They went. The grass swatted Tomas' legs. More artillery fire flashed and rumbled a few klicks away. He returned his gaze to the uneven ground, looking for Unis. He'd heard the talk from the more experienced men. Times like this, men died from complacency, missing an enemy playing possum, blundering through a trip wire, too visible to a sniper—

"Nothing," Sharma said.

Obermeyer added, "We're at our boundary."

"A quick breather, lads, then we get back to scoping out the wreckage." Marchbanks looked in the direction of the distant artillery fire, then grunted.

Motion in the fading smoke, coming from the road to sunright of their position. Tomas' shilling identified Sgt. Johnson in an overlay in his helmet display. "What are you stopping for, Marchbanks?"

"We've reached our limit, sergeant."

"We've reached a line on a map. If I and I talk to Lt. Tower, he'll talk to the captain, and we'll get back word to cross that line."

"It's free fire for the arty beyond it."

Johnson scowled, pointed. "Arty be chasing the Unis five klicks away."

"Did they drop mines twenty meters from here? Have some Unis from these abandoned vehicles formed a fireteam lurking in the grass? We don't know what's out there. We've fulfilled our mission, sergeant."

Sgt. Johnson shook his head. "Now be the time to edit the mission. The longer we wait, the greater the chance our intel opportunity will slip away. I and I need someone to go after them. You won't be doing it, Marchbanks?" The sergeant looked to the men before Marchbanks could answer. "Who will?"

"I'll go," Tomas said.

Marchbanks spoke with a vehement edge. "Lad, the sergeant didn't make it an order—"

"I'll go."

Marchbanks gave him a flat stare for a moment, then shrugged. "Alright, lad. We'll wait here."

"Keep your head on straight," the sergeant said. "You smell something off, get back to your team."

"Yes, sergeant." Tomas glanced at Marchbanks. Why did he resist the sergeant's decision? Tomas put the thought aside. Distraction could kill as readily as complacency. He lifted his rifle and started forward.

Bent grass showed the wounded man's path from the DeGaulle. Tomas walked slowly, peering for motion or the blocky shapes of artillery-delivered mines in the tall grass, pausing every few steps to listen for movement or breath. The only sound came from gnats buzzing past his ears and the rustle of grass blades in the cool wind from darkward. He checked around him, but even as his eyes adjusted to the landscape lit by starlight, he saw nothing. Step step pause. Nothing. Where was the trail? There? His fingers touched something wet and dark in the starlight. Step step step pause—

Pained, labored breathing, coming fast and shallow. Tomas crouched and listened to narrow its location. There, behind a swell in the ground. Tomas inhaled to calm himself. Unis can understand Confed, he knew from skills implantation. Rifle to shoulder, go.

Tomas snapped on his flashlight and ran a few steps forward. "Don't move! Surrender!"

"*Sí*," said a pained voice. "*Me entrego.*"

Disappointment nibbled at Tomas the instant he saw the wounded Uni. He'd expected some exotic figure, tweaked by genetic engineering for a bizarre homeworld, or normally shaped but dripping of the evils he'd committed in his occupation of New Liberty. The only thing to make the man in front of him look foreign was a different array of insignia and unit patches on his suit. His faceplate was up to show a thin mustache, just long enough to wax and curl up the tips. Double bars at his collar, a captain. Excitement surged in Tomas. He'd captured the Uni company commander! Marchbanks would praise him for that.

The wounded Uni captain squinted and weakly raised a hand, dropping it, unable to lift it to his brown eyes. He pressed his other hand to his belly. He grimaced. "*Soy idiota, olvidando... mi poción de Leteo.*" He groaned and pressed harder at his belly.

Tomas' excitement faded. He needed to get his prize back to their lines in one piece, but more than that daunted him. The Uni captain was another man, hurt. Don't let him end up like the two scorched men in the supply vehicle. Tomas fingered his shilling. "I've found a Uni captain. He's wounded, maybe badly. I'll get him back if I can."

"Roger," Marchbanks said flatly, then dropped from the call.

Tomas looked at the Uni captain. "Can you walk?"

He gritted his teeth. "*Demasiado dolor.*"

Tomas had no grasp of Andalucian. "Do you speak Confed? *Plappern Sie Sankt-Benedikts-Sprach? Parles-tu la joséphinais?*"

The Uni captain shook his head. "*Entiendo los tres. Hable solamente Andalucían. No puedo ir.*" He shook his head again. "*Demasiado dolor.*"

Sounded like the Uni captain couldn't walk. "I'll drag you."

"*Soy una tia.*" The Uni captain grunted again, louder and more pained. He nodded and said, "*Arrástreme*" through gritted teeth.

Tomas stepped closer and crouched next to him. First, ensure the prisoner is disarmed. He took the Uni captain's pistol from its holster. Without looking away from the Uni, Tomas unzipped a pocket over the small of his back, and stuffed the pistol into it. The zipper closed most of the way, but left two centimeters of the butt exposed.

He then patted the Uni captain down for knives and hidden pistols. None. Along the way he swatted the Uni's hand away from his abdomen, and glimpsed the wound in scanted beams of the flashlight. Torn fabric, ends drenched with blood. More groans when Tomas pressed his fingers near the wound. A faint stink of shit.

Tomas sat near the Uni's right shoulder and hooked his left elbow under the man's armpit. Time to drag. He turned his shoulders to his right, rifle wavering. Slow progress, scooching on his rump half a meter at a time. The Uni groaned with each motion. Sweat beaded on the wounded man's pallid face. "*¿Veré nunca mi sol dorado?*"

Mercy and pity struck Tomas. *I should have called for help while I had a free hand.*

A few more scooches and he realized he had to call now, better late than never. Tomas let go of the Uni captain and reached for his shilling. He froze halfway.

Three meters to the right of his line of travel, a Uni with a rifle lay prone in thick grass. He too looked surprised; his rifle pointed to the side.

Tomas aimed his rifle as best he could one-handed as the Uni aimed his. Both looked over their barrels at each other, but neither moved. *Pull the trigger Tomas how hard would it be what's wrong with you—* Next to Tomas, the wounded captain cried out.

The Uni's rifle wavered. "*¿Capitán?*"

"*Me rasguñan. Soy un preso de este Contrapelo.*"

"*¿Rasguñado?*" The Uni rifleman's tone revealed worry. "*¿Cómo gravemente?*"

Heart pounding, Tomas said, "No talking."

The Uni ignored him. "*Capitán, vino volverle a nuestra unidad.*"

Another groan from the captain. "*Madre de dios, el dolor. No puedo ir.*"

"No talking!"

"*Contrapelo. Contrapelo!*" Tomas realized the Uni rifleman spoke to him, and part of him wondered what *contrapelo* meant. "*¿Usted lo conseguirá a un médico aprisa?*"

Did *médico* mean *medic*? Tomas guessed what the Uni rifleman asked. "Our medic will treat him."

The Uni rifleman let out a long breath. "*Vaya con dios, mi capitán.*" Grass rustled. Tomas peered into the grass but caught no sign of him.

Tomas remembered why he'd stopped. He touched his shilling and said, "I need assistance returning wounded Uni captain to squad."

Johnson replied a few seconds later. "Roger. I be sending two men from my team."

Tomas dragged the Uni captain a few more times before he heard rustling from the direction of the road. His shilling overlaid onto his helmet display the names of two of Johnson's men. "Good job," one said.

"You two carry him," the other said. "I'll provide security."

Tomas reached for the Uni captain's legs. He would give the Uni rifleman a break. "All the other enemy are long gone." He and the first of Johnson's men picked up the Uni captain. He grunted and groaned as they carried him across the thick grass.

A minute later they crossed over the dirt road and soon reached an ambulance, a modified Badger stripped of armament and bearing the red cross of the medical service. They set the Uni captain down on a thin stretcher in the back of the vehicle. In a single harsh light, beads of cold sweat stood on the Uni's face. A shiver gripped him and he groaned again.

"We've got him from here," said the medic, a bearded, turbaned Ambarsari.

"Will he make it?" Tomas asked.

"He will if you let us do our job, private," the Ambarsari said. An al-Aqsan woman bustled over from a rack mounted on the front wall of the space and the two of them turned their attention to the Uni's wound. "Watch for septic shock," the medic said to the al-Aqsan woman. "If his symbiotic bacteria sense it's time to jump ship…"

Tomas left the ambulance and followed an overlay on his helmet display to his squad. He passed a human remains team pulling Uni dead from the wrecked Bismarcks and DeGaulles. They wore face shields and surgical masks, and scrunched their faces as they laid the dead into body bags. A dozen body bags already lay in a row along the roadside. A GF chaplain signed crosses over them and muttered something Tomas didn't catch.

A few more steps took him by a supply team tearing down one of the destroyed Bismarcks. Diamond blades keened and alloy hissed and popped under cutting lasers. Two men with thick gloves flung cut slabs of alloy into a truck bed.

When Tomas neared his squad, Johnson and Marchbanks stepped forward. Their helmets were up, exposing their faces, and Tomas realized he'd never opened his. He did so as Johnson spoke.

"Well done, Neumann. We should get some good intel from your captive. I and I'll talk to the lieutenant. There ought to be commendation coming your way." He angled his head, clearly listening to something in his earbuds, then hurried off to the main body of the squad.

"A commendation," Tomas said to Marchbanks. The latter looked unmoved. Tomas went on, more urgently. "The sergeant thinks I did well. You have to agree I did well."

"No, lad. I don't." Marchbanks scowled. "You got lucky. A commendation means you did something stupid and someone lived to tell the tale. You want your biggest legacy to be a medal in a display case on your mother's mantel, so she can cry every day she sees it the rest of her life?"

"I—" Tomas couldn't imagine his mother crying, not even over his corpse. And he thought back to his encounter with the Uni rifleman. "You're right."

"If we have a line on the map, don't cross it if you don't have to…. you agreed pretty quickly."

Tomas nodded, then saw Johnson about to speak to the squad. "In a minute."

Johnson spoke. "Idrin, we have new orders. We will remount and accompany the 1st Graywolf platoon in a sweep around the right flank of the arty kill zone. If Jah be willing, we just be along for the ride. Back to our Badgers!"

The men trooped toward their vehicles. Marchbanks and Tomas were ahead of the group. "What happened out there?" Marchbanks asked quietly.

"I met a Uni rifleman." He nodded at one of their comrades. "Closer to me than Cohen over there."

"Christ! We heard no rifle fire. You bayoneted him? Christ, sometimes you have to, but that's nasty work—"

"He was trying to recover his captain, I guess. We stumbled on each other. Aimed our rifles but neither of us fired."

"Why not?"

"It didn't seem appropriate."

Marchbanks kicked at a tuft of grass. "Christ, you were incredibly lucky. Maybe some Unis are rum lads, but you can't bloody assume that. And even if they are rum lads, they're strangers to us and us to them. None of them are going to tell their grandsons what a fine sonofabitch old Marchbanks was."

"I know," Tomas said. "Maybe he did it to save his captain's life."

"Don't try to learn their motives," Marchbanks said. "Wait, where is he?"

"He wanted to make it home and I let him go."

Marchbanks shook his head bemusedly. "Lad, I know God looks out for fools and drunks…. I'm wary of saying he looks out for you."

Wary? Why would Marchbanks think he disrespected his deity? "I don't observe the gods of others, but I observe how others act out their beliefs in their gods. If you think your god protected me…."

Marchbanks' face grew solemn. "He didn't. I'm telling you, you were lucky. Once. For the love of Christ, don't let it go to your head. Whether your luck was God protecting you out of love, or some evil pagan god of war sparing you out of cruel sport, or just blind chance, is no matter. All I know is that good luck is one of the worst things that can happen to a man in his first few times in the field."

Tomas squinted at Marchbanks. "One of the *worst*?"

"'Cause he'll come to believe his skills, or worse, his fate, will keep him alive through everything. There's no guarantee of survival in this for anyone. All you can do is enhance your odds of making it out of here. Remember the rules."

They approached their Badger, still hull down in a pit dug by the engineer platoon. Lt. Tower had the hatch open and talked down to Sgt. Johnson on foot, while Delacroix and MacInnis, in the back, carted fresh ammunition from one of supply platoon's vehicles. "Work with the team," Tomas said, "and keep your head down."

• • •

KEEPING your head down is a lot easier when you have encouragement. Tomas sat with his back to a boulder, chest heaving and heart thudding, while Uni bullets thudded around him. Ten meters away, Marchbanks was a hazy figure in the dim light. Without his helmet display tuning the video, Tomas wouldn't be able to see him. Marchbanks crouched behind another boulder and craned his torso, apparently to scope routes uphill. Another burst of Uni fire pinged nearby and Marchbanks dropped prone.

"I don't see a way up," Marchbanks told the team. "Lads, do any of you?"

Tomas rolled onto his stomach and peered around the boulder. He was near the upper limit of the boulder field; the next hundred fifty meters of shaded hillside were bare of rocks, and bore stumps cut a hand's-breadth above the ground. The Uni defenders had stripped the hillside to deny the GF cover. His shilling overlaid the impact points of the squad's rifle fire, telemetered by their rounds, as well as probability contour maps of the source of incoming Uni fire. Two Uni machine guns nested up there, along with riflemen in foxholes and a pair of grenade launchers. A grenade had already wounded Cohen and delayed the squad's climb through the boulder field while they evacuated him.

Tomas gave the bare hillside another glance. No swells or folds of terrain to give a man enough cover. "I don't." The others echoed his words.

Marchbanks widened his connection to the squad's net. "Sergeant, we don't see any safe way up."

"Neither does my team. Hang tight, Marchbanks. I'll see what we can do."

A lull fell over their part of the battlefield. Occasionally, a Uni rifleman or grenadier would fire to keep their squad pinned down in the boulder field, and from time to time, Tomas or one of his comrades would answer.

Meanwhile, the bulk of the battalion probed apparent weak spots in the Uni defenses about a kilometer to sunright. The roar of ordnance echoed off the hills. Tomas' company had been assigned to keep the enemy occupied in their sector, on the sunleft side of the dirt road leading back to the ambush site. Being a sideshow meant expecting no support from battalion's artillery battery or the air wing's Kestrels on station high above.

"Squad," Johnson said, "they be giving us some orbital assets. A fire mission liaison be coming up soon."

Soon stretched out for fifteen minutes. The roar from the main probe to the sunright mounted in volume while they waited for the fire mission liaison. The sergeant and Marchbanks gave no word of his arrival, just directions for Tomas and the rest of the team to provide covering fire for the liaison's entry into the boulder field. A few minutes later, Tomas heard gravel crunching behind him. A glance over his shoulder showed a man in full chameleonskin coming his way. He dropped next to Tomas and peered over the top of the boulder at the Uni defenses.

"What can I do?" Tomas asked.

"It's all me, soldier." The fire mission liaison reached into a pocket for a tablet and a small wand. He played the wand in the direction of a Uni machine gun nest, then checked numbers on his tablet. The screen showed a few alphanumerics in a deep red.

More Uni fired came downslope. A grenade rocketed over Tomas' head, and shrapnel clattered off rock.

The fire mission liaison touched his shilling. "FML two-one golf to *Boyd* FCO, do you read?" His face looked attentive in the dim light from Constitution's rays refracted through the sky behind the hilltop. "Prepare to receive coordinates." His hand neared his shilling, then paused as he squinted at his tablet. "Target one, coordinates, meters neg fife oh eight seven niner two, degrees two eight niner point four eight fife fife six. Read back."

Sgt. Johnson's voice over the squad net took Tomas' attention away from the fire mission liaison. "The main attack is stalling out sunright of the road. Prepare to advance by teams under cover of orbital fire mission."

Tomas peeked around the base of the boulder at the Uni machine gun nest. A few rounds barked out. Would they know what hit them?

"Fire for effect," the fire mission liaison.

A light flashed and a boom punched Tomas and pounded his ears, a shockwave of air heated in the beam. The sound climbed toward the orbiting ship, like a rocket launching, and echoed off the hill. Electricity crackled through the air and the hair on Tomas' nape rose. He peeked at the Uni machine gun nest, expecting to see electric arcs, molten soil, vaporized men. Screams muffled by the ringing in his ears came from somewhere. How much pain could the Unis be in for him to hear them at their distance?

A chill crawled over Tomas' skin. The screams came over the squad's net.

"FML two-one golf to *Boyd* FCO, hold fire! We have friendly casualties! Goddammit, you stupid sonofabitch, we have friendly casualties!"

Tomas looked to his left. A dust cloud swirled about forty meters away. Members of the sergeant's team held that position. His shilling overlaid location and medical diagnostics on his helmet display. A yellow man-shaped icon throbbed, showing Bar-Ruda, an al-Aqsan, had been badly wounded. A dull red icon lay nearby, immobile. Voloshenko's shilling reported no vital signs.

"You need more than impped skills to do your job," Tomas muttered to the fire mission liaison.

The man set his mouth in a grim line. "Shirley Foxtrot fucked up at fire control. I gave him the right coordinates. I'll swear on all the saints I gave him the right coordinates. Now shut up and let me put photons on the damn Unis."

"Bar-Ruda and Voloshenko are down!" Sgt. Johnson shouted over the squad net. "Who's closest?"

Tomas checked his shilling. "I am."

"Go to them, Neumann. We'll cover you."

Tomas crouched and ran behind boulders. His rifle's stock banged against his shoulder with each step. His squadmates fired their weapons uphill. The Unis made no response. They had a Marchbanks too, didn't they, telling his comrades to keep their heads down? The misplaced orbital fire had warned them to take cover before the fire mission liaison and the *Boyd*'s FCO corrected their error. A few meters of soil could protect a man against a pillar of laser fire from the SF's ships.

Meters of soil Bar-Ruda and Voloshenko had lacked.

Tomas took cover behind a low boulder five meters from the crater gouged by the orbital laser. The air smelled hot and dirty. Bar-Ruda's screams hit Tomas with wrenching agony both live and through the squad net. "The medics are on their way," he called aloud, useless words. Bar-Ruda kept screaming as Tomas ran the last steps.

Bar-Ruda lay limp against a boulder near the edge of the the crater. Dirt covered him. The chameleonskin outer lining of his suit and helmet had failed in spots, leaving gray patches, and blood soaked the front of his suit. Tomas lifted Bar-Ruda's helmet. More blood flowed from his nose, mouth, and ears. Bubbles of blood burst when he opened his mouth to speak. Tomas realized his screams were harsh, guttural words, maybe some al-Aqsan prayer.

"The medics are on their way," Tomas said again. Bar-Ruda didn't seem to hear. "I'll give you painkiller." Tomas reached for his emergency medicine kit. When in doubt, numb their pain. He pulled the emergency kit from its pocket and reached for Bar-Ruda's sleeve. Fabric tore. The laser had turned dirt into shrapnel, shredding his clothes. Probably his skin, too.

Tomas pushed the sleeve up Bar-Ruda's arm. A dirty film of oozing blood covered his skin. Tomas took Bar-Ruda's hand in one of his and snapped a self-tightening tourniquet around his upper arm. Bar-Ruda clenched Tomas' hand, painfully tight, pressing blood and soil against Tomas' skin. He screamed again, clearly a prayer. Tomas curled his feet inside his boots in powerless sympathy. *At least I can make him more comfortable.* He aimed the needle of the painkiller syringe toward a vein engorged by the tourniquet, then drove it in.

Bar-Ruda screamed twice more. Tomas shut his eyes hoping to soften the agony he heard. He could only bear so much. The painkiller soon took hold; the screams changed to a groan, then a whimper. Bar-Ruda's grip on Tomas' hand remained strong.

Tomas glanced toward the rear and checked the display on his helmet display. "The medics will be here soon." The helmet display showed them as icons picking their way through the boulder field.

Bar-Ruda whimpered in al-Aqsan.

Another look around showed Voloshenko's icon a dozen meters

away, with several boulders intervening. "What happened to Voloshenko?"

Bar-Ruda took a shallow breath and gasped. He looked a little more aware of his surroundings, and spoke a few words of Confed. "Don't know. SF beam knocked me back. Can barely breathe. Can't move legs."

The same medics from the dirt road, the Ambarsari and the al-Aqsan woman, crept up. She muttered something guttural and Bar-Ruda replied in the same language. The Ambarsari reached for Bar-Ruda's collar and yanked, tearing a strip of fabric away. Bar-Ruda's chest and his shilling were reddish-brown with dirt and blood.

"Private, get him naked. I have to hemostop the whole front of his body."

Tomas nodded. Bar-Ruda's suit came off in strips over his chest and arms. His pants were stubborn; the Ambarsari cut them with a reciprocating, diamond-bladed knife. Tomas pulled the cut pants off Bar-Ruda. Blood oozed from the man's *biroute*.

"Blast overpressure. Ruptures blood vessels," the Ambarsari said. "He's bleeding in his lungs."

The al-Aqsan woman knelt and fed a clear plastic tube into Bar-Ruda's mouth. Both medics acted with precise motions. Their faces were intent and focused, but Tomas saw anguish lurking around their eyes. How many men had died in front of them?

"I'll retrieve the other," Tomas said.

"We've already triaged him based on his shilling output," the al-Aqsan woman said, voice cold. "He's lost. We can only save your man here."

"I know Voloshenko is probably dead. I won't leave him if we can help it."

She worked the tube at Bar-Ruda's mouth and her body wavered. "You stupid men and your stupid honor."

Tomas slipped away. As he rounded the next boulder, another flash of light, another hammer of air roared nearby, fading as it climbed into the sky. *Hey Shirley, am I the victim of your next error?* but being able to think those words meant he wasn't. A glance uphill showed a bright red overlay in his helmet display marking an orbital laser impact on a Uni machine gun nest.

Behind another boulder, the icon representing Voloshenko stretched across Tomas' helmet display. Voloshenko's body wasn't there. Tomas pressed his shilling in the right spot and the overlay vanished for a moment to reveal unannotated video from his helmet-mounted cameras. Where the icon's heart would have been lay a shilling, scuffed and bloody, but otherwise intact enough to feed data into the squad net.

Where was Voloshenko? Was the shilling's report of zero vital signs an artifact of it losing contact with his body? Was he alive somewhere? Tomas glanced around the nearest boulders as hope buoyed his chest.

Something lay closer to the impact site. Hope fell, leaving hollowness. Tomas crept closer. It didn't look like a human body, at first. The blast had badly mangled Voloshenko. His throat had been torn open and his head lolled back. His face had been ripped up from under his chin to his nose. A fly landed and scampered along the wound.

The blast had turned his shilling into a weapon, gouging his face as it flew over his head.

Tomas went closer. One of Voloshenko's eyes remained intact, staring lifelessly at the blue-black sky. Tomas sat down and moved his hand numbly to his shilling. He hadn't liked Voloshenko, but no man deserved this. "Voloshenko is dead. Separated from his shilling, at my position."

"Roger," said Sgt. Johnson. "Mark it for the human remains team."

Tomas had seen dead bodies before, but he suddenly realized the Unis didn't count. The corpses in the Uni supply vehicles had been men, yes, but strangers. Whatever his opinion of Voloshenko, Tomas knew him. Had known him. "Sergeant, I request permission to wait with him."

"No, sergeant," came Alvarez's voice. "He was my friend. Let me wait with him for human remains."

"We can both wait," Tomas said.

Another laser strike pounded the hillside above them, this one at the second Uni machine gun nest. After the echoes subsided, Marchbanks spoke. "Sorry, lads. We have orders coming through."

"That's right, idrin," Johnson said. "Link up with your teams. We be going uphill."

CHAPTER 7

"That's it?" Tomas said when he saw the view from the Badger's front camera after their vehicle crested the pass.

"Aye, lad. New Boston."

"We've been fighting for a couple of months to get there?"

Alvarez echoed the sentiment. "If that's what we're trying to liberate, why not let the Unis keep it?"

"Quiet back there," Lt. Tower said over the Badger's net. "All the people of New Liberty are sympathetic to the Confederated Worlds and desirous of liberation from Unity oppression."

Marchbanks and Tomas shared a disbelieving look. Yet it didn't matter whether the lieutenant believed the propaganda or lied for their sake. They knew enough to publicly acquiesce in an officer's words.

The town of New Boston had a few thousand residents, according to the GF's wiki on the planet and its settlements. Smaller even than Portage. Squat mycocrete houses surrounded a central district of taller, handbuilt buildings, a college campus, and a public square. The only charming thing about the town was its location, on a sunlit slope of a foothill of the range of hills the GF had just fought across. Tomas hadn't seen direct sunlight in weeks. He might lament the permanent late afternoon the next chance he had to sleep, but for now, he welcomed it.

The slanted rays drove his memories of dead men a little further away.

Their platoon's four Badgers followed the dirt road down from the pass into the valley where New Boston lay. The dirt road tee-ended at an asphalt road, down which, hundreds of klicks and three months ago, the Unis had ambushed them. The GF had paid the Unis back with interest since then. Tomas briefly wondered why he failed to exult over that latter fact, then let it go when their Badger turned onto the asphalt road.

Hills to sunward dappled the asphalt with uneven shadows. Further to sunward, fully shadowed at the valley bottom, a stream ran down a winding gully roughly parallel to the road. The Badger bobbed and dipped with the terrain underneath, and Tomas dozed for a few minutes.

He woke when the Badger lurched to a stop. "On alert," Lt. Tower said. "Intel says the Unis are long gone, but I wouldn't trust them with my life."

Tomas and the other infantrymen rose and slung their rifles over their shoulders without speaking. They set their suits to camouflage mode, showing mottled patterns of urban colors. They knew to enter medium alert among non-friendly civilians; they didn't need the paper tiger to tell them what to do. The ramp dropped and they tramped from their vehicle.

Their platoon's Badgers had taken up a defensive position around the center of the public square. Each of the four vehicles covered a different cardinal direction with its main gun and machine gun. Yet the defensive posture was incomplete: vehicle commanders and gunners stood in open top hatchways. Other than vehicle crews and two dozen dismounted infantrymen, no one occupied the square.

If the Unis occupied Portage, I would've stayed indoors too.

Except for intersecting streets, buildings fronted the square. In the middle of one side, lit by Constitution's rays, a mural covered a six-meter-high wall. It showed a human shape, probably male, dressed in a puffy white vacuum suit with a gold reflective face shield on its helmet.

The man stood on a gray, pitted, lifeless plain, under a black sky, next to a rigid sheet on a pole. The sheet looked a little like the Confederated Worlds flag, except the white stars stood on a rectangular, not circular, blue field, in the upper left, not the center, and the red and white bands ran horizontally instead of radiating outward.

The man in the vacuum suit was not alone. The bust of another man floated in ghostly outline in the black sky behind the suited one. The ghostly figure featured narrow eyes and wavy hair in front of a nimbus of light. He gazed with serene confidence on the man in the vacuum suit.

"Is that a saint?" Obermeyer asked.

"He's a president," Tomas said. "Don't you read any briefings about the NLs?"

"I don't have to. I've got you for that." Obermeyer laughed.

"Fine. I won't answer your question." Tomas took a couple of steps away and stretched his arms overhead. A clock tower a few hundred meters away, in the direction of the college, sounded the local hour.

Obermeyer paced over. "What do you mean, you won't answer? You said he's a president. That means he isn't a saint."

"Can't the NLs think he's both?"

Obermeyer frowned, then shook his head. "On Challenger we respect the ancient presidents, but we don't worship them."

Tomas said nothing. Marchbanks squinted at the mural. "Obermeyer, d'you think we're on Challenger?"

Before Obermeyer could reply, Lt. Tower's voice echoed around the square. "Johnson, I will take Marchbanks' team into the city hall and meet the civilian authorities."

"Yes, sir. Look lively, idrin," the sergeant said. The team fell into two columns behind the lieutenant and he led them across the square.

The city hall had basalt-block walls, laser-polished to a sheen. The busts of more presidents, four of them, were carved in relief above the lintel. One bearded, another with a mustache plus rings over each eye. It looked vaguely familiar to Tomas from some ancient history class at the *lycée*.

Inside the building, a reception area greeted them. Empty chairs, blue with frayed piping and worn wooden slats on the arms. A desk bore a dark tablet. Tomas and the other soldiers swiveled their heads, looking for booby traps and hiding places. A hallway ran deeper into the building and a sign pointed arrows that direction. It took Lt. Tower a few seconds to decide the captions of the arrows read *Council Chamber* and *Mayor's Office.*

Down the hallway, they passed glass-walled offices. Lozenges of light ran along the floor, shading joints between beige tiles. Tomas peered to each side, seeing no one in visual or infrared.

The glass walls gave way to gypsum board. Tomas' heart sped up and he craned his head more. The gypsum board blocked his sight, but if a Uni lurked with a rifle, its rounds would pierce the gypsum board as if it were paper.

Lt. Tower held up his hand outside the council chamber's closed door, then raised two fingers and waved them forward. Marchbanks tapped Obermeyer and Cohen's shoulders. They nodded and padded into place. Obermeyer kicked the door open and Cohen led the way in.

"We yield up the town of New Boston," said a weary male voice from the far end of the room.

Tomas followed the rest of his team in. The council chamber reminded him a little of the briefing room at the spaceport near Reagantown. Straight rows of seats faced the town council's curved table. Yet here, instead of the seats sloping down toward the front, the floor was flat except for a dais on which the town council sat, elevated forty centimeters above the common citizens Tomas imagined coming into this room.

Behind the council table sat five people, four men and a woman. The weary-sounding man sat in the center. Purple bags puffed under his eyes and his brown hair, tinged with gray, lay disheveled on his head. All the seated council members looked exhausted. The only local in the room who showed any vigor was a tall, gaunt-cheeked man in a red turtleneck and faded blue jeans. He stood behind the weary-sounding man. He leaned forward and his hooded gaze swept over the GF men before settling on Lt. Tower.

The weary-sounding man spoke again. "I'm Mayor Schmidt. Seated here are the other four members of the New Boston City Council." He named the woman and the other three men. "Also here is Chancellor James of New Boston College."

Lt. Tower gave his name, rank, and referred to their brigade by its formal title. "As you may know, Unity infantry forces have vacated the area. In our pursuit of them, the Confederated Worlds Ground Force has taken possession of New Boston. My unit will be here for a few days to facilitate reconstitution of New Boston's political life into the provisional planetary government."

Mayor Schmidt swallowed. "We will be glad to work with you in bringing New Boston into the provisional planetary government." Behind him, Chancellor James sniffed out a breath and stretched his neck. The mayor nervously glanced in the Chancellor's direction before speaking to the lieutenant. "Please tell us what you require us to do."

"First, we will shut down the municipal fab for a few days."

"Our people won't be able to eat?" one of the seated men said. Mayor Schmidt jutted a hand toward him, palm down, and made a strangled hissing sound through his teeth.

"A team will review the fab's control system to ensure it cannot be used to fab material of military relevance."

Chancellor James leaned forward. "The Constitution is not a homicide pact," he said in a voice of settled finality.

Lt. Tower squinted at him. "Try again, in plain Confed."

Mayor Schmidt quickly said, "The Chancellor means to say the municipal fab lacks the ability to produce weapons. Planetary law."

"'Material of military relevance' includes more than weapons. Body armor, chameleonskin, armor plating for vehicles, components of target acquisition systems, and more. We'll print a full list. And no townsfolk will starve. The Ground Force will provide basic minimum rations to all civilians if the review lasts more than three days."

Lt. Tower went on. "Second, for the next forty-eight hours, residents may surrender firearms to us under a no-questions-asked policy. We'll set up a collection point in or near the square and publish and broadcast more detailed rules for the surrender."

"What happens after forty-eight hours?" Mayor Schmidt asked. A bead of sweat ran down his temple.

"After that time, possession of a firearm by a non-uniformed person will be taken as proof of irregular combatant status. Such a person has no right to prisoner-of-war status or other protections for regular combatants under interpolity law. We'll shoot him on sight."

Mayor Schmidt swallowed. "I'll tell our citizens. But don't take it as a sign of hostility if our citizens only surrender a few old hunting rifles. We don't own many firearms to surrender."

"That's because the people of New Liberty are smart enough, and loyal enough to the time-honored American spirit, to know the Constitution is a living document," the Chancellor said. "There's no need for a militia here, so the Second Amendment no longer applies. We're not the rednecks our ancestors left behind on Challenger." He gave icy stares to the infantrymen. Obermeyer, the only Challengerite among the team, scowled back.

Mayor Schmidt worked his mouth in agitation. "Lieutenant, all we mean is there aren't many firearms in town."

"That should make it simple to surrender them. Third, all offices of the town government are hereby vacated, pending a new election to be held as soon as possible. We will identify all townspeople who held positions of political authority under the Unity. Such people will be barred from holding any elected or appointed position in any town, regional, or planetary government for a period of five standard years. To be clear, that means all five of you council members."

They all looked crestfallen, but a few of them showed relief. Mayor Schmidt spoke in a measured tone. "We thank the Confederated Worlds for giving us the chance to retire to private life."

Chancellor James stood and stared at Lt. Tower. "Your logic is defective, lieutenant. The mayor and the members of the town council were elected by the people of this town. They were not given their authority by the Unity—"

"Would you be quiet?" Mayor Schmidt harshly whispered over his shoulder.

"The will of the people of New Boston would be thwarted—"

Mayor Schmidt spun his chair around and stood, grabbing the Chancellor's shoulder. "The will of the people of New Boston is that you. Shut. Up."

"The mayor has a good point, Mr. James," Lt. Tower said. "Hate the

Confederated Worlds as much as you want, but we're in charge here. All of you, go home, and await further communications from us about the municipal fab and the surrender of weapons."

"I have the college to lead," Chancellor James said. "It would shirk my duties to go home."

"All of you, clear the building." Lt. Tower's voice carried some heat. "Team, we'll follow them out."

Chancellor James went up the hallway first and gave a last, dismissive look at the mayor and council members behind him. The politicians trudged toward the reception area. "Can I clear my office?" one of them asked.

"No," Lt. Tower said. "We're locking the building until a civil affairs team arrives in a few days. Take it up with them."

The team trooped outside. Lt. Tower assigned some men to provide security, then gathered Johnson and the other sergeants to discuss how to take the surrender of firearms. "The rest of you, eat some breakfast."

Tomas looked around for Marchbanks. He angled his head toward their Badger, then led the way around it to the outside of the square. Cohen and Alvarez followed. They sat against the road wheels of the Badger's track and Delacroix tossed down their rations. The ghostly president watched them as they pressed their rations' heating buttons and peeled back the lids to let the smells of bacon and scrambled eggs escape.

"You aren't eating?" Marchbanks asked Alvarez.

He shook his head. "My rations will keep unheated for a week, right? If the town fab's down more than three days, you know the minimum ration we'll give the locals won't be much. If a local girl needs food, I'll make her a fair exchange."

"You're a master of seduction," Tomas said with dry sarcasm. He forked scrambled eggs into his mouth. "Let me take notes."

Vehicles rolled into the square on the same road they'd taken. Tomas and the others craned their necks. Supply vehicles, trucks and refitted Badgers with St. Martin's cloaks on their front bumpers. The men slumped back against their Badger's wheels.

"Alvarez, lad, stay away from the local lassies. I've a bad feeling about this town." Marchbanks nodded at the ghostly president.

"The head of the college is attached to his desire for Unity control," Cohen said.

"He mightn't be the only one."

Tomas kept eating. He hadn't realized how hungry he was, and how enjoyable it could be to sit in open air with a hot meal and an expectation no one would shoot at you. Even the firm alloy of the road wheel digging into his back gave him a trickle of joy.

Sgt. Johnson strode around the Badger. "You be studying the local artwork? Up, idrin. We've set up the firearms surrender drop for the locals and you've drawn the first watch."

One of the supply trucks had parked between two of the platoon's Badgers. The truck's bed faced the outside of the square. The tailgate was down and the chameleon cloth rear flap had been rolled up. "Simple," Sgt. Johnson said. "See those lines?" He pointed to sprayed paint on the asphalt. The lines defined three sides of a rectangle, about the size and shape of a football goal box. The supply truck's bed was the goal. "Have them stop behind the line, lower the weapons to the pavement, and back away. Then pick them up and toss them into the truck. Supply will melt them down after that. The lieutenant be broadcasting the drop procedures right now. We should see locals soon."

The day wore on. Tomas repeatedly checked his chronometer, trying to gauge the passing time. No one came. Maybe the mayor had told the truth, and no one had firearms to surrender—

Wait. Footsteps. Dozens of them, coming toward the square from the direction of the college. Students and professors were heavily armed? Tomas shrugged. So long as they refused to back Chancellor James' bullheadedness, he didn't care.

A cool gust from darkward swept around Tomas as the crowd entered the square. Chancellor James strode front and center. He kept his disdainful look, a look now shared by the dozens of professors and students, male and female, accompanying him. They were unarmed. Each carried only one rectangular object in their hands. The Chancellor and those nearest him reached the line and stopped.

The crowd from the college carried books.

Marchbanks took a step forward. "This drop point is for the surrender of firearms only."

"We wanted to comply with the spirit of the Confederated Worlds' order." Chancellor James stretched himself taller. "We will surrender the most dangerous weapon we possess." He tossed the book he carried toward Marchbanks' feet. Marchbanks danced away as it flopped on the asphalt. It slid and made a last quarter-turn before stopping. Tomas glanced down. *The Constitution of the United States of America 1789-2209.*

"We surrender the truth!" Chancellor James said. "The highest truth ever known by humankind! Revealed to Jefferson, Lincoln, FDR, and JFK in the sacred halls of Harvard University! Published by them on the front page of the *New York Times*!"

He turned away from the soldiers and addressed the crowd accompanying him. "A truth spurned by the Challengerites! They cling to a few of its words taken out of context to justify their tyranny, yet deny the spirit of the revelation to the presidents! They—" He jabbed a finger toward the soldiers. "—are our enemies! My fellow scholars and seekers of truth! Surrender your most dangerous weapons!"

Near the Chancellor, the crowd acted with vigor. Books spun through the air, landing near the soldier's feet. Not just copies of the Constitution, but heavier books as well, ancient history, commentaries on ancient law, and others. A few books slid past the soldiers and under the truck. One hardbound book flew into Obermeyer's shin. He hopped in place and cursed.

"They are cowards!" the Chancellor shouted. "They deny the truth yet know to cower from it!

The crowd cycled so people further back could fling their books as well. As they came up, many cast appraising looks at the soldiers' slung rifles and the Badger gunners looking out of the hatches next to their main guns. The Chancellor continually exhorted the crowd. "Cowards, I say! They will not harm a one of you!" The appraising looks faded, to be replaced with glazes of certainty as more books flew at the soldiers' feet.

When the crowd stopped flinging books, the Chancellor surveyed the people, then turned around. He sat down on the asphalt, crossed his legs like a yogi, and gave the soldiers a contemptuous look. A wave of sitting radiated out from him.

Someone in the crowd began to sing. Other voices joined in. Words about a banner, and stars? "Hey!" Obermeyer shouted. Veins stood on his neck. "That's the Challenger planetary anthem!"

"It's ours from time immemorial," Chancellor James said. "We have more right to it than do you false patriots from Challenger!"

Motion came from around the front of the truck. Lt. Tower sputtered to a stop near the soldiers. His mouth opened and his head swiveled from right to left to take in the crowd. "What's going on?"

"Civil disobedience," Marchbanks said.

Lt. Tower kept looking around. His face bore plain indecision.

Sgt. Johnson sidled closer. "We might alert Capt. Marcinkus—"

"No." Lt. Tower shook his head like a reptile shedding an old skin. He gave the chancellor a cold look. "We can resolve this on our own." He raised his voice. "Mr. James! Get your people out of the square right now!" His words echoed off the dark windows and locked doors of the buildings ringing the square.

"We have complied and will continue to comply with your broadcast rules for the surrender of weapons," the chancellor said. On the front rank, a few places to his left, a man with salt-and-pepper hair and a tweed jacket eyed Lt. Tower and, with deliberation, spat across the spray-painted line.

"You want to play it this way? I'll give you one last chance to think better of it."

Chancellor James lifted an eyebrow and said nothing.

Lt. Tower blinked a couple of times, then leaned forward with an intent expression. "You're sowing the wind." He lifted his tablet and swiped and tapped the touchscreen. Tomas glanced over and caught a glimpse of a broadcasting application's control panel. "To the residents of New Boston. Effective starting in five minutes, at eleven o'clock local time, a state of curfew is imposed on the town. All persons lacking prior approval from the GF local commander must remain indoors. Violation of the curfew is grounds for immediate arrest. Any resistance to arrest will be construed as an act of war by an irregular combatant. The curfew will remain in effect until further notice. Signed, Lt. Miles Tower, CWGF."

Glimmers of understanding lit some of the faces in the crowd.

Wavering looks appeared, but glances at the Chancellor dispelled them. The crowd remained seated as the time grew closer to eleven o'clock.

"Come on, you lot, move," Marchbanks muttered.

Lt. Tower paced behind the line of soldiers and talked to himself. "Don't make us do this, Chancellor," he whispered on one pass behind Tomas. On the next, his quiet voice sounded far more bellicose. "We will tear you and your people apart and you are to blame."

The protestors will leave in time, Tomas thought. They aren't soldiers.

From a few blocks away, the college's clock tower struck eleven. The bells pealed slowly, echoing around the square. Tomas' heart pounded and he worked his dry mouth. He counted the chimes while watching the crowd for any movement. No one stirred, even when the last echoes of the eleventh chime faded from hearing.

Chancellor James gave the lieutenant an insolent look. "We appear to be in violation of the curfew."

Lt. Tower thrust his hands behind his back and walked two steps past Tomas. His right hand clutched his left wrist. The fingers of his left hand trembled, yet he kept his voice stern. "Which of your presidents said, never throw shit at an armed man?"

"Are we under arrest?"

The lieutenant turned around to face the soldiers. He brought his hands to the front of his body as he turned. "Warning shots." He paced out of the line of fire.

"You heard the lieutenant, lads," Marchbanks said. "Aim above the buildings behind this lot."

Tomas brought his rifle to his shoulder with the muzzle pointing toward the sky, then put his eye to the sight. A distant cloud scudded to darkward high in the indigo sky. A few murmurs passed through the crowd, but Tomas' peripheral vision showed everyone remained seated. *We mean this. We'll show you how much we mean this.*

"Fire!" Marchbanks said. A three-round burst rattled from each rifle. In Tomas' helmet display, telemetry streaks sliced shallow arcs over the buildings and down the sky.

His teammates lowered their rifles. Tomas did the same. His impped skills slid the fire selector toggle to safety. The chancellor and those nearest him kept their positions, and unreal calm stayed on their faces. At least some people further away showed fear. A few at the fringes of the crowd slipped away, shoulders hunched away from the mass of their fellows. Tomas suddenly realized the ones leaving now would never again oppose the GF occupation of their town, of their planet.

"Hold fast!" the chancellor shouted. A few people on the edges sat back down with guilty expressions. "From time to time, the tree of liberty must be watered with the blood of patriots. Regret that we have only one life to give for our planet!"

Lt. Tower moved between Marchbanks and Obermeyer. "Your last chance, Mr. James. Evacuate now or the blood of all these people will be on your hands!" His voice had a plaintive hint to it.

"On my hands?" Chancellor James replied. "I won't be the one to give the order. I won't be one pulling the trigger."

A sullen look formed on Lt. Tower's face. "Fire on the crowd. Not James, though." He unsnapped the flap of his holster, pulled out his pistol. He sighted down it onto the chancellor's chest. "Leave him for me."

More people fled the rear and sides of the crowd. Doubt and fear filled faces near the chancellor. Yet he himself gave the lieutenant the same contemptuous look he'd harbored all morning.

"Goddammit, you sons of bitches," Lt. Tower shouted at Tomas' team, "I gave an order!"

A few of the men raised their rifles. "It's his order," Marchbanks said. His voice sounded dull.

"They're irregular combatants," Sgt. Johnson said. "It's irie."

No, it wasn't alright, but Tomas' rifle wedged its stock against his shoulder and pointed its muzzle on the crowd. Don't lie to yourself it didn't move on its own, don't blame the skills imps either, you moved it to firing position, observe what you're doing you're going to shoot unarmed civilians… Panic clawed at the inside of Tomas' chest. He didn't set his eye to the sight this time. Maybe he would miss.

His fingertip found the fire selector toggle. It was still set on safety. He could leave it there. Lt. Tower might notice the lack of telemetry from rounds from his rifle, if he ever reviewed the data, but he wouldn't, why would he? The men around him who would fire would be enough to send the surviving members of the crowd fleeing from the square. Tomas moved his finger to the trigger and set his eye to the sight. A young man, about Tomas' age, sat there. His close-set eyes were wide and his narrow chest heaved with breaths.

I grant you life, Tomas thought.

Lt. Tower fired his pistol.

Chancellor James slumped back with pain and disbelief on his face. A woman screamed and bodies rustled at the back of the crowd. The young man in Tomas' sights showed a face contorted with fear and hate.

One of the soldiers fired his rifle, then another followed suit. Protesters fell. More people, male and female, screamed. The middle and back of the crowd broke apart, people turning and running for the square's exits. More rifle fire felled some of those fleeing. The runners sped up; one tripped over a fallen protester and sprawled face down on the pavement; another knocked over a woman with blood pouring down her arm.

More fire from some of the soldiers. Tomas returned his attention to the young man he'd spared. Where was he? There, crawling on his backside, face showing agony, one hand pressed against his belly.

Other than the dead or dying, the square soon emptied. Lt. Tower went forward, kicking the pile of thrown books aside. He stopped first at Chancellor James. The latter's wounds had stripped him of his contempt. Only pain and fear showed on his face, in the moments before the lieutenant shot him between the eyes.

Lt. Tower turned to the soldiers. "Irregular combatants forfeit prisoner-of-war protections, including the right to expect medical treatment. Come on, you sons of bitches." Tomas gaped. It seemed like a giant's cold hand grasped his legs. Icy fear froze him in place. No other soldiers moved either.

The lieutenant's pistol hand shook. "Fine. Goddammit. I'll administer the mercy shots myself." He took two steps and killed the gutshot young man. A coil of sympathy and despair knotted tighter in Tomas' gut.

When all the protesters were dead, the lieutenant looked across the square without seeming to recognize what he saw. After a time, he blinked and scowled. "You son of a bitch. You made these people throw their lives away for nothing."

He spoke to the dead chancellor? Tomas followed Lt. Tower's gaze to the president on the mural, staring down from his nimbus at the man in the vacuum suit.

"There's a three-day pass for the man to destroy his image," Lt. Tower said.

"Hell yeah," Obermeyer said. He trotted over.

"Wait!" shouted Alvarez, hurrying after.

With a scowl, Obermeyer backed him up. "This cockbiter is mine." To the image, he shouted, "You think all us Challengerites are rednecks?" He lifted his rifle and fired a burst at the president's image, then another, another. Soon he shattered the image in a haze of mycocrete dust.

When the last echoes of Obermeyer's fire faded away, an uneasy silence fell. Tomas kept his gaze on the pile of books near his feet, occasionally straying up for a hurried glimpse at one of the dead protestors. What kind of Observer did only that? He lifted his gaze and studied the bodies. It might be the cleanest way to die: a bullet destroying the brain before its hundred billion neurons had time to generate the experience of pain and death. Had Mother said that? He couldn't remember.

He stepped closer to the dead chancellor. Perhaps the cleanest way to die, but the survivors gazing on the remains could only see the jagged entry wound, the cracked skull around the exit, and the smear of gray and reddish-brown of brain tissue and drying blood. The chancellor's brown eyes stared into the sky. Tomas wavered on his feet, and his stomach clenched around the bacon and scrambled eggs, yet somehow he kept them down.

"You don't have to look, lad." Marchbanks had stolen up on him.

Tomas turned to Marchbanks and noticed the other's gaze shied away from the chancellor's corpse. Had Marchbanks fired on the protesters? Had he shot the young man in the gut? Or had he done as Tomas had and kept his rifle's safety on? A wave of acceptance flowed down Tomas' skin. Whatever Marchbanks had done had been the right thing for him to do. He would accept Marchbanks even if he had shot the young man Tomas had spared. Sympathy for his teammate filled the muscles of Tomas' face.

In response, a glimmer of hope showed on Marchbanks' features, only to vanish inward and be replaced by a gruff, avuncular expression. Tomas ached as his sympathy surrendered to sadness. Whatever Marchbanks had done, he felt he could not speak of it.

Not even to me? But then Tomas realized he could say nothing either. Admitting he hadn't fired would lead his peers who had to scorn him. *I got my hands dirty*, he imagined them saying. *Are you better than me to keep yours clean?* He knew too that those who had fired feared Tomas and any others who had refused would think of them, not as soldiers, but as monsters. Each one of them stood alone, feeling unable to share the truth with anyone.

"We each do what we feel we need to," Tomas said, and he hoped his tone would somehow communicate what he really meant.

Lt. Tower sat down. Sweat beaded his face, now pale, and his breaths came quickly and shallowly. Sgt. Johnson drew closer and hesitated. "Sir."

"What, sergeant?"

"Your orders?"

"Orders?" Lt. Tower's gaze passed over the dead protestors without showing any recognition of seeing them. "We've done enough."

Sgt. Johnson stayed near the lieutenant and wetted his lips with his tongue.

"Goddammit, sergeant, do you see any irregular combatants? They all fled."

"Many did flee, absolutely. Yet some may have simply retreated to regroup and continue operations against us."

Lt. Tower shook his head. "We won, sergeant."

"I and I strongly suggest we aggressively patrol the town to enforce the curfew. No local will be loving us any time soon. At this point, I and I submit we be committed to making them fear us."

Lt. Tower huffed a few more breaths. His head slumped into his hands. "You do it, sergeant. I'll remain with B squad here in the square. Work out with B squad's sergeant when they will relieve you...." He cocked his head and raised his hand to his ear, pressing in on his earbud. "The captain's almost here with company's supply platoon. Two kilometers sunright of town, near the intersection with the dirt road, and moving fast." He staggered to his feet and brushed the front of his suit with his hands.

A couple of minutes later, the clack of Badger tracks sounded from the streets between the road and the square. The first vehicle pulled through the gap between two Badgers already parked there. Its tracks flung nuggets of asphalt at unarmed, refitted supply Badgers behind it. They stopped in the center of the square, surrounded by the platoon's four Badgers, and a few moments later, footsteps pounded toward Lt. Tower and the men near him.

Capt. Marcinkus had wavy gray hair. His helmet faceplate was up to show a face weathered and tanned like old leather. He glanced at the dead protesters. "What happened, lieutenant?"

Lt. Tower kept his hands at his sides—standard skill, don't salute in a combat zone, apparently even Academy graduates learned that—and stood attentively. "Our standard private weapons surrender drop point was attacked by a number of irregular combatants."

The captain looked at the soldiers nearby, then stopped at the sight of Marchbanks' rank insignia. "Were you involved, corporal?"

"Yes, sir."

"The lieutenant accurately reported what happened?"

"Absolutely."

Capt. Marcinkus coughed. "The GF has encountered irregular combatants here on New Liberty before, and it will encounter more after today." He looked thoughtfully at the unarmed corpses and the heaps of books on the pavement. "We'll have to call in a human remains team from battalion. They'll be here in probably two hours. But before that." He touched his shilling. "Lt. Sigurdsdottir?"

Lt. Sigurdsdottir soon came up from the supply vehicles. She was a sturdy woman with a guileless face. "Yes, sir."

"I have some suggestions for your report on supply platoon's activities today."

"I'm listening, captain."

"By about oh-twelve-thirty, supply platoon will have stripped irregular combatant KIAs of all weapons and…." He frowned and nudged a pile of books with his foot.

"Sir," Marchbanks said, "may I suggest, 'other implements of irregular warfare?'"

"A good suggestion, corporal. Anyway, in addition to these implements of war, lieutenant, a firearm from every irregular combatant KIA will have been tossed in the recycle hopper by oh-twelve-thirty. Your report will state that?"

She looked from one to another unarmed dead protestor, then nodded slightly to Capt. Marcinkus. "It will."

"I'm glad I can rely on you, Lt. Sigurdsdottir." The captain turned his attention back to Lt. Tower. "Before we discuss future operations here in the town, I have to send away one of your men."

"Sure." Tower gave no recognition of the order's oddness.

Capt. Marcinkus looked around and raised his voice. "I need a Private Neumann."

Tomas snapped his heels together and stood taller. "Here, sir."

The captain squinted at him. "I understand you got a close look at Shirley Foxtrot's fire control—" He cleared his throat, glanced at Lt. Sigurdsdottir. "—foul-up on the dark side of the mountains?"

"Yes, captain."

"The canned spam want to cover their mistake by blaming our fire mission liaison. Anyway, you've been summoned by the brass to a hearing on the matter in Reagantown. You'll catch the next vehicle driving to battalion headquarters, then fly the rest of the way. Lt. Sigurdsdottir, get him on the next outbound vehicle."

"Yes, captain." She gave Tomas a firm look. "Grab your pack and wait with my team."

"Yes, Ma'am." Tomas looked around, unclear what had just happened. *Reagantown? A hearing?*

Marchbanks stepped closer and nudged him with his elbow. "Your luck is holding, lad."

"Luck?"

"You get two days traveling back and forth, plus as long as the hearing might take. That gets you at least one night in a soft cot at the spaceport."

Tomas saw the downside of his summons. "I don't want to get involved in a hearing. Brass? What—"

Marchbanks put on a wry smile. "Och, lad, you've nothing to fret. Both our brass and Shirley Foxtrot's have their minds made up about what happened, and who's at fault. Whatever they decide will come out of a back room you'll never see. Just keep your head down and say 'I don't recall' until they dismiss you."

"But…." Tomas' gaze wandered to the dead protesters, then shied away. His earlier thoughts came back to him. He wanted to let Marchbanks know he accepted him. "I'd rather be here, part of the team."

Marchbanks swallowed once, then put on another smile. "Sorry, lad, you're stuck basking in our envy." He bumped Tomas' shoulder with his fist. "Now get going. Just promise me one thing."

"I'll say 'I don't recall.'"

"Oh, that too." He grinned, but the expression failed to reach all the way into the muscles of his face. "More important than the hearing: say hello to the Daughters at the spaceport for me."

CHAPTER 8

REAGANTOWN

TOMAS CHECKED the shine on his shoes and the buttons of his gray dress uniform for the tenth time when the door creaked outward. A military policeman stepped into the doorway. "Come with me, private."

He rose from a worn leather chair and in two steps left the room. The MP led him down a hallway. The soles of their dress shoes clacked on the tile floor. The two men turned a corner and a closed door waited at the hallway's end.

"The tribunal is seated on your right," the MP said. "Salute, give your name, rank—"

"I know what to do."

The MP showed surprise. "The skills imps have updated what they implant. Good. In you go." He opened the door and Tomas stepped through.

In front of a Confederated Worlds flag, and flags of the two branches flanking it on shorter staffs, five people sat at a long wooden table with thick square legs. SF dress blue outnumbered GF dress gray by three to two, although the highest-ranked officer was a GF colonel seated at the center, clearly presiding over the lieutenant colonels and majors of both branches sitting to his sides. Tomas reported to the tribunal. Flesh shifted against seats elsewhere in the room and the colonel raised a grizzled gray eyebrow in that direction before speaking to Tomas. "Take a seat in the witness box, private." He pointed to the far side of the room.

As Tomas went to it, he glanced around. Plain beige gypsumboard walls above a dark wooden wainscot. Two tables to his left. Behind one sat the fire mission liaison and a GF captain with a bookish demeanor. Behind the next—

Lucien LaSalle. He looked to be struggling to keep a solemn expression on his face, but a ghost of a smile touched the corners of his mouth when his gaze met Tomas'. Tomas knew that expression from years in Portage: a blind self-assurance that his peers from his town would fall into place and support him. Tomas kept his face impassive and entered the box.

Another MP, a pale, black-haired woman, approached Tomas. "Raise your right hand. Do you swear to tell the truth, the whole truth, and nothing but the truth, in full view of the officers and enlisted personnel in this room, any god or gods you may worship, and your own conscience?"

"Yes."

The MP went to the side of the room. The colonel leaned forward and cleared his throat. "Captain, your witness." He checked his chronometer. "You have thirty minutes."

"Thank you, colonel." The GF captain stood and came out from behind his table. "Private Neumann, before we discuss the incident that took place on 27th April 3011, I will ask you some formal questions to ensure the record is clear. Have you met any member of the tribunal before?"

Tomas swept his gaze across the tribunal's faces. "No."

"Have you met me or my SF counterpart before?" He gestured at a SF major with thick-lidded eyes and an imperious air, seated next to Lucien at the second table.

"No."

"Have you met Corporal Scobee before, and if so, under what circumstances?" The captain gestured at the fire mission liaison.

"Yes. On 27th April, before and during the incident."

"Finally, have you met Lieutenant LaSalle before?"

Near the tribunal's table, a transcriptionist tapped and swiped her tablet with solid strokes of her fingers. Tomas waited for the sound of her data entry to die down. "Yes."

The captain double-took. "You have? Under what circumstances?"

"We grew up together in Portage-du-Nord, on Joséphine."

The captain looked at Tomas with a gimlet eye. "Now, I must ask you a very important question. Despite knowing Lt. LaSalle, can you impartially and truthfully answer the questions I will soon ask you about the incident, and Lt. LaSalle's counsel will ask you after that? May I remind you, you swore an oath to tell the truth, so if you cannot answer our questions about the incident truthfully, you're obliged to tell us that now."

"Objection, leading the witness," Lucien's counsel said.

The captain bowed his head. "Let me rephrase. Private Neumann, despite growing up with Lt. LaSalle, can you impartially and truthfully answer questions about the incident of 27th April?"

Behind his table, Lucien watched Tomas with a glimmer of coconspiracy. *Of course you'll say you can,* Tomas imagined him thinking, *but I know you'll look out for your own.*

Smug self-absorbed Josie. Your ancestor's name is on the founder's monument in Couronnement and you think that compels every joséphinais to lie for you? There's a man dead and another in the healing vat because someone fouled up, and those men have something you never will: a GF shilling.

Tomas would lie the other way. He would spin his answers to pin the blame for the incident onto LaSalle. *See if you can win election to the Chamber of the People after serving out the war under a cloud.*

But before he could answer the GF captain's question, another presence welled up inside the part of Tomas' mind where his models of other people dwelled. Not Marchbanks, not even his mother. Instead, a brown-haired man with disappointment turning down the corners of his mouth. His father. Tomas imagined him saying a man was better off serving a higher truth than lying for a petty gain.

Tomas drew in a breath and sat straighter. "I can and I will."

Lucien kept a hint of a smirk on his face. *He still thinks I'll lie for him.* Tomas no longer felt anger; now, instead, he felt pity.

The GF captain walked back to his table and picked up a tablet. "Very well, private. Now let's talk about the incident of 27th April. You already stated you met Cpl. Scobee that date?"

"Yes."

"That meeting was during action between your company and elements of the 2nd Nueva Andaluciano Regiment of the Unity Army?"

"I only knew at the time they were Unity Army. It was my understanding from my platoon lieutenant and squad sergeant they were from that regiment."

"Thank you for your precision." The next few questions rehearsed the situation in the hour before the misplaced laser fire. Tomas answered as best he could recall.

"After rangefinding the Unity machine gun emplacement, did Cpl. Scobee make radio contact with a fire control officer on the CWSFS *Boyd*?"

"Yes."

"How do you know that?"

"I was within a couple of meters of him. I could hear his side of the conversation."

"When he made radio contact, did he relay a set of coordinates to the fire control officer on the *Boyd*?"

Tomas thought for a moment. "He gave a series of numbers."

"A series of numbers." The captain lifted his tablet. "Was that series of numbers 'meters neg fife oh eight fife niner two, degrees two eight niner point four eight fife fife six?'"

Tomas squinted, trying to remember. This wasn't one of Madame Martin's quizzes, he realized. There was no right answer, only the truth. "I don't recall."

"Did the FCO on the *Boyd* read back that series of numbers to Cpl. Scobee?"

"I don't recall."

"Was there any further conversation between Cpl. Scobee and the FCO on the *Boyd* before the beam inflicted friendly casualties?"

"I don't recall."

The captain arched an eyebrow. "You don't recall either of those? You were under cover behind the same boulder as Cpl. Scobee, yes?"

Tomas' nape felt sweaty. "After Cpl. Scobee gave the series of numbers to the *Boyd*'s FCO, there was a lot of chatter on the squad net. I had to pay attention to my squad."

"Very well. What was Cpl. Scobee's demeanor after the beam inflicted friendly casualties?"

Tomas thought. "He was very angry. He called the *Boyd*'s FCO to hold fire."

"Thank you, private." To the tribunal, the GF captain said, "Nothing further for this witness."

The colonel took notes on his tablet, then looked at Lucien's table. "Major?"

"Thank you, colonel." The major slid back his chair and gave Cpl. Scobee and the GF captain a haughty look. Tomas pressed his lips together in disapproval, and steeled himself to face the same disdain from the major; but the major turned a congenial expression to him.

"Private, thank you for taking the time to talk to us today. First, I'd like to make sure I understand your account of the incident...." The major spent the next few minutes rehearsing Tomas' answers to the captain's questions. Tomas puzzled about the repetition, until Marchbanks' parting advice came back to him. They would talk, he would answer, and soon it would be over.

"You said Cpl. Scobee acted angrily after the beam struck the coordinates he communicated to Lt. LaSalle?"

"Objection," the captain said. "The question implies it's settled that the error arose on Cpl. Scobee's part."

The major studied the tribunal for a moment, then raised his hand. "Colonel, allow me to rephrase the question. Private Neumann, you said Cpl. Scobee acted angrily after the beam struck?"

"Yes."

"How else did he act after the beam struck?"

Tomas thought back. "He said something like, 'I swear I gave him the right coordinates.'"

Lucien perked up as the major went on. "In other words, he acted defensive? Guilt-ridden? Remorseful?"

Tomas assayed his memory as accurately as he could. "He recognized the situation as a grave one."

The major's affable demeanor flickered for a moment, but returned before he spoke. "Would that recognition suggest to you that Cpl. Scobee knew he had erred?"

A motion at the table drew his gaze. Lucien tightly closed his mouth and made a small churning motion with the fingers of his left hand. Come on, help me out, Tomas read in the gestures. Yet he had sworn an oath. "No," Tomas said.

"To be clear, are you saying you're certain Cpl. Scobee believed he was blameless?"

"I don't know what his thoughts were either way."

"All you can say is, Cpl. Scobee said, 'I swear I gave him the right coordinates?'"

"Yes."

"Alright. I have one last question." The major went to his table and picked up a tablet. "You previously said you don't recall if Cpl. Scobee gave to Lt. LaSalle the coordinates—" He read the numbers from the tablet. "Has anything in the past few minutes happened to jog your recollection?"

"No."

"Anything at all?" the major asked. Lucien made the same churning motion with his left hand, as small as before but faster.

The captain spoke from the other table. "Objection, asked and answered."

The colonel's voice rumbled. "Sustained. Make your point, major."

"Let the record show the witness offered no testimony supporting the corporal's claim to have read to Lt. LaSalle the coordinates generated by the rangefinder app on the corporal's tablet. No further questions at this time."

The colonel made more notes. Head still down, he said, "Do either of you want to keep Private Neumann on base until this hearing is closed?"

The major and Lucien shared a look, then the major spoke to the tribunal while Lucien looked properly reticent. "We reserve the right to reask certain questions to which the witness answered he could not recall during this session."

To the captain, the colonel said, "Any objection?"

"None," the captain said. "Though I would remind everyone present that any willful meeting with Private Neumann, whether to discuss the subject of this hearing or not, would be a violation of the witness tampering statute of the Confederated Worlds Code of Military Justice."

The major slapped his hand on his table and turned a withering glare on the captain. "Are you impugning the ethical standing of a Space Force officer and a member of the Confederated bar?"

The captain stared back, face calm. "If you would never do such a thing, major, then no, I am not."

"Keep the trash talk on the playground," the colonel said. "Private, we may summon you to return here with as little as thirty minutes' notice between oh-eight-hundred and seventeen-hundred over the next three days. So don't lose both your shilling and your tablet in a craps game or at the Daughters. Dismissed."

Three days with nothing to do? Tomas left the hearing room in pleased bewilderment. He returned to his tiny room in the base's temp quarters. He pulled the bed down and sat at the foot of it, his knees almost brushing the wall. Marchbanks would doubly envy him. He sent Marchbanks a text message, then shucked his dress uniform for a garrison cap and plain gray-green fatigues, and set off.

The base at Reagantown had amenities far beyond those at brigade headquarters. Rock climbing walls, a fifty-meter swimming pool, a billiard room with two dozen tables, and a chess club with open games every half hour, plus seven restaurants each devoted to a particular planet's cuisine.... yet even as he drifted through these diversions, something nagged at Tomas. Marchbanks didn't reply to his message after three hours, which was part of what nagged him. Was the squad in a real fight, against irregular combatants armed with more than just books and an urge for martyrdom? Had Marchbanks been hurt? Or worse? Yet more bothered Tomas, and he couldn't articulate what.

It was in that troubled mood that Tomas made a chance encounter in the mostly unoccupied billiard room. As he walked in, an armored grenadier private near the door played a solitaire game, poorly. *"Scheisse."* The cue thunked against other balls in a side pocket. He rapped his knuckles on his temple. *"Halt das Spielball aum Tisch."*

Tomas stopped. *"Kommen Sie aus Sankt-Benedikts-Welt?"* Do you come from Sankt-Benedikts-Welt?

"Yeah," the other soldier replied in Sankt-Benedikts-Sprach. "You too? Where on Sankt-Benedikts? I can't place your accent."

"I mostly grew up on Joséphine. We went there when I was very young. I don't remember Sankt-Benedikts-Welt at all." A thought quickened his heart. "Maybe a few things from there. An oak tree, and Sankt-Benedikts-Stern casting a golden light."

The other frowned. "Golden sounds off. I'd call it orange."

Tomas' mood fell even further. "Maybe I'm misremembering. I was very young."

A shrug. "We all see the worlds through our filters." Tomas prickled —he was an Observer, he saw the worlds as they were. He eased when he realized the other's statement about filters was a filter of his own.

The other gestured at the constellation of balls on the green felt. "Care for a game?"

The next day, in the early afternoon, Tomas found himself near a restaurant named Maison DuBois when he realized he hadn't yet had lunch. Constitution's slanted rays through the front windows and the glass door lit up an interior of honey-brown carved wood. Curious, he stepped in. A chime rang at the top of the door. From a stool behind the counter roused the proprietor, a rotund civilian with a trimmed mustache and swept-up hair. *"Bonjour,"* the proprietor said, hello.

"Bonjour, Monsieur DuBois," Tomas replied. *"Es-tu de Nouvelle-Québec ou Joséphine?"*

The proprietor smiled. "I'm from Joséphine," he replied, "just like you."

"How could you tell?"

"Nouvelle-Québeckers still use *'vous'* when talking to strangers."

Tomas bowed his head. "Of course."

"So where on Joséphine are you from, Private—" The proprietor squinted at the nameplate on the front of Tomas' fatigues, then shrank back, looking faintly puzzled. "Neumann?" He pronounced it *New-maw*, with a ghost of an *n* at the end.

"My family moved to Joséphine when I was very young. We settled in Portage-du-Nord." The proprietor's eyes widened at the words. "You know Portage?" Tomas asked.

The proprietor coughed and slapped his chest with his palm. "Portage? I'm from, ah, near there."

"Where? I didn't travel much as a kid, but I've been to Bois d'Orme half a dozen times."

The proprietor's arms spread in regret and his face relaxed. "I'm from the other direction. Sainte-Therese-la-Petite-Fleur."

Tomas dimly recalled that town from his bus ride to Couronnement upon his enlistment. "What led you to leave? Your pardon if I'm prying."

The proprietor waved off any need for Tomas to be pardoned. "There were things I had to do as a man that I couldn't do back home."

"I understand completely," Tomas said. He'd probably reminded the proprietor more than enough of Joséphine. He studied the chalkboards on the wall behind and above the counter. "What do you recommend?"

The proprietor relaxed further. "*Soupe à l'oignon* and a *croque-provençal*. With my compliments." Tomas nodded and the proprietor tapped on a tablet. Dishes clanked and hot water hissed in a room behind him. Yet despite giving Tomas a free lunch, the proprietor seemed diffident, especially considering the restaurant was otherwise empty. Or was that Tomas' own down mood coloring his perception? In either event, Tomas gulped down the soup and grilled sandwich, and only paused to beam a few Confed dimes to the restaurant's tip box before leaving.

Perhaps the Daughters would liven his mood? Their salon here was far more ornate than the one at brigade headquarters. Lace curtains covered dormer windows in the mansard roof. The foyer was five times larger, and next to the donation tablet, a life-sized statue of the goddess rested on a plinth. Her dilated *vulve* was at eye level and aimed at the front door.

The excess carried through the salon, and after a Daughter took his hand, upstairs. The carpets felt like maroon sponges under his feet; atomizers puffed floral scents every few meters in the hallway; the bed changed firmness at the Daughter's voiced commands. She activated some downtempo electronic music—he raised his hand. "Please don't play that. I'm an Observer. I avoid recorded images and sounds."

The Daughter angled her hips and put on a faux-naïve look. "I didn't know. Music, off." She snapped her fingers.

She stripped, stripped him, pulled him to the bed. Her long blond hair had dark brown roots, and her breasts felt oddly firm. "You work so hard out there, defending us from the Unity," she said breathily in his ear. "Lie back and let me do the work."

He did. She flung her leg over his and mounted his *biroute*. Her hips bucked and she worked her hand through her hair, eyes heavily lidded, a constant flow of moans from her mouth. Artifice. The act meant nothing to her, Tomas realized. He accepted that, but her pretense of arousal and surrender annoyed him. He lay with his hands on her hips as she bucked faster and faster. Finally she drew out his orgasm.

He said a few polite words and left. His down mood dogged him through the rest of the day and into his bed.

He found himself on the square in New Boston. The young man was in his sights again. Tomas' heart thudded and his finger slid the fire selector to safety.

"Och, lad, I'm stained with blood," Marchbanks said from his side. "Don't you want to be part of the team, by staining yourself too?"

Tomas turned to Marchbanks, but it wasn't Marchbanks. A brown-haired man with a narrow jaw stood there. "Father?"

"Over here," came from the young man's place. There sat the brown-haired man. *How could he be in both places?* and then Tomas woke up to rain tinkling the window.

He stayed in his room that morning and wrote another letter to his mother.

I trust my previous message reached you. All is well. I continue to combine service in the Ground Force with the maintenance of your standard of behavior for an Observer. The censors would probably take out the next lines. Our campaign against the Unity Army here on New Liberty goes well. We should have them mopped up shortly and be available to press the war against the Unity on another front.

He watched raindrops creep down the window. A far cry from the sunny day in his memory, under the oak with his father. *As I mentioned last time, I have memories of a man I assume was my father. I remember a sunny day on some world other than Joséphine. I have assumed it was Sankt-Benedikts-Welt, but I met a Benedikter the other day who described Sankt-Benedikts-Stern in a way that makes me think my memory is not of our home-world after all. Before Joséphine, and while my father was alive, did we stay on some other planet?*

Tomas pondered more things to say, then shook his head and jabbed the *send* button. She would respond, or more likely not, and nothing could make her reply. He watched a transport shuttle make its landing burn toward the spaceport. The rain smeared his view of the shuttle's fusion exhaust.

His tablet chimed with a request for a video call. It came from the tribunal's clerk. Tomas sat upright and pressed *answer*.

"Private Neumann? The tribunal has no further questions for you."

"You mean they reached a decision?"

The clerk shook his head. "I can't tell you that. However, it does appreciate your testimony. I'll send you orders to return to your unit."

The clerk ended the call, and moments later, the orders arrived on Tomas' tablet. Report to the airfield, departure at oh-ten-twenty— Tomas quickly packed and hustled through the drizzle to the airfield. No one lingered outside, but at several places along his route, knots of personnel stood in doorways or under awnings, conversing with guarded faces.

Had something happened? He reached the airfield and found the Bluejay due to take him back to the Blackjacks' headquarters. Two other men had already boarded, a scout and an engineer. Their faces showed a heated discussion.

"It makes no difference," the engineer said. "The NLers won't answer the guerrillas' call."

"I don't know if the enemy story is accurate or not," the scout responded. "But I know if the Unity were occupying Nuevo Nuevo León, and there were reports, true or false, they desecrated a shrine to the Virgin of Guadalupe, tens of thousands of locals would take up arms against them."

"What happened?" Tomas asked.

"You haven't heard?" the scout said. "It's on the home page of *Stars and Rays*," the armed forces news site.

"I've been enjoying some liberty. Haven't bothered reading it."

"Liberty's going to end for all of us in a hurry." The scout checked Tomas' armored grenadier insignia and the Blackjacks' patch on his sleeves. "For you most of all."

"You're overreacting," the engineer said.

Tomas pulled his tablet out, then stowed his pack. After strapping in, he called up *Stars and Rays*. The headline read *Pro-Unity NL Leaders Call For Civilian Volunteer Militia.*

He read more as the Bluejay lifted off. A group calling itself the Provisional Free Government of New Liberty had issued a communiqué. Citizens could not rely on the Unity Army to protect them from the Confederated Worlds forces. Among its evidence, the communiqué pointed to a massacre and desecration at New Boston.

Tomas sat straighter and followed links to a page with photos. His first response turned his head away, but he set aside his hesitation. You could see a photo of something you'd already seen in real life, couldn't you? Not a violation of Observer precepts.

And what he would see couldn't be worse than his memory.

He opened his eyes. It showed dead protesters—he could make out the young man he'd spared, and Chancellor James as well. He thought about the angle of view. Perhaps with a zoom lens from a high building on the college campus? Taken in the few hours between the killing of the irregular combatants and cleanup by the human remains team. An extreme zoom showed a grainy image of a woman's face, her forehead caved in by Lt. Tower's mercy shot. The communiqué alleged *unarmed civilians were executed in cold blood.*

A cold feeling washed down Tomas' body. One zoom lens. The cold feeling heightened. Sgt. Johnson had been right. Pressing the fleeing protesters would have killed or broken the resistance of all of them. Instead, the platoon had dithered, giving one survivor time and space to make a world of trouble.

Images of our presidents were desecrated as well. The next photo showed the president, his face crumbled to powder, looking down on the man in the vacuum suit in the mural Obermeyer had vandalized.

Tomas returned to the main story about the communiqué. The Provisionals called upon New Liberty's citizens to form militia units to resist the Confederated Worlds.

Tomas mused for a moment. Even if the scout were right about the number of volunteers, the NLers only had a few hunting rifles and other hand weapons, and the only skills to use them they would have acquired the hard way, through long practice, one mind at a time. So he saw where the engineer had come from in the argument. Perhaps the scout worried because he was most lightly armed and most likely to blunder into those few rifles. Even with only a hunting rifle and poor training, an NLer could still kill a soldier.

He read on, and his minor concern grew like a malignant cyst. The Provisionals had set up stations to broadcast fab blueprints for heavy weapons, including copies of the Unity Army's fighting vehicles. They also broadcast instructions for implanting soldiering skills using the general purpose civilian implantation machines found in most schools. More than hunting rifles and poor training would oppose the GF.

Tomas set the tablet down and watched the passing landscape through the video displays mounted above the seats in the Bluejay's cabin. If the Provisionals got just one percent of the locals to join the militia, that meant twenty thousand people. The surviving Unity Army regiments had less than that. The Blackjacks' work wouldn't be over anytime soon.

He blinked and images from his dream fleeted across his mind's eye. There was one bright side. If the NL volunteers carried rifles, there would be no question whether they were innocent civilians or irregular combatants.

CHAPTER 9

STRATEGIC REDEPLOYMENT

"WHY THE HELL ARE WE RUNNING?" Obermeyer said over the squad net. "We had the Unis by the scrotes, and now we let them go?"

"Can't say I particularly want to grab a Uni's testicles," Alvarez said, "but I don't care what floats your boat."

"Fuck you."

"Save the chatter for after we've been relieved," Sgt. Johnson said. "Right now, we be on watch."

Tomas lay behind a long, low dirt mound tufted with soybean plants and squinted against Constitution's bright disc in front of him. The Blackjacks had already traveled five hundred kilometers to sunright from New Boston as part of a 'strategic redeployment' ordered by the GF commanders on planet. They had hundreds of klicks further to go. A few kilometers sunright of a small town, their company had pulled to the side of the main road for a night of sleep and vehicle maintenance.

The low sun cast long shadows of a forest of maples and elms toward them across the soybean field. Tomas' team occupied a slight elevation, maybe five meters higher than a meandering creek dividing the soybean field from the forest. Distant birds chirped and a breeze rustled soybean leaves in their rows.

Two hundred meters to darkward, the platoon's Badgers backed up Tomas and his mates with heavy machine guns and lidar surveillance. Mechanics shouted and revved power tools as they did simple maintenance in place.

Long days of travel weighed down Tomas's eyelids. He squeezed shut his eyes and shimmied his head to stay awake. Just a few hours. Probably nothing will happen—

A distant blip on the creek's far bank, at Tomas' eleven o'clock, flickered on his helmet display, then vanished.

Tomas squinted, then reached for his shilling to call up more information on the blip. A lidar unit on one of their Badgers had registered a walking human with 40% confidence for less than a second.

"Anyone else see that blip?" he asked over the squad net.

"What blip?" said Obermeyer.

"I and I saw it." Johnson paused. "I and I'll call the mechanics to check out the lidar units."

"There's obviously no one there," Sharma said. "Chameleonskin doesn't block lidar."

Tomas peered forward over the sights of his rifle. Sound and motion pulled his attention up to the flapping wings of a passel of birds rising from the forest and wheeling in the sky above.

He spoke in the squad net. "Spooked birds at my one o'clock, three hundred meters."

"Birds?" Obermeyer asked. "We're not here to watch the wildlife."

"Shut up and listen," Marchbanks said.

Tomas peered at the forest, looking for motion. Maybe Obermeyer would hassle him for jumping at shadows, but in the Badger's rear compartment there had been a lot of quiet speculation about the New Liberty militia, *mike* from the phonetic alphabet word for the *m* of *militia*. He would take no chances.

"Nothing," Obermeyer said after a time.

"I told you, Neumann," Sharma said, "if mike's in the forest, he has fab blueprints for chameleonskin. The lidar would pick him up."

"Keep your eyes open, lads." Marchbanks' tone silenced the chatter. "If mike's there in chamleonskin, you might see side-angle distortions."

Tomas kept watching the edge of the forest. The low sun made him squint. Would he be able to see any distortions against Constitution's glare?

He squinted again. A hundred meters away, a couple of soybean plants rustled with a passing breeze. But how had the breeze left the other plants in that row, and in the rows nearby, unruffled?

"What if they aren't in chameleonskin?" Tomas said into the squad net.

"We'd see them, Josie." Alvarez spoke with annoyance.

The low sun seemed to blur for a moment. Was that a man's shape passing in front of it?

Tomas' cheeks grew clammy as he remembered the physics printout he'd skimmed in the hours before he'd met Capt. Schreiber. "Not plain fabric. Not even camouflage. Fiber optic wrap?"

Cohen shouted, "Motion at a row of soybeans, my twelve o'clock, twenty meters!"

"The sun's in your eyes," Obermeyer said. "There's nothing—"

Small arms fire barked at a spot down the line. From Obermeyer's position. And Tomas knew the sound: the Unity's standard issue rifle. A red icon throbbed dully at the side of Tomas' helmet display, coming from Obermeyer's position.

"They're wrapped up head to toe in optical fiber!" Tomas shouted. He slid the fire selector toggle and fired a burst at the direction of the movement he'd seen. He swept the muzzle across twenty degrees of arc, firing more bursts. Cohen fired as well. "It's wrapping light, including lidar, around their bodies!"

Another lidar blip, and more Unity rifle fire sounded, roughly parallel with Tomas. Mike was already in the line!

Tomas rolled over with a panicked expectation a rifle muzzle was aimed at his head. No one there. He forced himself to draw a breath. Without sunlight in his eyes, he'd be able to see the distortions resulting from the placement of optical fibers around a mike's body. Tomas returned to his belly and crawled three meters to his right to confuse any mike who might have been watching his position.

There: a wave of distortion shifted into position behind a row of soybeans. A thin distorted line with a dark round tip emerged from between plants and aimed at Tomas' former position—

Tomas fired two bursts at the man behind the wrapped rifle. "They have a bead on our initial positions!" he shouted into the squad net. "Move!"

He scrambled a few more meters down the row of soybeans. Dust wormed in between his collar and his helmet and he fought down a cough. More rifles fired up and down the squad's line and he felt faint relief they were all GF issue. From his new position, he glimpsed the mike who'd targeted him. The rifle, dimly visible as a line of distortion, lay slanted down the front of the dirt mound the mike had used for cover. Most of the mike's body remained shrouded by fiber optic wrap, except for jagged tears at the shoulder and head. Blood soaked the soil under him.

Tomas' helmet display needlessly showed telemetry from where his rounds had struck flesh.

Tomas caught his breath for a moment. Another dull red icon had appeared in his helmet display. Sharma. Dammit. But telemetered hits showed four mikes had already been killed or wounded. Mike's plan had failed. Time for him to turn tail and run off with hopes the GF couldn't track him.

But if mike was in retreat, why was he singing? The same song the protesters had sung came from a voice thirty or forty meters from Tomas. He aimed his rifle and fired in that direction. Someone else fired at the singer too. Neither Tomas nor his squadmate hit through the soft cover of soybeans and chameleon cloth; the singer kept on. His voice added a mocking lilt.

From the other side came more voices, but these did not sing. "Remember New Boston!" someone shouted, and echoes of "New Boston!" and "Martyrs for the Constitution!" came from nearby. A glance showed distorted figures running over the uneven terrain of the soybean field at Marchbanks.

Tomas fired at the running men, three bursts. One of their rifles swung wildly but remained in hand, and telemetry showed one of his rounds had been stopped by a body armor layer under the mike's fiber optic layer Tomas reached for a fresh magazine and his shaking hands jammed it into his rifle.

Bursts of fire came from Marchbanks. The mikes' rifles tumbled to the ground, and Tomas' helmet display reported all three had been hit.

"You okay?" he called to Marchbanks over the squad net.

"Those crazy mikes. What in the bloody hell were they think—"

From the edge of the soybean field came a shrieking sound. A missile streaked by, roaring in Tomas' ears and making him duck. Two more missiles followed. Tomas glanced back. The missiles pitched up. Their new flight path took them over the line of Badgers behind them toward fighting vehicles undergoing refit and crew rest. Sgt. Johnson shouted an alarm into the platoon net as the missiles pitched down and banked for the thinner rear armor of the vehicles. Explosions erupted from a Badger and a Graywolf.

"Sir, we need intel on mike," Sgt. Johnson called to Lt. Tower. "I and I suggest call a bird to give us some visuals and infrared."

Lt. Tower sounded like a dull knife. "Roger. Making the call."

"Keep your eyes open, lads," Marchbanks said. "Sergeant, the Badgers ought to pepper the field with their thirteens. It will get mike on his belly. If he's wrapping light around him, we'll see through him to the ground and getting something better to shoot at."

"Good call," the sergeant said. "Idrin, on your bellies too. We don't want mike to see what a thirteen can do from your example."

Tomas squirmed into the soil. The machine guns on the Badgers rattled out rounds. He slid the fire selector to single shot to save ammunition, and peered into the soybean field for distortions or shadows. He fired at phantoms and tricks of light. His telemetry showed no hits.

Overhead, an aircraft's wings beat. Eight distant icons of enemy appeared in his helmet display at the edge of the soybean field. Four or five more mikes had already crossed the creek and were slipping into the woods. The Badgers banged out more rounds. One of the mikes at the edge of the field tumbled and the rest scrambled across the creek.

"We're holding here, men," Lt. Tower said. "Dismounts from the other platoon will passage our lines and conduct pursuit operations."

A few minutes later, the pursuit force went forward. Tomas' squad's net carried echoes of words spoken to the pursuers. "Godspeed." "Go get 'em." Muffled replies followed. Tomas held out his hand and shook a pursuer's. "Stay safe."

"You too."

What could go wrong back here? Before Tomas could think of anything more to say, the other man had taken a couple of steps and become a vague ripple of chameleonskin against the backdrop of the forest.

Sgt. Johnson ordered the squad to search the field for dead mikes. Tomas and the others went forward in silence, broken by the thrash of boots kicking soybean plants, and comments on finding the dead. "Hey songbird, you cockbiter," Alvarez said. "I got you for Obermeyer."

Tomas found the man he'd killed. Faceplate shattered, shoulder torn, he levered him up with the muzzle of his rifle and flipped him onto his back. Flies buzzed at the disturbance. Tomas knelt and studied what he could see of the dead man through the faceplate. Man? How young was he? The skin around his undamaged eye was pale and smooth, as if he'd spent all his brief life indoors.

I don't blame you for doing what you think you had to. Tomas felt mild pity. A wave of numb regret soon washed the pity away. A shame he and this dead mike could only meet this way. *Better you than me* soon followed. Tomas sought more words to define his thoughts, but Marchbanks' voice over the squad net distracted him.

"You whoreson. Were these your sons? You threw your own sons into battle? May God damn you to hell and the devil make you his catamite."

Tomas gave the dead mike a final glance, then went to Marchbanks. Marchbanks was his teammate, not a stranger, and alive, not dead. Moral circles can only stretch so far. He stepped over soybean plants and stopped alongside Marchbanks.

He silenced his shilling. "You alright?"

Marchbanks nodded his chin at the three dead mikes near him. "Such a damned stupid waste."

Their helmets had been pulled off. Pain and surprise were frozen on their slack faces. One looked familiar. Had he been one of the sullen faces watching the company's passage through the small town up the road? They all looked young to Tomas. "Maybe a high school—"

"Father or teacher, he's still a whoreson." Marchbanks jabbed his rifle's muzzle at one of the dead mikes. He pressed down, lolling the dead man's head, then pulled his rifle back. A dull, distant look formed on his face.

Cohen came up. "Are you alright, Marchbanks?"

"Bloody hell, why's everyone asking me that?" A breath sloughed from Marchbanks. After a moment, he fingered his shilling to drop his microphone out of the squad net, then gestured with his chin at the dead mikes. "Christ, lads, this is nae good."

"We got them," Cohen said.

"Two million locals? Military tech out of every fab and fighting skills out of every schoolhouse? How can we fight that?"

Tomas' breath caught. He'd never heard Marchbanks sound so pessimistic.

Cohen sounded confident. "We get rid of bacteria, don't we? It's the same."

"Nae the same. Getting rid of mike is impossible," Marchbanks said, voice flat.

Tomas lifted his head. He saw the insight they had missed. "I don't know about that, but Cohen, you're wrong about one thing. We don't get rid of bacteria at all. We're inundated with them all the time. But they almost never infect us. It's in their best interest not to. Remember what the sergeant tried to get the paper tiger to do in New Boston?"

Cohen said, "Hmm," then walked on.

Alone with Marchbanks, Tomas wanted to speak more. "You understand what I'm saying?"

"If we kill enough hotheads the rest will lie low. But how many of us will they get before then? Two of us right here, against a dozen of them. All they need do is whittle us down till the politicians on Challenger cut their losses." Distant rifle fire came from the forest. Marchbanks glanced up. The line of his shoulders showed a little more vigor. "Och, I'm thinking about things above my pay grade. We're here, and the only way out is to go straight ahead."

Tomas gave a tight smile and clapped his hand on Marchbanks' shoulder. "I'm looking out for you."

"Thanks, lad. Tell you one thing I could use your eyes for. I know it's against regs for him to carry it, but does Alvarez have his usual flask of rotgut? I could really use a nip."

AFTER THE ARMORED bulldozer stopped moving in front of the pillbox, Marchbanks shouted at the pillbox's rear entrance. "Do you yield, mike? We'll bury you alive if you don't!"

Prone behind a fallen tree, Tomas sighted down his rifle at the rear entrance. Thick walls cast deep shadows over the entrance. His finger rested outside the trigger guard. They would give the mikes a chance to surrender.

From inside the pillbox, a mike yelled back, "You'll label us irregular combatants and gun us down on the spot!"

"Haven't you heard our broadcasts? We extend lawful combatant protections to you now, mike!"

Muffled talk leaked out the rear entrance. "You said before you would respect our laws and customs! Tell that to President Kennedy!"

"Why won't they just surrender?" Marchbanks muttered into the squad's net. The gain from his microphone dropped, and he shouted his next words over the pillbox to the engineer driving the bulldozer. "Cpl. Komatsu, keep pushing soil into their firing slits!"

The bulldozer went back into motion on the other side of the pillbox. The blade scraped more soil, pushing the top of the pile higher than the pillbox's roof. Dirt clots tumbled down onto the concrete surface.

"We yield!" the mike shouted. "We yield!"

"Leave your weapons inside, take off your helmets, and set your chameleonskin on orange," Marchbanks said. Mike had switched away from fiber optic wraps for the lighter and more versatile chameleonskin. "Come out, hands up, single file, five meters apart. Form a circle five meters across in front of me and sit facing outward. Keep your hands up all the time."

The mike called, "We have two wounded. They can't walk on their own."

"One unwounded man can help each wounded one. Still, hands up or in front of your body, even the wounded. And move slowly."

The first mike came out, one arm around a wounded comrade, the other raised. Blood spotted the wounded mike's orange chameleonskin as he shuffled forward on his good leg. Both mikes looked exhausted. "Will you bring us a medic?" the unwounded one asked.

"Get yourselves on the ground first," Marchbanks said. "Keep your hands in sight."

The unwounded mike helped the other sit down. The wounded man grunted when his leg touched. The first mike sat down two meters to his comrade's left. Tomas glimpsed quiet resignation on his face.

Marchbanks murmured through the team net to Tomas, "Escort a medic here."

Tomas didn't move or speak.

"Did you hear me, lad?"

"Leaving a man alone is against procedure—"

"You have to adapt what the skills imps taught you to the circumstances. Get going. I can watch this lot." Marchbanks rose to a seated position and slid down the side of the boulder. He went to the wounded man and patted him for weapons.

Tomas came from behind his fallen tree and held his rifle loosely in both hands. More prisoners exited the pillbox and trudged toward the circle. Their shaved heads bowed, fatigue plain on their faces, they moved into position without questioning. Certainly Marchbanks could handle it, but procedure was there for a reason. "Are you sure—"

"I'll be fine, lad. These ones are beaten." Marchbanks moved to the wounded man's comrade to the left.

Tomas kept going. Heaped soil covered the front face of the pillbox. The heaps bore the scrape marks of the bulldozer's blade. Gouges in the forest floor left by its tracks marked the path downslope, toward the main road where a destroyed Badger still burned.

"We need a medic for at least two wounded prisoners," he said to Sgt. Johnson.

"We'll get you one. Come on down to the road. Where be Marchbanks?"

"Guarding prisoners taken from the pillbox."

Sgt. Johnson hmphed. "He can handle it, but get back there quick. I and I'll send a medic your way now."

Tomas slung his rifle over his shoulder and kept going. The slope had a gentle grade, but the bulldozer's tracks made footing uneasy and the branches of trees toppled on its ascent to the pillbox scratched as he brushed past.

From the direction of the company's headquarters and supply platoons, a medic came his way. The red cross on her sleeve stood out in the forest of browns and blackish-greens.

As they more closely approached, his eyes widened in surprise. He'd expected the al-Aqsan, but this woman was taller and more buxom. Her skin was fair and blond ends showed under the rim of her helmet. His surprise kept him from checking her nameplate.

"Come with me," Tomas said. They started upslope. Her long sturdy legs kept pace with him. "You're new…?"

"I landed three days ago."

"And you're from?" He spoke idly, watching the forest beyond the pillbox for any mikes.

"Sankt-Benedikts-Welt. You?"

"Born there, but grew up on Joséphine." He wondered why he felt no excitement at meeting another Benedikter, then shoved the thought aside.

She stumbled on a track left by the bulldozer. He grabbed her hand and his arm tightened to keep her upright. "You okay?"

The medic put weight on her foot. "I should be fine." She glanced at her hand, still grasped by his. "Thanks."

He let go. He realized she was the first woman, other than a Daughter, he'd touched while on planet. "They're just around the pillbox. I only know of two wounded but there might be more."

They rounded the corner. Marchbanks crouched behind the last prisoner in the circle. With a bored look on his face, his hands ran down the prisoner's flanks.

Behind him, one of the prisoners turned to face into the circle. The prisoner put his left hand on the ground and raised his weight off his backside. In his right hand, something glinted.

"Hey!" Tomas yelled. He lifted his arm to point at the prisoner behind Marchbanks. Marchbanks gave Tomas a puzzled look.

The prisoner sprinted across the circle and lunged for Marchbanks.

His left hand reached around Marchbanks' head to grab the top front of the helmet, while the prisoner's right hand moved toward Marchbanks' neck. That close, the gap between his helmet and would be apparent. Another glint in the dappled light, from what Tomas knew with dread intuition was a knife, and both Marchbanks and the prisoner fell.

"Hey!" Tomas pulled his rifle off his shoulder as he ran toward the circle. The prisoner rolled to the balls of his feet and brandished his knife. No glint now; blood slickened the blade. A feral expression contorted his face.

Still running, Tomas fired a burst into the prisoner's chest. The mike stumbled backward. His eyes were wide with confusion and he froze in place. Tomas stopped and fired another burst at his face. His rounds tore open the back of the prisoner's skull and he tumbled backward, crushed head smacking the ground near one of his seated comrades. His limbs jerked and his body lay still.

Gurgling sounded near Tomas' feet. Marchbanks had his hand at his neck, and his eyes bugged in fear. Blood gushed from his neck in pulses.

The medic ran up. Tears welled in her eyes. "*Gott im Himmel.*" She reached for her medical kit. Her hands shook so much she took a few seconds to unsnap the flap before kneeling next to Marchbanks.

One of the prisoners cried out, a high wavering sound. His hand fluttered like a wavering bird to his shoulder. Blood and brain tissue from his comrade stained his suit. He pulled his hand back in front of his face and his expression showed horror. He turned to Tomas, and the horror turned to fear.

A cold feeling froze Tomas' face into an affectless mask. Inside, his heart pounded, and parts of his subconscious never before heard voiced themselves in words for the first time. *Yes, fear me, and die anyway—*

He fired a burst, destroying the prisoner's face, collapsing his body into the dirt. The next prisoner in the circle showed the same fear. Inside, Tomas exulted, like some ancient gladiator thumping his fists on his chest; but his face remained expressionless. A squeeze of his finger and he killed the third man.

The other prisoners reacted now. One stood and ran for the woods. His bright orange suit contrasted starkly against the browns and dark greens of the forest. Two bursts into the back of his ribcage. He tumbled and groaned once before falling still and silent.

The fifth prisoner had fallen to his knees and raised his arms high. "It's not our fault. I didn't know he had a knife."

Cold steel encased Tomas' emotions. He angled his head toward the mike who'd slashed Marchbanks' throat. "We thought he was unarmed too." Another burst through the face. Five down.

How many more? Too few. Two wounded men. The one with the thigh wound had a trace of hope in his expression, but the line of his mouth showed he knew he would die. Tomas shot him in the head.

The last one lay limply, his eyes rolled back and shivers gripping his body. The medic knelt next to him, her bloody hands working at torn cloth over his torso. "What are you doing?"

Tomas killed the wounded mike. "You can't help him anymore. Take care of our own."

"It's too late," she said. Her voice bore a gravity he could not resist. Tomas blinked and looked down at her. He expected to see fear. Even his mother would fear him if she'd seen what he'd just done. Yet the only emotion he saw was disgust.

He leaned back and finally took a half-step away from her to keep his balance. His handiwork lay all around him, drawing his gaze. Dead prisoners. Marchbanks' body lay motionless among them, his eyes vacantly staring at the canopies of oaks and maples overhead.

Tomas' breath came fast and ragged. *No, it's justified, I did this all for you.*

Can seven dead mikes bring me back, lad? he heard in his mind's ear. Tomas continued to breathe shallowly. Spots swam in his vision and he sat down. His head dropped between his knees and his heartbeats roared in his ears.

Barely-heard footsteps. "Neumann, what happened?" Johnson asked.

Tomas kept his head down. "He had a knife. I don't know how Marchbanks could have missed it. He had a knife. Slit Marchbanks' throat."

"If one did, they all might. It be irie—"

Tomas laughed and cried at the same time. "None of them had a clue what their man planned! None of them knew what was going on, until I gunned him down. Then they all waited for me to shoot them."

"Sounds like they wanted you to kill them," Johnson said.

Incredulous, Tomas looked up. Tears in his eyes refracted his view of the sergeant. His voice crackled. "How can you say that? Who could want to die? Who? Who? Who." Tomas' head slumped and he cried. Tears dripped down his cheeks and sobs came out of his mouth. He reached for his shilling and cut off his microphone. His shame burned intensely solely from the medic's disgusted look. It would explode if his squadmates heard him cry.

"I and I don't know the facts," Sgt. Johnson said. "What I and I see, some prisoners surrender under false pretenses, rise against the personnel guarding them, kill one, but be neutralized by the survivor."

Tomas pushed down his tears, grateful for a chance to be angry. "Shit! You're talking like I deserve a fucking medal!"

Johnson's voice sounded firm. "We need you, Neumann. We be alone on a planet of fanatics who want us dead. The only people we can rely on be our idrin. You got to pull yourself together. Feel whatever you want when we ride the transport home. Here and now, the only thing you can do is act."

Other men—Cohen, Alvarez, a few others—walked up from around the pillbox. They hesitated, then hurried forward when they saw Marchbanks' corpse. "What happened?" Cohen asked.

Tomas looked away. He stared through the forest without seeing it. "I did what I had to do."

"About time," Alvarez said.

Tomas rankled at his tone. A glare formed on his face, but by the time he turned his head to look at Alvarez, the glare had faded. "Do something for me. Toss me your flask."

CHAPTER 10

SUNRIGHT DECATUR

THE COMPANY'S new base was near a town called Sunright Decatur, twelve hundred kilometers from Reagantown. A river spawned from the glaciers on the planet's dark side flowed past, and the wind from that direction always seemed to blow cold. Even facing Constitution made no difference; the chill stealing over Tomas' back seeped deeper into his body than the sun's low rays could expel.

In addition to operations against mike units seen in the vicinity by obs wheels, scouts, or the SF, at least one squad patrolled Sunright Decatur twice every day. Dismounted teams headed and tailed a column, with the squad's two Badgers in the middle. Their path varied, but they always stopped at the municipal fab and the town hall.

A detachment from the company's supply platoon accompanied them to or from the municipal fab and worked there between patrols, feeding the town and monitoring arriving civilian trucks for any broken military material a mike sympathizer might try to recycle.

The mayor was a woman with wrinkled eyes and dirty blond hair showing gray streaks. She had a warm alto voice Tomas heard once in a while, if she met them at the town hall's front door. The squad leader would speak privately in her office while the squad waited on the street outside. Their helmets were off, clipped to their belts, and their suits were set to a gray and brick-red urban camouflage pattern.

Despite these tokens of trust they extended the locals, pedestrians mostly turned onto side streets to avoid the GF soldiers. A few boys, released from school by the GF's ban on skill implantation units, mingled around, gazing awestruck at the idling Badgers and daring each other with whispers and nudged elbows to talk to the soldiers. Mothers and older sisters would call with nervous voices for their boys to come home. Sometimes the soldiers would see one of the women in a doorway or around a corner of a house, holding a boy behind her with one hand while the other clutched the collar of her blouse.

"Look at them, worried for their virtue," Alvarez said. "Like they could stop me from taking what they've got."

Tomas wanted to stay silent, but maybe some response would mollify Alvarez into shutting up. "I'll stick with the Daughters."

"You might have a long wait for liberty to see them."

"Daughters won't jam a knitting needle through your ear during the act."

That shut up Alvarez. Cohen caught Tomas' gaze and gave a curt, appreciative nod. Tomas made no response. He wished he could be alone.

"Where are the men of the town?" Lundergard asked. He was a tall, gangly Österbotterman. Not technically a virgin—a mike had shot in their direction during a seek-and-destroy mission in the woods sunleft of town a week before.

"In a mike unit up in the hills," Ryan said. Ryan was a virgin, and he took the squad's stories about mike with dread seriousness.

Cohen looked at the front door of the town hall. "Look lively. The sergeant."

Sgt. Johnson came up to them. "Form up, idrin. We'll walk further than usual back to base."

The squad headed into an industrial quarter, with Tomas' team on point. The cooling towers of the municipal fab dominated the skyline. Along the streets stood single-story mycocrete buildings. Intersections with side streets showed open loading docks and carried the sounds of woodworkers' saws and sculptors' arc welders to the squad. Some workmen looked up with guarded expressions, while others kept to their jobs. Tomas wanted to put his helmet on and set all his chameleonskin to full camouflage. He had no fear of the locals; he just wanted to go unseen.

"Hold a minute," Sgt. Johnson said through the squad net from his position at the tail of the column. A green arrow popped into Tomas' helmet display, pointing around a corner. "Cohen, your team follows the green arrow. My team, stay with I and I and follow the blue arrow." Tomas craned his neck. A blue arrow pointed down an alley in the same direction as the other. "Badgers remain here. The third building be a metalworker's shop. We meet inside it in forty seconds. We expect the occupants be unarmed. Go!"

Cohen led Tomas' team around the corner. As their boots pounded down the street, the green arrow yawed to the right. It pointed at a small metal door in a tan mycocrete wall. A prop held the door open and a barely pubescent boy sat on a red plastic chair outside the doorway. His eyes widened and he scampered in the doorway. He kicked the prop aside as he went.

"We've been made," Cohen said.

"Faster, idrin!"

The team ran. Ryan yanked open the door while Cohen led the others in. "Hands up! Freeze! Don't move!" they shouted, and swept their muzzles across the interior space. Across the workshop, members of Sgt. Johnson's team stood on ground level outside a loading dock, elbows and rifles on the shop floor. Metalworking equipment occupied the half of the shop furthest from the door. A closed-off loft stood above them.

Four boys, the youngest being the lookout and the oldest appearing about twenty standard, shuffled together into the center of the space with their hands up. "Check them for weapons," Sgt. Johnson said.

"I'm on it," Tomas said. "Cover me," he told Alvarez. He patted the boys down while Alvarez held his rifle at the ready. Tomas was thorough, pulling out pockets and ordering the boys to kick off their work boots. *You won't get me like you got Marchbanks.* "Clear, sergeant."

Behind Sgt. Johnson, some men of the squad checked a forging press and a turret lathe, while others pried lids off crates. To the local boys, Johnson said, "Who be in charge?"

They looked nervously among themselves. The oldest one took a half-step forward. "Me."

"Not you. Where be your father?"

The oldest boy lifted his chin. "I'm in charge here."

Behind him, one of the younger boys glanced at the loft above the tools, then started guiltily and stared at the floor. Sgt. Johnson stepped back and looked up and down the shop. "Check there," he said to one of his team as he pointed to the loft.

"On it." A few of them looked around and one found a pulldown ladder. Two men started up the ladder while a third aimed his rifle at the top.

"What are you here for?" the oldest boy said.

Alvarez snorted. "You got a big mouth for a little mike."

Tomas waved his fingers and Alvarez, looking chastened, shuffled back a step.

"Son," Sgt. Johnson said, "we not be stupid." He nodded to one of his team, who handed him a thin metal object about sixty centimeters long. Generally cylindrical, about forty centimeters of it were unadorned except for a raised, notched flange. A rectangular blocky portion made up the rest. The barrel of a standard issue Unity rifle. "You'd best tell us what you know."

"They know nothing!" called a pudgy man climbing down the ladder. Two rifles were aimed at him. He jumped off and hustled over. "My sons, my nephew, his friend. They're just boys."

"You be building rifle parts for mike."

"Sir, no, I mean, yes." His face was red and his breath labored. "But they forced me. The militia. I didn't choose it. They threatened me late in the night. Kicked in my front door and rounded us up at gunpoint. 'You have a metalworking shop and a lovely family. Which one will serve us?' What could I do, sir? Please, sir, what could I do?"

One of Johnson's team came up. "Just barrels. No other parts."

"Call supply. Get someone here who can check the equipment's programming. Maybe they fab different parts in batches."

"No, sir, I swear it. On all the presidents and the constitution itself I swear it. Just barrels. I don't know where the militia—mike—makes any other parts, or where they take these when they pick them up."

Sgt. Johnson sloughed out a breath. "You tell a nice story. It might even be true. We will corroborate it. All five of you will come back to base for scans of your mental activity."

The metalworker nodded. "Of course, sir, of course. We will prove this wasn't our idea. We just want to ply our craft in peace."

The oldest boy spoke. The family resemblance was plain. "Is that some code?" he asked Johnson. "Are you going to take us into a field and shoot us?"

His father hissed. Sgt. Johnson gave the boy a cold look. "Depends. Be you innocent civilians or irregular combatants?" He then looked to men of the squad. "Tie their hands and put them in the back of a Badger for the return trip. The other Badger will carry every rifle barrel we can fit inside over to the municipal fab. Toss the office for any paper or tablets that might tell us something about this operation."

A few minutes later the squad set out. Tomas' team now brought up the rear, behind their Badger carrying the metalworker and his sons. "We should've just shot them right there," Alvarez said. "Right, Neumann?"

"No."

"Oh, yeah, you're right. We should shoot the whole goddam town. You want to kill them all, don't you?"

Tomas kicked a pebble down the pavement. "Just the ones who deserve it." His voice sounded cool, but when he blinked, images of the prisoner on his knees, the medic's look of disgust, appeared to him. *A killing machine or a remorseful man. Which me is real and which false?*

Half an hour later, the other team trooped out of the municipal fab after tossing eighty rifle barrels into the recycling hopper. "Finally we can head back to base," Alvarez said.

"Idrin, we have one more stop on the way out of town."

Lundergard groaned. "My feet already hurt."

Cohen chuckled. "Detach yourself from your desire to lounge on your bunk the rest of the day. We have our orders."

They went through a residential quarter, under live oaks with green-black canopies canted like satellite dishes to catch Constitution's light. Behind fences of black alloy, the mycocrete houses were painted to look like stucco. The soldiers' shadows stretched up the driveways. The garages, ordered kept open by the GF command, held cars, a few pickup trucks, a trailer holding a boat.

After an intersection, the view opened up. A block held a long brick building in the center of a wide lawn. *Sunright Decatur High School*, read permanent letters on the bezel of an LED sign. The LEDs were dark. A breeze pulled seeds off dandelion heads along the edge of the sidewalk.

Near the school's front entrance, a circular driveway curved around a lawn where a GF obs wheel stood. The Badgers parked back-to-back on the driveway and Johnson led the men to the half-glassed doors. Rain-borne dust speckled the windows and the tops of the locks holding the door handles. Men waved their shillings at the locks. "This one checks," said a soldier, and the other locks checked as well. The doors had remained locked since their last visit.

"We look around even so." Johnson handled his shilling through his uniform. "Three go in and the rest check the perimeter. You have a preference, speak."

"I'll go in," Tomas said. It would be darker in there, and distant from most of the squad. Cohen and Bar-Ruda also volunteered.

Inside, the only light came from the windows. Electrical power had long since been cut. Dust lay like gray snow on the sill of a window at the principal's office and the frame of a trophy case. The building was laid out like a capital E, with the main entrance in the lower left corner. "I'll take the far wing," Tomas said, the wing furthest from the sun.

The distance from the rest of the squad was not complete. Their chatter entered Tomas' ears and data from them popped onto his helmet display. Couldn't he be alone, even for a moment? "A grate over a crawlspace entrance is loose," Ryan said.

"Good eyes," Johnson said. "Put a lock on it."

Tomas kept walking and rounded the corner. Shaded by the other wings, this hallway was the darkest of the three. Classrooms and rooms with low-power implant stations opened off the hallway. Dusted coated the vents of the lockers. Tomas carried his rifle loosely in his arms. How long ago had the mikes behind the pillbox been schoolboys in a place like this?

A noise came from one of the implant station rooms. He froze and lifted his rifle higher. Maybe nothing, perhaps the building settled or a rat sought food. Hopefully all it was. He padded closer to the open door, then ran three steps in, swinging up his rifle as he went.

In the dim light seeping around the lowered blinds, the whites of the boy's eyes grabbed Tomas' attention. The boy stood behind a table bearing an implant station. The arm holding the station's TMI helmet was up, exposing the helmet's inner lining.

The boy's chest heaved. He lifted his hands from a metal plate bearing squat cylinders, a solar panel, and insulated wires leading below the table to the electronics driving the implant station. He might have been sixteen standard.

"What are you doing here?" Tomas asked.

Eyes wide with fright, the boy said, "I wanted to use an implant station."

"You know that's forbidden." Tomas' face hardened. "I could shoot you as an irregular combatant right here."

The boy's hands wavered. "I'm not doing anything wrong. I just want to learn."

Tomas lowered his rifle. "What do you want to learn?"

"Confederated Worlds languages."

"Confed and NL are mutually intelligible—"

"No, no. Languages from your homeworlds." He put on a declamatory face. "*Il mio nome è Theodore. Parlate Nuovo-Toscano?*"

Tomas shook his head in a wide, slow motion.

"What then is your language—"

"Every GF soldier or Confederated Worlds civilian you'll ever meet on New Liberty can speak Confed," Tomas said. Theodore's mask of naïve idealism began to crumble. "You're risking your life for something that doesn't matter. Shut down the implant station and lie low until we're gone. We're locking the crawlspace grate you used to get in, so you'll have to find another way out. Do what I'm telling you or you'll end up dead."

Theodore gulped and nodded. Tomas left the room and headed toward the front door. He glanced back a few times, but the boy had no knife and no urge to slit his throat. Tomas relaxed just enough to feel how tense his shoulders still were. *There's been enough killing on this planet. Let's make peace where we can.* He trudged onward.

Cohen and Bar-Ruda waited near the trophy case. "Nothing," Cohen said. "You, Neumann?"

"Nothing either. Let's get out of here."

THE NEXT WEEKS passed in a routine. The company ran missions into the woods and hills to sunleft of the town. Most of their activities involved checking obs wheels and dismantling irrigation systems to wither away shrubs and thin out the forests. Mike generally lay low, but sometimes emerged from his bunkers to snipe at dismounted infantry. Makeshift landmines damaged vehicles from time to time. *Hikes with a risk of gunshot,* Cohen called these missions. Sniper attacks and other mike activity were met with fire from the vehicles and Kestrels on station above.

Patrols in Sunright Decatur were generally quiet. Tomas never saw Theodore. He never saw the metalworker or his sons again, but he heard scuttlebutt from another patrol. They found the metalworker dead on his residential street, gunshot residue on his lips and brain mixed with bone and blood on the pavement under his head. A paper note pinned to his shirt said the militia had executed him for treason.

A few days later, Tomas' squad was due to patrol. He was one of the last to fall in, arriving at the assembly point a few minutes before departure hour. As he approached, Sgt. Johnson stepped up. "Neumann, a word."

Tomas checked his chronometer. "I'm timely arriving, sergeant."

"Did I and I say you weren't? We need a few men for a special task today and I and I know you can handle it."

They were going to gun down unarmed civilians. The intuition rocked Tomas on his feet. "What's the task?"

"Can't get into it yet. It requires fire discipline and keen observation. Can I and I rely on you, Neumann?"

"Yes."

"I and I'll tell you when you're needed. Prepare to head out."

In the assembly area, only one of the squad's Badgers waited with the dismounted men. The men's suits were set to urban camouflage. Tomas found his team and noticed Cohen wasn't there. "I'm team leader today," Alvarez said.

"You? Where's Cohen?"

"What, you jealous? I must be leadership material."

Tomas shrugged. The situation would come clear eventually. Sgt. Johnson acted as if nothing was amiss; the squad rolled out the base's main gate at the usual hour.

The patrol started out as usual, but after dropping a supply team at the municipal fab, the sergeant beckoned Tomas and two others behind a corner of the fab's main fence. "Helmets on, and full chameleonskin head-to-toe," he told them.

Tomas put on his helmet and pressed the controls at his wrist. He looked down and barely saw his legs. It relieved him to be almost invisible. Any looks of disgust aimed his way would pass right through him.

A ping sounded in Tomas' helmet. "Here be your destination coordinates," Sgt. Johnson said. "You go parallel with the patrol, but stay at least a block away from us and move as stealthily as you can. Each one of you will have responsibility for one external door of a building. Attempt to take the person of interest prisoner, but protect yourselves foremost."

A green arrow appeared in Tomas' helmet display, along with yellowish ones pointing to his squadmates' destinations. On the far side of the street parallel to the squad's main path to the town hall, they hugged the front walls of workshops. A car turned the corner and they froze until it passed. Further on, they walked sideways to present the smallest visible angle to a woodworker taking a break, drinking water on a loading dock.

Near the town hall, their paths diverged. Tomas followed the green arrow to a two-story building a couple of blocks behind the town hall. In a corner of the building's front, a door had been propped open. The arrow led him inside.

A narrow entryway gave two routes deeper into the building: to his right, into a glass-doored clerical space where two young women worked with rigid backs turned to the door; and up a stairwell. The arrow pointed up. The treads were solidly built, and made no sound as he climbed.

The second story lacked internal dividers. The one large room had bare carpet and a dusty smell. Low in the corners hung spiderwebs bearing flies bound up in silk. A pair of French doors overlooked the street, opened to the breeze and the town's few sounds. A closer look showed no balcony past the doorsill; Tomas could stand in the doorway and jump easily down with a power assist from his suit. The room was dark enough that passersby would be less able than usual to see distortions in the chameleonskin.

Across the street stood another two-story building. An LED sign next to the front door read *Office Space for Rent; Entire Building Available.* Tomas' helmet display projected a red target onto the front door. Behind the building, weeds tufted an empty lot. Beyond the empty lot, across another street, the town hall's brick fence rose two meters above the sidewalk. Above the rear fence, someone sat in a corner office upstairs. Dirty blond hair streaked with gray spilled down her back. The mayor. Her motionless body language suggested she worked intently on the papers on her desk.

More icons appeared on his helmet display, telling him the bulk of the squad had arrived in front of the town hall.

"Ready yourselves, idrin," Sgt. Johnson said to Tomas and the others.

A few seconds later, motion came from the mayor's office; the sergeant walked in.

A rifle cracked the neighborhood's silence. Not GF or Uni standard issue. It came from the building for rent between Tomas and the town hall. In the mayor's office window, cracks radiated from a bullet hole. The mayor herself was slumped forward and blood stained her paperwork. Tomas couldn't see Sgt. Johnson, but his icon in Tomas' helmet display glowed green.

You knew it was coming and ducked but why let the mayor die— Tomas shook his head to clear his thoughts. The red target remained on his view of the building for rent. "Three meter fall," he said to his helmet, and jumped. Smart fibers in the legs of his suit cushioned his landing on the pavement below. He crossed the street and crouched on one knee, then aimed his rifle at the door.

"He went out the door on my side!" one of the other men said. "Neumann, he's heading for the corner near you!"

Tomas crouched and padded toward the corner. His helmet display projected icons on his view of the building's front wall, one for his squadmate, one for the shooter. The shooter would round the corner in moments—

He cross-checked him with his rifle, swinging the stock with his right hand into the shooter's chest. The shooter tumbled to the sidewalk and Tomas brought his rifle back to firing position. His squadmates pounded to the scene, rifles drawn, shouting at the shooter to remain still. Tomas didn't speak.

The shooter was Theodore. He'd lost the naïve expression from the encounter in the school. Now he gave each of the soldiers a defiant look. "You fuckers got me. But at least I shot that bitch in the head. Patriots outnumber traitors, so it's a good exchange, my life for hers."

One of Tomas' comrades sniffed out a breath. "Not a good exchange for you, mikey."

"The constitution is bigger than my life," Theodore said. Idealism glazed his voice and he stared at each of them in turn. Tomas quailed when their gazes met, but Theodore couldn't see his face through the chameleonskin on his helmet's faceplate.

More footsteps sounded, along with the whirr of tires from a Badger's road harness on the pavement. "Good work, idrin."

"Thanks, sergeant," said one of them. Tomas nodded.

The Badger's brakes squeaked and the ramp clanged open. Cohen came out, accompanied by a woman with hair tucked under a camouflage helmet. It took Tomas a moment to identify her from her crow's feet and the lines of her face. The mayor? "Sergeant, thank you for agreeing to my plan," she said. Her voice confirmed her identity.

Theodore's defiant look vanished. "I shot you in the head."

"The GF personnel and I set up a dummy. A wig on a basketball stuffed with sacks of ketchup and toothpaste."

A glimmer of defeat on Theodore's face gave way to continued defiance. "You fucking whore. Which one of these do you spread your legs for? Or do you not bother selling yourself to sweaties and noncoms, and save your illusory virtue for officers?"

She looked coolly at him. "Teddy, that's no way to talk to your aunt."

Aunt? What could lead someone to try killing his own aunt?

Theodore said to her, "You forfeited any respect I should give you when you committed treason."

She set her fists on her hips. "I keep this town alive, Teddy. All you would do is bring down on it the Confederated Worlds' wrath." To Sgt. Johnson, she said, "What do you do with irregular combatants?" Her tone made clear she already knew the answer.

"Summary execution." He looked around. "I and I think the side wall around the corner should do."

"What?" Theodore said. His eyes showed whites. "You take prisoners—"

"We take mikes in uniform prisoner on a battlefield. You be in civilian clothes and tried assassinating an official of the local government."

Theodore's eyelids fluttered. "You have to interrogate me first. A brain scan would give you intelligence on mike activity. I can cooperate, tell you what I know—"

The mayor's hazel eyes bored into Theodore. "How do you think we knew what you planned?"

Theodore looked pale and a grimace froze on his parted lips. "You could have stopped me and didn't. You'd rather shoot me? What's my mother going to say?"

"Sunright Decatur can only survive this war if the townsfolk know I hold their best interests above my own. If my sister will hate me for that, that's just another of my own interests I have to set aside for the good of the town." To the sergeant, she said, "I'm done with him."

"Tie his hands behind his back, idrin. Who has a blindfold?"

The other soldiers got Theodore to his feet and shoved him face-first at the building's front wall. Tomas tied his hands together and cinched the rope tight. He gave the knot a final tug and Theodore grunted in response.

A pain in Tomas' mouth caught his attention. He'd been biting his lower lip. After a shake of his head, he grabbed Theodore's arm and frog-marched him around the corner.

The building presented a gray wall to the alley. Tomas and the other soldiers stopped four meters from the front corner and the same distance from the small door in the back Theodore had fled from after the shooting. Cohen carried a length of bandage Tomas recognized as being scavenged from a medkit in the Badger. He folded it in half lengthwise, then again. When he moved closer to Theodore, the boy bucked his head to keep Cohen from blindfolding him.

One of the other soldiers punched the boy in the stomach. Theodore bent over in pain and moaned as Cohen tied the blindfold over his eyes. "Face death like a man," the other soldier said.

Theodore slumped to his knees. His moans of pain became sobs. "Form up, idrin," Sgt. Johnson said.

Tomas, Cohen, and the other two soldiers formed a line across the alley.

"Any last words?" Sgt. Johnson asked Theodore.

Tomas' heart slammed and his stomach felt ill. Theodore would say he met a soldier in the school, who let him violate the ban on skills implantation and gain the skills to shoot the mayor. The sergeant would investigate. A court-martial would sentence Tomas to five standard years in a terraforming battalion on one of the raw worlds near the Progressive Republic. If they did he would deserve it—

Theodore stopped crying and stood tall. His voice wavered a little as he said, "'I regret I have but one life to lose for my country.'"

After his words echoed away, Sgt. Johnson said, "Ready."

Tomas lifted his rifle and slid the toggle to single-shot before he could think about it. The skills imps had prepared him to be part of a firing squad.

"Aim."

A cold, remorseless feeling filled Tomas as he sighted on the middle of Theodore's chest. Memories of the prior mercies he had shown to this boy and the student in New Boston mocked him. He had been a fool. He would never again show pity to anyone. Not even himself.

"Fire!"

CHAPTER 11

THE HEMP FIELD

Between a swell in the rolling plain eight hundred meters to sunleft of their foxhole, and a pair of distant forested hills tinged red-orange by Constitution's light, the prevailing wind from darkward carried a faint plume of dust across the sky. From sunleft came the low rumble of many tracked vehicles. Enemy vehicles, moving slowly down a gravel road that was mike's axis of advance.

Tomas and Ryan stood in their foxhole just behind the crest of a low contour parallel to the road. Tomas watched the swell to sunleft, looking for shimmers of active chameleonskin when the first vehicles would top the swell.

"I've never faced tanks before," Ryan said.

"Don't worry about them. They'll be too busy trying to return fire against the Graywolfs." Two hundred meters to their sunright, the gravel road curved to the left around a low hill. A tank platoon, four Graywolfs, waited hull-down on that hill, along with his platoon's four Badgers. "You just cover me against mike dismounts while I fire the grenade launcher at their tanks." The launcher leaned against the side wall of the foxhole. Two racks of four grenades each hung from hooks hammered into the stony soil next to it.

"Dismounts? Maybe we'll catch them in their DeGaulles." Ryan's voice switched from fearful to hopeful in five seconds.

"No such luck. You can tell they're moving slowly, can't you?"

Ryan looked at the dust cloud, but Tomas could read from his face he didn't grasp it. "Oh, yeah."

"Their infantry is on foot, looking for obs equipment, landmines, and ambushes." The foolhardy mikes had already been killed in places like the soybean field. The ones they faced today had learned how to fight like professionals. He angled his head toward Ryan. "You clear on what you need to do?"

"Yeah. Dismounts. Cover—"

Ryan shut his mouth when Tomas called for silence with a chop of his hand. The clack of tracks on the dirt road grew louder, and the first mike vehicle appeared at the top of the swell. The active chameleonskin obscured the vehicle's outline, but nothing could mask the sound of the tracks on gravel or the sight of dust rising from the tracks. The rumble of the drive wheels made it as a Marlborough, a tank.

The Marlborough came at walking speed down the gravel road. Tomas' helmet display projected a line of hostile infantryman icons rustling through waist-high hemp in the fields on both sides of the road. The software assembling the projections required some minimum probability that a shimmer of light and motion through the crop was actually a mike, and the icons flickered into and out of existence depending on sight angles and the position of the enemy's arms and legs.

"Shouldn't you get the grenade launcher ready?" Ryan whispered.

"Lamp's still red." Just as in the foxhole he'd shared with March-banks, the engineers had run wires to an intercom and a tablet in their foxhole. The tablet mounted on the wall of the foxhole now showed a traffic light. Red meant hold fire; yellow would mean prepare the grenade launcher; green would mean fire grenades at the mike vehicles.

"You didn't even look."

"Don't need to. The Graywolf platoon commander's in charge of this mission, remember? He's no paper tiger. He knows there's only one tank over the swell and he wants to wait for more."

A few minutes later, Ryan murmured, "How many more does he want?"

Twelve vehicles, a mix of Marlboroughs and DeGaulles, had topped the swell, as well as two more lines of dismounted infantry. The lead tank was about two hundred meters up the road from their foxhole. A glance to sunleft showed a strong dust cloud still rising from out of sight. Mike had at least a company moving against them, maybe two. We might be outnumbered four to one. The ambush couldn't stop mike's advance, just harass it and hope Shirley Foxtrot could put photons on it. There were fewer ships in orbit now, thanks to mounting tensions with the Progressive Republic. This ambush had low priority for any orbital fire mission by those ships remaining.

"As many as we can get. Now shut up." His helmet display projected a parabolic microphone onto a half-ellipsoid smear held by someone in the second line of mikes. "If they catch us talking, the mission is dead."

Ryan hunkered against the front wall of the foxhole. Tomas peered out the gap between the lip of the foxhole and the edge of a sheet of chameleonskin stretched over their heads. The column of mike vehicles crept forward, drawing even with, then passing, their hiding place. In the distance, more topped the swell in the ground and the dust cloud in their rear remained as dense as before. Two companies, at least.

On the touchscreen of the tablet, the traffic signal switched from red to yellow. Tomas tapped Ryan's shoulder and pointed. Ryan nodded and hefted his rifle, while Tomas lifted the grenade launcher to his shoulder.

Guns boomed from the low hill to their right. Moments later, reactive armor on the front slopes of the mike tanks, and shells penetrating that armor, thundered. Large strips of chameleonskin on the lead tank lost their images and showed only the 'skin's gray base material. Smoke poured out of a hole in the turret.

A few Marlboroughs near the head of the column fired back. Rounds missed, pounding the hillside below the GF vehicles or sailing over them. The mike vehicles further back in the column remained silent, their vision presumably obscured by dust, smoke, and their comrades ahead of them.

The Graywolfs and Badgers kept firing, and soon another mike tank at the column's head poured smoke into the air. Ryan lifted his rifle toward the lip of the foxhole—

Tomas jabbed his fist at Ryan's shoulder to get his attention, then shook his head. *Not yet,* he mouthed.

It took mike a few more minutes to respond to the fire from the Graywolfs and Badgers. Marlboroughs and DeGaulles back in the column veered off the gravel road and flattened the hemp fields on both sides. The mike vehicles traveled in bounds, two firing at the top of the hill for every two advancing, until they formed a line whose ends curved in toward the hill. A tank stood within forty meters of Tomas and Ryan with its thinner flank armor facing them.

Now, Tomas mouthed, as the traffic light on the tablet's touchscreen turned green. He calmly sighted on the seam in the chameleonskin between the tank's main body and the turret. An easy squeeze of the trigger and the grenade roared out of the tube, kicking his shoulder. He didn't see the rocket fire a few meters away, but heat washed his face in the instant before the grenade impacted.

The explosion thundered to their foxhole. "God damn!" shouted Ryan.

"Keep your eye on their dismounts and cover me." Tomas popped the next grenade out of its rack. The supply of eight grenades represented wishful thinking and the fecundity of molecular fabrication. He'd be lucky to fire three before mike reacted and forced them to withdraw. He mounted the second grenade on the launcher and sighted on the next tank, at seventy meters. Ryan fired bursts at infantrymen Tomas had no eyes for as he aimed and launched the grenade. Another hit.

Tomas popped out the next grenade. Uni standard rifles chattered nearby. He mounted the grenade and nodded at Ryan. The other showed fear but his hands efficiently pushed the next magazine into his rifle. Ryan swallowed and rose up to fire out of the foxhole.

The smoke from the damaged tanks drifted their way on the

prevailing wind. Tomas grimaced. It would add to the increasing distance to make the next hit even tougher. Uni rifles fired their way, but not close. Tomas peered into the smoke and glimpsed his target. He launched the third grenade. The sound of its impact was lost in the cacophony of gunfire, but telemetry showed it had struck alloy. Tomas reached for the next grenade.

"Isn't it time to fall back?" Ryan said. "The sergeant said three grenades."

"He said expect three, but use your judgment. I'm using my judgment."

Uni rifle fire rattled nearby. A buzzing sound passed overhead. A fifty-centimeter rip in the chameleonskin showed a sliver of deep blue sky.

"They're on to our position!" Ryan said.

Tomas mounted the grenade on the launcher. His gaze was on the cloud of smoke in front of them. "Go if you want."

Confusion stooped Ryan's shoulders for a moment. He crawled up the sloping rear wall of the foxhole.

More rifle fire struck the dirt around Tomas or flew overhead. In a lull, Tomas stepped up and sighted another mike vehicle in the smoke, a DeGaulle with tracks visible from the front. His helmet display estimated it aimed its armament in his direction. He'd drawn their attention. *Come on, try to get me,* Tomas thought in a one-sided conversation with the DeGaulle. *I'm not afraid to die.* He fired a grenade and his arm twitched as he pressed the trigger. Reactive armor roared, blowing out a chunk of chameleon skin on the front of the DeGaulle. The vehicle kept coming.

"Neumann!" shouted Cohen through his earpiece. "Get back here on the quick!"

Tomas hunkered down and reached for the next grenade. The mike riflemen held their fire. He stepped up to launch another grenade at the DeGaulle, but didn't aim, just pointed in the vehicle's direction. He squeezed the trigger as a burst of large caliber rounds from the DeGaulle's machine gun shredded the rest of the chameleonskin cover and smacked the ground just in front of the foxhole, flinging dirt at the cameras on his faceplate.

He sagged against the wall of the foxhole and gasped for breath. They'd found him. He'd waited too long to leave the foxhole. *I don't wanna die I don't wanna die I wanna die wanna die got to get out of here...* He picked up his rifle and activated a self-destruct timer on the grenade rack, then hurriedly crawled out the back.

He slithered between rows of hemp sloping away from the foxhole, barely out of sight of the DeGaulle. Rifles fired from a few dozen meters to sunleft, splintering hemp fibers thirty centimeters above his head.

Tomas fired back, wild bursts chewing through the plants obscuring the enemy from vision. He crawled away from his firing position before they could triangulate on him. He heard them calling to one another. "Loop around to cut him off! There's only one Confed left!"

Punctuating their cries, the grenades remaining in the foxhole exploded. Dirt flew and fragments of metal snicked the foliage around him.

Got to get back to the platoon. Tomas crawled that direction as spotty fire rattled above him. He listened for the rustle of movement to the sides. His helmet display showed a low probability of mikes that far forward on his flanks. Software won't lose its life if it's wrong. He fired bursts wildly to his right until the clip sprung out of the rifle's stock. He crawled forward on his knees and right elbow while reaching for the next clip in his pack. As he groped, he realized he pulled out the final clip he carried.

He couldn't hold them at bay for much longer. He could surrender... but what would the militia do after they captured a member of the Blackjack platoon that killed irregular combatants in New Boston? A show trial, an execution.

Maybe that would be for the best—

Tomas shook his head. He had to get to the platoon before he ran out of ammunition. Still on his belly, he fired one more burst at the mikes he thought were on his flank, then rose to a crouch. "Power burst, speed!" he said to his helmet, then ran a zigzag pattern through the rows of hemp.

His feet loped across the field as the flexing fibers in his suit assisted his legs. Rifle fire smacked the plants around him as the power bar in his helmet display shrank and changed to yellow. Was he pulling away from the mikes? Their rifle fire sounded more distant—

A pain lanced through his right arm and he lost his grip on his rifle. He couldn't move his arm. His sleeve was tattered, and torn skin showed the white of nicked bone for a moment before blood poured out the wound. The pain made him want to vomit, but he kept his lunch down. He squeezed his left hand around his upper arm, thumb in his armpit, and kept running. The power bar shrank further, into the warning zone, and turned red.

Tracks ground and creaked nearby. Tomas glanced over his shoulder. The DeGaulle had crested the contour line and its weapons were aimed right at him. He crouched lower and changed his zigzag pattern just before the DeGaulle fired its machine gun.

Pain bloomed in his left thigh. His left foot struck the ground and black spots swam in his vision. He stumbled and rolled through hemp stalks, landing on his back. Wound indicators lit up his helmet display and the pain in his arm and leg made him whimper. A few shreds of muscle held his knee and lower leg to his body. Torn white heads of bone showed and ebbing pulses of blood gushed from his leg. He moved his good hand to the inside of his left thigh and pressed to slow the loss of blood. He felt cold and his breaths came quick and shallow. Agony, agony. Maybe it would be better to die.

Shells arced over him on flat trajectories, detonating thirty meters away. Reactive armor roared on the front slope of the DeGaulle. Rifles fired nearby, and Tomas recognized the sound of GF standard issue. *They're coming for me. No, don't, I don't deserve rescue, this is my recompense for all the lives I've taken….*

A head obscured by chameleonskin appeared above him. *You got me, mike.* The thought softened the harshest edge of his pain.

"Tourniquets first, leg then arm," said a familiar voice. Cohen. "Then we get blood substitute into him."

"Right." Ryan's voice sounded thin and high. His hands moved over Tomas' thigh. "Oh, god, he's so cold."

"Nein," Tomas said. *"Deine Hände sind zu heiss…."* Ryan's hands were hot, didn't he know that?

"Keep going," Cohen said, voice firm. "He's in shock. If we don't stop the bleeding soon he'll die before we can get him to the medics."

Why didn't they understand him? Right, they spoke New Tuscan. Or was that someone else? Tomas wondered who but his train of thought kept derailing. A man with a narrow jaw watched with fearful alarm. *W'aus kommst du, mein Vater?* Tomas thought as his mind slid down a dark hole away from the men tending him.

CHAPTER 12

PETERS-STEIN TECHNIQUE

Tomas stared at a trapezoid of light on a white surface in front of and above him. Flanking the white surface, cypresses outside a window swayed in a breeze.

Thoughts snapped into place. The hemp field. The ambush. He'd survived.

He flexed his arm, his leg. He lay in a bed and his limbs slid between crisp sheets. Tomas grabbed the near end of the top sheet with his right arm and flung the sheet toward his feet. His arm twinged and he lost his grip. The upper meter of the sheet tumbled into a rippled heap at his waist, exposing the hospital gown covering his chest.

With his left hand, he pushed the gown's right sleeve up to his armpit. A baby-pink band of hairless flesh ringed his upper arm. He turned his elbow and winced at the discomfort of motion. His right biceps was concave, shrunken under the pink band of skin.

Tomas kicked with his right foot and soon had the sheet down to his ankles. He lifted his left leg half a meter above the bed and held it trembling in air for a few seconds before he had to drop it. From the middle of his thigh down, pink skin covered thin and wobbly muscles.

He was whole and would have time to heal.

Shame gripped him.

He'd put Ryan and Cohen's lives at risk. He'd gambled with the GF's tenuous hold on the planet by pitying a mike assassin. He'd killed innocent men behind the pillbox. He didn't deserve to live....

He looked around. A hospital ward, ten beds jutting out from each of opposite walls. A few sleeping men. He sensed this room was part of a large building. A hospital would have general anesthetics, scalpels, a high roof one might access. If he didn't deserve to live, he could take his own life.

A wave of gooseflesh rippled down his sides. He couldn't kill himself. He feared death too much. The realization flooded him with more shame. Tears rolled from the corners of his eyes.

Footsteps padded nearby. He opened his eyes to see a nurse. She wore her hair pulled back under her bonnet, a severe look not dispelled by the warmth in her brown eyes. "Glad to see you're awake, Private Neumann."

He didn't want to see warmth, from her or anyone. "How long?"

"You were in the cocoon four weeks while they rebuilt your arm and leg. They moved you here last night."

Four weeks. He could have forgotten much in that time, but instead, all his memories remained fresh. Tears welled up in his eyes again.

Her eyes crinkled in sympathy. "Are you in pain?"

"Pain? No. A few aches when I move."

"That's normal. Your new muscles are less developed than your original ones, and your brain hasn't learned how to control them. You have a couple of weeks of rehab before you'll be physically cleared to return to your unit."

He wanted to get back as soon as he could. Make it up to Ryan and Cohen. Face down mike. He widened his hands and glared at her. "You've got to be kidding. Two weeks?"

Unperturbed, she said, "You have to pass a fitness test before they'll clear you for front line duty. Two weeks is usually how long it takes after a man with new limbs comes out of the cocoon."

"Sorry. I know it's not your fault." He kicked the sheet all the way off his feet and slid his legs toward the side. "Let's get started."

The nurse pressed her hand onto his chest to stop his movement. "The therapist will come for you. Two two-hour sessions every day. The rest of the time you can sleep, relax, play games… talk…."

The few other awake men in the ward seemed little interested in speaking. Her emphasis on her last word raised his defenses. "Talk? About?"

Her face turned into a sympathetic mask. "I've only seen the hospital and nearby parts of the base. I haven't even gone into Reagantown. I don't know what it's like out there. I'd be happy to listen to you if you want to tell me what you've seen, what you've done—"

"There's nothing to talk about."

She smiled sweetly. "If you change your mi—"

"I won't. There's nothing to talk about."

"Thank you for telling me your boundaries. I respect them."

He ground his next words through his teeth. "Don't patronize me."

"Patronize? Never. I respect you." She touched her warm fingers to the back of his right hand, then left. She hesitated near the door of the room to pull out a tablet and swipe in a note before exiting.

The physical therapist came a few minutes later with workout clothes and a powered wheelchair. He led Tomas to a fitness room where sweating men in hospital gowns lifted four-kilogram weights and walked between waist-high rails while holding on with both hands. "Go light and don't push it," the therapist said. He worked chewing gum with circular motions of his lower jaw. "You want to exhaust the new muscles without damaging them. You want to do the same with your mind too. The muscle memory's still there, but it's got to learn how to cross the nerve junctions to your new muscles. That's enough biceps curls."

"No." Tomas kept going, even though his arm wobbled. He had to get back, to his unit, to combat. Even though he didn't want to die, back in combat, fate would take that decision from him.

At the top of a biceps curl, the therapist gripped his wrist and pried the weight from his hand. "You're done with these, Private."

"I want to get out of here."

The therapist's jaws mashed his gum, then stopped. "I'm going to get you out of here as quickly as possible. I won't let you malinger by overworking and setting back your progress. Now grab a weight in each hand and try some squats."

After the therapy session, Tomas wheeled back to the ward for a meal of chicken breast and protein smoothie, then fell asleep.

He woke when a captain with a white armband bent over a bed on the opposite side of the ward, talking to a soldier whose face was hidden behind a tablet he held upright on his chest. The captain gave a parting word of encouragement that the soldier ignored, then stretched to his full height. The sides of the captain's garrison cap touched fringes of gray hair, and when he faced Tomas, the sunlight striking his face from the window next to Tomas' bed washed out his wrinkles.

The new angle showed Tomas the rest of the captain's armband. It bore a *taijitu*.

The captain met Tomas' gaze, glanced at a tablet in his hand. His eyes widened and he hastily came to Tomas. He fumbled the tablet into a slot on his belt and extended his hand. "Greetings, Private Neumann." At least he pronounced his name correctly.

"Captain..." Tomas gave the officer's hand a minimal shake and checked his nameplate. "Lindemann."

"As you might guess—" The captain tapped the *taijitu* on his armband. "—I'm an Observer chaplain, posted here to minister to the spiritual needs of our wounded and our medical staff. I see you're an Observer too."

Tomas frowned. How could the captain tell? The intake forms at the station in Challenger orbit, he realized with a sinking feeling. He should have left the checkbox blank. "That doesn't make me special."

"No. I minister to all our wounded, regardless of their spiritual community. But I'm particularly trained to minister to your spiritual needs. Mind if I sit?"

Tomas shrugged. Capt. Lindemann took a chair next to the bed. His face looked as if he was uncertain what to say. "It's uncommon to meet an Observer serving in a combat position."

"Tell my mother."

"Your mother...." Wheels of thought churned behind Capt. Lindemann's eyes. "You grew up on Joséphine? 'Neumann' doesn't sound like a *joséphinais* name."

"I was born on Sankt-Benedikts-Welt, but my parents left when I was very young."

"*Wirklich? Ich komme daraus auch.*"

Tomas' desire for solitude doubled. He put on a false frown. "Is that Sankt-Benedikts-Sprach? I don't speak it."

Capt. Lindemann went on in Confed. "I'm from there too. Actually, there's a chance I knew your parents."

Tomas felt a pang of desire to hear about his father, but not if it meant exposing his thoughts to this stranger. He scratched his right hand on the sheet and said nothing.

"The Observer community on Sankt-Benedikts-Welt is relatively small, and Neumann is an uncommon surname. I knew a couple named Neumann, who had a son who would be about twenty standard today."

"I don't remember you," Tomas said.

"You were too young. I wouldn't expect it even if that had been your family I knew. The wife had a real shine of dedication to our precepts. She glowed with a passion to share our message with the worlds." Capt. Lindemann thought further. "Her husband did too. He had wild brown hair and his face looked triangular, very pointed to the chin. Do those people sound like your parents?"

A ridge of pressure tightened across Tomas' eyebrows. "My father died when I was young. I don't know what he looked like."

"You haven't seen a photograph?"

Tomas scowled. "We're Observers—"

Capt. Lindemann angled his head. "I wouldn't judge anyone, not even an Observer, for keeping a photograph of a loved one." His sage tone thinned out, letting a wistful note come through. "It sounds as if your mother is very dedicated to our precepts."

The captain must have some attachment to his mother, if he could remember her after fifteen standard years. "She lives near the town of Portage-du-Nord, if you want to go to Joséphine on your next off-planet leave."

Startled eyes, a cough. Capt. Lindemann leaned back and his chair creaked. After a time, he said, "She was probably not the wife of the couple I knew. The settled galaxy is small, but not that small. No matter. You're still an Observer and I'm here to minister to your needs."

"My only need is to get back to my unit as soon as possible."

Capt. Lindemann's demeanor switched to one of solemn inquiry. "Why?"

"I have work I need to finish."

"What sort of work? Why do you need to finish it?"

"There's a war on. We have to fight off mike. I'm not going to leave my comrades to do it alone."

"Did something happen out there? You can tell me about it."

Tomas' face blanked. "Nothing happened."

Capt. Lindemann drew a breath and turned to the window. "Combat is the most harrowing experience anyone can go through. It raises strong emotions—fear, sorrow, pity, guilt—and keeps them at a high intensity for a long time." He turned back to Tomas with a waiting expression.

Stilted words. As if he knew anything about strong emotions. "You read that in a book, captain?"

"I got that from the skills imps. It's not accurate? It doesn't tell the whole story? Maybe you can tell me more."

"You wouldn't understand."

Capt. Lindemann sighed. "Maybe I wouldn't. But let me tell you something. This ward does more than rehab body parts. That's the easy bit. We also need to make sure you're psychologically ready to return to combat."

"That's what skills imps are for."

"We've tried that. It doesn't work. From what you've told me, I conclude you need to talk to someone before you go back to the front."

Tomas shifted his weight. A wince tightened around his eyes.

"You don't have to talk to me." Capt. Lindemann emphasized his words with open, conciliatory palms. "I sense your reticence. There are plenty of chaplains and psychological staff who are not Observers or not from Sankt-Benedikts-Welt. I don't care who you go to, but talk to someone about what you've experienced."

"Maybe. I mean sure, I'll think about it."

With folded arms, the captain gave Tomas a cool look. "I'm the senior Observer chaplain on site. I have the power to veto an Observer's return to his unit until he's psychologically fit. I know you want to return to your unit. But you will have to participate in a spiritual consultation first." He stood and let out a breath. "And I'm sorry to hear your father's dead. We've slowed aging so much and cured so many diseases that news of every death is shocking."

As soon as Capt. Lindemann left, Tomas tried to go back to sleep, but instead he could only enter a restless nap where indistinct impressions of his squadmates and his foes drifted past. After a time, he gave up and grabbed his tablet with his left hand. A few awkward swipes got him to the hospital's spiritual and psychological services.

He skimmed until he found an entry. *Warrant Officer L. Younger, Peters-Stein Technique, no spiritual tradition required*, just a four-hour block of time on one of four afternoons a week. Not an Observation; from his name, the warrant officer wasn't from Sankt-Benedikts-Welt; and a long stretch of time away from the monotony of his bed, the same quadrilaterals of sunlight on the far wall, the backs of tablets and sleeping faces of his fellow inmates, appealed to him.

Tomas pressed the *Make Appointment* button. A notification popped up in response. *We will coordinate with your physical therapist for a time when you are ready for potentially strenuous activity.*

Strenuous activity? Maybe he wouldn't have to talk to anyone. Relaxed, he set the tablet on his nightstand and soon fell asleep.

He spent a week diligently following the therapist's instructions and eating his protein-rich meals. His new limbs felt and looked stronger every day. When the therapist mentioned he could be discharged a few days ahead of schedule, he felt a faint relief. The sooner he returned to his unit, the sooner fate would do with him what it would. By dedicating himself to the rehab regimen, a crust formed over his shame and guilt. No one would ever see his emotions. He would go to the warrant officer's consultation room, do the jumping jacks or whatever else the Peters-Stein Technique entailed, and get the stamp of approval for his return ticket to the front.

Even bad news broadcast by *Stars and Rays* failed to blunt his focus. Late in his first week of rehab, the Progressive Republic declared war on the Confederated Worlds. The rumor mill soon speculated about the number of ships the Space Force would withdraw to bolster the new second front. Tomas ignored the speculations. He would return to the fight against mike and the Uni remnants soon enough, and whether or not Shirley Foxtrot could engage in space supremacy missions would not change his destiny.

Except for restless, sweaty sleeps, punctuated by vague dreams that left his mouth tasting like cotton, the week of rehab passed easily.

One noontime, after a productive session in the fitness room, he waited for his lunch. And waited. Orderlies finally brought in food for the other soldiers, but when they reached his bed, one apologized to Tomas and gave his partner a recriminating look. "You forgot his lunch."

"I didn't load the cart—"

"You didn't count trays, either. Do I have to do everything?"

The second orderly looked sheepish. "Private, sorry, we'll get on the kitchen right away to get your lunch cooking."

"Good," Tomas said. "Because I am hungry."

Yet still he waited, while plates and utensils clanked around him and his stomach growled. How had the kitchen fouled up so badly?

His tablet chimed. Tomas picked it up, expecting a message from the kitchen. The man on the other end introduced himself as a corporal in the hospital's spiritual and psychological services department. "Chief Younger will see you in thirty minutes."

"I haven't had lunch yet."

"You won't need it. Get here as soon as you can."

He was hungry, and though the endorphin buzz of strength training dulled the sensation, he still fumed after the corporal ended the call. *Making me skip lunch….* His irritation stoked up when he realized Chief Younger had planned the whole event. *He'll bribe me with the promise of food if I tell him what he wants to hear.* A piston of anger worked in his chest as he followed a map on his tablet to the chief's consultation room.

He entered a small office on the hospital's sunward side. Light spilled around a shade drawn low over a single window. Stacks of paper on an extruded foam desk, two chairs with worn padding on thin metal arms. A faint clean smell of soap. A door in the far wall had a tablet mounted in the gypsum board next to it. *Welcome, Private Neumann. Palm scan required for entry.*

He pressed his palm on the tablet. A magnetic lock released and the door thudded free of the jamb. Tomas went in.

The room was much larger than the office. Thick curtains, featuring an outer layer of gray chameleonskin, covered the walls. An oval of can lights in the ceiling shone down around a smaller oval of a half-dozen chairs. On the longer sides of the oval sat four people, two men and two women, in civilian trousers and short-sleeved shirts, skimming and swiping tablets with intent expressions.

At the nearest short side of the oval sat the only GF member present. Tall and with feminine curves under her gray fatigues, her blond hair curled from under a garrison cap. Her head was bowed over a tablet; she gave one last authoritative swipe and dropped it into a pocket between the right-hand legs of her chair. She stood, extended her hand, and as she turned toward him said, "Private Neumann, I'm Warrant Officer Younger...."

Tomas froze. He wanted to flee. All the shame and guilt he had masked with physical therapy and fatalistic surrender flooded him, like the surge of some vast storm. Only the fact that he had go through this to return to combat kept him in the room.

She was the medic from the pillbox.

She recovered first. "Welcome, Private."

Her face was impassive, yet her eyes showed she paid him the fullest attention she could. Skin crawled on his back. "Am I?" His voice sounded thin.

"All are welcome here. I will say to you what I say to everyone: as you followed the path that led you here, you made the best choices you knew how to make. You are perfect as you are. If you're willing to change something that troubles you, we can help you. If nothing troubles you, or if something does and you are unwilling to change it, then we celebrate your perfection."

"Why are you mocking me? Perfect as I am? You know what I've done."

Some of the civilians shared puzzled looks behind her.

"Yes," Chief Younger said. "We've met before. Yes, I know one thing you've done. Does that thing trouble you?"

"What do you think?"

"I think you should have a seat." She gestured at the empty chair across the oval from hers. The chair was firm plastic and lacked cushions. The civilians watched him with intent faces. "So does something trouble you?"

As she spoke, a bright can light came on over his seat. A boom of electronic equipment the size of a launcher grenade hung from the ceiling next to it, angled at his head. He squinted and lowered his gaze. "Why are we playing this game?"

"Game?" Her calm expression hardened. "If you want to play games, this isn't the place. You can head back to the ward and I'll get to my paperwork."

"You're going to force me to talk about it? I don't have a choice. I need you to sign off on my psych evaluation."

Her face remained aloof. "If you want a signature, you can find someone else. A lot of my peers would sign off on you right now. Does something trouble you or not?"

His stomach growled and he felt light-headed. Tomas couldn't resist her firm voice. "Yes."

"What?"

The foot on his new leg started tapping the floor. Its rhythm worked up his body, rocking his upper torso back and forth. "Don't make me say it."

"Tell her about it," murmured a male civilian on his right.

"Keep quiet," muttered a female civilian on his left. "Tell her nothing."

"—tell her, tell her all—"

"—don't say a word—"

"—reveal everything—"

"—keep it in you and never let it out—"

Tomas wanted to turn his head from one to the other, but couldn't decide which. He stared at Chief Younger as the civilians kept muttering. His mouth opened but he couldn't speak.

"I won't make you say it," Chief Younger said, "but if you can't say it, I don't know how to help you with it."

"Please…" The tapping and rocking sped slightly and grew in amplitude. He shut his eyes against the bright light overhead.

"—say it all—"

"—you can never tell a soul—"

"Private, if you don't want to do this, that's fine." Chief Younger's voice sounded dispassionate. "Like I said, I have paperwork—"

"I killed them!" He kept tapping his foot and rocking his torso. "They had surrendered! I killed the one who slashed Marchbanks' throat, but then I killed them all!"

After the curtains surrounding the room swallowed the echoes of his words, their chameleonskin turned a deep glacial blue, except for a patch behind Chief Younger. Spiral arms of red and white swirled behind her head. Over a slow, thudding rhythm Tomas felt as much as heard, she asked, "What makes that a problem?"

His body froze. His mind followed the path of her words and ran headlong into their absurdity. "How can it not be a problem?"

"Some men can kill without remorse."

His tapping and rocking started back up again. "You think I'm like that?"

Her voice stayed dispassionate. "I don't know. Are you?"

"No!"

"Then what's the problem?"

"If only I could go back—"

"And stop yourself from killing them? Do you know of a time travel wormhole? I don't. What's the problem?"

Dammed emotions burst out of his subconscious. They clogged his throat with mucus and congealed around his voice. "I don't want to live! I don't want to die! I'm frozen in shame and guilt and anger and I can't get out!"

"Do you want to change that?"

"Yes!" The flooding emotions overwhelmed the tap of his foot. Both his legs flexed back and forth, lifting the front of his chair off the floor. His head thrashed forward and backward in counterrhythm to his legs. When his eyes were open, the red and white spiral arms swirled faster, an accretion disc around the vast gravity of her eyes. The slow thudding struck up a resonance in his mind that stretched out his consciousness too thin to remain. He was only a sea of emotions.

"Go!" shouted someone. From another, "You can do this!" Tomas heard only encouragement. "More, more." Chief Younger's was the strongest, most encouraging voice of all. "Turn it up!"

His legs flexed faster and higher. The chair's plastic back creaked when the rigid plastic flexed behind his back. When his head thrashed forward, his fists smacked his thighs. He grunted, long and loud, a bellowing animal. Around him, the voices kept up their encouragement.

"Freeze that feeling!" shouted Chief Younger. Tomas dropped his head and hands to his lap and stopped moving. His thoughts swirled, like sediments in a glass too turbulent to settle. Her voice turned clear and compassionate. "What's the earliest you remember feeling the same feeling you have right now?"

Sensations bubbled up. Memories never recalled before. Off in the distance, far from consciousness, rang the intuition these memories were true. "I'm four. We're leaving Sankt-Benedikts-Welt. I don't want to go."

"Tell us more."

Sadness lumped in his throat. A rustic interior of honey-colored wood; oaks outside, branches bare, and a dusting of snow on the ground; blocks of fabbed wood in the fireplace; the brown-haired man with the narrow jaw. Tomas spoke Sankt-Benedikts-Sprach without noticing. "I'm telling my father I don't want to go. I don't know where we're going but it's far away. He's talking but it's all big words and he's pretending to listen to me but I can tell he's pretending and nothing I say matters and I keep crying and screaming and my mother tells me to be quiet and accept his decision just like she's doing and then he gets angry at her don't you really want this I gave you every chance to protest and she says I'm doing this for your sake and isn't that good enough and I'm crying and screaming more why can't we stay...."

Chief Younger replied in the same language. "Was it like this, Tomas?"

He lifted his face. Chief Younger seemed a million miles away yet still the center of his attention. Behind her, the chameleonskin showed the mottled gray of an overcast afternoon all around the room. "Almost. We were indoors. Warm brown paneling." The chameleonskin changed colors. "A little warmer. Sankt-Benedikts-Stern is over there." He pointed to his ten o'clock. "And the fireplace—" His pointing hand moved to his eight-thirty. Colors bloomed in the appropriate spots on the walls.

"And your parents?"

One of the male civilians, with black hair and soft eyes, stood in front of Tomas, on his left side. On his right, one of the women, blonde and hunched, stood with her hands folded in front of her torso. Tomas stuck out his forefinger and middle finger and rolled his wrist back and forth. The civilians switched places. "And my mother looked stronger. She's steel, always steel. I don't know he could have hammered her into the shape he wanted." The woman lifted her shoulders and a rigid look filled her face. "Yes."

"And you?"

The other male civilian was short, stocky, red-haired, freckled. He looked nothing like Tomas, except his face showed so well the confusion and frustration Tomas had felt that distant day, felt that present moment. Tomas' speech fell away and tears filled his eyes. He managed to nod.

"Was it like this?"

The three civilians acted out the scene, in precise, impped Sankt-Benedikts-Sprach. The fourth, the other woman, waited behind Tomas' shoulder and murmured clipped, jargony Confed into a lapel microphone in response to his mutters and his body language. He felt as if he watched his childhood self from a distance, crying and screaming. Why must we go? I want to stay! His father's expression pretended to be attentive, but all he did was use big words about duty and purpose to bulldoze his younger self's resistance, without success.

Then his mother spoke. The woman's portrayal sounded through him like a hammer on a Badger's hull. Like a magnet, it pulled out and aligned memories of his mother's commands to him over their years alone on Joséphine. Be quiet. We're doing what your father wants. Her tone showed she didn't want it either, and then his parents argued. The heat of their argument mounted and soon led into harsh words, plus threats and bluffs of irrevocable rupture between them.

The actor portraying Tomas trembled, eyes red as some mutant raccoon's. Tomas pitied the boy he had been, a boy still inside himself somewhere. Tears rolled out of his eyes. He grieved, and the grief swelled. It wasn't just for the past him. For the current him, for Marchbanks, for all the other dead, whether GF, mike, or Uni.

"Was it like this, Tomas?" Chief Younger's voice rang sweetly through the room.

"Yes." His voice sounded clear despite the emotions burning behind his face.

"Did you learn that day to shut down and hide what you're feeling?"

"Yes."

"Would you like to learn a different way to handle situations like this?"

His train of thought, still unsettled, stumbled again on the absurdity. "There can't be a different way."

"There is."

"What?"

Her eyes remained attentive on him. "May we show you?"

Tomas shrugged, nodded.

"I didn't catch that."

He met her gaze and loudly said, "Yes. Show me."

The civilians began from the start of the scene. His father spoke past Tomas' childhood self in big words and the redheaded actor's face showed the seed of a tantrum. But instead of screaming and crying, he said, "Father, may I tell you what I'm feeling?"

His father blinked a few times. "What? Of course."

"I feel confused and frustrated." His hand broke character, beckoning Tomas closer.

"Confused? Frustrated? You don't need to feel those things. We're moving and it's for the best."

Tomas hesitated as he moved forward. He knew the actor had the truth of his father. He ached to be so close to his father, yet so rebuffed by him. He wanted to bury his confusion and frustration and hope they would go away, but Tomas' childhood self stood resolute. "Thank you for telling me what you think I should feel. I feel confused and frustrated. What do you feel?"

His father's usual mild expression grew a little colder. "I feel you should accept that we're moving."

"I hear that's what you're thinking." The redheaded actor beckoned more and Tomas realized he wanted the two of them to speak together. Intuitions crystallized in Tomas' mind while shivers thrilled his skin. "What are—" Tomas joined his voice to the actor's. "—you feeling?"

His father's shoulders slumped. "Feeling? I'm frustrated. Not with you, with me. I explained why we're moving but I guess not clearly enough. We're Observers. You know what that means? We have a special calling to see clearly. Not just with our eyes, but with our minds. Our hearts. We have to see clearly so everyone else, on every human world, can learn to see clearly too. The people here on Sankt-Benedikts-Welt don't need us as much as the people on Nueva Andalucia."

Nueva Andalucia? A Unity world? What crazy script did this actor read? But those questions came from a distant corner of his mind, where the questioning judgmental part of him had been chained for the moment.

His father went on. "I think you'll like Nueva Andalucia. I'm not making that up to deny what you're feeling. I know you, son. I know what you like. The sun over Nueva Andalucia is a lot like Sankt-Benedikts-Stern, maybe a bit more yellow. The people are friendly—"

"Are they?" his mother asked. Her arms were folded protectively across her chest and she peered at his father. "There's no Observer presence there now. Why? Will we be the first to ever land?"

"Mother," the redheaded actor said. He said the word with an open final tone, which hooked Tomas.

More intuitions slid into new positions in his mind. He looked at the woman and saw his mother in the glint of the can lights in her cheekbones. Even if he projected a resemblance that wasn't there, perceiving the resemblance made Tomas' heart pound. Still, he knew what he had to say. "Mother, tell me what you're feeling."

She stepped back from his father, but kept her arms defensively across herself. "It doesn't matter what I'm feeling. We're leaving for Nueva Andalucia tomorrow."

Chief Younger cut through the tableau. "Don't let her avoid your question."

"Thank you for telling me what you're thinking. What are you feeling?"

"Feeling? About Nueva Andalucia? I can't say it. It would frighten you."

Across the room, Chief Younger opened her mouth to speak. Before she could, Tomas nodded for her sake and kept his gaze on his mother. "Thank you for thinking of me. Please tell me what you're feeling."

His mother looked alarmed. "Isn't it clear what I'm feeling about Nueva Andalucia?"

"I can only know for certain if you tell me. Please tell me what you're feeling." A joyous, potent feeling welled up his neck and into his head.

His mother's face froze and her voice came softly. "I'm afraid."

"There's nothing to be afraid of," his father said. The annoyance in his tone was plain.

"What are you feeling, father?"

His father looked between the two of them for a time, tension mounting in his face all the while, before speaking. "I'm even more frustrated." He turned to Tomas' mother. His hands suddenly rose to his cheeks. His face slumped against his fingers and his tension yielded to sadness. "I've done a horrible job explaining this to you, too, dear. Nueva Andalucia is a civilized place. Settled by ancient Europeans, just like Sankt-Benedikts—"

"I'm still worried," she said. "The ancient Europeans committed plenty of atrocities against one another. I know you think I'm over-reacting."

Chief Younger said, "Tomas…."

"Tell her what you're feeling, father. Please."

"I feel impelled to do this. Excited we could establish our tradition on Nueva Andalucia. Surprised you are so worried. How long have you worried? I should have noticed—"

Tomas knew what to say. "Thank you for telling us how you judge your own behavior, father. Please tell her what you're feeling."

"—I'm sad I never noticed how worried you are." His father drew a breath and opened his shoulders to her reply.

Tomas had never imagined his mother could say her next words. "I'm embarrassed. I know in my head they aren't going to lynch us. If they were that primitive, they couldn't have survived a sublight settlement trip or terraformed their planet. Yet I worry for legitimate reasons—"

"Tell him what you're feeling, mother." He'd had enough practice now for the thought behind the words to flow more vigorously, just as the physical therapy over the past week (somewhere, out there, a vast distance from this moment) made the movements of his new limbs stronger and more assured.

"I'm worried. A new language, new customs. What if we say something foolish, or offend the wrong person? I'm worried we'll fail. I'm worried we'll come back here in shame and everyone will know we failed."

His father went to her and put his arms around her. "How can we fail if we have each other?"

In the next quiet moments, Tomas dimly noticed the redheaded actor had backed away a while before. The thudding rhythm had been going on the whole time. Yet these notices soon drained away to whatever part of his mind held his judgment and his questions. His parents, channeled somehow by these actors, held each other close and looked lovingly into each other's eyes. Sharing feelings was all it took? He wished he'd known that—and he laughed.

"Tell me what you're feeling," Chief Younger said.

"Longing. It's like a warm belonging in my chest, on the cusp of deflating. This could have been my family, instead of—" He waved as if he shooed a fly, to indicate the prior scene. "Sorrow. I can't change what I did when I was a child. No time-travel wormholes. I feel resolved. I can't change my family's past, but I can change my future." He let his feelings come and go. "I feel alive."

The chameleonskin abruptly switched to an angry red all around the room. "What about—" Chief Younger's voice caught. Her eyes glistened in the can lights. "—the problem that troubled you when you came here?"

"I killed men who deserved to live. I can't change that, as much as I want to. That hurts. All I can do is act differently if I ever again enter a situation like that." Another intuition struck him. "And though I chose to kill them, they chose to die. The mike with the knife could have struck when Marchbanks was totally alone with them. He waited to be seen by me. The mike who begged for his life, he surrendered to his fate. He wanted to die."

Tomas' torso rocked with another intuition. "Marchbanks wanted to die too. He had the skills to disarm the mike with the knife. He didn't." *Why? Does 'why' even matter? If he sought to die, he got what he wanted.*

"And I wanted all this too. I wanted to kill them." He swallowed at one thorny thought. "I wanted Marchbanks to die? What did I want to hide from him so much that part of me wanted him dead?"

Chief Younger said, "I don't know the answer, Tomas."

"And I wanted to be smothered in shame and guilt for killing them. And I wanted you to see me kill them, so I could feel feared and hated. By my mother, but she wasn't there, so I made do with you. I regret treating you like an object instead of your own person."

The chameleonskin around the room slowly transformed from red to blue. She gave him another look of pure attention. "Thank you for telling me what you feel. What comes up when I ask about your return to combat?"

Could he face Unis and mikes? Could he stand at the side of his squadmates? "I feel a mild regret we're at war. It's pulling down the muscles of my right cheek."

"I can see it from here."

He let out a breath. "We've all chosen to be soldiers. Me, my comrades, the Unis, the mikes. We've all chosen to risk death and try to kill each other. That's painful to contemplate, but it would be more painful to quit. I don't mean it would be painful to break rocks in a terraforming battalion. I need my squadmates to know I'll stick with them no matter what."

"Thank you for telling me those things," she said. "Is there anything else you'd like to tell us?"

His consciousness was moving back into the full volume of his mind. It stumbled over memories of the experience as it went. Questions about the Peters-Stein Technique occurred to him, but he let them go unasked. Hypnosis, skillful observing, acting, it didn't matter. Just its results mattered.

There was one question, though…. He turned to the actor who'd played his father. "Where did you get Nueva Andalucia? Do you have some records on my family that I don't know about? I have no memory of ever living on a Unity world."

The man set down a cup of water and swept his hands through his black hair. "I don't know why I said Nueva Andalucia. We're hypnotized a little when we're playing our roles, kind of like you are. It just came to me and made sense. I can't say that's what happened—"

"My only memory of my father is from a world with a golden sun. I used to think it was from Sankt-Benedikts-Welt, but your description of Nueva Andalucia fits better." The blue chameleonskin ringing the room seemed to glow. His head felt clear and his body, full of energy. He could return to his unit, not to surrender to his fate, but to work with it to become the kind of man he'd imagined Captain Schreiber and Marchbanks to be. "Thank you, all of you."

Chief Younger crossed the oval toward him. He rose and waited as she worked with her tablet. His new knee ached, a glorious ache, an ache of effort and well-earned rest. A moment later, his tablet pinged, and he reached down for it. A message from her.

"That's the official psych consultation document. Private Neumann, I approve your return to your unit." Her voice sounded calm and professional, but her next word came with audible feeling. She rested her hand on his forearm and said, "Godspeed."

CHAPTER 13

GRANT RIVER BRIDGE

"I'M GONE for six weeks and you lot can't hold the line?" Tomas dropped his pack on the ground next to his team's Badger.

Cohen set down his ration kit and stood up. His face had fresh lines and it took him a moment to grin. He hugged Tomas, slapping his hands on Tomas' back. "Good to see you. Looks like they glued your leg back on good as new."

"I'm glad to be back. I missed all of you. Even Alvarez."

"Fuck you." Alvarez grinned around a forkful of mashed potatoes.

"You had a safe flight up from R-town?"

Tomas backed out of the hug. "Mike had a few flyboys up, but my Bluejay pilot knows what he's doing." He spoke to Cohen more seriously. "Can I tell you something?

"Of course."

"In the hospital, I felt lonely a lot. Our team has been through a lot together and I felt bitter wondering why no one wrote me. But then I remembered I never wrote you when you were in the hospital, before New Boston. I can imagine you felt some of the same things then. I want to apologize for not writing you when you were laid up."

Cohen looked sheepish. "That was a long time ago."

"Sure, but my experience reminded me of it. If you ever want to talk—"

"I know how tough it is to send messages from up here," Cohen said. "I didn't expect any when I was recovering."

"I hear you. But I know now, when I was up here, writing you in the hospital would have reminded me the same could happen to me, and I wanted to hide from that. I don't want to hide anymore." Tomas clapped his hand on Cohen's upper arm, then surveyed the other men sitting alongside the Badger. Constitution lit their stubbled, dirty faces. They chewed lamb kabobs and roasted eggplant quickly, taut muscles bulging over their jaws. Haunted looks hovered behind their eyes. "Lundergard."

The Midgarder barely raised his left hand, then returned his attention to his meal.

Two new guys sat at the end of the row. New, but in less than six weeks, they'd seen enough to have the same hard-bitten look as the team's old hands. Cohen introduced them as Iommarino and Monroe. Iommarino wore a crucifix pendant outside his suit. Facets of the pendant flung reflections over his messkit when he moved. Tomas remembered the medal on the chest of the SF recruiting officer in Portage, then laid the thought aside. He'd known Iommarino for five seconds, which was long enough to know he was Tomas' teammate. Any comparison with a canned spam orificer would only make the SF recruiting officer look worse.

"We heard a lot about you," Monroe said.

Tomas shook their hands. "Some of it might even be true." He looked around. "Where's Ryan?" His tone fell at the end. He already knew.

"Mike got him," Cohen said.

A cold feeling washed down his torso. "I hope not on the day you guys came for me."

"Two weeks later. One of the new mike units. I hear there's twenty mike regiments now."

Tomas puffed out his cheeks and sagged against the side of the Badger. "Twenty? They outnumber us three to one?"

"They got bold when the Progressive Republic declared war." Iommarino spoke as if he knew everything going on in mike territory and the PR capital.

If we can't control things, we want to believe we can at least predict what will happen. "The hospital buzzed about the SF withdrawals of ships to bolster the PR front."

"We don't need Shirley Foxtrot anyway," Alvarez said. His voice hinted at anger and fear.

"She'd just put photons in the wrong spot again," Tomas said with a tone of agreement he didn't truly share. His earlier complacency about SF redeployment had been a mistake. The less help the team got from orbit, the worse their chances in combat. He lied for the sake of the new men on the team. A shared glance with Cohen showed each of them the other knew the truth.

Chatter came over their earbuds. "Saddle up, fifteen minutes," said Capt. Marcinkus.

Cohen reached for a cold ration pack. "You need to eat?" he asked Tomas.

Tomas waved away the offer. "Ate on the truck coming in from battalion headquarters." That, and he'd written a letter to his mother, asking if his family had ever lived on Nueva Andalucia. He didn't expect an answer and set the thought aside. "I'm going to hang my pack and find the platoon commander. It's still—?"

A glum nod.

Tomas hung his pack on one of the hooks mounted on the outside of the Badger. He trooped around it, looking for Lt. Tower. The lieutenant and Sgt. Johnson stood twenty meters away, in the shade behind another of the platoon's vehicles. They looked up as Tomas approached.

He snapped his heels to attention. "Private Neumann reporting, sir."

"At ease." Tower's face showed his martinet side had come out today. "Ready to get back on your bike, Neumann?"

"Yes, sir."

"The war's changed while you were sipping protein shakes and visiting the Daughters. There's a shitload of mikes out there now. But it makes it easy to know who are enemies are. Anyone we see. You listening?"

"Yes, sir." Tomas wanted to share a glance with Sgt. Johnson, but kept his attention on the lieutenant until Tower looked away.

"He's yours, sergeant. Get ready to roll out." Tower walked away.

Finally Tomas gave the sergeant the glance. Johnson shook his head in a broad arc. "He didn't say we kill everyone. We only fight mike. We still be on New Liberty to liberate its people from the Unity."

"That's what I read in *Stars and Rays*," Tomas said carefully.

"You'll see it here too. We still fight clean." Sgt. Johnson glanced around. "I and I know Lt. Tower be a poor platoon commander. I and I tell the company sergeant major at every chance. But we have the lieutenant until Capt. Marcinkus comes down the bifrost bridge and plucks him away."

"Where are we rolling to?" Tomas asked.

"When you be flying here from Reagantown, did you see all those rivers flowing darkward to sunward? We be heading for the far side of the Grant River, about a hundred-eighty klicks back. It be a wide deep river across the whole habitable zone."

Tomas pictured the map in his mind's eye. "The whole brigade's retreating."

Sgt. Johnson raised his eyebrow. "Retreating?"

"Sergeant, can't us soldiers call it what it is? If the louie were here I'd say 'redeploying.'"

"We be falling back. Not just us Blackjacks. Every brigade to sunleft of Reagantown. Now get in the Badger. Our platoon be right behind the Graywolfs at the point of the company's column."

MacInnis leaned and twisted backward to shake his hand when he boarded their Badger. Delacroix shouted greetings down from the turret. Tomas took Sharma's old spot in the back of the Badger, as well as his old assignment, grenadier. He and Monroe rubbed shoulders as the vehicle lurched forward. Whenever Tomas glanced to his left, the reflection of the video screens shone on Monroe's cheeks. Still young enough to need to see everything.

Skirmishes had taken place along the road: every few klicks, the cold, broken hulls of reconnaissance vehicles slumped along the roadside. Wrecked mike vehicles, speedier and lighter refits of the DeGaulle model, outnumbered demolished Weasels by about two to one; but mike had more fab cores on his side to crank out replacements.

Also common along the roadside were the toppled poles of obs wheels. The cameras, microphones, and related hardware in the cases had been either smashed or carried off. Dozens of meters away from the toppled poles, craters and scorch marks showed where the SF had put photons on the ground, following some indication of toppling telemetered by the poles. "Shirley Foxtrot must have gotten some mikes," Monroe said.

"And mike cleaned up all his dead?" Iommarino replied.

Tomas pointed at one of the toppled poles. About a meter and a half above the base, roughly hand height on a standing man, a dent marked the side of the pole. He'd seen the same dent on other fallen poles. "Looks like mike hitched a vehicle to them and pulled them out of the ground."

"Observation posts mean nothing if we can't put rifle fire on a mike trying to clear them," Cohen said. "Same with obstacles. Remember that."

They continued onward. The high gray cloud grew thicker, blacker. Either the atmosphere's dominant convection current played with mike's aerosols, or mike had more smudge pots to sunward of this location. The low rays of Constitution, slanting under the dark cloud, from time to time glinted off the wings of mike's aircraft.

In the turret, Lt. Tower said something indistinct. Delacroix replied, over the vehicle's net, "Yes, sir, full stop." The Badger's motor grew quieter and the clatter of the tracks stopped.

"What's going on?" Iommarino said.

Tomas put his hand on his rifle and grenade launcher, standing on the rack just inside the rear ramp. "We're probably getting out soon."

The lieutenant gave orders through the squad net. "Johnson, your squad has a recon mission. Drop the ramp," he added in an aside to MacInnis.

The ramp dropped. Tomas and his teammates picked up their weapons and went out. Behind their Badger, the one carrying Johnson's team had also stopped. The sergeant and his men rounded their vehicle and joined them.

"Twelve hundred meters to sunright, the road enters a valley," Lt. Tower said. At the mouth of the valley, the road fell out of sight amid the upper branches of a stand of pines on a hidden downward slope. A caution sign rippled with heat shimmer just before the road started its descent. To either side of the valley, wooded hills rose, forming a line vanishing into the distance. "We need to know if the enemy are in the valley. There are no obs wheels remaining on station anywhere nearby. Go on foot and take a look. You have forty-five minutes. No radio beyond squad net. Get going."

They set out in two columns on opposite sides of the road, each about forty meters from the living asphalt. Tomas' team was on the darkward side. After crossing the swell behind which the vehicles waited, the ground sloped slightly downward to the valley mouth. The column wound past low, brown shrubs. A trickling sound came from a gully to his left. Cool water would be a huge relief…. Even with all the infrared ports open on the back of his suit, the warm day already drenched him. He blinked away sweat and winced when it hit his eye.

They reached the mouth of the valley without incident. Cohen waved at them to get down and spread out. Tomas went prone behind a shrub and took a look.

To his left, the gully opened up into a jumble of rocks and muddy pools, tumbling toward a stream on the valley floor. The road took a sharp turn and descended into the valley at an angle through the pines covering the slope. The war had touched the woods; downhill from a pair of toppled obs wheel poles, SF fire had shattered a score of trees and stripped a hundred more of branches.

The road and the streambed met again about two klicks ahead, in a town of several hundred houses. Tomas' helmet display named it Sher-manville. The largest structures were the municipal fab, two churches, and a school. Buildings crowded the road and a single bridge crossed the streambed. The ambush on the New Boston road had been in terrain far more spacious than the streets of this town. A mike with a grenade launcher could lurk within a few meters of a passing Graywolf or Badger. For that matter, a mike could emerge from hiding with a bucket of paint to blind the vehicle's cameras, or with a crowbar to wreck a drive wheel.

Going around Shermanville would be a poor option as well. Such a route would run between the wooded hills on one side and the town on the other. Flank and top armor would be exposed to grenades and missiles from mike teams concealed in the woods.

If mike was here at all. Tomas peered at Shermanville, zooming in with his helmet display. The town lay still. No cars traveled the streets, no pedestrians followed the sidewalks, no children played in the parks. Had mike ordered them to stay indoors? Or did the people cower in basements of their own accord in view of rumors of the GF movement nearby?

He couldn't tell by looking.

His helmet display showed they had three minutes before they needed to form up for the return to the platoon's vehicles. Tomas shifted to try scratching an itch on his sweaty back with the pack tucked inside his suit. As he moved, something metallic half-buried under a black sage shrub caught his eye.

"Found something," he said into the squad net. He crawled forward to take a closer look. As he guessed, a GF observation wheel. It hadn't fallen here when mike had toppled the elevated ones closer to the road. One of their scouts had placed it here. The front cameras were free of dirt. A glance toward the town showed the obs wheel had an unob-structed view. He announced his discovery to the squad.

"We can't upload it by radio," Sgt. Johnson said. "Louie's orders."

Tomas' heart thudded. Someone had to see what was stored on the obs wheel. He could call one of his squadmates, but how much of their remaining time would it take for someone to come over? More impor-tant, could he look his mates in the eye afterward?

A contrary thought came to mind. *If you were going to watch prere-corded video, you could have joined intel from the start, and saved yourself a lot of blood and pain.*

A final realization settled his mind. He wouldn't trade his experi-ences as an infantryman for all the easy duty in the Confederated Worlds.

He flipped open the obs wheel's access port. Thanks to impped skills, he knew what to expect. A retracted reel held a data cable having a male connector with a trapezoidal cross section. The external control panel in the chest of his suit had a mating female connector. His hand reached for the flap in the chameleonskin covering the external control panel. He remembered his mother's words, at the pews when he told her he would enlist. *They'll make you watch recordings....*

No, mother. I choose to watch this recording. I'm doing something more important than saving my teammates from virtual fugue. I'm giving them a better chance to stay alive. Tomas opened the flap and pulled the data cable from the obs wheel. The male connector snicked faintly in his suit's external control panel.

Through his helmet display, his view of the valley below and the sky above abruptly changed. The sky was brighter, free of the high gray cloud of mike's smudge pots. A time stamp in the lower right corner dated the image he saw to eight days before. Despite his decision, his heart pounded. This was a photograph. He sensed the traps laid by the technology: vortices of nostalgia and obsession, false beliefs that a thing could be grasped by freezing its image. He gulped a breath. He was man enough to be able to use it and set it aside.

How many other things did he fear and hate at his mother's bidding?

Available video appeared in his helmet display. *204:14:39* and after a long moment the second incremented.

By touch, Tomas worked a stick-wheel on the control panel. Time lapse, six thousand to one. He started playback.

A hundred minutes passed in every second of video. The main streets blurred with motion at the busiest times of day. The sky darkened appreciably when mike's aerosol cloud reached the vicinity. Nothing much—wait.

For a couple of seconds of playback, the parking lot of the school filled with a crowd of people. What would lead so many people to stand around for three or four hours?

His fingers worked the stick-wheel, pausing, rewinding, zooming, playing back more slowly. His helmet display picked up the outlines of three chameleonskinned trucks. Two rows of implant stations stood nearby, powered by temporary cables laid on the asphalt. Uniformed mikes guided people from the crowd to the stations, and from there to the school's football field.

Tomas panned the view. At one end of the field, a wooden mock-up of a Graywolf sat with its flank facing mikes and civilians at the other end. Though the civilians fired dummy grenades and missiles, smacking and splintering the wood, the launchers were real.

"Mike's here, in force!" Tomas said into the squad net. "Grenade launchers and anti-tank missiles, a lot of them. Impped skills and three hours of blank firing exercises."

"Where did you get that?" Alvarez asked.

"Video from the obs wheel."

"Video?" Cohen asked. "Did you watch…?"

Sgt. Johnson spoke. "You be certain, Neumann?"

"Absolutely, sergeant."

"Then we go back to platoon. On the double."

They crawled out of view of the town, adjusted their infrared ports to dump heat out the front of their suits only, and jogged back. Sgt. Johnson sought out Tomas and linked a cable between their two suits. "Send I and I the video."

Tomas did. The sergeant said nothing for a few seconds, then whistled. "We won't drive into this, idrin." About six hundred meters from the vehicles, the extreme range of the squad net, Sgt. Johnson spoke again. "Lt. Tower, do you read?" His voice carried urgency. He repeated the call several times, without answer. The paper tiger had to be listening to the squad, didn't he?

If he did, he didn't reply until the squad could make out the chameleonskinned machine guns of the Graywolfs at the head of the column. "Tower here. What, sergeant?"

"Mike has set an ambush in the town. We have video of civilians getting impped skills and testing fabbed anti-tank weapons. We can't go forward."

"Are you certain?"

"Two of us have seen it, including one of my sharper soldiers, Neumann."

Lt. Tower said nothing. Picked up by the lieutenant's microphone in the confines of their Badger's turret, Delacroix's muffled voice said, "Neumann?"

Finally, the lieutenant said, "Get that video to me. I can't call Capt. Marcinkus without an officer seeing it."

"Sir, maybe I and I was unclear. I and I've seen it as well—"

"It's not your career if we hugely deviate from our movement axis because we're spooked by phantoms. Get me that video. Tower out."

Johnson slumped his head for a moment, then shook it clear and beckoned the squad to hurry to their Badgers. Once inside, the infantrymen opened up all their infrared ports, lifted helmets, and mated air conditioning lines with the intakes on their suits. Sgt. Johnson entered Tomas' team vehicle, crowding the rear compartment even more than usual as he plugged a data cable from the wall into his suit and talked live to the lieutenant.

MacInnis writhed around and stuck his head out of the driver's compartment. "Neumann, did I hear this right? You watched video from an obs wheel?"

"That's right."

MacInnis double-took. "I thought it was against your religion."

Tomas shrugged. "The thing I most want to observe are you lot in civilian clothes on discharge day."

No one spoke for a moment, until Cohen chuckled. His actions released laughter from Lundergard and MacInnis, followed by the new guys.

"Cut the chatter!" Lt. Tower's voice echoed down from the turret. "We have orders from Capt. Marcinkus. The company will take a new route to the Grant River bridge. This will be longer than we expected, but the bridge will be destroyed at the same time. Everyone, strap in and prepare to move!"

Shouts of "yes, sir" filled the vehicle. Sgt. Johnson disconnected the data cable and moved for the ramp, then turned back to Tomas and gave a fist tap to Tomas' upper arm. "You did good, Neumann."

"I'm glad I could help the squad, sergeant."

"Was I not clear?" Lt. Tower called out.

Sgt. Johnson gave the underside of the turret a hooded glance, then trotted out. MacInnis shifted back into his usual position in the driver's compartment. The ramp closed behind him and the men strapped themselves into their seats.

The Badger lurched into motion. Alvarez spoke. "You bastards need to tell me something." His enunciation of *bastards* larded the word with a slight insult.

Cohen crossed his arms and turned to look at Alvarez. "What?"

"Why are you acting like Neumann did something great?"

Anger spiked in Tomas, but he also sensed sadness, partially masked by the anger like the surface of New Liberty under mike's aerosol cloud. The emotions flooded him. He couldn't respond.

"He violated a strong religious precept," Cohen said, "to save us from a potential ambush. Does that mean anything to you? Do you have any religious precepts?"

"Yeah. One," Alvarez replied. "Our team better be more important than anyone's god. I won't congratulate you for doing something you should have been doing from the day you joined us. You hear me, Neumann?" He glared at Tomas.

"I'm not asking for congratulations," Tomas said. He'd done the right thing. Maybe it would have been better for no one to know. He sought something more to say, to bring Alvarez to his side; but the other tucked his hands into his armpits, shut his eyes, and rested his chin on his chest.

"Haven't they set the explosives?" Iommarino said. He raised his voice over the burble of the river at the foot of the bluff. He stood next to a concrete structure showing a meter-high wedge above the ground. An alloy cable, thick as a fat man's thigh, ran from a hole in one side of the wedge to the top of the nearest tower of the Grant River bridge. He slapped the cable to emphasize his words.

"Over there." Cohen pointed to the river's sunright bank, six hundred meters away, where blurs of chameleonskin showed the bulk of the company's vehicles moving into defensive positions. A few tiny human figures worked at the cable anchorages near the foot of the tower holding the suspension cable on that side. "You only have to blow one anchor per cable for the whole thing to fall."

"Is blowing up the bridge going to be enough?" Monroe asked. "How high and steep are the bluffs?"

"Mike can't drive down," Tomas said. He stood at the edge of the bluff overlooking the river. A steep slope bearing pines dropped twenty meters over about fifteen meters of distance. A dirt trail forty centimeters wide switchbacked down the bluff, ending at a flat strip of sandy puddles before the river's main channel.

"You're certain?"

"I'm certain."

"Alright, idrin, enough sightseeing." Sgt. Johnson gestured. Four vehicles, two Graywolfs and two Badgers, sat hull down in tank scrapes. Beyond them, a quarter-circle of foxholes ran from the top of the switchback down the bluff to the sunleft shoulder of the road. "The engineers gave our task force some nice holes. Time to get to them."

The squad split into buddy teams and started toward the foxholes. "Sergeant, how close is mike?" Lundergard asked.

"Not as close as our scouts and rear guard." The sergeant sounded testy. "We be here until the entire battalion gets across."

Tomas and Iommarino settled into the foxhole nearest the road. The view out the firing port showed sparse tufts of grass all the way to the sunleft horizon. Interrrupted lengths of the road showed over rolling hills.

Above, mike's aerosol cloud covered the far half the sky. Icons superimposed on Tomas' view showed seven Crows, airmobile hussar transport thopters, wheeling to sunright. Their wings swatted the air when they passed over the foxhole.

In the silence after the Crows passed, the ground level wind moaned as it carried wisps of sand across the road's living asphalt. In lulls, the rumble of distant gunfire reached them.

"Is that them or us?" Iommarino asked.

Tomas angled his ear that direction. "That's mike. Hear that whoosh, though? Our antitank missiles."

"So mike's sending armor our way." Iommarino's voice sounded hesitant.

"He's sending everything our way. Maybe we'll be across the river by the time he arrives."

A few minutes later, the first friendly vehicles appeared in their helmet displays. Three Weasels from a scout platoon, one of which had a blank panel of chameleonskin. The icons representing the scout vehicles remained visible even when the Weasels dipped out of sight behind rolls in the landscape.

The Weasels slowed when they neared the foxholes. Although their identity beacons could not be forged, mike still could have patched up wrecked Weasels he'd found on the battlefield. But when the hatch on the lead Weasel popped open, Tomas' helmet display identified the head sticking out as belonging to the lieutenant commanding the scout platoon. "Soldier, where's the task force commander, Lt. Tower?"

"In the scrape behind us nearest the road," Tomas called. "If I may, what's going on?"

"Mike's tanks are on our tail. They knocked out one of us and nicked another. Three thousand meters behind us, before we lost sight of him. The terrain rolls too much. Keep your eyes peeled. He might sneak up on you." The scout lieutenant looked inside the hatch and swatted his hand on the turret. The lead Weasel lurched into motion and the remaining ones followed.

"How close could mike get to us without us seeing him?" Iommarino sounded nervous.

"Too close," Tomas said. "He knows the terrain, and we don't have obs wheels away from the road."

"He couldn't pop up right in front of us. We'd see his dust in the distance."

"Would we? Assumptions are a good way to end up dead." Tomas pondered. "Even if he snuck up on us, he'd have to worry about fire from our Graywolfs. If our tanks and mike's start dueling, keep your head down. We're in the safest place we could be."

Iommarino gave him a look mingling incredulity with a dollop of fear. "You're not scared?"

Tomas looked him straight in the eyes. "I'm very scared, and I'm glad for it."

"Glad?"

"Because it reminds me not to take stupid chances." Tomas gestured out the firing port. "Now let's watch for mike."

Lt. Tower soon came on the task force net. For the benefit of everyone other than Tomas and Iommarino, he relayed the scout lieutenant's report that mike might be within three klicks and closing. He also reported another scout platoon was still beyond their perimeter and due any moment. "If mike gets here first, we'll hold the bridgehead as long as we can or until the scouts report they can't reach us. Stay calm, all of you."

Tomas peered across the landscape. At a hill's crest seven hundred meters out, patches of air shimmered. He grabbed his grenade launcher. Those shimmers had to be... but they didn't look like chameleonskin. Instead, sunlight dazzled in them as if they were a mist of water.

He zoomed in on one of them with his helmet display. The patch showed vertical streaks, like water from a sprayer. Below the vertical streaks, dirt grew darker, and tiny puddles formed on the ground. Water indeed, soaking into the soil.

Tomas yanked on Iommarino's arm. "Get down!"

A cannonade boomed from the far hill. It sounded louder than the gun of one Marlborough, or even a platoon of Marlboroughs. How many tanks had mike sent after them? The ground shook when mike's shells struck near the hull-down GF fighting vehicles, rattling dust out of the foxhole's walls and making the two men waver on their feet.

"I know why we didn't see mike's dust!" Tomas shouted but still could barely hear his own voice. "He's rigged up sprayers to wet the ground in front of his tracks!"

The two Graywolfs fired, and a missile whooshed from a Badger. The task force's vehicles were still in the battle. Mike would need fortunate hits to strike their turrets while the ground around their shallow holes hid the bulk of their hulls.

The reverse was true. The crest of the distant hill covered most of the front slopes of mike's tanks. The distance made Tomas' grenade launcher ineffective. He leaned it against the wall of the foxhole and picked up his rifle, in case mike had infantry nearby.

Voices shouted in the task force net. "Goddammit, how many tanks does mike have?" Lt. Tower's voice sounded high and thin. "A company? We've got to get across the bridge now!"

"Tower, we still have scouts outside the perimeter," said the Graywolf platoon commander, Lt. Lampenius.

"Four Weasels can't get past a company of tanks!" Lt. Tower sounded frantic. "We've done all we can. I'm ordering a withdrawal."

"Withdrawal? The scouts can get through, if we help them. We're relatively safe in our scrapes and can launch smoke over the whole area."

"I was given command of this task force," Lt. Tower replied. "We're withdrawing. Infantry, remount now."

A lull in the tank guns' fire let Tomas hear Iommarino's fast, ragged breaths. "Is he serious?"

"—We're on our way." Radio chatter from Alvarez partially masked Iommarino's words.

"He's in command." Tomas worked his suit's controls for the infrared ports. Open the ones in front, close the ones in back. He waved his hands over his torso and legs to confirm as he said, "He made a valid point. Better to write off the scouts than get us all killed or captured. The longer we wait to head for the bridge, the more time for mike to find a better firing angle against us. Get your infrared ports set."

Iommarino moved his hands closer to the infrared ports on his chest. "I got them. I can feel the heat."

"Did you close the rear ports?"

"Of course I—damn." Iommarino fiddled with the control panel, then waved his hands behind his back. "Damn. I almost forgot that? My back would've been covered in bulls-eyes—"

"We caught it," Tomas said. He clapped Iommarino on the shoulder. "Get going. I'll follow in a second."

Iommarino scraped over the loose rock. Pebbles clattered to the foxhole floor. Tomas looked out the foxhole's firing port. No mike infantry; not even vague smears of low probability calculated by the computers in his helmet and shilling. Maybe they would make it across the bridge. He turned and crawled out.

Guns boomed around him. He followed Iommarino around tufts of hardy grass, on a line that would take them about as far between the nearest Graywolf and the front of their Badger as possible. An armor-piercing shell shrieked into the dirt near the Graywolf, thirty meters away, kicking up dust but not detonating. Relief relaxed his shoulders. They would be able to remount without much trouble. The vehicles would then drop some thick smoke and call in harassing fire from the formations on the other side of the river. They could make it across in one piece.

The guns lulled again. Through the relative silence came the hydraulic whine of a Graywolf turret adjusting its position, followed by the thwock of a thopter's wings.

Thopter? Tomas looked up. A red icon flashed in his helmet display and warning tones sounded through his earbuds. Not GF—mike. An Immelmann fighter floated three hundred meters overhead, gliding from station to station like a kite. Flashes on its belly showed the muzzles of its machine guns. Tomas flinched and pulled his knees toward his chest. A second later, the sound of its fire reached the ground. It sounded like a flock of woodpeckers hammering a hardwood tree.

Dust kicked up behind the dropped ramp of the lieutenant's Badger, followed by twinned screams through the air and the squad net. Alvarez and Monroe had been the first members of the team to reach the vicinity of the Badger's rear compartment. Tomas' helmet display showed their icons, both dull red and throbbing. Side ports of their suits glowed in infrared.

"Shit! I'm hit!" Alvarez shouted. "Somebody, help me."

"Oh lord Jesus help me," said Monroe. His voice sounded tight with pain. "Help me lord Jesus. Please sweet Jesus."

Lt. Tower shouted more frantically than before. "Mike air on an antipersonnel mission. I don't have anti-air assets! Don't you bastards have any deployed?" Sounded like he spoke with the rest of the company's platoon commanders and had forgotten to close the channel to the task force. "I can't remount the infantry if you don't clear the sky!"

The Immelmann's machine guns fired again. Tomas' helmet display marked the target area, behind the other Badger on this side of the bridge. Alvarez continued to shout for aid. Tears choked Monroe's voice.

"High prob a mike tank platoon peeled off the end of their line," said a Graywolf crew chief. "We've lost them on lidar, infrared, and visual."

"I can't remount the infantry and mike's armor is trying to outflank us!" shouted Lt. Tower. "We have to save our vehicles and crews! Vehicles are withdrawing now!"

Tomas snapped his gaze to his Badger. Had he heard right?

Lt. Tower kept shouting. "Goddammit, MacInnis, that's an order and you'll be court-martialed if you don't lift the ramp and put this sonofabitch into gear!"

The Immelmann's machine guns fired another burst as Sgt. Johnson said, "Sir, we can hold until company drives off mike's bird. Sir. Sir?"

Lt. Tower made no reply. The Badger backed out of its scrape.

"Don't leave me and watch where you're driving you almost hit me!" Alvarez shouted. The Badger slewed sharply, a deft motion for a forty-ton vehicle, then shifted gears and moved forward, right at Tomas. He quickly crawled to the side. The Badger passed three meters from him. MacInnis knew how to drive. The Badger picked up speed and headed for the roadway leading onto the bridge, followed by the platoon's other Badgers from both sides of the road. Mike shells chased them but missed.

"How will we get across the river?" Lundergard asked into the squad net.

"Ride the Graywolfs!" yelled Iommarino with naïve confidence.

Cohen replied, "The Graywolfs will be prime targets for all those mike tanks. You don't want to ride a Graywolf when its reactive armor goes off." The guns of mike tanks fired to emphasize his words. Shells roared overhead.

"We aren't leaving yet." Lampenius, the Graywolf commander, spoke. "We're men with skills, not paper tigers." Some cheers followed his words through the task force net.

"Dammit, where's a medic?" Alvarez shouted. "I need a medic!"

Tomas glanced up. The Immelmann flitted from point to point in the air above, continuing to fire bursts at the ground. A burst shredded the chameleonskin roofing his former foxhole. He crawled in the other direction, toward the wounded men.

Alvarez writhed, clutching his left leg. A round had shattered his knee, but he'd managed to get a self-wrapping tourniquet around the middle of his thigh. He'd live. "You're not a medic!" he yelled at Tomas.

"You did a good enough job on yourself," Tomas said. "You don't need a medic."

"Wait! I need help!"

"So does he." Tomas crawled toward Monroe.

Blood stained the ground and slicked Monroe's tattered suit. His shilling telemetered signs of severe shock. Rapid pulse, rapid breathing, low body temperature. His slurred voice sounded like it came from far away. "Take me, lor' Jesus. Grea'-mee-maw, course you here by His throne...."

Grief washed over Tomas. "You'll be okay," he said, and the grief was chased by guilt.

"More'n okay. I'm in the arms of the lord." Monroe fell silent, and his icon in Tomas' helmet display darkened to deep red.

Tomas gripped his gloved hand. *I wish I could mourn you now, Monroe—*

An odd sound came from behind him. He let go of Monroe's hand and looked over his shoulder.

A loud twanging sound came from the anchorage, followed by the double-crump of nearly-simultaneous explosions at each of the cable anchorages on the far side of the bridge.

The twanging grew louder. The cables, pulled taut across the river, were now free to relax. The relaxing tension pulled them from the top of the tower on the sunright bluff. The sheared cables plunged toward the bridge deck. The deck writhed as it crumbled into the river below.

"They've blown the bridge!" Tomas shouted into the task force net.

For a moment, no one spoke. Even mike's tank guns fell silent. Then men erupted into babble on the task force net, some plaintive, some frantic, but a few—Johnson, Cohen, Lt. Lampenius, and Tomas—calm. "There's a switchback down the bluff!" Tomas shouted repeatedly, until most of the soldiers stilled their babble. "We can make it to the riverside and swim across."

"And abandon our vehicles?" Lampenius asked.

"Sir, seems to me we can fab tanks, but we can't fab brains to learn the skills to drive tanks."

"Good point—shit! Mike tank platoon, on our flank!"

Two Graywolfs swung their turrets and fired their main guns. Too late for one—a mike shell pierced the top deck near the bottom of the turret. The hatch popped. Two crewmen leaped out frantically as fire licked the edge of the hatchway. The men wore simple camouflage patterns, no chameleonskin, no infrared wicking. The sky silhouetted them as they scrambled for cover. Some of the main line of mike tanks fired their machine guns. One of the Graywolf's escaped crew toppled.

"We must abandon the position, sir," Sgt. Johnson said.

Lampenius grunted. "Agreed. What about mike's bird? A mass of men at the top of a switchback would be prime targets."

Wisps of sound came from across the river. A glance at the sky showed missiles streaking toward the Immelmann. Finally someone had answered Tower's call for anti-aircraft fire.

The Immelmann left its hover and accelerated to sunleft, spitting out a cloud of reflective particles in an attempt to confuse the guidance packages on the missiles. The missiles detoured around the reflective particles. The Immelmann lurched from side to side like a clumsy hummingbird. It avoided the missiles, but was soon a shrinking speck heading into the distance.

"All right, that settles it." Lampenius said, "Infantrymen, get down that switchback. We're going to destroy our vehicle, then follow you."

"I'll throw smoke canisters," Sgt. Johnson said. "We still need men with grenade launchers to cover us against mike's armor."

Tomas blinked. He was one of those men. But I need to get Alvarez —No. *We* need to get Alvarez across the river.

"Iommarino!" Tomas shouted. "Help Alvarez to the switchback!" No answer. "Iommarino, you can do this! The team needs you!"

"Yeah, yeah, I'm coming, I'm coming." Iommarino soon scrambled to them. He wrapped his arm over Alvarez' chest and started crawling, dragging the wounded man, all without meeting Tomas' gaze.

"Good job, Iommarino," Tomas said. A few dozen meters away, a canister arced end-over-end through the air. It clacked on the stony ground and spewed gray smoke. Another canister followed. The last functioning Graywolf chuffed out more. Tomas peered into the gloom and held his fire. He only had four grenades and didn't want to waste them. Soon a thick pall covered the area, obscuring the GF soldiers as they crawled and dragged their wounded to the top of the switchback.

The enemy could probably guess what the GF was trying to do. The mike tanks fired their machine guns through the smoke, wounding one man by luck. The number of GF soldiers at the top of the switchback dwindled. Tomas' helmet display showed icons of descending soldiers on his view of the ground between him and the bluff.

The surviving Graywolf fired one more armor-piercing round into the gloom. The blast from its gun's muzzle flashed like lightning amid the smoke. A few moments later, its hatch opened. Lampenius laid it quietly against the turret, then jumped to the ground and waved the crewmen out. "Forty-five seconds until it self-destructs," he told the task force. "Get down the bluff face before it goes." The Graywolf crew, starkly visible in their camouflage uniforms, crouched and ran for the switchback. Their commander followed.

Tomas and the other man with a grenade launcher took turns bounding for the switchback. Tomas was first to reach the top of the bluff. He hid behind a shrub four meters from the top of the trail as the other man made his final bound.

The ground rumbled. Tracks clacked somewhere in the gloom. A vague shape, flickering with probability estimates aided by the lidar still functioning on the last Graywolf, coalesced out of the smoke. A Marlborough. Its gun traversed and elevated like a sniffing aardvark nose. Tomas aimed at the front drive wheel. Time seemed to slow in the moment before he fired. He ran for the trailhead. It took a few seconds for him to realize the grenade had telemetered a hit.

The rumble deepened and the clack of tracks heightened, soon followed by a colossal roar when the Graywolf exploded. Shards of metal whizzed over the edge of the bluff, some on steep trajectories. "Hunker, hunker!" Tomas shouted into the task force net. Men pressed themselves against the face of the bluff as metal splintered branches and clattered against the slope. "Go!" he yelled after the last fragments of the Graywolf's hull fell to the ground.

The men hurried down the slope. Tomas slung his grenade

launcher over one shoulder and brought his rifle to his hands from the other. At the first switchback, he glanced back the way he'd come. The gun of a mike tank was visible above the bluff's edge. Though close to it, the men were safe; Marlboroughs couldn't depress their armament low enough to fire down the slope.

They could probably fire on the middle of the river channel, but that was a problem for a few minutes from now.

The men formed up on the sandy flat. "I'm the last one down," Tomas said. "Let's get across."

Sgt. Johnson spoke with his usual aplomb. "Idrin, start swim—"

"Sergeant," Tomas said, "with respect, imped skills are no guarantee of success on an open water swim. A soldier might know the motions but lack the knowledge in the bone of how to handle the current. I suggest we buddy up. The strongest swimmers buddy with wounded and the next strongest buddy with weaker swimmers. Before you get in the water, drop anything you don't need. We can fab it later."

"Good ideas, Neumann. Who be my strong swimmers?"

Tomas said, "I'm pretty strong; I'll take Alvarez. And men, if your buddy flails, take care of yourself first." He dropped the grenade launcher to the damp sand. He went to Alvarez while the rest of the men buddied up.

Alvarez clutched the thigh of his wounded leg with both hands. He thrashed his head side-to-side when Tomas approached. "I don't need help."

"Do I have to get the sergeant to order you?"

"Alright." Alvarez shifted his weight, then his upper body froze, head facing the top of the bluff. "Shit, we've got more mikes at the party."

Tomas glanced up long enough to see mike infantrymen at the top of the bluff, shouting at one another and drawing their rifles.

"Idrin, in the water, now!" Sgt. Johnson shouted. He fired his rifle at the top of the bluff. "Lieutenant, can we get some cover—"

"Working on it," Lampenius said. "Company, we need anti-personnel suppressing fire on the top of the bluff. Do you read? We need anti-personnel suppressing fire. Don't let them get down the bluff!"

Rifle fire came from the mikes atop the bluff, pinging the ground around the clearest targets, the Graywolf crewmen. A mike team started down the slope.

Tomas put his arm around Alvarez and lifted him to his good foot. They hobbled across the sand, Alvarez cursing with every step. The river babbled down the main channel. Blurs masked by spray showed where the first swimmers had entered the water. The river's current looked stronger from up close. Machine guns on the sunright bank drummed out rounds against the mike infantry.

Tomas and Alvarez waded in. "Son of a whore it's cold!" Alvarez said.

Tomas grabbed Alvarez' right arm with his left and dove. He started a sidestroke, working the water with his right arm and towing Alvarez with his left. A few rifle rounds smacked the water nearby.

The river was indeed cold, the product of glacial melt from the icecaps covering New Liberty's dark face. The water seeped between the collar of Tomas' suit and the bottom of his helmet. Too long in the river and something would get them, either hypothermia or the extra weight soaking their suits. Glances at the bluffs showed the current rapidly pushed them downriver. Tomas adjusted course toward the sunright base of the bridge.

"Still with me?" Tomas asked Alvarez.

Alvarez didn't reply. Suddenly worried, Tomas checked his helmet display to see if the other's vitals had gotten worse. He almost asked again when Alvarez finally spoke. "Go ahead, say it."

"What?"

"Don't lie." Alvarez sounded resigned. "You caught me and you know it."

He wanted to feel guilty, Tomas realized. About what? "I want to hear it from you in your own words."

Machine guns and the main armament of tanks fired atop both bluffs. Tomas listened for the fire of mike rifles, or the smack of Marlborough machine guns striking the river, and heard none. The GF suppressing fire did its job.

"I talked so much shit about you," Alvarez said. "That your god outweighed our team. But shit, who am I to talk? My god has outweighed the team too. At least your god was something bigger than you. Mine wasn't. My god was nothing. It was me."

Tomas stroked and kicked, adjusted course. "You."

"Dammit, how much are you going to make me say? Me. My own fucking ego. All I've given a damn about is getting out of here. I kept my head down and didn't help anybody else. I didn't even help Monroe. I saw his wounds and the telltales on my helmet display—"

The shoals at the foot of the sunright bluff were too low to the river for Tomas to gauge the distance. "You couldn't have helped him."

"Shit, don't say that. I could've helped him just as much as you did. Human contact, a consoling voice." Alvarez' voice caught. "All I wanted him to do was die so I didn't have to hear his words as he hung on. I'm not like that. I'm no saint but I swear to god I'm not like that."

Tomas took more strokes. "Yeah, you're no saint. You're something better." He stroked again and his outstretched right arm brushed sand beneath him. He stretched his legs toward the shallow bottom, then helped Alvarez to stand up. "You're my squadmate."

"Shit."

"Listen to me." He put his arm around Alvarez and helped him hobble onto the shoal. A cool wind from darkward made Tomas shiver. "You've made the best choices you've known how to make. If you want to make different ones, I will gladly help you. If you want to make the same ones, I will gladly help you do that too." At the top of the bluff in front of them, GF machine guns and ordnance boomed out fire against the mikes across the river. Other men from the squad, as well as the Graywolf crews, crawled dripping and shaky-legged onto shore. "Now let's get dry."

CHAPTER 14

THE NEW LIEUTENANT

"TEN-HUT!" Sgt. Johnson called. Tomas and the rest of the platoon came to attention as the new lieutenant took his place in front of them on the parade ground.

The new lieutenant surveyed them for a time. His brown eyes shared a palette with his tanned face and the dusty greens and khakis of the camouflage pattern on his garrison cap. He stood stiff-backed, with pressed camouflage fatigues and shined boots. *Do we have another Academy grad?*

"At ease. I'm Lt. O'Brien. I'm replacing Lt. Tower, who I'm sure you've heard has been reassigned." He studied them more. Tomas kept his face blank.

Lt. O'Brien smirked. "Every platoon I've served in has had a man with his ear to the rumor mill. I don't need to know who serves that function here, but I'm no paper tiger you can lie to. Play straight by me and I'll return the favor."

Tomas let out a breath. The new lieutenant had come up through OCS.

Lt. O'Brien delivered a brief speech. He'd reviewed the platoon's record. Any black marks on it were attributable to previous poor leadership. The platoon had good men and he was honored to lead them.

He then greeted each of the soldiers in turn. Tomas kept his eyes mostly forward, but occasionally let them stray as he tried to overhear the new lieutenant's conversations. He'd studied their dossiers, Tomas realized, asking Cohen about his home region on Shambhala and talking with Iommarino about their high schools' rivalry in the McAuliffe city sports leagues on Challenger.

Yet he had little to say to Tomas. O'Brien mainly scrutinized him and muttered small talk. A measure of disappointment grew in him until O'Brien said, "Come with the sergeant to my office after we're done here." O'Brien then moved on to the next man in line.

Disappointment vanished, replaced with fear. Had he done something to irritate the new lieutenant already? In the rank ahead of him, Iommarino turned with boggled eyes and mouthed *what?*

Tomas accepted his fear and shrugged. He'd find out soon enough.

After the inspection, Sgt. Johnson waited in front of the platoon while the other soldiers left the parade ground for the shelters. Word had somehow spread about Tomas' orders, and each man took it differently. Cohen bumped Tomas' shoulder with his fist and murmured "Good luck," while Lundergard avoided Tomas' gaze and walked a long arc around the sergeant to keep at a distance.

"Sergeant, do you know what this is about?"

Sgt. Johnson showed a poker face. "I and I have an inkling."

"Sergeant, tell me."

"Better you hear it from Lt. O'Brien himself. Let's go."

The company's new base was a cluster of shelters bermed to the eaves with dirt. No windows here. Constitution stood a hands-breadth above the top of the innermost of the razor wire fences forming the base's perimeter, higher in the sky than anywhere else Tomas had seen it on-planet. The more intense rays of the sun compounded his nervousness, sending sweat streaming down his neck as he approached the cluster of shelters housing the platoon commanders' offices.

The LEDs in the ceiling were fabbed to match the output spectrum of Epsilon Eridani, Challenger's sun. After all his time on New Liberty, the light struck Tomas as too white, too austere. It made the text displayed by the tablet and stacks of paper on the lieutenant's desk too stark. It sharpened the lines of Lt. O'Brien's face and the scrutiny in his eyes.

Tomas snapped his heels together and saluted. "Private Neumann reporting, sir."

O'Brien returned the salute. "At ease. I'm sure you're wondering why I called you here. I've been reading your dossier. Coming into the GF, it was clear you were smart and had some good aptitudes. Your early record as an armored grenadier is solid. But since your return from the hospital in R-town.... Some men get wounded and they come back to the front fearful it will happen again. Others come back foolhardy, thinking death had its best shot at them and missed. You avoided both those traps."

"I had an excellent psychological and spiritual consultation at the hospital in R-town, sir."

"Whatever the reason," Lt. O'Brien said, "you've become an excellent soldier. Sgt. Johnson has written pages and pages of favorable reviews."

Tomas' eyebrows rose. Sgt. Johnson stood a little taller. "Don't let it go to your head, Neumann."

Lt. O'Brien went on. "Lt. Lampenius hadn't met you before the day you crossed the river, but he has great praise for your actions. Lt. Tower didn't say much about you... and all else being equal, that's another point in your favor." He leaned back and laid his hands on his desk.

"Favor? Sir, are you putting me up for a medal? Are we pitching hero stories to the media to fluff up the war effort?"

Lt. O'Brien crossed his arms and leaned back further. "You're telling me you think you deserve a medal?"

"Sir, no. I'm telling you, I did my duty because it was the right thing to do."

"Did your duty? You went beyond your duty. You violated your religious precepts and avoided an ambush that would have wrecked this company as a fighting force. After Tower blew the bridge early, you showed initiative. You gave the sergeant and Lt. Lampenius sound advice. You led twenty-five men across the river."

"Sir, I only made suggestions to my superiors."

"Well phrased." Sgt. Johnson chuckled.

More sweat dampened Tomas' nape. "Whatever I've done well, there are too many men in the GF who would've done as well in the same situation. I don't deserve more recognition than they do."

With a smile, Lt. O'Brien shook his head. "As it turns out, I am putting you up for a medal. But I didn't call you in here to talk about a new bauble for your dress uniform. I'm here to talk to you about a promotion."

Tomas took in the words and noted his feelings. "I'm flattered, and confused. The platoon has a full complement of corporals—"

"No, Neumann. Not corporal, or even sergeant." Lt. O'Brien regarded Tomas levelly. "I recommend you apply to officer candidates school."

Tomas blinked a few times, and his gaze wandered over the interior of the office. He'd never thought about OCS before. His thoughts churned in an effort to understand the hesitant feeling pooling behind the muscles of his face. He let out a breath. The hesitation gave him all the understanding he needed. "Sir, I'm flattered—"

"But you want to say 'no.' Neumann, I understand. I was in your position, only eight months ago. You're worried about maybe someday giving orders to your former squadmates? That won't happen. You won't get assigned to the Blackjacks, let alone to this battalion, company, or platoon."

Tomas observed his hesitation through the framework of Lt. O'Brien's words. "Thank you for the clarification, sir, but that's not what's holding me back. In fact, what you've said makes me even more hesitant."

"How so?"

"For me, the GF more than anything is the half-dozen of us in the fireteam riding in your Badger. I feel like I'd be skipping out on them for easier duty. Not that being an officer is easy, sir." He remembered Tower in the plaza in New Boston, coldly murderous one moment and passively apathetic the next. "I understand you have commitments and responsibilities we don't. But I have a bond to the team."

"There's a role you play here. You don't want to take that away from your team."

"Yes, sir."

Lt. O'Brien pursed his lips. "As your new platoon commander, I should be glad to have a man with that attitude riding in my Badger. But I'm disappointed you define your position in the GF so narrowly. At our best, we are a team that spans all our deployments, from here to the worlds bordering the Progressive Republic, and from the private who just took his shilling to the highest ranking general who's had his for decades. Being in our team means finding the role we are best suited to, and playing it for our sake and the sake of everyone else with this thing—" He tapped an index finger on the front of his fatigues, over the shilling riding on his chest.

Tomas' mind expanded from a realization of the truth of the lieutenant's words. The team would find another grenadier. If his actions were worth emulating, the team would emulate them even if he wasn't there. His duty to his teammates, both those living and those dead, was to do the most he could to win this war and affirm their sacrifices. If he could best do that by becoming an officer, he owed it to his teammates to follow the lieutenant's recommendation.

But what about after the war? "Sir, you make many good points. But I never thought about making a career out of the GF."

"You would be committed for five years," Lt. O'Brien said, and his voice grew softer as he added, "or the duration of this war if it runs longer than that. After your commitment ended, you could retire to civilian life and become, whatever you want, an Observer minister or anything else. Or it's thirty years to a full pension. Think about it, Neumann. If you need more information to make up your mind, ask me…. What's this?" An alert appeared on his tablet's display, just as Tomas' shilling throbbed.

Lt. O'Brien scrolled the display. "We're being ordered to start our patrol of our river frontage ahead of schedule. This is a readiness drill ordered by Capt. Marcinkus. He wants us out the gate in ten."

Sgt. Johnson showed no sign of finding the order challenging. "We will be in the Badgers in seven, sir."

The lieutenant pushed his chair back from his desk and reached for his earbuds and helmet in a wall-mounted case behind him. "See you there, Johnson, Neumann."

As they trotted to the squad's shelter for their helmets and suits, Tomas asked, "Do you have another inkling, sergeant?"

"All I know is what you know. Looks like Capt. Marcinkus wants us to keep ready."

"Ready for what?" Tomas asked. They reached the squad's shelter and Sgt. Johnson went to his locker without replying.

The patrol left on schedule. Despite the rushed departure, nothing out of the ordinary happened after they left the base's gate. They rode their Badgers up to the river, then spent the next six hours alternating between the hot, cramped rear compartment and foot patrols to the bluff's edge. On the sunleft side of the riverfront road, the engineers had rigged sheets of chameleonskin over tall alloy struts. While on the road, their Badgers were invisible to cameras and radars on mike's side of the river.

They were obscured to mike's birds, as well. The GF ran its own smudgepots, on the darkward side of each brigade's zone. Their aerosols rode the prevailing low-altitude winds. Whatever benefit they provided in obscuring GF movements from mike's aircraft was bought at the cost of black dust. The dust coated the Badger's windows and camera ports and wormed in through the breathing ports on the soldiers' helmets.

On a foot patrol to check a cluster of obs wheels on the edge of the bluff, about five klicks upriver from the blown bridge, coughs racked Lundergard. "Why the aerosols?" he asked. "Are our brass planning an attack and want to hide our preparations?"

Tomas watched eddies in the dark haze. "They're planning something."

"To attack we'd need to throw a new bridge across the river. Have you seen any prep for one? I haven't."

"Me neither." Tomas watched the far bluff for traces of movement. "But they might be planning an attack outside our zone. Or not planning an attack at all."

Lundergard coughed again. "You're no help."

"I don't like uncertainty either. But all we can do is be ready for whatever order comes down."

When Alvarez returned from the Reagantown hospital, recovered from his wounds during the river crossing, he reported a wide range of rumors had circulated the wards, like competing strains of infectious diseases. Peace negotiations with the Unity; a crushing defeat of, or by, the Progressive Republic in an SF action near Péngláishān; a massive reinforcement being prepared by the GF for New Liberty. Alvarez also told them about an odd duty he'd been assigned his last two days of rehab: he'd fed papers into a whirring, humming machine that spat them out unchanged. "What the hell was that about?" he asked the men in the squad's shelter.

"They were digitally capturing information from the papers," Tomas said. A perfectly sensible reason for Alvarez' task drove out his breath. "They're preparing to evacuate the planet."

"What?" Cohen asked with curiosity.

Tomas hefted his tablet. "It's easier to carry this into orbit than a million sheets of paper."

Alvarez shook his head. "That can't be it. They put all the paper back where it came from."

"Time will tell," Tomas said. His tablet chimed with an incoming message. "Later." He went to his bunk and called up his messaging app.

New message from Annike Neumann, Portage-du-Nord, Joséphine.

His heart quickened. Finally Mother had written back. Maybe now she was ready to give him some information about his father. Tomas forced himself to slowly open the message.

Dear Tomas,

I am relieved to read you survived your wounds. Yet every day, when I see a car on the Bois d'Orme highway slowing near the turn-off for the parsonage, I fear it's a 'family relations officer' (such a ghastly euphemism) coming to tell me you have been killed. When the car passes, I relax for a moment, until I imagine you returning to me after your discharge with your body whole, but your mind broken. I can tell when you try to hide things from me. I can read between the lines. You've hidden many things from me. When you hint this 'Peters-Stein Technique' helped you regain your mental wholeness, it's clear you are protesting too much. I don't know how broken your mind is now, or how much worse it will be when you return to me, but you at least will have a place to stay once the GF casts you away.

I've inquired about the Peters-Stein Technique. It's misguided foolishness. I don't know why they made up those absurd stories about your father and me.

I know you should have heard from me the full story of what happened to your father. Our family never went to Nueva Andalucia. We instead went to Challenger. Your father had grandiose dreams of bringing the Observer message to the underclass in the big cities. Yet some people don't want to be helped. Your father got a knife in the back for his grandiose dreams. That's what happened. Remember, Tomas, I have never lied to you.

In one of your earlier letters, you mentioned running into a Monsieur DuBois from Sainte-Therese. I don't know any DuBois family in that town. The only DuBois I know is the widow in Portage. Obviously she's no relation to him.

Please stay as safe as you can. I don't approve what you've done, but I want you to come home alive. I'll even care for you if you're broken inside. I'm the only person who ever loved you.

Love Mother.

Tomas kept the message open for a time, flicking the text up and down the display as he thought about what she'd said. Gooseflesh prickled his cheeks. She'd lied about Challenger, and his father's death at some petty criminal's blade. He must have died on Nueva Andalucia. Did she want to hide that fact because Nueva Andalucia hung in hostile space? Or had his father died in some circumstance too embarrassing to repeat? Tomas imagined a lurid story, an affair with an Andaluciana in a flamenco dress ended by pistol fire from a jealous husband with a waxed mustache—

None of it mattered. His father was dead. His corpse fertilized the soil of a planet in enemy space. Even if Tomas redeployed to Nueva Andalucia later in the war, he would never find his father's grave. He had no father. The thought hurt, but carried with it a restful feeling.

I thank you for what you were able to provide, he expressed to his father's memory. *Now I take that and build my own life.*

Tomas thought for a few more minutes, then swept away his mother's message and tapped the compose button on the messaging app. He scrolled through a directory of GF personnel on-planet and found the addressee he sought.

Dear Chief Younger,

I hope this message finds you well. I repeatedly think back on our session as a dividing line in my life. It's like a cocoon, where an insect transforms from a crawling worm to a winged flyer.

In light of the insights our session has given me into who I am and what I can do, I've decided to apply to officer candidates school….

CHAPTER 15

THE FINAL MISSION

Lt. O'Brien stood in front of the platoon, outside the main entrance to the base's fitness building. "Men, I don't know what's going on, but it's big. You've heard the battalion commander is here? He's not alone. The brigade commander is here as well."

A hush settled over the men. A summons to meet that much brass had never happened. Not just in the two months since they'd crossed the river, but since Sgt. Johnson had joined their unit. The lieutenant led them inside.

A clump of officers stood under the folded-up basketball goal at the far end of the gym. Their voices echoed off the mycocrete walls as they spoke among themselves. Tomas studied the group, looking for nametags and rank insignia among the dazzle of khakis and greens of the GF's garrison-duty fatigues. He glimpsed a single silver star on the collar of the brigade commander, Brigadier Kanagawa, near Capt. Marcinkus and a host of other captains and majors. A silver oak leaf marked the collar of Lt. Col. Bar-Talab, the battalion commander, who stood near an incongruous figure dressed in light blue. An SF uniform? Tomas craned his neck for a better look at the SF man but couldn't get one.

"Ten-hut!" Lt. O'Brien said. The enlisted men formed ranks and saluted.

The officers returned the gesture. "At ease," Brig. Kanagawa said.

Tomas dropped his hand, and then his whole face fell. The SF man was Lucien LaSalle. Lucien squinted his way, then leaned his head back with a glower aimed at Tomas.

Brig. Kanagawa had a weathered face and gray hair at his temples. "I commend you on doing fine work here. The base has been tip-top from the moment Lt. Col. Bar-Talab and I arrived, and men, you have turned out smartly. I am honored to command your brigade."

The brigadier cleared his throat. "You are of course wondering why the sheriff is here." He tapped the single star on his collar to explain the slang. He had to be older than he looked to use so archaic a term; Tomas knew the word but had never heard it spoken. "There is a mission of supreme importance that your platoon is uniquely well suited to take part in. But for me to talk about it, I must warn you, requires a level of secrecy we don't normally ask of our enlisted men. We know you have the will to keep it secret, but the higher brass in R-town ordered me to hand out lethe capsules to each of you before you can leave this room." Knots of staff officers filed out behind the brigadier and drifted to the exits. "Do you commit to this, men?"

"Yes, sir!" Sgt. Johnson said. Tomas joined his voice with the sergeant's about halfway through.

"I didn't catch that."

"Yes, sir!" The platoon spoke in unison.

"Thank you, men. You might also be wondering why one of our Space Force colleagues has come down from orbit to be with us." Brig. Kanagawa gestured at Lucien. The latter looked uncomfortable and cast hooded looks around the room. "It all fits together. The War Ministry on Challenger has made a decision and both our branches have to work together to execute it. We are evacuating New Liberty."

Gasps and murmurs came from the men around Tomas. He sagged over his stomach. So many months, so many dead, for nothing?

Tomas took a breath. No. They had learned valuable lessons no amount of impped skills or peacetime training could impart. If he was accepted and passed OCS, the lessons he had learned would make him a better officer for the rest of his career.

The brigadier grew stern. "Quiet, men. Your mission is to reconnoiter the landing zone for the SF's transport ships. I now hand the floor to Lt. Col. Bar-Talab to fill you in on the details."

The staff officers shifted to face the lieutenant colonel. Behind him, a gangly lieutenant unrolled a tripod-mounted display and stretched to lock it into place. The pause gave Tomas time to wonder. Why do they need an armored grenadier platoon to do reconnaissance? What's out there the scouts can't handle?

Lt. Col. Bar-Talab had a stout body and a blunt voice. "Thank you, brigadier." A map appeared on the display. Near the top of the map, Tomas read the icons of friendly units, mike formations, and the Grant River dividing them.

The river curved to the lower left and ended in a fifty kilometer long zone of intermittent lakes, where Constitution shone strongly enough to evaporate the river. Beyond the intermittent lakes was nothing but sun-scorched desert. Bar-Talab pointed a laser at a geologic formation on the cooler side of the evaporating river. "This is the Paiute Plateau, about a hundred-forty klicks behind us. It's thirty klicks by twenty, and averages four hundred meters above our current altitude. Its sunward edge is a high mountain chain that rainshadows the plateau. It's hot, dry, and mostly empty of NLer settlement, according to Shir—Space Force monitoring. It's the best place our brass and SF's have found to get all our forces on the sunleft front off the planet."

The display switched to a more detailed map of the plateau. " 'Mostly uninhabited' is another way of saying there is a permanent settlement we need to look at more closely." He circled the laser dot over a temple icon situated in the mountain chain between dense forest on the sunward slopes and the high desert of the plateau. "This temple is the Novus Homo Observation Society." Lt. Col. Bar-Talab peered at the platoon. "I understand Private Neumann is an Observer?"

And the reason his platoon had been tapped for this mission? Tomas said, "Yes, sir." His voice echoed flatly off the walls.

"The next images are based on SF photography of the site, further processed to give you men the view you'll have on approach. If that's a problem for anyone, shut your eyes."

Tomas took a breath and opened his eyes wide.

The temple reached for the sky. Perched on a cliff overlooking a pass, mycocrete outer walls showed *taijitus* to travelers approaching from the plateau. An Observer facility, all right. Behind the walls, a grassy courtyard held a number of buildings and a gracile tower of nanotubes and alloys. The tower held a platform twenty meters square, and a series of meshwork stairways leading up to it. Banners hanging from the edges of the platform showed more *taijitus*. The top of the platform might be fifty meters above the desert floor.

"Sir," Lt. O'Brien asked, "do you have a rendition of the view from the platform?"

"Here's our best calculation." The image flickered. Though shimmering with heat, the sunleft and darkward edges of the plateau were visible. Bar-Talab said, "You see why we need to reconnoiter this facility. If mike had surface-to-air missiles in that courtyard, and a man with a rangefinder on the platform, we could lose SF ships and GF men. Another question?"

Capt. Marcinkus spoke with a rehearsed tone. "Why not destroy the facility from orbit?"

Bar-Talab opened his mouth to speak, but stopped. Lucien fidgeted and turned his head to Bar-Talab, who said, "Lieutenant, care to answer?"

"Gladly." To the soldiers, Lucien said, "We easily could. We already have a plan to destroy every other structure on the plateau that's potentially usable by hostiles." He sneered at Tomas and disdain dripped from his voice. "Sadly, the Observer lobby on Challenger is insidiously powerful. They'd rather put GF lives at risk than let us blow up one of their temples from a safe distance."

Tomas swallowed thickly. Sweat dewed on his nape. You make me the bad guy? Still mad I didn't lie for you at the tribunal?

Lundergard whispered to Tomas, "This shirley knows a lot about your religion."

"He has it in for me. You heard about the friendly fire casualties we suffered near New Boston? He pressed the button."

Alvarez nodded. "SF exiled him dirtside, and he blames Neumann for it instead of himself. He's stirring shit. Won't work. Some Observer might be the reason for this mission, but Neumann is part of our team."

Capt. Marcinkus spoke. "You have connections in the War Ministry, Lieutenant LaSalle?"

Lucien blinked a few times. "Pardon me, Captain?"

"All I know is we have an order to leave the Observer facility on the plateau untouched unless mike's using it against us. I have no idea how that order was decided. Do you?"

Lucien looked belligerent for a moment, but then glanced at the sea of GF camouflage around him. "I do not."

Lt. Col. Bar-Talab said, "Alright, men. You will be departing tomorrow at oh-two-hundred. Along the way, you'll link up with a scout platoon from one of our sister battalions. Together, you will travel to the Observer facility, ETA oh-ten-hundred. If mike has forces present, the highest priority is to neutralize them. Next highest is silence them. We want to keep mike in the dark as long as possible about our plans. If he doesn't know what we're doing, our redeployment to the plateau will be easier and the odds of mike getting into surface-to-air missile range to bring down a shuttle will be lower."

The lieutenant colonel went on. "If mike has no forces present, then the highest priority is to maintain the neutrality of the facility's staff until the evacuation is essentially complete. Between you and the scout platoon, your task force will have three men from Observer backgrounds. Neumann, you and those two scouts will make sure we interface with the facility's staff in a cultural sensitive manner." Lt. Col. Bar-Talab studied them. "Pack anything you can't fab on New Nauvoo, because you won't be coming back to this base. Brigadier, anything further?"

Brig. Kanagawa shook his head. "Dismissed."

Lucien joined Lt. O'Brien at the head of the platoon. They filed out the gym doors, pausing to take lethe capsules from the brigadier's junior staffers. When Tomas took the clear plastic bag containing the capsule and its neck chain, his name and rank printed on it, knowledge filed away in his mind by the skills imps came to his consciousness. Bite through the capsule and swallow. In five minutes, his recent memories would be scrambled, unknowable to both his own recollection and a mike brain scanner should he be captured. The capsules were properly printed with a use-by date and time. Just under ninety-six hours from now.

Tomas read the implication. If the capsules would be useless in four days, by then they would be off the planet. He tore open the bag, hung the capsule around his neck, and tucked it inside his shirt next to his shilling. He dropped the empty bag into the maw of a recycling unit.

The platoon members spent the rest of the afternoon in their shelters. Tomas took a few minutes to sift through his belongings and dismiss most of them as being replaceable. After that, he checked his mail. Excitement bloomed in him when he saw a new letter from Chief Younger——Lissa. *Dear Tomas*, it began. They'd moved to first names a few weeks before. He read her letter carefully, savoring her choices of words, then composed a reply.

He spent the rest of the day reviewing intel on the Observer facility. Intel lacked floor plans of the buildings, but the layout reminded Tomas of facilities on Péngláishān he read about in his mother's old, hardbound volumes of the Observer Encyclopedia. A meeting hall, an office, and a parsonage built into a spur of rock. Broad-roofed breezeways connected all the buildings. From the size of the parsonage, the facility could have anywhere from zero to eight resident staffers.

He read further. There was probably at least one permanent resident. The facility's website stated *Visitors welcome daily, eight a.m. to eight p.m.* Video, from both orbit and obs wheels along one of the roads up to the plateau, showed a supply truck making weekly runs from the municipal fab in Hale Valley, the nearest town, sixty kilometers to dark-sunright of the facility.

Tomas felt some relief. A mike unit at the facility would have its own fab, and wouldn't need supplies from a town in GF territory.

Unless mike kept the supply truck coming to create an illusion of normalcy.

Around sixteen-hundred, Lundergard rose from a group of men playing a multiplayer game on their tablets, and strode toward the shelter's door.

"Where are you going?" Sgt. Johnson asked.

"I'm getting antsy. I'll just hit the fitness room—"

"Do some pushups in the corner. We will eat a late dinner in the mess hall, but otherwise, idrin, we won't leave until we board the Badgers."

"I'm not going to tell anyone we're bugging off-planet in a few days," Lundergard said with a frown.

Sgt. Johnson said, "Orders be orders."

Lundergard looked unconvinced. Tomas set down his tablet and said to him, "The orificers trust us not to voluntarily spill the information. But the rest of the company knows something's happening. They haven't seen us all day, right? If they now see one of us outside, the rest of the company will ask us what's going on. No matter how little we tell them, the rumormongers might glean the truth. Sequestering us is the best chance to keep the mission confidential."

After looking thoughtful for a moment, Lundergard grunted. He dropped to the floor between two bunks and did pushups.

Dinner came at nineteen-thirty. They trooped across the base, Lt. O'Brien and Lucien in front and Sgt. Johnson at the rear. Lucien wore an untailored GF uniform, so short that his shirttail quickly came untucked from his pants. Tomas glanced around, but this side of the base was empty.

The SSC enlisted personnel crewing the mess line asked the soldiers no questions beyond which meats and vegetables they wanted. Past the mess line, the officers led the men toward the far table. Tomas found himself walking alongside Lucien. He kept quiet. It wasn't his place to strike up a conversation with any officer, even one he'd known in his former life.

"Don't think I wanted to run into you," Lucien said.

"I hadn't expected to see you after the tribunal, sir."

Lucien glowered. "Don't rub my face in the tribunal. I didn't want you to lie, but you painted the truth in the drabbest colors possible. Why? Mudbugs closing ranks against Shirley? Are you envious I'm an officer? That I had a better life on Joséphine?"

Tomas stopped at the middle of the table, near his squadmates. At the table's head, Lt. O'Brien set down his fork and eyed Tomas and Lucien. Tomas said, "I told the truth as I best recalled it."

"Don't give me that Observer claptrap."

"You sound angry."

Lucien leaned toward him, lips pressed together. "You have to worship the goddam yin-yang symbol to figure that out?"

The soldiers around them watched, with clear sympathy for Tomas and wary dislike for Lucien. Lt. O'Brien came up. "Problem, lieutenant?"

"Ask your man."

O'Brien's voice became flatter, deeper. "I'm asking you. I know about the misplaced fire mission, and I know Neumann testified about it. What's your problem?" O'Brien looked down his nose at Lucien's collar. "You kept your rank."

Lucien sniffed out a breath. "Rank? You think that's my only concern? I got exiled dirtside. 'Mud sticks to your wings.' It's ten times harder to get a promotion down here."

O'Brien shrugged. "Looks like you have two choices. You can bitch about your fate, or you can work ten times harder to get back into orbit. I don't care which you do, so long as you do your job when we roll out."

With a haughty look, Lucien said, "Thank you for your advice, O'Brien. My dinner's getting cold. I'm going to eat." He took his tray to the far end of the table, isolated from the GF soldiers.

Tomas sat too, amid his comrades. Alvarez said, "Shirley has a task on this mission?"

Iommarino raised an eyebrow and glanced at Lucien. "He'll call in the orbital fire if we find mike's occupying the facility. That way he can't scapegoat any of us for getting the coordinates wrong." Iommarino laughed at his own words. Alvarez chuckled.

Tomas smiled weakly. He wouldn't argue with his squadmates' judgment, but he himself had nothing against Lucien. He wanted Lucien to play his role in the next day's mission as best he could.

After dinner and a few fitful hours of sleep, Sgt. Johnson roused the squad an hour before departure. They pulled on their chameleonskin suits with stiff motions and bleary eyes. Stepping outside didn't help; Constitution's reddish glow thumped on Tomas's mental sluggishness in the middle of the clock-time night, but couldn't dispel it. Along with his squadmates, he dragged his feet to the Badgers.

Near the vehicle storage sheds, the clanking of Badger tracks riding onto their road carriages quickened Tomas' thoughts. The platoon rounded a corner and went in. Now a little more awake, Tomas noticed the mechanics had worked on the platoon's Badgers while the soldiers had waited in their shelters. Thin alloy struts formed a frame over the turret and top armor of each vehicle. Mechanics clambered over the Badgers, unfolding bulky rolls of chameleonskin over the outside of the frame. On one Badger, already framed over, the chameleonskin showed a civilian motor home.

"We're going incognito," Tomas said.

Iommarino looked surprised. "That makes us irregular combatants. If mike captures us, he could shoot us on sight."

"There's an easy solution to that," Tomas replied. "Don't get taken prisoner."

Cohen chuckled and guided them to their Badger. In the chameleonskin covering each side of the vehicle, a hole gave access to a gray half-globe the size of a football. Finger taps on the chameleonskin above and below gave proof of framing struts holding the half-globe in place. The half-globe's translucent cover obscured some articulated devices inside it. "What's that?" Lundergard asked. No one knew.

The chameleonskin over the rear of the vehicle had a slit up the middle, like a stage's curtains. Inside the rear compartment, Monroe's old seat, the one between Cohen and Tomas, remained empty. After they filed in, Cohen said into the vehicle's net, "MacInnis, we're all mounted."

"Can't shut the ramp yet."

"Why not?"

"Waiting on a passenger."

Tomas' mood fell; he knew who that passenger would be. A moment later, Lucien and Lt. O'Brien came into view at the foot of the ramp. "This is your ride," Lt. O'Brien said.

Lucien took a step, then scowled. At Tomas, at the other soldiers, at O'Brien. "Is this the only one?"

"We outfitted it for your needs. It's the only Badger with an empty seat."

"Someone's skipping this mission?" Lucien asked.

O'Brien looked away. Tomas spoke. "His name was Monroe. He's skipping this and every mission, sir."

Lucien's eyes widened and he grew a little pale when Tomas' meaning sank in. He trudged up the ramp and strapped into Monroe's old seat, while O'Brien loped up the ladder on the outside of the vehicle to the turret hatch. His footsteps overhead rang through the hull.

At the appointed hour, the Badgers rolled out. Though it was a combat mission, the smooth flow of the road carriage tires on pavement lulled the men. Soon, most were dozing. Tomas occasionally opened his eyes enough to glimpse Lucien, bleary-eyed but awake, watching the displays and craning his neck to look around the compartment.

They met the scout platoon on schedule at a crossroads, then turned onto the road leading up to the plateau. The plateau's shadow caught them a minute before they started climbing a road slanting up the darkward rim. The view in the displays showed lamps on tall poles lighting up when their vehicles drew near. A meter-high guardrail hugged the edge of the road. It could stop a civilian car, but the massive fighting vehicles would plunge right through. Iommarino looked away from the display and squeezed his fists until his knuckles turned white. His nervousness tinged the entire compartment. Tomas, awake now, pushed himself into sitting upright.

Lucien, meanwhile, pulled out his tablet and scrolled through an app. His motions and the glow of the screen drew Tomas' attention. Many pages of text, control buttons, an SF logo.

Tomas remembered his thoughts about Lucien during dinner the night before. "Anything I can help with, sir?"

Lucien scowled. "You think I can't do my job?"

A nugget of anger formed in Tomas' gut, but he let it dissolve. "Sir, I'm certain you can do your job perfectly. I have nothing else to do right now and would be happy to help."

"My job is to scope out prospective landing sites on the plateau. The ground-penetrating radar modules on the sides of the vehicle are linked to my tablet. There's nothing you can help with."

Soon, they reached the top of the plateau. The side views showed dry, rocky terrain, interspersed by green tufts of cactus. Lucien looked bored at first, but he kept glancing at Tomas until he set his face and hunched over his tablet, swiping and tapping, as colored lines traced seemingly meaningless patterns.

"Whoa," Lucien said.

"We need to stop, sir?" MacInnis asked.

Lucien studied his display for a moment. "No. I've seen enough." He tapped a button, then drew a circle on his tablet's display. Once complete, the circle filled with bright warning red. "Unstable terrain," he murmured. "Easily could have missed it," he added, even more softly.

MacInnis switched one of the displays on the inside of the ramp to a forward view. In the distance, a faint gray smudge in the heat shimmer of the desert marked out their objective from the sandy brown palette of the plateau. As the last kilometers rolled by, the Observer facility grew more clear. The *taijitus* facing darkward were plainly visible at two klicks out.

The caravan of fighting vehicles turned from the main road onto a paved driveway leading to the Observer facility. The driveway climbed a slope scattered with boulders and shrubs. Tomas studied the forward view for traces of mike activity while his hand reached to the side of the compartment to be near his rifle and grenade launcher on their rack. The Badgers grumbled as they climbed toward the facility. The slope was empty of mike.

At the top of the slope, the gate in the facility's outer wall stood open. The black alloy gate rested its lower corner on the ground at the side of the track. The mycocrete wall looked pitted by years of wind-blown dust. *Taijitu* banners fluttered against the wall.

The disguised Badgers slowed to ease through the gateway. MacInnis deftly drove through, keeping the ground-penetrating radars' housings clear by a few centimeters on each side. The vehicles parked in a line facing the buildings.

The forward view showed a man standing just off the parking lot, on a paved walkway leading to the meeting hall. He dressed more casually than Tomas expected of an Observer minister—blue denim pants and a short-sleeved plaid shirt in a paler shade of blue. The task force's arrival seemed to have hurriedly brought him outside: his chest heaved as he caught his breath, and he reseated the arms of his sunglasses more solidly on his ears. Roughly Tomas' height, he had brown hair edged with gray and a narrow jaw.

"Neumann," said Lt. O'Brien, "leave the grenade launcher and your helmet in the back. Keep your rifle over your shoulder and your suit on plain gray-green. Along with the two scout Observers, greet him. The officers and sergeants will be right behind you."

The ramp dropped. Tomas watched the display as the viewing angle grew steeper and then too steep to watch. But by then, he'd seen enough of the man to know. Not an illusion, nor mistaken identity. New Liberty was a single wormhole from Nueva Andalucia.

"Neumann?"

"Sorry, sir. I'm on it." Tomas stood, slung his rifle over his shoulder, and tromped down the ramp. He parted the halves of the chameleon-skin cloaking the Badger's rear. His heart pounded as he rounded the vehicle and walked toward his father.

The man's arms moved nervously, crossed over his chest one moment, at his sides the next. As Tomas and the scouts approached, he asked, "What can I do for the Confederated Worlds military?"

One of the scout Observers, a Péngláishān native named Wong, glanced at Tomas and the other scout. His peer shuffled a half-step back.

Tomas studied his father. *He doesn't recognize me. Of course he doesn't, he left when I was five.* Words fled his mouth.

Wong stepped forward. "Our respects, *dàoshi*. On behalf of our officers—" Wong waved at the vehicles behind him, where the two GF lieutenants and Lucien gathered. "—we ask your permission to search your facility."

Tomas' father took off his sunglasses and squinted at the approaching officers and the fighting vehicles behind them. "This isn't Péngláishān. You don't have to call me *dàoshi*."

The heat of the pavement made Tomas' feet sweat. The man's eyes were deep blue and hooded on the upper eyelid, just like the man he'd envisioned in the skills imps' chamber. *You're seeing things. How do you even know what your father looked like? A subconscious burble? And you have no evidence your family was ever on Nueva Andalucia....*

"As you wish, honored sir," said Wong. "How should we call you?"

"Mr. Newman is fine."

Tomas' heart pounded more. He had to speak. His throat clenched to spew out his words. "Did you anglicize it from 'Neumann' when you came here from Nueva Andalucia?"

Everyone around Tomas drew in breaths and stared at him. Though aware of the others in passing, Tomas focused on his father. The man blinked, mouth open, face slack with surprise. "How do you know that?"

A dozen years of longing stampeded out of Tomas' subconscious. How many times as a small boy had he cried himself to sleep, wishing for even a minute with his father? Here he had one.

A few more blinks and his father recovered his wits enough to look for the nameplate on Tomas' suit. His eyes widened and he lurched back a step. "Tomas?"

"Mother said you were dead."

His father stepped closer. Tears glistened in his eyes and he reached toward Tomas. "I'm sorry she lied to you. She was always selfish. I should have known she would cringe from the stigma of divorce. Easier to pass herself off as a widow—"

"*She* was selfish?"

His father looked puzzled. "The divorce was her idea. We were on Nueva Andalucia and, and...." He turned his head to the officers standing behind Tomas.

Lt. O'Brien said, "I would be glad for the two of you to catch up, but we do need an answer to Pvt. Wong's question, Mr. Newman. May we search your facility?"

"Search?" Tomas' father looked at the fighting vehicles. The infantrymen stood on the pavement and the front chameleonskins had been furled to reveal the main armament of the Badgers and Weasels. "I would never harbor the militia. This place is a haven from the war."

"Your words are promising," Lt. O'Brien replied. "May we search your facility?"

Tomas' father shrugged. "You have my permission, but you'll find nothing." He gestured at the meeting hall.

Lt. O'Brien curtly moved his head in acknowledgment, then turned to the sergeants gathered a couple of meters behind them. "Your squads have their assignments. Johnson, you'll be a man down, any issues?"

Sgt. Johnson gave Tomas the warmest look Tomas had ever seen from him. "None, sir."

"Let's move."

With the rustle and creak of swaying equipment, and the scrape of boot soles on asphalt, the soldiers filed across the parking lot and fanned out to the different buildings. Lt. O'Brien, the scout commander, and Lucien went to the shadow of the meeting hall, a discreet distance from Tomas and his father. Lucien's expression cycled from smirks, to narrow squints, even occasional flashes of compassion, and who cared what he thought? Fate had opened a window for Tomas that would soon shut forever.

"Tell me what you're feeling," Tomas asked.

His father extended his hands toward Tomas, then dropped them when Tomas didn't reciprocate. "Like I said, the divorce was her idea. We thought Nueva Andalucia would be a fertile ground for spreading the Observer message. It shared a Roman Catholic cultural background with Sankt-Benedikts-Welt, so we knew how to pitch our message in terms the locals would understand. But the Andalucianos didn't heed it. We tried and tried, but we finally had to admit we weren't gaining converts. Maybe the saber-rattling coming from Challenger made them leery of foreigners. This was a year or two before the Confederated Worlds STL ship dragged the wormhole here from New Nauvoo." He caught his breath. "Your mother wanted to go back to Sankt-Benedikts-Welt, but I told her we had to revise our task, not drop it. So she left with you and I came here."

How many of his words were lies to Tomas or himself? Had 'we' done what he'd said, or did he try to spread responsibility for his bad decisions onto Tomas' mother?

Lies or truths, all he could do was accept his father as he was. "Thank you for that information," Tomas said, "but I'd like to know what you're feeling."

"Feelings? I'm surprised, of course. Aren't you? To meet you again, like this… and you joined the military…."

"Tell me more."

"I'm angry at your mother." His father's face showed mild bewilderment, as if he surprised himself by saying more. "She took you and then lied to you. That's wrong." His father's gaze fell to the pavement, and his shoulders hunched. "And I feel bad she never told you why she left me. That must have hurt."

Memories pushed into Tomas' consciousness, like lava seeping onto a world's surface. "I missed you when I was a child. I wished I could somehow have you back, even for a moment. I remember, after we moved to Joséphine—"

"Joséphine?" His father looked thoughtful. "She too couldn't face the shame of returning as a failure to Sankt-Benedikts-Welt."

Tomas glanced up at the *taijitu* banner fluttering from the deck of the elevated platform. The parallel with his active memory lifted the corners of his mouth. "I went into the Saint-Girard church, lurked in the corner, and I prayed to the crucified Christ behind the altar you were really alive and would come for me. Mother would have harangued me for months if she'd ever found out."

"I'm sorry you felt the need to pray to other people's god over what your mother did to us."

"It was years ago. I see the world as it is, now." Tomas looked into his father's eyes. "I know coming here was the best decision you could have made."

His father smiled weakly. "You need to understand something, Tomas. A man has to work for something bigger than himself. It's the only thing that gives his life any meaning. Otherwise he's sleepwalking and will wake up some day wondering where his life went. I had to come here. I had to spread our message and be an example of how to dedicate one's life to the higher truth within each one of us."

Spreading the Observer message by working alone with whatever few visitors journeyed here? His father denied so much. The wind rustled sand across the parking lot and Tomas vowed again to accept his father as he was. "I understand," he replied. "For us soldiers, the GF can be that thing bigger than ourselves."

"Your mother never understood me when I told her that." His father lacked any sign of hearing his reply. "If she had, she would have known we had to keep bringing the Observer message to worlds that needed it, and she would have kept the three of us together. We're fortunate we had this chance to meet despite her." He slowly turned his head to take in the line of fighting vehicles. "What could have brought you here? I don't mean New Liberty. I mean here."

Tomas wished he could tell him, but the mission and the team outranked even family. "You know I can't tell you."

"But I'm your father." His face showed reconsideration. "Who's been out of your life for over a dozen years. I accept that you might be angry."

After a moment to gauge his feelings, Tomas shook his head. "I'm not."

"You're a better Observer than I am." Red rimmed his father's eyes.

"Thank you for the compliment. My commitment to my fellow soldiers is the reason I can't talk about why we're here."

His father shifted his weight. "Like I told the officers, the militia's done nothing around here. Your ships—" He glanced into the sky. "—would see it if they had. All that empty desert...." He waved in the direction of the main gate and the asphalt road leading darkward across the plateau. After a time, he looked once more in the general direction of the SF ships in orbit. His gaze flickered over a tiny portion of the vast sky for several moments. Tomas couldn't read his thoughts.

Eventually, his father spoke. "I suppose the military has to see for itself the militia isn't here. Do your superiors doubt the competence of the spaceship fleet?"

"No more than the Space Force doubts ours."

His father smiled weakly, over an agitated demeanor. He turned his shoulders to look for the GF personnel working their way from building to building. Tomas followed his gaze and saw the purpose in his comrades' motions, purpose his father wouldn't see. Quiet chatter from the task force net came sporadically through Tomas' earbuds. "Meeting hall secure."

"Office building secure," Cohen said.

"Parsonage secure."

Lt. O'Brien broke in. "With the buildings secure, I want the scouts to go up to the observing platform to look for mike activity and set some obs wheels. Johnson, have you seen a way out of the facility on the sunward side?"

"No, sir."

"Take your squad out the way we came in, circle behind the facility, and scout that side. Shirley's orbital eyes show piney hills dropping down to the river, with no mike activity, but I want boots on the ground to confirm."

"Yes, sir," Johnson said. "Idrin, you heard the man. Foot patrol."

Sgt. Johnson and the rest of the squad came out of the office building and trudged along the walkway toward Tomas and his father. Iommarino stared at Tomas' father, and Cohen gave Tomas a compassionate look. "We'll take care of the assignment," he said to Tomas.

"You're certain? Sergeant?"

Johnson nodded. "You have bigger things to take care of."

I do? Tomas had longed for the chance to talk to his father every day between his arrival on Joséphine and his enlistment in the GF. Yet now that he had the chance, how little he could do with it. The questions that had gnawed at him for over a dozen years, variations on what happened? and why? now lacked importance. His father, watching the line of men walking between two Badgers on their way to the facility's front gate, was a stranger to Tomas, and vice versa.

"Son...." The word struck Tomas with a self-conscious tone, and his father's expression showed the older man knew how it sounded. "I want to talk more, but I need a few minutes in the restroom."

"I'll walk with you."

"You don't have to do that."

Tomas squinted at Constitution just above the parsonage's low shed roof. Even with his suit set to plain gray-green, the fabric was heavy and hot. "I would take a few minutes in the shade."

"Oh. Your uniform must weigh a lot. I'll get you a glass of water too. Follow me." His father led him down the walkway.

The office building was a long, low structure of reddish-brown mycocrete. Inside, cool air whooshed from the vents, and drawn window shades kept the interior pleasantly dim. Past a spotless reception area and near the beginning of a long, dark hallway, his father showed Tomas into his office. "Have a seat. I'll be right back with your water."

Soon, from someplace nearby on the opposite side of the hallway, came the thump of cabinet doors shutting and the gurgle of a cooler dispensing water. While he waited, Tomas looked around his father's office. It reminded him of his mother's study at the parsonage back home: behind a worn wooden desk, shelves bowed under the weight of books, among them a complete set of the *Observer Encyclopedia* and the leading missionary guidebook, *Showing Others the Way*.

Unlike his mother's study, though, dust stood thickly atop the books, and a tablet stood in a charging cradle on his father's desk.

From the doorway came his father's voice. "When I was your age, I loved the old books. Their weight, the rustle of their pages, the typefaces…. I can still remember where on the page certain passages from the *Tao Te Ching* could be found in the old hardback edition your grandfather gave me. 'Those who know the Tao are not extensively learned; the extensively learned do not know the Tao.' But the digitized version on the tablet is so much more convenient and powerful." His father looked pensive. "Here's your water. Please excuse me. I should only be a few minutes."

Tomas sipped the water. "Thank you. Father."

Another weak smile. His father pulled his tablet off its charging cradle and left the room. The sound of his footsteps faded down the hallway.

Tomas drank more water and listened to the task force's chatter in his earbuds. The scouts on the elevated platform saw a terrain free of mike for tens of klicks in every direction. They had mounted obs wheels and now ran the initial tests and calibrations. So far so good.

The GF still had a great chance to get off the planet without mike finding out in time to interfere.

Somewhere down the hall came a dim sound, like hard objects clanging into each other. Not a typical latrine sound. And how long had it been since his father had left the room? Tomas rose from his seat and stood in the open doorway. Silence filled the hall.

Tomas padded in the direction his father had gone. Every door he passed was closed. He leaned his head toward each door, listening for sounds or voices. Nothing.

He paused outside a unisex restroom, the only one in the entire hallway. He held his breath and pulled out the earbud linked to the task force net. Still nothing.

Tomas frowned and kept going. Next to the nearest door on the opposite wall, a placard read *Storage*. A noise came from within.

After leaning closer, Tomas heard a voice, quiet and muffled. He cupped his hand around his ear. The voice was definitely his father's.

"Concerned citizen to Militia Headquarters Shermanville, do you read?" The voice was quiet and muffled by the door. "Concerned citizen to Militia Headquarters Shermanville. Come on, pick up. Come on. Concerned citizen to Militia Headquarters Shermanville, do you read?"

Tomas' heart slammed. His hand shook as he replaced the earbud in his ear. He pulled the rifle off his shoulder and to his hands, hoping the sound of plastic and metal hitting his palms would go unheard. He took a deep breath. A clammy feeling crawled over his skin.

He kicked in the door.

His father stood in a far corner, behind an open metal shelving unit in the middle of the room. Tomas saw his father between a small cardboard box and some electronic parts in a thick plastic bag. The older man's face was pale. His mouth hung open and his eyes were wide.

Tomas rounded the shelving unit and aimed the rifle at his father. In his left hand, the older man held a radio headset. Static hissed in the earpiece. His right hand rested on the controls of a hand-crank radio. The radio sat at the end of a shelf. On the tile floor between him and Tomas, metal and plastic desk accessories spilled out of a cardboard box with a crumpled corner.

"Turn off the radio," Tomas said.

"Tomas. Son. I can explain—"

"Turn it off." Tomas' voice sounded cold to his ears. The part of him that had acted behind the pillbox stirred again. He took a breath. He didn't expect to need it, but its availability straightened his back.

His father rocked a switch on the radio. The static in the earpiece cut off.

"Send the radio over."

His father held out the headset.

"Not the headset. Put the radio on the floor and kick it my way with your foot. Easy motions."

A nod, and then his father bent down. He shoved the radio with his foot. It came most of the way to Tomas and he left it on the floor between them.

"I can explain," his father said again. "The Confederated Worlds army is leaving New Liberty, isn't it?"

Tomas glared and said nothing.

"Not answering means 'yes.' The supply drivers from Hale Valley, and the people who come here for spiritual retreats, all talk about how outnumbered you are and how much territory you've yielded to the militia. People down here with telescopes can count the ships in orbit. Everyone knows the Confederated Worlds have sent away ships ever since the Progressive Republic declared war. You're leaving. Why else come to the plateau? The militia has done nothing up here. Why else could the plateau matter to your superiors than as a place to leave without the militia seeing you go?"

"We can't stop you from speculating," Tomas said. "But we won't let you share your speculations with mike."

His father took a breath. "If you were leaving, would you have taken me with you?"

The answer came immediately to Tomas' mind. No. Impped knowledge told him civilians were to be denied transport in a withdrawal from a hostile planet. Beneath the impped knowledge, another thought emerged. *You should have thought of that when you abandoned me to Mother.*

"No. Don't try to deny it. I know what happens to locals the militia thinks collaborated with you. The mayor of Sunright Decatur was lined up against a wall and shot. I'm the nearest civilian to where you'll jump off the planet. The militia will find me and scan my brain. I'm a native of the Confederated Worlds. I knew you were here and I guessed why you came. If I didn't tell them, they'd kill me on the spot."

He reached out for Tomas. "Our work is too important. The Observer Way is rarely followed here, but that's all the more reason we have to keep doing it. A drip of water over ten million years can make a canyon. We—"

"We?"

"Come with me. The militia will welcome you. You can reveal everything you know to the Unity when their fleet returns to New Liberty."

The thought disgusted Tomas. "My loyalty is to the Confederated Worlds and the Ground Force." He stood taller. "Come with me."

His father's eyes widened. "What are you going to do with me?"

"I'm going to march you to Lt. O'Brien and tell him what happened. I suspect we'll keep you in custody until we depart. Mike can't fault you for failing to inform—"

"Yes he can!"

Tomas shrugged. "Then you should have succeeded."

"But, but, I'm your… father…." The older man's face fell.

Tomas squatted, bracing the rifle against his hip as he groped for the radio with his left hand. He took his gaze off his father for a moment—

Cardboard and plastic scraped on the shelf above his head. Tomas looked up and jerked his left hand between his head and falling boxes. The shelving unit leaned toward him. Footfalls and a glimpse of brown hair from the other side of the shelves showed his father had ducked around the end of the unit when Tomas had looked away.

The shelving unit tipped further. Tomas jumped up and stood against the wall to his right. The top of the unit crashed into his left forearm. He winced and the door to the room slammed behind his father.

Tomas squirmed backward. The top of the shelving unit pressed against his arm. Awkwardly, with his right arm squeezing his rifle into his armpit, he worked his shilling with his right hand through the fabric of his suit. "Sergeant! Lieutenant! Newman is unarmed but hostile. Repeat, Newman is unarmed but hostile. I prevented him from attempting contact with mike but he escaped my custody. Look for him. I will follow."

Finally he reached the end of the shelving unit. His breath hard, he ran to the door, yanked it open, ran out. The hallway was empty. At the end furthest from his father's office, a vertical sliver of daylight narrowed and disappeared as a door to the outside swung shut.

Tomas ran that way. He squinted when he reached the outside. Confused chatter and questions filled the task force net. He ignored them. A glimpse of motion around the corner of the parsonage caught his attention and he followed.

He found a patio of stone pavers and a round, raised firepit behind the parsonage. A sliding glass door gave access to the building. Behind the glass panes, thick curtains hung from floor to ceiling.

He could be hidden there, armed and willing to shoot.

He could have a radio there, too, and even now be trying to call mike.

Tomas tugged on the door handle. Locked. He reversed his rifle and butted it against the glass. Cracks formed like thin ice under a heavy footstep. He butted again, again. The crack pattern spread and the glass buckled away from the blows. He reached in and worked the handle open.

Once the lock snicked, he pulled back his hand, yanked open the door, and swept the curtains aside with his rifle muzzle. The room held a worn brown chair facing a video screen on the wall. The odor of smoked hashish came from a hookah in the corner. Empty.

Tomas went into a narrow hallway. The doors were all shut, except one to a bedroom. A queen-sized bed, neatly made; carpet with straight lines left by a vacuum cleaner. To Tomas' right, near a window looking out on the spur of rock, stood a closet door. A strip of light leaked out from beneath it. Tomas flung open the door and burst into the closet, muzzle up.

The scent of cedar hit him. A light in the ceiling was on, illuminating cedar planking and built-in storage on all four walls. Shoe racks, hanging rods, a floor-to-ceiling wardrobe. Small outdoors gadgets—

powered binoculars, a GPS receiver, a self-folding tent—shared space with his father's shirts and pants.

Tomas glanced behind him, suddenly fearful his father was sneaking up on him. No motion, no sound. Where was he?

The wardrobe. Tomas moved as quietly as he could. He braced his rifle against his body and yanked open the wardrobe door.

No hiding man. No clothes. Instead, the rear panel of the wardrobe had been mounted on hinges. The rear panel stood open now, revealing a passageway eighty centimeters in diameter carved out of the rock. The scrabble of motion came from somewhere down the tunnel.

Tomas activated his shilling. "Mr. Newman is taking a tunnel. Presumably to the outside. I will follow."

"I'll get the idrin outside," Sgt. Johnson said. "We'll look for him and you."

Tomas crawled into the tunnel. The rough surface pressed his shilling against his chest. Dim light followed from the closet, and after a turn, it soon left him in darkness. The tunnel sloped down and wound through more turns. Tomas shoved aside a thought of the tons of rock around him on all sides. Alone in the dark, all he could hear was his breathing. His helmet, now stowed in the Badger, would be worth its weight in gold for its night vision capability right now. His father might have turned to make a stand and he would never know until it was too late.

After a couple of minutes, a glimmer of light came from around another turn. He crawled faster and rounded the turn. An entrance to the outside showed the side of a boulder and the trunks of pines rising from below.

Tomas scurried out and oriented himself. The facility's mycocrete wall behind him lacked taijitu banners. In front of him, glimpsed between pines, the salty flats of the evaporating river lay a few klicks away, and beyond them, a dry rocky plain stretched toward the fat red ember of Constitution. "I'm behind the facility," he said. After looking downslope, he said, "Mr. Newman is in view."

A blue-clad figure hurried down the slope, amid clattering pebbles and thwacking shrubs. He kept his right arm straight, wavering a little to balance himself. His left hand held a small gray box to the side of his face. The box reached from mouth to ear.

Tomas raised his rifle's sights to his eye. "Stop!" he shouted. "Put down the radio! Hands up and come to me!"

His father glanced back in a blur of pale face, then kept running.

"Stop!" Tomas shouted again. He fired a burst over his father's head. Rounds smacked a tree trunk. The older man crouched, startled. He hesitated, but for only a moment.

The part of Tomas that had come out behind the pillbox stirred again, but it was not alone. Another part of himself, wiser, more mature, came out of his subconscious. The two merged together and filled him with certainty. He checked his father's direction of motion, then sighted again. Pale blue plaid filled the aperture. He fired.

His father sprawled on the slope, face down. The small gray radio lay a few meters from him. His elbows dug at the dirt and his right arm reached for the radio, but his motion ceased in moments.

Tomas stood and hurried down the slope. "We need a medic back here! Fifty meters my sunward. Now!"

His father's threat had been neutralized. Maybe the medic could get here in time. If medical corps finds them alive, they'll stay that way.

Tomas breathed hard. And if not? *I can still get that one minute with him if I hurry.* He ran faster and slid on his rump the last two meters downslope. He scrambled onto his knees next to his father.

The older man still lay on his belly, one cheek against the dirt and one arm stretched out for the portable radio. Blood soaked the dirt under him. Thick red wounds gaped on his back. He didn't move.

Tomas touched the underside of his jaw with the backs of two fingers. No pulse. He moved his fingers around, trying to find a pulse. None. His father's lifeless eye stared into the pine forest.

Footsteps of many men came from up the slope. Tomas turned to see a medic and his squad filing toward him. His squadmates looked shocked. Their gazes flickered from Tomas to his father. The medic rushed forward and knelt by Tomas' father.

Sgt. Johnson clapped Tomas on the shoulder. "Good work, Neumann. The other squad found the radio he used in the building. Lt.

O'Brien and the scout commander checked its outgoing buffer. He didn't get a message off to mike."

"He had another radio," Tomas said. He gestured at the gray portable one lying in the dirt nearby. "I don't know if I stopped him before he could use it."

"We'll check it out too."

Cohen stepped closer. "How are you, Tomas?"

Had Cohen ever called him anything but 'Neumann?' Tomas welcomed the closeness implied by Cohen's choice of words. "I'm okay."

"Tell me more."

Tomas looked at his father. The medic leaned back on his haunches and dropped blood-stained hands to his lap. He'd shut his father's eyes along the way. "I'm angry at him for trying to alert mike. Sad, too, that he felt he had to. Sad I had to shoot him. I gave him chances to surrender. And all my life I'd wanted to talk to him, just for a moment, to hear what wisdom he could give me. From everything he said before he sneaked off to call mike I know there wasn't any wisdom and why did I think there was and is this what I really wanted...." He dropped his rifle to the ground and hung his head in his hands.

"It's okay," Cohen said. "Let it out."

Tomas kept his eyes shut and took deep breaths. From the shadows of his subconscious, his twinned parts, the murderous and the noble, watched him with acceptance. He returned the acceptance to them. Beyond them, around them, he sensed the squad nearby. His senses expanded. He visualized the rest of the task force, up at the facility. Lissa in her office in the base at R-town and he hoped she would make it off-planet with the rest of them. And all the dead men: Voloshenko, Sharma, Obermeyer, Ryan, Monroe. Marchbanks. Their bodies rotted but they lived on as virtual souls, emulated in his memory and the memory of every other soldier who'd known them. He accepted all of them, just as they were, and he knew they accepted him.

He opened his eyes. "I feel those things, and I know I did the right thing. Thanks."

"I know." Most of the others nodded.

Most, but not all. Words caught in Iommarino's throat before forcing their way out. "The right thing? What the hell is wrong with you? Maybe he was a mike simp, but you killed your own father!"

Tomas gave him a level look. "There are things more important than family."

Iommarino recoiled. "What could be more important than family?"

"None of us chose our families." Tomas set the flat of his hand on his chest. "Every one of us chose to take the shilling."

ABOUT THE AUTHOR

Hi, I'm Raymund Eich. I write science fiction that takes readers on journeys from middle America to the ends of the universe.

My most popular titles are military science fiction series **The Confederated Worlds** (novels *Take the Shilling*, *Operation Iago*, and *A Bodyguard of Lies*) and the **Stone Chalmers** series of science fiction espionage adventures (novels *The Progress of Mankind*, *The Greater Glory of God*, *To All High Emprise Consecrated*, and *In Public Convocation Assembled*).

I've also published over twenty other book-length works and more than forty short stories. My short fiction has appeared in *Odyssey*, *Analog*, *Boundary Shock Quarterly*, and the anthology *Surviving Tomorrow*, and has earned honorable mentions and a semi-finalist award in the Writers of the Future contest. My works are available worldwide in ebook, trade paperback, and audiobook editions.

After circling the world by age five, I grew up in the Ozark Mountains of southwest Missouri. I attended Rice University, where my academic career culminated with a Ph.D. in biochemistry. Though I'm no longer a working scientist, hundreds of papers cite my graduate research.

In addition to my writing career, I've worked in patent law, won a national quiz bowl championship, enjoy boardgames, and love my family. In case you're wondering, my last name has one syllable and is pronounced "eye-sh."

Connect with me at **www.raymundeich.com** or follow the QR code below.

Online and brick-and-mortar bookstores around the world list millions of books, with thousands more published every day. I'm glad you discovered this one.

If you'd like to know when I release a new book, instead of leaving it to chance, join my Readers Club. I'll email you monthly with publishing news and a short personal update. Plus, from time to time I'll let you know about an older book of mine you might have missed.

Yes, please! I'll go to **www.raymundeich.com/mailing-list** or scan the QR code below.

No thanks. I'll take my chances next time I look for your books.

OTHER BOOKS BY THE AUTHOR

Available wherever books are sold.

Learn more about these titles at our website, **www.cv2books.com,** or follow the QR code below.

Learn more about these titles at **www.cv2books.com**.

THE CONFEDERATED WORLDS

The purpose of all other combat arms is to put the infantryman in sole possession of the battlefield.

A thousand years from now, while Earth sleeps in virtual reality, three polities —the Confederated Worlds, the Unity, and the Progressive Republic—strive to connect the scattered, terraformed worlds of humankind by artificial wormholes.

When they meet, they clash, in a decades-long struggle of arms that will embroil every human world, in which dedication to duty liberates worlds— and oneself.

Learn more about the Confederated Worlds series at **www.cv2books.com/the-confederated-worlds**, or follow the QR code below.

Take the Shilling

The Confederated Worlds implanted in his brain the skills to make him a soldier. Tomas Neumann had to learn for himself how to survive interstellar war.

Operation Iago

The Confederated Worlds lost the war. Can Lt. Tomas Neumann win the peace against elusive, deceptive foes out to turn the Confederated Worlds against itself?

A Bodyguard of Lies

Assigned to the halls of power, only Capt. Tomas Neumann can save the Confederated Worlds from the ultimate treachery.

THE INCEPTI CATACLYSM

The entire galaxy knows about the Incepti Cataclysm. The occupation force from Vela destroyed a planet with nanotechnology. Only a few Inceptis fled the wave of death in time to join their brethren scattered across the Democracy.

Everything the galaxy knows is a lie.

Anara Orden. Daughter of survivors. Recruited by fellow Inceptis to join Democracy intelligence. Though young and good of heart, she kills without qualms. She knows her employers only order her to terminate Velan agents threatening the Democracy.

But when her next target is a fellow Incepti, she questions everything and chooses a new mission. She will share the truth with friend and foe alike.

Yet powerful forces across the galaxy will do whatever it takes to cling to power. Even if millions of innocents must die.

Escape from Conatus (Book One)

When Anara learns the truth, a simple mission becomes a flight for survival.

Revelation in Vela (Book Two)

Instead of a refuge, Anara and her companions end up in the cross-hairs—of two sides.

Victory for Carina (Book Three)

As war comes to the galaxy, only Anara's desperate plan can bring a just and lasting peace.

STONE CHALMERS

One man can make—or break—Earth's iron grip on its galactic colonies: Stone Chalmers. Spy. Assassin. Earth's top operative.

Stone's missions take him through artificial wormholes and on warpdrive ships to colonies bound to Earth—whether they like it or not.

Though undercover, with cover personas overlaid on his mind and disguises engineered by nanotechnology into his bones and his cells, Stone's missions are never easy. In the eye of a storm of intrigue and conspiracy, Stone's actions make the difference in whether open rebellion threatens the galactic order imposed by Earth…

…and threatens Earth itself.

Join Stone on his pulse-pounding adventures across a galaxy spiraling out of control, in this complete four-novel series.

Learn more about the Stone Chalmers series at **www.cv2books.com/stone-chalmers**, or follow the QR code below.

The Progress of Mankind

To maintain order in the 22nd century, Earth relocates undesirables through artificial wormholes onto colony planets. Everyone benefits… except the planets' original colonists.

Now, the newly rediscovered colony of New Moravia learns Earth's plan and fights back.

The Greater Glory of God

Thousands fled the chaos of the 21st century on rogue warpdrive ships to settle colony planets. When Earth reunified in the 22nd, its fleets rediscovered the colonies and hunted down the warpdrive ships.

Every warpdrive ship but one.

To All High Emprise Consecrated

Unified Earth has rediscovered the colony of Minerva. Prosperous and technologically advanced, Minerva quickly submits to Earth supremacy.

Surprisingly quickly…

In Public Convocation Assembled

Earth's government controls all human colonies scattered through the galaxy by means of wormholes, warpdrive ships, and ruthless operatives. Operatives working to strengthen Earth's grip.

Or destroy it.

THE FALSE FLAG WAR

Concordia's mission reflected the best of the human race. Crew and scientists from both of Earth's rival factions, Humanists and Traditionalists, journeyed for years at relativistic speeds to reach Bravo Charlie, a life-bearing planet orbiting Alpha Centauri B, to expand the frontiers of knowledge for all.

Concordia's mission also reflected humanity at its worst. Corrupt bureaucrats and ambitious political leaders in both factions maintained a status quo backed by weapons of mass destruction. The faction commanders on the mission each sought to seize advantages for their side alone.

Then the ship received transmissions. Signs of an ancient, powerful alien presence on the planet below.

Exploration 2127

Sent to explore, **Jaeger** and **McIlroy**, born and raised in a Texas divided by razor wire and minefields. Men torn between the mission's ideals and orders from their respective faction commanders.

Then Jaeger and McIlroy discover how to bring Earth's factions together... using knowledge given by aliens dead over a million years.

Invasion 2132

Concordia fell silent. Mission control now detects an unknown ship leaving the Alpha Centauri system. Heading to Earth at relativistic speeds. Silent about its purpose. Its crew unknown.

Earth's one chance: Its rival factions must work for mutual defense. While shadowy figures strive to use the unknown ship for their own faction's gain.

OTHER NOVELS

The Blank Slate

Neuroscience entrepreneur Clay Shieffer must stop a tyrannical president…
because he unwittingly gave the tyrant power over the human mind.

New California

After New California's founder committed suicide, two men vied to rule the
colony.

Ashwin George, supported by the colony's elite and the Chinese company
dominating half the settled galaxy.

Against him, Desmond Park, nanotechnology engineer, armed with the most
formidable weapon of all.

A single idea.

The Reincarnation Run

Skeptical spacejock Landry Krieger knows exactly how to smuggle the
"reborn" spiritual leader of an oppressed people past their conquerors... but the
boy's priests—and governess—shake up his orderly plans.

Azureseas: Cantrell's War

Ross Cantrell joined the animal control mission on the newly-discovered planet
Azureseas to earn the money to start married life together with his girlfriend.

Then Ross discovers the truth about the planet's "animals."

SHORT STORY COLLECTIONS

The First Voyages: The Complete Science Fiction Stories 1998-2012

From 21st century asteroid settlements to World War II Romania, from an Earth dominated by immortal aliens to Christ's empty tomb, a fresh, distinctive voice in science fiction will take you on journeys to the photosphere of the sun, the coding regions of DNA, and the complexities of the human psyche.

Stage Separations: The Complete Science Fiction Stories 2013-2018

In these pages, you can...

...race against time to solve mysteries hidden in a planet's vast desert—and in a woman's heart

...learn the true story of a president's assassination

...journey 14,000 miles to a high-tech fountain of youth

...win or go "home"—to an Earth you've never seen

and explore six other worlds created by a distinctive voice in twenty-first century science fiction.

Orbital Maneuvers: The Complete Science Fiction Stories 2019-2020

In these pages, you can join–

A mission to terraform a lifeless, rocky planet | A private detective uncovering the ultimate crime | A woman called by an ex-boyfriend… who's been dead twenty years | A President breaking his country's highest law | A star athlete discovering the true price of a championship

–and enjoy five more tales, in the latest installment of the Complete Science Fiction Stories of Raymund Eich.

Extravehicular Activities: The Complete Science Fiction Stories 2021-2022

Leave the safety of your space capsule for the dangers of billion-year old alien derelicts, intelligent insects with mysterious motives, espionage in an alternate 1920s Paris, and rogue reconstructed dinosaurs.

These wonders and more await in the fourth volume of the Complete Science Fiction Stories of Raymund Eich.